Jonathan L. Howard is a game designer, scriptwriter, and a veteran of the computer games industry sinc[...] ited Kingdom with his wife and da[...] wing the devilishly funny JOHANN[...] and JOHANNES CABAL THE DI[...]

Praise for Jonathan L. Howard

'Readers, rejoice; Johannes Cabal is back . . . Howard's Dreamlands will thrill fans of H.P. Lovecraft, but Cabal leaves a permanent mark on even the most fluid of landscapes, and Howard's writing shines, sketching out a personality both fascinating and heartbreaking, on an adventure that reverberates from Dreamlands to the waking world, with a future that every reader must hope involves many more stories to come' www.bookgeeks.co.uk

'I loved the original offering from this author and with its wit, cracking pace and above all else, its larger than life principle protagonist it's a tale that is literally a huge chunk of fun' *Falcata Times*

'Howard's ear for witty banter and his skill at rendering black comedy bode well for the future' *Publishers Weekly*

'Cabal, the detective and necromancer, is full of charismatic amorality, making him both a classical and a refreshing antihero' *Time Out*, Chicago

'In Johannes Cabal he has created a thoroughly unpleasant lead character who somehow the reader is rooting for – a real achievement' *Fortean Times*

'A thoroughly entertaining and hugely fun book populated by great characters . . . intelligently written and very funny' www.sci-fi-london.com

'A charmingly gothic, fiendishly funny Faustian tale' www.goodreads.com

'Not only does Howard deliver a devilish mystery but he also wraps it all up in a gorgeous "steampunk noir" atmosphere' www.graemesfantasybookreview.com

'Just as fast and funny as its predecessor. I loved it, and hope another one comes along "as fast as a rabbit from a trebuchet" as the author so prettily puts it' Tina Rath, The Dracula Society

'I had no reason to expect this sequel to be even better than that steamalicious first book. Yet it is' www.warpcoresf.co.uk

By Jonathan L. Howard and available from Headline

Johannes Cabal the Necromancer
Johannes Cabal the Detective

JOHANNES CABAL

the FEAR INSTITUTE

JONATHAN L. HOWARD

headline

Chapter heading illustrations by Snugbat

Map by the author, using Campaign Cartographer 3

First published in Great Britain in 2011 by
HEADLINE PUBLISHING GROUP

First published in paperback in 2012 by
HEADLINE PUBLISHING GROUP

3

Cataloguing in Publication Data is available from the British Library

ISBN 978 0 7553 4800 8

Typeset in Goudy old style by Avon DataSet Ltd,
Bidford-on-Avon, Warwickshire

Printed and bound by CPI Group (UK) Ltd, Croydon, CR0 4YY

Headline's policy is to use papers that are natural, renewable and recyclable products and made from wood grown in sustainable forests. The logging and manufacturing processes are expected to conform to the environmental regulations of the country of origin.

HEADLINE PUBLISHING GROUP
An Hachette UK Company
338 Euston Road
London NW1 3BH

www.headline.co.uk
www.hachette.co.uk

For Marsha and Michael Davis

Contents

Foreword:	A WARNING TO THE CURIOUS	ix
Chapter 1:	IN WHICH THE FEAR INSTITUTE VISITS AND CABAL IS CONFRONTED BY THE POLICE	1
Chapter 2:	IN WHICH THE UNITED STATES ARE VISITED, THOUGH BRIEFLY	25
Interlude:	*THE YOUNG PERSON'S GUIDE TO CTHULHU AND HIS FRIENDS: NO. 1 GREAT CTHULHU*	48
Chapter 3:	IN WHICH CABAL LEADS AN EXPEDITION BEYOND THE WALL OF SLEEP	49
Chapter 4:	IN WHICH THE FAUNA OF THE DREAMLANDS PROVE UNPLEASANT	67
Chapter 5:	IN WHICH CABAL WANDERS FROM THE BUCOLIC TO THE NECROPOLITIC	86
Interlude:	*THE YOUNG PERSON'S GUIDE TO CTHULHU AND HIS FRIENDS: NO. 2 NYARLOTHOTEP, THE CRAWLING CHAOS*	109
Chapter 6:	IN WHICH THE EXPEDITION CROSSES THE SEA AND CABAL TAKES AN INTEREST IN THE LEG OF A SAILOR	110
Chapter 7:	IN WHICH THE EXPEDITION EXPLORES A NAMELESS CITY OF EVIL REPUTE	128
Chapter 8:	IN WHICH CABAL HAS A SURPRISINGLY CIVILISED CHAT WITH A MONSTER	147
Chapter 9:	IN WHICH A HERMITAGE IS DISCOVERED AND A GREAT TERROR REVEALED	165
Chapter 10:	IN WHICH THERE IS A BATTLE AND CABAL MAKES IT QUICK	184

Interlude:	*THE YOUNG PERSON'S GUIDE TO CTHULHU AND HIS FRIENDS: NO. 3 AZATHOTH, THE DEMON SULTAN*	202
Chapter 11:	IN WHICH IT TRANSPIRES THAT DYLATH-LEEN IS NOT VERY NICE	203
Chapter 12:	IN WHICH THERE ARE MONSTERS AND CATS, WHICH IS TO SAY, VERY MUCH THE SAME THING	222
Chapter 13:	IN WHICH THE DOMESTIC WONTS OF SORCERERS ARE INVESTIGATED AND CABAL CANNOT BE CONCERNED	244
Interlude:	*THE YOUNG PERSON'S GUIDE TO CTHULHU AND HIS FRIENDS: NO. 4 YOG-SOTHOTH, THE LURKER AT THE THRESHOLD*	263
Chapter 14:	IN WHICH WE CONTEMPLATE THE LIFE AND DEATH OF JOHANNES CABAL	264
Chapter 15:	IN WHICH LITTLE IS SAID, BUT MUCH IS CONVEYED	285
Chapter 16:	IN WHICH CABAL PLANS IN THE LONG TERM AND LAUGHTER PROVES TO BE THE WORST MEDICINE	286
Interlude:	*THE YOUNG PERSON'S GUIDE TO CTHULHU AND HIS FRIENDS: NO. 5 AN ABC*	306
Chapter 17:	IN WHICH CABAL EXPERIENCES OMOPHAGIA, ANNOYS THE VATICAN, AND ENDURES MUCH	308
Author's note		331

Foreword: A Warning to the Curious

Gentle reader, what follows is the third novel in the series of stories concerning Johannes Cabal, a necromancer of some little infamy. There will doubtless be some of you have come here seeking some fanciful little tale for your amusement, to furnish you with a smile or two, perhaps even a giggle. You are fools, as are the benighted wretches who ever suffered the poor judgement to spawn you. What follows is, in truth, a horrible story of madness and corruption, of lost hope and new destiny, of vicious but stupid crabs. You will not read this and walk away untouched.

Or perhaps you will. People are so insensitive, these days. Once upon a time, all you had to do was finish a story with a revelation in the form of a single short declarative sentence paragraph in – and this was the powerful part – *italics* to shred the sanity away from anyone more psychologically vulnerable than a lamppost.

It was his own face.

Or . . .

There were still two glasses upon the mantelpiece.

Or . . .

The library book was terribly overdue.

Not so these days. Everyone is so desensitised that the potency of artfully deployed italics has long been lost. It was good enough for H. P. Lovecraft, but apparently it isn't good enough for the modern world, filled as it is with obtuse bastards.

You know what? Forget the warning. Read the book. Go insane. See if I care.

JLH

If poets' verses be but stories
So be food and raiment stories;
So is all the world a story;
So is man of dust a story.

Colum Cille

A Region of the Dreamlands
Based upon the notes of J. Cabal, esq.
(After Gaughan & Schultz)
X Mormo, possibly
Cerenarian Sea
X Mormo may be here
X Potential location of Mormo
X Mormo?
Mtal
Mt. Aran
Celephais
Gak
X Here Be Monsters
The Stony Desert
Hlanith
Mt. Hatheg-Kla
Dark Wood
Liranian Desert
R. Oukranos
Enchanted Wood
Mt. Thurai
Mt. Sidrak
Ulthar
Mt. Lerion
Mt. Dlareth
Cuppar-Nombo Desert
Aulonian Plain
Golthoth
Dylath-Leen
X Here Be Monsters Too
Baharna
Ruined City
Mt. Thorin
X Sunken City
Oriab
X Here Be More Monsters
Mt. Ngranak
Lake of Yath
R. Zuro

Chapter 1

IN WHICH THE FEAR INSTITUTE VISITS AND CABAL IS CONFRONTED BY THE POLICE

It was not such a peculiar house in and of itself. A three-storey townhouse – four, if you counted the attic – Victorian in design, tall and thin and quite deep. To the fore, a short path ran from the door (to the left of the frontage) perhaps ten feet past what might have been intended as a rose garden in some long-past year. Now it was overgrown, but in a strangely artful way, as if chaotic minds had planned a new and not entirely wholesome horticulture for the little garden. Indeed they had, but we shall return to that aspect of the house shortly.

Although at one point it had clearly been a middle terrace house, its neighbours were no longer in evidence but for broken half-bricks protruding from the end gables. A single house, the lone survivor of a terrace, marked darkly with the smoke of nearby industrial chimneys, a short front garden and a somewhat longer back one, the former bounded by a low wall, the latter by a tall one. Not a common sight, but neither one to excite much comment in the normal run of things. If, that is, it were sited within an industrial town or city. It was not.

The house rose solitary and arrogant on a green hillside some few miles from the next dwelling. The nearest factory chimney capable of layering the soot on the house was further still. If one were to see the house in its rural location, apparently scooped up by some Goliath and deposited far from its proper place, one might feel inclined to investigate, to climb the pebble and earth trail that leads to the garden gate, to walk up the flagstoned path beyond it, and to knock upon the door. After all, somebody must live there. The building is well maintained and smoke curls from its chimney.

This is an inclination to be fought at all costs, for this is the house of Johannes Cabal, the necromancer. There are all manners of unpleasantness about the place, but the front garden is the foremost.

Johannes Cabal was sitting in his study, making notes in the small black book that he customarily carried in the inside pocket of his jacket. They were pithy to the point of acerbity – Cabal was not in a good mood. That in itself was no rarity, but he was particularly ill-tempered today as his latest attempt to secure – which is to say, steal – a rare copy of de Cuir's very useful *Enquêtes interdites* had failed. Cabal was used to his frequent necessary descents into criminality coming to nothing, but it especially galled him on this occasion.

'*Verdammt* kobold,' he muttered, as he crossed a '7' with unnecessary vigour. He had faced many horrors in his life, many ghastly supernatural guardians, but this was the first time he'd been bested by a blue goblin, especially one with poor diction.

The blue goblin (specifically – as may be understood from Cabal's mutterings – a Germanic form known as a kobold), had acted as a guardian of sorts for an unusual library. Where most libraries are content to sit by or near a road, this one had occupied a pocket existence of its own, slotted neatly between the world of men and the world of the Fey. It was an extensive and useful library, but it did not encourage lending or even browsing. After a few bruising encounters with heavy volumes flung at him from shelf tops, Cabal had discovered the book he sought and made a hasty but victorious retreat. His victory lasted exactly until the moment he had had the time and leisure finally to examine the looted book and found that it had unaccountably become a small manual on the subject of waterproofing flat roofs. He belatedly thought of the Fey's ability to alter appearances, and then he thought of a kobold vivisection, which cheered him up a little.

So absorbed in his writing and muttering was he that the pebble that bounced off the window failed to draw his attention. The second, thrown vigorously enough to threaten the glass, succeeded. Cabal sighed, put down his pen, took up his revolver and went to the window. Given that it was pebbles rather than bricks, and given that nobody who lived within ten miles would be so stupid as to irritate Cabal, who was not only a necromancer but, in the vernacular, 'an utter bastard', it seemed likely that the thrower was a child on a dare. Cabal intended to shoot to miss, albeit narrowly. He was therefore surprised when he saw three soberly dressed men standing on the other side of the garden gate. One looked like an undertaker and Cabal, who had had a similar experience once before, checked his pulse just to be sure. Pleased to find he wasn't dead again, he went to the front door.

The three men, who had been watching the house with polite if slightly distant attention, now turned it upon Johannes Cabal. They saw a clean-shaven man with short blond hair, physically in his late twenties though he carried an air of cynicism and worldliness that would have seemed premature in a man twice his age. They saw his black trousers, black waistcoat, thin black cravat, white shirt, tartan slippers, and they saw his enormous handgun.

The last time Cabal had been to the gunsmiths' in town to buy more cartridges for it, the man behind the counter had told him that the pistol, a Webley .577 Boxer, was 'guaranteed to stop a charging savage', according to the literature. Cabal had replied he didn't know about that, but it could stop a Deep One with its dander up and that was good enough for him. The man behind the counter had considered this, and then talked about the weather. It was, in short, a fierce and unfriendly gun, and its very appearance was usually enough to cause nervous shuffling among spectators. The three men, however, seemed no more put out by it than by Cabal's slippers, and those hadn't caused any obvious consternation either.

Cabal considered. He did not encourage visitors, he had no colleagues *per se*, he had no friends, few acquaintances, and his family were all either dead, or had disowned him – or were dead *and* had disowned him. Occasionally other necromancers turned up to try to steal his researches in much the same way that he tried to steal theirs, or assorted self-elected paragons of virtue arrived to slay him as if he were a dragon. He was not a dragon; he was a much better shot than most dragons and the paragons' last sight was of the fierce and unfriendly Webley .577 Boxer and Cabal's irked face sighting over the wide muzzle at them. The three men seemed to fit none of the categories. 'Who are you?' asked Cabal. 'What do you want?'

One of the party, a short middle-aged man with receding hair, snowy mutton chops, and the open, sanguine air of a defrocked priest spoke up: 'We wish to make you a proposal, Herr Cabal.'

'A proposal?' Cabal pushed his blue-glass spectacles back up his nose and regarded the trio suspiciously. 'What sort of proposal?'

'That,' interrupted the tall man in the top hat, who looked like an undertaker, 'is better discussed in private.' He pursed lips that looked well used to it. 'Our immediate concern is to reach your front door.'

'My front . . . ? Oh!' Cabal understood and laughed. He looked down. Just over the tile-ridged edge of the garden alongside the path was a faded circular for patios and conservatory extensions. There had probably been others, but they had blown away long since, this one staying only because it was trapped beneath a discarded human femur. The surface of the bone was pocked with tiny bite marks. He looked back up at the men, a sardonic smile on his face. 'You're concerned about the denizens of this little plot. Gentlemen! They are only pixies and fairies! You're not afraid of them, are you?'

'Yeah! We're harmless!' piped a tiny voice from beneath a hydrangea, until it was shushed by other tiny piping voices.

For his answer the tall man stepped back and read the notice on the gate out loud: '*No circulars, hawkers or salesmen. Trespassers will be eaten*. We are not afraid, sir. We are showing rational caution.'

'Yes,' conceded Cabal. 'Put like that, I see your point. Very well.' He spoke to the garden. 'Let these men by.' There was a muted chorus of dismay from the hidden watchers, but the three were allowed to walk up the path unmolested. By the time they reached the doorstep, Cabal had already gone inside.

He was waiting, seated, in his study when the three men caught up with him. They stood gravely clustered around the door, unable or unwilling to sit without their host's invitation. Cabal was entirely unaware of a host's duties, and contented himself by sitting with one leg crossed over the other and the pistol held idly in his lap. He looked at the men and they looked back at him for several uncomfortable moments. 'Well?' he said finally.

'My card,' said the funereal gentleman, producing one from his pocket and offering it. Cabal did not rise to take it, but suffered the man to advance, hand it over, and then withdraw in the manner of a priest delivering a votive sacrifice.

'Mine also,' added the third man, speaking for the first time. He had, to Cabal's eye, the air of a recovering alcoholic who now ran a small printing company dedicated to the publication of religious tracts.[1] He, too, had mutton chops, but these were black and as lustrous as a dog's coat. His eyes were quick and dark, and he wore the disreputable shortened form of a top hat known as a 'Müller'.

'Mine too!' added the one with the appearance of a disgraced priest.

Cabal studied the cards casually. 'So, you are Messrs Shadrach,' he thumbed the card from the top of the small pile

[1] It is illustrative of the workings of Cabal's mind that he readily associated religion and moral dissolution.

and allowed the funeral director's card to flutter to the floor, 'Corde,' he dropped the former alcoholic's, 'and Bose.'

'It's pronounced *Boh-see*,' said the unfrocked priest, although – disappointingly – it appeared from his card that he was actually a dealer in artworks.

'You were never a priest, were you, Mr Bose?' asked Cabal, just to be sure. Mr Bose shook his head and looked confused and that was that.

Mr Corde was – equally disappointingly – a solicitor and not a reformed alcoholic publisher of religious screeds, but Mr Shadrach really was a funeral director. This also disappointed Cabal, whose grave-robbing activities in search of research materials were often complicated by the eccentricities of those who carried out the burials. One doesn't want to spend all night excavating down to a coffin only to discover that it is lead-lined, sealed with double-tapped screws, and proof against crowbars.

'All very good, but none of which answers the question that I believe I implied when I said, "Well?" An art dealer, a solicitor, and a funeral director. What business have you with me, sirs? Indeed, what business have you with one another?'

'We belong to a society, Herr Cabal. A very special society, dedicated to a noble but arcane purpose. It is this purpose that has brought us to your door.'

Cabal looked at them with a raised eyebrow. '*Grundgütiger*! You don't all want to be necromancers, do you? It's thankless work, gentlemen. I advise you strongly against it.' Their blank expressions assured him that, no, this was not the purpose of their visit. 'Well, what, then?'

'Let us start from a hypothesis, Herr Cabal,' said Mr Bose, with wheedling enthusiasm. 'And let that hypothesis start from a question. Is the human creature as perfect in function as it might be?'

'Meaningless,' replied Cabal, 'with no definition as to what that function might conceivably be. We are good communicators, passable runners, middling swimmers, and poor at flying.'

'Just so. But even there, we are capable of communications of great subtlety over very long distances, we build locomotives that can outrun the fastest animal, steam launches that can give even dolphins a good run for their money, and aeroships that have formed our conquest of the skies. You see my point, of course. But do you take my greater meaning?'

'*Natürlich*. You are suggesting that the function of the human creature, to use your phrase, is to adapt itself to its environment or even to adapt its environment to itself by virtue of its intelligence. Then my answer is no. Humanity is nowhere near perfection even with regard only to its intellect. Have you ever looked at your fellow man? It is not edifying. I have hopes that time and evolutionary forces may improve matters or, failing that, eliminate us and give something else a chance. I think the insects deserve a turn.'

'But in the shorter term, how may we improve ourselves?'

Cabal shrugged. 'Eugenics. Kill the lawyers. Vitamins. There have been all manner of suggestions.'

Corde had been growing visibly exasperated with Bose and cut in: 'Think rather in terms of what limits us, Herr Cabal. What holds us back in our everyday lives? What Mr Bose is trying to say is that our little society seeks to eliminate the most profound of all these limiting factors.'

'Death,' replied Cabal, without hesitation. 'You *do* wish to become necromancers.'

'No, sir!' said Corde, a little heatedly. Gentlemen do not wish to hear themselves described as nascent necromancers, even by a necromancer. 'I mean the little death that eats away our lives from the moment we are old enough to realise that a final death certainly awaits us.'

Cabal frowned. He was aware of the phrase 'little death', as used by the French, but it seemed very much out of context here, where the context consisted of Messrs Bose, Corde and Shadrach. 'I am bemused.'

'I mean, Herr Cabal,' and here Mr Corde took an unconsciously dramatic step closer to Cabal, '*fear*!' Satisfied that he had made his point with sufficient emphasis, he stepped back again. 'Every waking moment of our lives we spend as hostages to the terrible "perhaps". We dread the unnameable that lurks beyond our doors. We collapse into ridiculous phobias with the most fleeting provocation. Clowns! Birds! The number thirteen! Each one a nail driven into the fabric of our lives, limiting our movement, hemming us in, draining our futures of possibilities. How many better tomorrows have been lost because of natural human timidity? How many wonders have never seen the light because those who dared dream them could never dare build them?'

Cabal laughed: a humourless sound. 'You wish courage, gentlemen? I believe it may be found in any public house, by the pint. Good day.' He rose to escort the men out, but then Mr Shadrach spoke, and Cabal listened.

'We have considered long and carefully before coming to you, Herr Cabal. You are quite right. A sufficient measure of liquor will drive out fear from any man, but it will take all rationality with it too. My companions have not perhaps made our aim quite as clear as they might. We understand the role of fear as a safeguard, but we dispute its effect on a higher creature such as the human being. A rational man should be able to look upon a situation and weigh its dangers – physical, moral or financial – as coldly as if weighing tea on a scale. That is denied us because fear is essentially irrational. We seek nothing more or less than to remove it. Our dream is that one day the human race will walk this good Earth, free from the invisible tethers of fear, subject only to the kindly effects of rational caution.'

Cabal sighed and sat down again. 'You mentioned a society. What sort of society? Do you hold annual general meetings, raise funds by selling cakes, and all go on a charabanc holiday together with funds raised by subscription?'

'We do not,' replied Shadrach, a little icily.

'Ah,' said Cabal. 'Yours is the other sort of society, then. The type with impractical handshakes.'

Shadrach also regarded their society's secret handshake as unnecessary, infantile and not even very secret, as it looked like the first shakee was attempting to put the second into a half-nelson. Thus, he did not dispute Cabal's description, but said, 'Our numbers are relatively few, but contain men and a few women of influence and insight. Scientists, logicians, entrepreneurs. Our resources, both intellectual and monetary, run as deep as our ambitions.'

'No churchmen, I notice. Of course not. What use have they for a world without irrational fear? And how did an undertaker, an art dealer and a solicitor happen to join such a society?'

'Irrelevant,' said Corde, a little snappily.

Shadrach, however, was happy to elucidate. 'My own interest was founded in the lack of fear of the dead that I feel, a lack created by my long familiarity with the practicalities of dealing with the recently departed. One cannot do such business without wondering at the fear the public hold for a population that can offer them no harm.'

Cabal, whose experience with that population indicated that they were perfectly capable of offering harm in the right circumstances, held his silence.

'Mr Corde, if I may speak on your behalf?' Corde jerked his head in an impatient affirmation, so Shadrach continued: 'Mr Corde deals with people every day who make bad decisions based upon fear and not logic, whether to create a fund here, or a trust there, even fear of writing a will in case it should tempt Fate in some ill-imagined way. In both our cases, you see, we watch people blunt their lives with silly fears, fears that offer them nothing, not even safety. And Mr Bose . . .' here, Shadrach did not ask permission '. . . is fascinated by the deeper mysteries, of life, of death.'

'I meet all sorts in my job,' smiled Bose, as if discussing the vagaries of collecting matchbox labels. 'One of my clients told me about the society, and I said, "Oh, that sounds like fun!" So here I am.'

Shadrach looked at Bose for a long moment, unsure how to proceed. Cabal filled the silence a little impatiently by saying, 'Yes, it's all very laudable I'm sure, but I am still at a loss to understand my part in all this. How do you intend to achieve your goal? Brain surgery?'

Bose grimaced. 'Tried that. It didn't work,' he said, before being shushed by Corde.

'We have conducted much research, Herr Cabal,' said Shadrach, 'both experimental,' here he shot a sideways glance at Bose, who looked suitably abashed, 'and theoretical. It is the latter that has led us to a possible – indeed probable – solution. What we intend is nothing less than to isolate the very spirit of fear and, thence, to focus our energies on finding its anathema. The antibody to fear, if you will.'

Cabal smiled or, at least, his face creased in a manner only suitably described as a smile, but there was little warmth there. 'You wish to isolate fear. Ah, well, if only I'd realised your ambitions were so simple. Perhaps we can work up to it by capturing faith, bottling hope, and presenting love to the world as a commodity, available by the pound, wrapped in greaseproof paper and topped with a bow.' He sighed. 'How can you possibly hope to isolate the incorporeal? If it were a true spirit, you could amuse yourself with salt and pentagrams, but fear, sirs? You waste your time and mine.'

Surprisingly, the three men did not seem at all put out or taken aback by Cabal's response and he realised that they'd anticipated it. Indeed, they seemed to relish it. 'Sir, our researches are conclusive. We are certain, absolutely certain, that fear may manifest and be captured. But not, sir, in this world.'

'There is another place, Herr Cabal,' said Bose, 'another world where things are not as they are here. Where the most fanciful concepts may prove sterling truth, and the incorporeal take form.'

Cabal straightened a little in his chair, interested despite himself. 'You speak of the Dreamlands.'

The name notwithstanding, the Dreamlands are neither a retailer of mattresses, a retirement home nor a particularly nasty permanent funfair in a rundown coastal resort. Neither are they where our minds go when they sleep. Those are merely dreams, and the Dreamlands are too strange and, in their own curious way, too noble to trouble themselves with endless variations on wandering the corridors of one's old school on the first day, alone, lost, naked, and having just discovered that an exam nobody told one about had started ten minutes ago. No, the Dreamlands were formed by dreams, but are not a dream themselves. They are a world of curious and exotic sights, a collision of myths, of lands as ancient as thought and oceans as deep as imagination. They are home to those who have abandoned their waking bodies, or been abandoned by them. But, as the Dreamlands are true and material even though they hide behind the veil of sleep, there have been other immigrants from other realities, and here lay Cabal's interest. One of those immigrants was a fierce and protean magic that might, just might, carry a spark of itself back into the waking world, should it be brought by somebody strongly willed enough to shade it from the mundanities of the everyday. Somebody like a well-motivated necromancer.

'Yes, I researched them exhaustively myself years ago. But they are beyond reach.'

'They are not, sir.'

'To trained or talented dreamers, no. To the users of certain highly dangerous and unreliable drugs, no. To the holder of the Silver Key, no. I am none of these things, *meine Herren*, and neither are you. The Dreamlands, while an interesting destination, are beyond the reach of any of us.'

Alarmingly, the three men still seemed splendidly unconcerned and, indeed, rather smug. Cabal ran the alternatives through his head rapidly and settled on the most likely, though staggeringly unlikely it was. 'You . . . have the Silver Key?'

It was Shadrach who spoke. 'We do, sir. We have the Silver Key of the Dreamlands. We may enter and leave as we will.'

Cabal tried to keep the quiver out of his voice. 'You . . . How . . . did you come by it?'

'As a bequest. An explorer of that world learned of our endeavours and, I'm delighted to say, passed it on to us.'

'As a bequest,' Cabal echoed. 'How did he die?'

'Oh, he may not be dead. He was simply declared deceased by the coroner's court. He'd been missing for some time and, well, I'm sure you know how these things work.'

Cabal, who was very familiar with the workings of all the institutions that dealt with death, grunted. 'It does not worry you that this gentleman probably died in the Dreamlands?'

'Worry,' said Corde, evenly, 'is a product of fear. We will not submit to it. Instead, we will add this datum to the rational caution that such an enterprise must engender.'

Ah, thought Cabal, *now we come to it*.

'There are many possibilities, many things that may go awry in the Dreamlands,' said Shadrach. 'This may be the only opportunity that we of the Institute will ever have to venture there. We must maximise our chance of success in every way that we can.'

'And this, I would guess, is why you have come to me,' said Cabal. Although he showed no sign of it, he was impressed by their methodology. If irrational fear had something approaching a physical form, then it could surely survive only in a world formed from dreams where the rules of existence were intuitive rather than scientifically rigorous. From there it could leak its influence back into the sleeping minds of the mundane world to soak into their waking lives and colour every decision with delicate shades of uncertain terror. It all sounded very interesting, Cabal was sure. There was, however, a problem. 'I'm afraid that I must disappoint you. I have no experience of the Dreamlands. I have never been there.'

'We know,' said Corde. 'You're alive and sane. It seemed very unlikely that you'd ever visited.'

'So, why . . .?'

'Because we have little use for a dead or insane guide. You may not have immediate experience of the Dreamlands, Herr Cabal, but you do have plentiful experience of the, ah, occult,' he said apologetically, 'and the unusual. You also have a reputation for formidable *sang-froid*, which will come in useful given the stressful environment.'

Cabal smiled, a little less humourlessly this time. It always amused him that, when you wished to flatter somebody, you would describe them as possessing *sang-froid*, whereas if you wished to sting or insult them, they were simply *cold-blooded*.

'Our proposal is that you should lead an expedition into the Dreamlands, Herr Cabal,' said Shadrach, 'to seek out, capture and bring back into this world the archetype of fear, its principle, the very phobic animus itself.'

'And if it refuses to come quietly?'

'Then it will be put down.'

There was a heavy silence after that for some seconds. Then Cabal said, 'You are asking me to risk my life and sanity. What am I to gain from this?'

Bose coughed. 'The Silver Key, Herr Cabal. Once we have the animus, we shall have no further need of the Key. Indeed, rational caution dictates that it is never used without good cause, and our cause would already be fulfilled. We think that you, however, would have cause to use it again, in future, in the continuance of your own field of research.'

Cabal considered. Then he spoke: 'Gentlemen, your

proposition is not without interest. I should like to think upon it. You will make your way back to the village and, if you have not already done so, take rooms there. I would suggest that you don't tell them you have any dealings with me or the standard of service will suffer. I shall send word of my decision to you some time tomorrow. Good day.' And so saying, he shooed his visitors from his house, ensuring first that they successfully negotiated the path without being ambushed from the tea roses.

Later that evening, Cabal was to be found at the table, the contents of a box file labelled 'Dreamlands' spread out before him. He had been accruing data on the place for years, although never as a definite piece of research. After all, while the usefulness of the Dreamlands in his work was beyond dispute, accessing it in a safe and reliable way had always been little more than . . . well, a dream.

Others had attempted it, and some had even done so successfully. As a group, however, they were a bunch of arty sorts – Orientalists and sensualists, who could be depended upon to be undependable, sitting around in silken robes with a book of poetry in one hand and a hookah pipe in the other. They disgusted Cabal for their practical rather than moral shortcomings; if Cabal was to go exploring, he would be inclined to do so with a sola topi on his head and an elephant gun loaded for tyrannosaur in his hands.

Practicality, however, was the enemy of the Dreamlands explorer. He would be standing around in the mundane world until his sola topi bleached and his elephant gun rusted, while in the meantime the disgusting woolly-minded artistic types were off writing bad sonnets by the lake at Sarnath, having wandered into the Dreamlands by the very virtue of being woolly-minded artistic types. It was as intolerable as, for example, the British Library suddenly enforcing a 'Monkeys Only' rule, leaving serious scholars fuming outside while, within the sacred walls, macaques made merry with the Magna Carta, and capuchins defecated on the Gutenberg. It galled Cabal beyond belief that those of analytic mind who could make most use of the strange resources of the Dreamlands were, by their very nature, denied entrance.

There was one way through, however: the Silver Key – always capital S, capital K because it truly was that important and that unique. There may be only one Holy Grail, but it is part of an entire junk shop's worth of similar relics – fragments of the One True Cross, the Spear of Destiny, the Burial Shroud in Turin, and more miraculous bits of dead saints than bear thinking about. The Silver Key, however, was truly unique – the only artefact that allowed physical rather than psychic entry into the Dreamlands, and the only artefact that could be used by absolutely anyone with the will to do so, regardless of opium consumption.

Finding it, however, was the natural prerequisite to using it, and finding it had proved impossible. It seemed to have an irrational fondness for ending up in the hands of the very wastrels who could just as easily have reached the Dreamlands by the narcotic route, and as drug-addled wastrels make poor documenters, the trail of hands through which the Key had passed was as ephemeral as footprints by the low-tide mark.

And now, having been dismissed as, at best, unfindable and, at worst, non-existent, the Silver Key of myth and legend was almost in his hands, certainly within his reach. Cabal considered walking to the village in the night, murdering the men in their beds and stealing the Key, but discarded the notion. After all, they might not have it with them. Besides which, the idea of leading a funded expedition into the Dreamlands appealed to him. He could use the hunt for this 'Phobic Animus' of theirs as an opportunity to scout out the land, and gather intelligence for his own subsequent explorations. He did not even mind having three unctuous men following him around: he agreed with their aims and if, wonder of wonders, they succeeded, the mortal world would be that much more rational, and therefore personally bearable to Cabal. Also, he was confident that he could outrun any of them, and if the party ended up being pursued by one or other of the Dreamlands' many horrors, it was good to know that there were three alternative meals that he could leave in his wake.

The village – it had a name, but Cabal rarely used it – lay some four miles away from where his house stood in its sheltered little valley, a location calculated to prevent the slightest tone of a church bell reaching it even with a tailwind. Four miles is also, incidentally, an awkward distance for a torch-bearing mob to cover: torches gutter, pitchforks grow heavy, and the length of the walk robs a lynching of its necessary spontaneity. Not that the villagers did very much of that, not after the last time.

Cabal kept his visits there to the bare minimum, and for their part, the villagers tolerated him with a forced civility that said as much for their Englishness as for any fear of him. The grocer would take his order in polite silence, only speaking to make the mandatory opening conversational gambit of greeting and comment upon the weather, then to clarify any ambiguities as he transcribed Cabal's list of requirements, and finally to bid him a sincere and relieved goodbye. People on the street ignored him. Even the most wilful teenager knew the stories and avoided eye contact.

The only individual who sought Cabal out when he visited was Sergeant Parkin, the senior officer of the village's police force, consisting of Parkin, two unambitious constables, and an ageing Alsatian called 'Bootsy'. People liked Sergeant Parkin and were grateful for the calm way in which he dealt with the Cabal problem. 'He knows better than to throw his weight around here,' Parkin would say, while drinking on duty in the saloon bar of The Old House at Home. 'We treat him polite, like, and he's here and gone, and good riddance.' The villagers might have been less pleased to know that Parkin's public-relations efforts were entirely focused upon them, as Parkin himself was in Cabal's employ. In return for a suitable emolument in a brown envelope every Christmas, Parkin kept the village in a state of delicate uncertainty, as a Swiss village might be beneath a mountainside deep in snow: providing they remained calm and quiet, no avalanche would descend upon them. Parkin saw no clash between his role and his actions. After all, his primary concern was to keep the peace, and this he did.

Parkin was talking football in the pub when Mr Jeffries, whose home overlooked the dusty and rarely travelled road that ran by Cabal's house, entered, approached the sergeant directly, spoke quietly and calmly in his ear, and left again.

Parkin frowned and looked at the calendar hung behind the bar. Beneath a gaudy McGill painting of an exasperated judge and a smirking divorce case co-respondent ('You are prevaricating, sir. Did you or did you not sleep with this woman?' 'Not a wink, my lord!'), the date caused him some mild consternation.

He buttoned up his uniform tunic, put on his helmet, said, 'Duty calls,' to the landlord, slung the last inch of his pint down his throat, and went out to face the dreadful Herr Cabal.

Cabal was unsurprised to see Sergeant Parkin waiting by the pump, trough and rarely used well on the village green, his arms crossed, his expression vexed. He walked directly to the policeman, aware that every busybody in the place was watching them. It did not help Cabal to undermine Parkin's authority, so he exhibited enough deference to maintain the sergeant's standing, and just enough coldness to remind the onlookers just who they were dealing with here.

'Funny time of the month for you to be out of your bailiwick, isn't it, Mr Cabal?' said Parkin, loudly enough to be heard by the watchers. Then, more quietly, he added, 'Bugger me, chum, a word of warning would have been nice.'

'Of course, Parkin,' replied Cabal, also quietly. 'I should have sent a member of my extensive household to tell you. The under-butler, perhaps, or a footman, or possibly one of the many grooms.'

Parkin, who knew that Cabal was the only inhabitant of his house, or at least the only living human inhabitant, grunted, and let the point go. 'All right, so you're here now. What is it you're after? You only had your groceries last week. You haven't run out, have you?'

'No. I have had visitors. I believe they are staying at the tavern. I wish to speak to them.'

'What?' Parkin shot a glance at the Old House at Home. 'The undertaker, the unfrocked priest and the bloke who looks like an alky? I knew all that codswallop about butterfly hunting was bollocks, but I didn't know they were anything to do with you. I don't recall you having any visitors before, Cabal.'

'I have visitors, just not often, and they don't normally stop here.' Cabal was aware of hostile eyes upon him, and of the delicate *status quo* of the relationship between the villagers and himself seesawing dangerously. 'Is this a problem, Sergeant?'

'If you go blundering into the pub, yes. That's sacred ground, Cabal. Don't ever go in there. That's somewhere safe where they can whine about you to their hearts' content, safe knowing you'll never show your face in the place. Going in would be . . . provocative. No, I've got a better plan.'

The villagers watched the doughty Sergeant Parkin and the vile Johannes Cabal negotiate quietly until, with dangerous anger showing clearly in his body language, the necromancer turned and strode back out of the village in a cold fury. Parkin stood, arms crossed and haughty, and watched Cabal go until he was past the post office. Then, duty done and the village once more safe, he strolled back to the pub to be bought a pint on the house, a suitable reward for a conquering hero. While the landlord pulled the pint, Parkin made his way into the snug and there found Messrs Shadrach, Corde and Bose eating lunch and muttering to one another in conspiratorial tones until Parkin's entrance plunged them into an embarrassed silence.

'Afternoon, gentlemen,' he said jovially. 'If you wouldn't mind eating up smartish, like, packing your bags, and pissing off out of it, the parish would be grateful.'

There was a shocked silence. Shadrach made as if to say something, but Parkin leaned down and said, close enough to

Shadrach's face that he was momentarily overcome by pipe tobacco and beer fumes, 'It's not a request, sir. It's *not* a request.' Then, dropping easily to a penetrating whisper, he added, 'You gentlemen have an appointment,' and quickly pressed a folded piece of paper into Shadrach's hand. 'I wouldn't be late if I were you, squire.' Parkin rose, shot them a cynical salute, and went off to claim his beer.

They found Cabal sitting on a fence by the road a mile out of the village, shying stones at a crow. He didn't appear to be working very hard to hit it, which was just as well since the crow was remarkably good at dodging, and indeed seemed to regard having lumps of rock cast at its head as a show of affection on Cabal's part. 'Kronk!' it cawed joyfully, as a lump of flint the size of a baby's fist hissed by the tip of its beak.

'You received my communication, I see,' said Cabal, as they approached. He climbed down and went to meet them. As he did so, the crow belatedly realised the game was over and flew up to land on Cabal's left shoulder. He shot it a glance from the corner of his eye that it chose to ignore.

'You have a crow for a pet, Mr Cabal?' asked Corde.

'Hardly that. More a fellow traveller. You want my decision?' The three men nodded, more or less gravely. 'I agree to your proposition. I shall guide you into and through the Dreamlands. I emphasise that the knowledge on the Dreamlands I bring to this enterprise is based upon the writings of others, and can only be considered as reliable as they are.'

'Of course,' said Shadrach.

'So, if we get lost, I do not wish to hear a single solitary word that the failing is mine. If I do, I shall feed the complainant to the nearest gug.'

'What is a *gug?*'

'Exactly my point. I know, and you do not. My knowledge of the Dreamlands may be flawed, but it is still magnitudes greater than yours. With that caveat, do you remain committed to this undertaking?'

'We do,' they chorused, a little shakily.

'You *are* sure?' said Cabal, smiling slightly at their quavering voices. He fed the crow an aged macadamia he had found in his jacket pocket. 'I ask merely because I have a sense that the Phobic Animus is here with us now, for some reason.'

Not trusting themselves to speak, the three men nodded their assent.

'Good. Well, now. I assume you have easy access to your institutional funds, as I shall be spending a lot of them immediately. Equipment is by the bye: the Dreamlands will provide what we need, at least to begin with. We shall need to travel, however.'

'Travel, Mr Cabal?' said Bose. 'But surely the Dreamlands are coterminous with all space and time? We can enter them as easily from here as from Timbuktu.'

'I do not recall suggesting Timbuktu,' said Cabal. 'Yes, you are right, but simply standing beside a boundary does not allow you to move through that boundary. A high wall allows no access, not until you find the door. I cast lots before I came out today, and I have found a place where the veil between this world and the Dreamlands is suitably fine that the Silver Key will make short work of it. That is where the Gate of the Silver Key lies, gentlemen, and we should make haste before it decides to relocate to the heart of the Sahara, or the depths of the Antarctic, or – gods forfend – Wolverhampton.'

'And where does it lie now, Mr Cabal?'

'Somewhere beneath the sagging gambrel rooftops and behind the crumbling Georgian balustrades of Arkham, in the state of Massachusetts. Arkham, that lies upon the darkly muttering Miskatonic. I have not been there since . . .' He paused, remembering, and that faint ironic smile twitched across his mouth. 'Since for ever. Witch-cursed, legend-haunted Arkham. Ah, how I've missed it. Oh, and the university library has a copy of *Enquêtes interdites*. I must remember to steal it, time permitting. That is for later, however. Can your organisation foot the bill for our travel and accommodation?'

'It can, Mr Cabal,' said Shadrach, with encouraging firmness. 'Ever since its creation some thirty years ago, the Institute has been saving its resources for this great endeavour. We shall have all we need, and more.'

'Good, good,' said Cabal, distractedly shooing the crow from his shoulder.

'We will alert the treasurer of the Fear Institute by telegram immediately, and . . .'

He paused: Cabal was holding one index finger up in a gesture of enquiry. 'The Fear Institute?'

'Yes.'

'Is it named after a Mr Fear?'

'No.'

Cabal laughed, a dry, cynical noise that stirred and died in his throat. 'There is nothing mealy-mouthed about you, is there, gentlemen? Good. I approve.

'To the Fear Institute, then, I offer my services.'

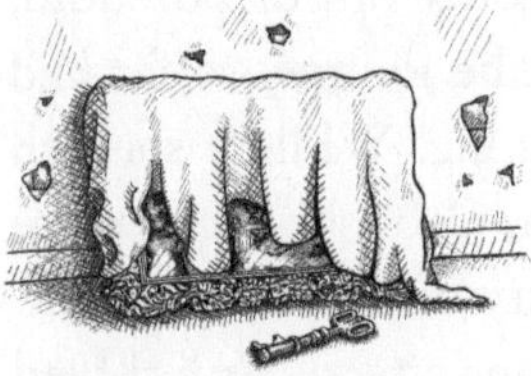

Chapter 2

IN WHICH THE UNITED STATES OF AMERICA ARE VISITED, THOUGH BRIEFLY

Neither were the claims of Shadrach, Corde and Bose unfounded. Money was requested, and money was forthcoming. They travelled by train to a major port, and there took passage across the Atlantic. Corde suggested they travel by aeroship, but Johannes Cabal made a face, said that air travel was very overrated and that he would prefer to go by surface ship. Thus, forty-eight hours after their first meeting with Cabal, the party was steaming across the ocean, due for arrival at New York in eight days.

'From there, we take the New Haven railroad service to Boston, and thence . . .' Bose consulted the back and front of a train timetable for some moments, dropping it to the table in the lounge in favour of another before going back to the first '. . . and thence a short trip, also by train, to Arkham station, which is in, ah . . .' he read the fine print carefully '. . . Arkham.'

Shadrach and Corde nodded sagely at this intelligence. Cabal, for his part, had left his cabin only out of boredom, and was now considering this a folly. The journey so far had been low in incident and high in planning. While a staunch proponent of at least some preparation, Cabal had long since learned the utility and frequent necessity of extemporisation. Once one went beyond that, however, one effectively hobbled oneself, leaving oneself vulnerable and liable to one becoming zero, and one wouldn't like that. Contingency plans were all well and good, but they were going into a very *incognita* sort of *terra*; it all seemed like just so much wasted effort.

When Cabal made a comment along those lines, however, Shadrach said, 'We must expect the unexpected,' before laying out his scheme to deal with pirates riding stilt-legged elephants to the others. It was a good plan, as it happened, but then, so had been the plans to deal with giant platypuses and killer begonias. Cabal wondered if they were simply going through the dictionary and evolving procedures to deal with every noun they came across. He hardly cared, having belatedly realised that the more planning they did, the less he had to talk to them.

He also realised, and this he kept to himself, that the Animus travelled with them. These men were afraid, so they planned for the silliest eventualities simply because it kept them occupied. They denied themselves pause for reflection, because fear breeds in the quiet moments.

Cabal also had a small fear: that eight days of their nonsense would drive him insane. He was regretting having been quite so efficient in his preparation that it left him few distractions.

He had copies of two very rough maps and a notebook filled with the distilled wisdom of any number of laudanum-enhanced poets with respect to useful knowledge of the Dreamlands. It was a very thin notebook.

He was flicking through it when the others finally agreed on a plan in case of attack by soft furnishings, and Corde asked, 'What was that creature you were speaking of the other day, Cabal? The gog, was it?'

'Gug,' replied Cabal, without looking up. 'It's called a gug.'

'Well, I was just thinking, gentlemen,' said Corde, addressing Shadrach and Bose, 'that we should also plan for known threats in the Dreamlands. After all, it is that sort of information that Mr Cabal has at his fingertips.' The others agreed, with much humming and stroking of chins, that addressing real threats might be a good idea. Having secured their agreement, Corde turned back to Cabal. 'So, what can you tell us about this *gug* fellow, then?'

Cabal merely flicked through his notebook until he came to a sketch, and passed it over to them. He was gratified by their sudden pallor and widened eyes.

'Yes,' said Shadrach, finally. 'Well . . . that looks . . . manageable.' And the three of them started muttering about deadfalls and bear pits.

Cabal made a mental note that 'manageable' could apparently be applied as a euphemism for a furry monstrosity with too many forearms, a vertical slit for a mouth, poor dental hygiene and an uncritical worship of dark gods so debauched that even other dark gods would blank them at dark-god parties. He also decided not to burden them with the knowledge that 'gug' was the name of a race and not an individual, or to point out that the sketch bore no scale and so their assumption that a gug stood only at about man-sized was profoundly optimistic. He would wait until they had finalised their plan before politely enquiring how the gug would react on finding itself shin deep in their trap or, indeed, how any of its many friends might.

The eight days of the sea crossing became more bearable as the Institute members grew by degrees both bored of their over-planning, and cognisant of its futility after Cabal had dropped a few more bombshells into their sessions.

The final straw was when Cabal innocently enquired of them, 'What is your plan for cats?'

'Cats?' said Shadrach.

'Cats?' echoed Corde. 'Are we likely to be set upon by cats?'

'I don't know,' said Cabal. 'That rather depends on your plan.'

Bose, the least enthusiastic of the three when it came to covering every conceivable contingency, tapped the box file that lay on the table. It was stuffed with plans, and there were another four just like it in Shadrach's cabin. 'Which plan?' he asked morosely.

'Your plan for cats.'

Shadrach frowned. If Johannes Cabal had not previously demonstrated beyond any reasonable doubt that he was disinclined to frivolity, then Shadrach would have been sure that they were being made fun of. 'Do I understand you correctly, Mr Cabal? Our plan for cats, which has not yet been formulated, depends upon our plan for cats?'

Cabal nodded sadly. 'It might.'

Shadrach and Corde looked at one another for a long moment. Then, with a heavy heart, Corde took up his pen and wrote upon a virgin sheet of paper, 'Cats'. He had barely had time to underline it when it was whipped out from beneath his nib by Bose, who tore the sheet into halves, then quarters, then eights, before letting them flutter on to the table. 'I am having a drink,' he declared. 'And I do not mean tea.'

They watched him go off in the direction of the bar, so did not notice Cabal's quiet smile of triumph before it vanished behind a two-day-old newspaper.[2]

On the eighth day, New York appeared on the western horizon, glittering monoliths caught in the morning sun. As the ship approached and the famous skyline became more distinct, Cabal's expression became more sour. Finally, he declared it the most phallocentric conurbation he had ever seen or even heard of, and that they should escape from it as quickly as they could because 'These subcultures get ideas of incipient superiority, combined with decadence across the social strata that make them psychologically inhuman. They will be tribalised and not subject to recognisable norms. We may even have trouble communicating with them. Mark my words, if we don't escape that hive as soon as we possibly can, things could go badly.'

Neither did their subsequent experiences undermine Cabal's expectations. The customs official they met on landing used 'youse' interchangeably for not only the singular and plural second-person personal pronouns, but also for the nominative, accusative, dative and possessive forms. A man

[2] And in the end the burgesses passed that remarkable law which is told of by traders in Hatheg and discussed by travellers in Nir; namely, that in Ulthar no man may kill a cat. *The Cats of Ulthar*, H. P. Lovecraft, 1920

they asked directions of also claimed to be a native, but his speech drawled on as if he were giving a running commentary on glacial shift. In contrast, the woman in the ticket kiosk at Pennsylvania station spoke rapidly and without pause for almost three minutes, leading Cabal to suspect that she was simultaneously inhaling through her mouth and talking through her nose.

Only when they were safely aboard the Boston train and it was *en route* did they relax. 'I feel that much more prepared for the Dreamlands, now,' commented Corde.

'I don't know,' said Bose, as he watched New York thin out around them. 'It didn't feel *that* alien.'

'You can't get a decent bacon sandwich there, you know, old man.'

'What?' gasped Bose, scandalised. He glared at the slowly diminishing tall buildings. 'Barbarians . . .'

Their first impression of Boston was that it had a far more European air about it, and was therefore patently more civilised and much more to everyone's taste. As it was already mid-afternoon, they decided to break their journey there and find a hotel. They would reach Arkham the next day, and that would be soon enough.

That evening after dinner, they repaired to a private room, taking a large pot of coffee with them. Corde, Shadrach and Bose ranged themselves along one side of the table, cups and notebooks to hand, while Cabal stood opposite them in the manner of a lecturer.

'It has been said,' he began, 'that what you do not know cannot hurt you. This would come as a revelation to many, if it were not for the fact that what they did not know had already torn them to shreds and giblets.'

'I'm not sure that's the context that—' began Shadrach, a little prissily, but Cabal was not listening.

'Our motto for this expedition, then, is *forewarned is forearmed*,' he continued, neglecting to mention that his personal motto for this expedition was *The devil take the hindmost*. He paused, wondering where would be a good place to start and, as he did so, he saw Bose's sheep-like expression and decided that brevity was the best policy.

'The Dreamlands are an inexact quantity. A cartographer's and a demographer's nightmare – or perhaps jobs for life – because the Dreamlands are constantly changing. Slowly, I grant you, but their tectonics are as hummingbirds compared to those of the waking world. I have maps, but their reliability must be suspect to a degree. Thus, we ask, and we ask often. Which brings us to the people.

'As we have already discussed, there are two ways for a mortal to enter the Dreamlands – corporeally or incorporeally. In the former case, their body accompanies them and all is straightforward. In the latter case, it is not clear where the matter comes from to form the dreamer's new Dreamland body, or where it goes to when the dreamer awakes. Many dreamers, of course, never return. Either due to accidents in the mundane world while they sleep, or by dint of the injudicious use of drugs to bring them into the Dreamlands in the first place, they die here, yet live there. It is impossible to be sure, but it seems likely that the indigenous population are all – or largely – immigrants from here. No, Herr Bose,' for Bose was looking around, startled, 'not specifically from this hotel. I mean from Earth and Earth's prehistory.'

'Wouldn't they be a bit . . . you know, old, by this time, Cabal?' asked Corde.

'Time is a more flexible asset there, Herr Corde, but I take your point. The current natives of the Dreamlands were born and bred there from ancient dreamers who either could not or would not return.'

'Is that fact, Mr Cabal?' asked Shadrach, making copious notes in a flowing cursive hand. 'Or supposition?'

'The latter,' said Cabal unabashed. 'It is difficult to explain the localised racial traits if it is true, but not impossible. Perhaps, millennia ago, immigrants from Ancient Greece or lost Mu came there and settled close together. That is human nature, after all. And so those populations naturally have Grecian or Muite characteristics to this day. It is impossible to be sure. The Dreamlands are . . .' he waved at his folder of notes, his distaste very evident '. . . very woolly.'

Corde, who felt too much orientation would dull the romance of it, was happy to change the subject. 'Then let us simply be on our guard and meet the Dreamlands as they meet us. We shall pick up the gist of them quickly enough, I have no doubt. Now, Cabal, the Gate of the Silver Key. You have its exact location.'

'Oh, yes.' Cabal was languid as he put the loose notes carefully back into their folder. 'I know precisely where the keyhole is.'

'Then . . .?'

'But I cannot give you a precise location.'

There was a silence, finally broken by Bose whispering to Shadrach, 'He's doing that thing again, like he did with the cats.'

'I thought you had cast lots or some such . . .' Corde resisted the urge to say 'nonsense' and instead said '. . . as a method for determining the current location of the Gate.'

'I have, indeed,' said Cabal, 'and my findings have been

precise and unambiguous. We shall catch the train to Arkham tomorrow morning and locate the Gate by evening.'

'Why leave it so late?'

'Because there will be less chance of witnesses.'

Shadrach regarded Cabal with the uncertain air of censure one might expect from a headmaster confronted by a boy who has smashed the atom, and the school with it. 'You mean to say, we shall have to break into somewhere?'

'No,' said Cabal. Then he thought for a moment longer and added, 'Yes. But no.'

'Are you being deliberately obscure, Cabal?' said Corde, his smile fading.

'Partially, but – *pace*, gentlemen – the answer is obscure in itself. Explaining it will . . . Suffice it to say that you hired me for my ability to deal with certain situations with a certain professionalism. I must ask you to trust me when I say that this is one such situation. I could give you a more exact answer, but in doing so I would endanger the success of the mission. You must trust me.'

And so, with ill-grace but no alternative, they did.

Oxford has its dreaming spires, and Paris its lights and love, but neither place exerts quite the same influences upon the poetic and susceptible as Arkham, the city of shadows. Shadows, literal and figurative, that lie upon the homes and upon the minds of that strange town's inhabitants. By European standards, of course, Arkham was a new town, not even half a millennium old, yet an air of ancient decrepitude had fallen upon the place scarcely after the first house was raised that baffled expectations and raised the hackles.

The land on which it had been built had been bought from

the indigenes for the usual trinkets, but in this case there had rapidly grown an unspoken suspicion that the former owners had got the better part of the deal. At first glance, there was nothing wrong with the land: it stood green and promising, rising gently from the sullen waters of the Miskatonic river that ran through it. Plots were quickly drawn up and dispersed, and eager settlers arrived to make new lives there. Soon, however, their eagerness tarnished and faded, replaced by an uncertain feeling that all was not well. But the land was good, and the location perfect, and practicality overcame vague doubts. Soon, other settlements were established, like Kingsport to the south-east, Innsmouth to the east, and Dunwich inland to the west. Soon after, the rumours began.

The whole region seemed indefinably tainted. Bad things happened. Brutality, drunkenness and petty crime stained the reputations of the towns, but there were whispers of worse things still. Witchcraft was afoot in Arkham, incest in Dunwich, murder and cannibalism in Innsmouth went the gossip. The towns seemed mired in degeneration and sin against which the burghers had no recourse. But then the witch hunters came from nearby Salem, and cleansed by fire and rope. Though they killed only the hapless innocent in Salem, nobody ever made such claims for Arkham or her near neighbours. Here, the self-styled inquisitors saw things that assured them of their righteous cause, even while it shook their faith in a benevolent God.

And so, Arkham and Innsmouth and the others were saved from the atavistic blight, all was light and joy, and evil ne'er again haunted these places. Certainly, that was the impression the towns were keen to convey, if only to save themselves all that bother again, and – in common with the best self-fulfilling prophecies – that was how things seemed. Some carried this feat with more assuredness than others: Arkham became home to the popular and renowned Miskatonic University, which in turn attracted learned and artistic communities to the town; Kingsport grew lean and ascetic, as though time had lost interest in it, thereby holding the twin illnesses of decay and progress from its door. Innsmouth, however, kept its secrets and grew cunning in that keeping, while Dunwich just rotted amid its fields like an unharvested pumpkin.

But it is Arkham that claims our interest, amid its quaint old-world houses and its famous university, which, if not quite Ivy League, still brings to mind things that climb and creep.

The vast majority of Arkhamites are pleased with their town in many respects. It is architecturally interesting, it has a good university, it is pleasantly placed, and if it has some small historical opprobria attached to its name, then these have mellowed through time to lend nothing more than a delicious notoriety to the town. In this last matter, the vast majority of Arkhamites are deluded.

Arkham lies in a region of reality where the weft and warp have worn dangerously thin. Here, people may think things they ought not, see things they ought not, and be seen by things that ought not be. There are those within the town who know of these facts, and who willingly research into them, either for purposes of knowledge, protection or, most frequently, personal power. It is a perilous path, and few survive it intact, either spiritually or physically, those who reach the end finding that the prize is rarely worth the cost. As they suffer and die and suffer some more, beyond the thin veil there are dark shapes that gibber and pipe, and one voice laughs and never stops.

Yet there are always more who come to try to draw the veil aside. Which suits the dark shapes, for they know a secret that was ancient long before even amoebae floated in the primordial oceans of Earth. An ancient truth that sings throughout this universe and the others that crowd around it, a secret that may be expressed in words as 'There's a sucker born every minute.'

One such sucker was Eldon Harwell, a young man recently dropped out of – before he could be sent down from – Miskatonic University. Eldon's path into moral disintegration had begun when he had attended a showing at the Pickman Gallery on the corner of Pickman and West. It had been a poorly attended affair, and Harwell had been quite full of nibbles and cheap white wine when the proprietor had taken a shine to him, and invited him to see the 'private' collection after the public showing was concluded. Drunk and bored, Harwell had readily agreed, hopeful that the collection would be sufficiently debauched to please the jaded senses of a citizen of Eldersburg, Maryland, such as himself.

Harwell, as a former undergraduate, was confident of his worldliness, but what he saw behind the threadbare velvet curtain kicked open several doors in his psyche that would better have remained locked. He was, for example, familiar with the theory if not the practice of bestiality, but the beautiful – and in pure aesthetic terms, in ratio and technique, in application and style, it *was* beautiful – painting of women sporting with hounds unsettled him more than he had expected. First in the recognition that the hounds were not exactly hounds and, later when he thought back, the realisation that the women were not exactly women.

He slept badly that night, and when exasperation finally

drove him from his bed, he looked out from his garret room across the junction of Lich Street and Peabody Avenue. There lay Arkham Cemetery, shadowed and silvered by the light of a gibbous moon that seemed to leer down upon the silent, empty scene.

But, no! What was that? In the corner of the burial ground, through the ivy-twined railings, he caught a glimpse of movement between the gravestones. It paused, as if aware of him, then stepped out into the cold moonlight, and he saw that it was a dog, only a dog.

And then it looked up at him, and rose on to its hind legs, and it walked like a man.

He awoke the next morning on the floor, a bump at the back of his head where it had struck the floor when he fell, fainting. This was a small blessing, as it allowed him to reorder the disordered events of the night in a form that caused him less distress. He had risen, and tripped in the darkness, banging his head in the fall. This had caused a horrible nightmare triggered by the paintings he had seen. There had been no dog in the graveyard. There had been *no* dog.

He was lying to himself and, in his heart, he knew it. What he did not know was he could never be the same man again. The doors had been opened, and they allowed transit in both directions. He began to have ideas, interesting ideas in the same way that the ideas of the Marquis de Sade or Samuel Taylor Coleridge were interesting. Perverse, out-of-the-usual-run-of-things ideas that buffeted around his head like especially muscular butterflies, seeking expression. This was of the greatest torment to Harwell for, though he was as debauched and worldly as a man of his age and means could reasonably expect, though he was now illuminated by the truth of everything and was mere baby steps from comprehension, he was entirely talentless.

Musically, his attempts at 'Chopsticks' sounded like Stravinsky in a temper, his art was inferior to a manatee's attempts at finger painting, and what his prose lacked in style, it also lacked in adverbs. The overall effect was that Eldon Harwell was a blocked spigot; a kettle filled with meaning and a cork down his spout.

Such a situation has driven greater men into the arms of madness, and opiates, and barmaids. Being a lesser man, Harwell succumbed to all three, before settling into a state of melancholia, from which his few remaining friends could not stir him.

In that dismal garret, he sat with his head in his hands, unable to articulate the vistas that moiled and slithered across his mind. At hand were a pen, ink and a half ream of cheap paper, for Harwell could at least spell and therefore clutched miserably at writing as an outlet. One day, he hoped and prayed, the boiling light he could perceive but not describe would resolve into coherence, and he would be its conduit. A great poem would pour from him, and leave him empty and peaceful. He also knew his next act would be to burn the manuscript before it could infect anyone else or, worse, reinfect him. As yet he had remained frustrated in this. Every attempt to shake loose the cosmic truth within him had resulted in a garbled mess or, on one occasion, a limerick about vicious but stupid crabs.

The curtains remained drawn at all hours. He feared seeing something else in the cemetery, so when the knock came at his door late one night, it surprised him terribly and he cried, suddenly fearful, 'Who is there? Who raps upon my chamber door at this late hour?'

Beyond the portal, there came the muffled sound of a whispered conversation. Finally, a sepulchral voice intoned, 'I . . .' There was another pause, amid fierce muttering. 'Which is to say, we . . .'

Then Harwell heard a new voice murmur something that sounded exasperated and possibly defamatory in German before saying, 'Oh, just open the door, Herr Harwell. We have business to discuss with you.'

Reassured by the matter-of-fact tone, Harwell unlocked his door and slowly opened it to reveal four men whose identities must surely be apparent to all but the most inattentive reader. Johannes Cabal was the first in, impatient energy written into his every movement. He looked critically but silently around the room as Shadrach, Corde and Bose filed in behind him and stood uncomfortably with their hats in their hands as Cabal wandered about the place with long strides. At the window, he twitched the curtain back a crack and looked out over the crossroad for perhaps half a minute, before allowing the curtain to fall back into place. He stood in silent thought for a moment before saying, 'We do not have a great deal of time, gentlemen. We are not the only party with an interest in Herr Harwell. We arrived barely in time.'

'An – an interest?' stammered Harwell. 'Who has an interest in me? Who are you?'

'Elucidation would be redundant,' said Cabal. He snapped his fingers peremptorily at Shadrach. 'The Key, sir! Quickly now.'

'The key . . .' It took a moment for Shadrach to take Cabal's meaning. 'The Silver Key?'

'Of course the Silver Key,' said Cabal, his patience burning away as quickly as a powder trail. 'You do have it, do you not?

If we have come all this way, and it is sitting on the dressing-table at home . . .'

'Yes, of course I have the Silver Key, but it is useless without a gateway. Isn't that true?'

Harwell glanced around the group, now at least partially convinced that he was hallucinating this indecipherable gang of men cluttering up his room. He hadn't realised it was possible to suffer absinthe flashbacks, but it seemed the most likely explanation.

'Yes, it is true, and there is a gateway here. The Key, if you please?'

'A gateway,' said Harwell. 'In my room?'

'Yes, indeed,' said Bose, as genial as Pickwick. 'Your garret is home to a gateway to another world! Isn't that wonderful? The land of dreams, no less.' Shadrach shushed him, to no obvious effect.

Harwell's expression showed dawning comprehension. 'The land of dreams . . . the land of . . . Of course! It explains so much! My dreams, my visions! I understand now!' He looked frantically around, turning on the spot. 'Where is it? Where is this gateway? It must be near – I can feel it.'

Cabal meanwhile had accepted the Key from a reluctant Shadrach and was in the process of sliding it from the long chamois envelope in which it was kept. He let it lie in his hand for a long moment, feeling its weight wax and wane, watching the bittings ebb and flow, like crystals melting and re-forming. It was silver, certainly, but only in colour. What it was made of was an entirely different question.

He tucked the envelope into his coat pocket while taking a firm grip of the Key. 'Yes, Herr Harwell. The Gate of the Silver Key is very close indeed.'

Harwell turned to him, his next question already forming on his lips, but he never had the chance to voice it. For Cabal raised the Silver Key to head height and, without hesitation, drove it between Eldon Harwell's eyes.

There was no crunching of bone, no spraying blood or cerebral fluid as the Key slid through skin, subcutaneous fat, flesh, skull and brain. There was no sound at all, but for the collective horrified gasp of shock from the onlookers. It is not true to say that the Key's passage between Harwell's frontal lobes left no mark: the flesh and bone crumbled and melted into thin white smoke and what was left was nothing more or less than a neatly defined keyhole. None of them thought this strange at the time, but only afterwards in reflection; at that moment it seemed that the keyhole had always been there, obvious and apparent to them as soon as they had seen Harwell, yet somehow they had forgotten about it. It was a curious, half-formed memory, their first experience of the nature of the Dreamlands while waking, as its influence escaped through the opening gate into the mortal world like jasmine-scented air escaping a garden.

Only Cabal and Harwell made no sound, until Cabal turned the Silver Key in its lock and Harwell made a soft sigh as of realisation or perhaps recognition. Certainly, his eyes widened as though he could see things that had lain hidden from him his whole life. 'It's . . . beautiful,' he whispered, and a solitary tear rolled down his cheek as the confused miasma of half-glimpsed possibilities that had haunted him since that night at the Pickman Gallery finally grew sharper in focus. 'It's all so . . .'

Then his face grew tense, the skin pulled back against the bone. 'There's something else, something else . . .'

Cabal finished turning the key and gently withdrew it from Harwell's head. The keyhole remained, and from it lines of liquid light rolled up vertically across the centre of the brow and down along the ridge of the nose.

'The Gateway . . .' said Corde. 'The Gateway of the Silver Key.' The silver line of light was extending over Harwell's head and down his chest, the glow becoming fiercer as it travelled. 'I'd naturally assumed—'

'Walls do not dream,' interrupted Cabal, and Corde fell silent.

The line had almost bisected Harwell and with every inch the line travelled, his expression of disbelief warped slowly into horror. 'No . . . no! I can see it! I can see it! I cannot . . . must not . . . God help me!'

'What can you see?' demanded Cabal, standing close to Harwell. He noted that the stricken man's eyes seemed to be growing further apart. The gateway was opening.

'I see . . . it all!' Harwell's eyes were focused on something far beyond Cabal, beyond the grubby little room, beyond this world and the realms of space that it sits within. 'Oh, mercy! Is there no mercy?'

And, with that, the tips of the line of light joined, the Gateway of the Silver Key opened wide, and that was the end of Eldon Harwell. He became something, but what it was, living or dead, was without definition. He shattered into crumbs that sublimed into gas that smeared into liquid that sublimed into something else again until all that was left was the gateway, burning in the air with the light of a bright afternoon into a dirty garret at midnight.

'You . . .' Bose was, for once, lost for words. 'You killed him.'

Cabal shrugged, as if Bose had accused him of using the wrong spoon at dinner. 'He was already dead. He'd allowed certain conceptual theomorphs to take residence in his mind. He would have killed himself or been killed within a few months in any case. At least this way he served a purpose.' He noticed some pieces of paper lying on Harwell's writing-table and studied them for a moment. 'He was a poet. No loss, then.'

'You are a cold man, Mr Cabal,' said Corde, not entirely disapprovingly.

Cabal did not answer. He was looking at the portal, stepping around it to gauge its width. 'This will not be a quick passage. I estimate it will take approximately a minute for each of us to complete the transition from here to there. We must start immediately.'

'We are leaving now?' Shadrach was shocked and a little angry. 'When we came on this little reconnaissance of yours, you gave us to believe that we would only be confirming the location of the gateway.'

Cabal waved a complacent hand at the tall, glowing ellipse hanging in the centre of the floor. 'As we have.'

'But what about our equipment? Our preparations? You are asking us to plunge into the unknown!'

'This entire expedition is a plunge into the unknown, Shadrach. Your equipment is useless. Your preparations are moot. The Dreamlands shall provide. The one thing they cannot give us is time.' He walked to the window and gestured for the others to join him. He drew the curtain back far enough for them to look out into the street. From the graveyard, dogs that were not dogs were streaming, running straight for the building in which they stood. They made a sound as they went, a strange gruff mewling unlike anything any of the men had heard before. It took little imagination to discern shifts in intonation that sounded worryingly like language.

'Why are the streets empty of people?' asked Bose. 'It's not that late. What . . .'

Cabal picked up his Gladstone bag, opened it and removed his revolver. 'Because we are in the borderlands of dream and nightmare, and in nightmares, there is never anyone there to help. Is anyone else carrying a gun?'

Shadrach, Corde and Bose shook their heads. Cabal growled with displeasure. 'Gentlemen! We are in the United States of America. Going armed is virtually mandatory. Quickly, then. Through the gateway. I shall hold off our visitors.'

He was halfway through the door on to the upper landing when Corde called after him, 'What are those creatures?'

'Ghouls,' said Cabal, and then he was gone.

Cabal looked down the stairwell, and weighed up the options for defence. It was not the first time he had fought in very similar circumstances and the knowledge that he had survived that time lent his actions confidence. He opened the revolver's cylinder and checked the load before reclosing it with a purposeful click. The sound of scrabbling at the door grew as the ghouls wrestled with distant memories of when they were human and knew how door handles worked. The door was locked – Cabal had made a point of securing it after they entered – but he knew the ghouls' impatience would overwhelm their caution soon enough, and then a cheap door with a cheap lock would present no barrier to them.

Nor did it. The scrabbling at the wood became faster and more violent and then, suddenly, the door was smashed open to the clatter of the striker plate on the tiled hallway. Cabal hoped for their sakes that Messrs Shadrach, Corde and Bose were making their way through the gateway because he would be needing it himself soon enough, and if any of them was not through by that time, he would personally ensure that they became the expedition's first casualties. The Gateway of the Silver Key was no longer just the immediate goal of their plans, it was now their only route to safety. Cabal drew back the revolver's hammer and aimed down the stairwell.

The black tide of fast-moving shadows swamped the lower flights, swirling anti-clockwise up the well. Cabal held his fire – he had only six shots and doubted he would be afforded an opportunity to reload. It was when they reached the landing below him that he aimed at the first ghoul up the flight of stairs directly beneath him, and shot it through the back of the head. The .577 round proved as efficacious against the vile dun-coloured rubbery hide of the ghoul as it ever had against Deep Ones or, indeed, people. The discharge was staggeringly loud in the confined space, and the plume of smoke that jetted down served to add to the creatures' confusion as their comrade slumped and rolled back down among them, leaving much of its vaguely canine face on the step.

Behind him, he heard Bose say, 'Mr Shadrach is through, Mr Cabal! Quickly, Mr Corde! Your turn!'

Cabal performed a rapid mental calculation and decided that he would have to hold the ghouls off for a little longer than he had hoped. Down below, he could hear chewing. Ghouls are a notoriously unsentimental race, and once one is dead it is immediately redefined in the minds of its friends and colleagues as lunch. It would seem that even their great desire to reach the gateway before it closed came second to a quick snack.

Cabal drew back the hammer again, the loud click as the lock engaged serving to reconcentrate the minds of the ghouls marvellously. There was some muttered speech, a disgusting meeping and glibbering that appalled Cabal's linguistic sensibilities. It appalled him even more to have to speak in the same tongue.

'You down there,' he garbled, aware that his accent was poor. Silence suddenly fell. 'I have no argument with your people. Go back, and no more need die.'

'You have the gateway,' barked a voice, presumably that of the pack leader.

'What need you of the gateway? Your people can travel to the Dreamlands easily. The gateway is ours for the moment. Leave us in peace.'

There was a pause. Then the ghoul said, 'I know you.'

Cabal's eyes narrowed. He could feel an uncomfortable tension uncurling like an electric eel across his neck and shoulders. It took him a moment to realise that it was fear. He stamped it down immediately: this was the very irrational terror that caused the Fear Institute so much exasperation. Yet it was the irrationality of it that concerned him more than the way his heart pounded or the sweat that suddenly beaded his cool brow. He had encountered ghouls before, and they had never given him more than momentary inconvenience. Why was he afraid?

With an effort, he brought his mind to bear on the situation at hand. This ghoul was a cunning one, but not nearly cunning enough. It would engage his curiosity to take him off guard and then charge the stairs. He braced his gun hand and prepared to fire. 'I don't know you.'

'You would not, but you knew me once,' said the ghoul,

and it said it in English. 'Oh, you knew me once, Johannes Cabal.'

Silence fell once more. The moment drew out. 'You knew me once, Johannes Cabal,' the voice repeated. Still, there was no reply. On the stairs, a hideous hiccoughing growl arose. The ghoul was laughing.

In the garret where Eldon Harwell once lived, and where a police investigation would later find no clues as to his disappearance but a bloodstain on the stairs that analysis showed not to be human, the Gateway of the Silver Key flickered and extinguished. Of Harwell and his four mysterious visitors, there was no trace.

Surviving fragments of Cyril W. Clome's manuscript for *The Young Person's Guide to Cthulhu and His Friends: No. 1 Great Cthulhu*

Now, best beloved, let us consider **Great Cthulhu**. He is the greatest of the Great Old Ones and is a god. Yes, he is. A real god. Not one of those pathetic gods that depend on silly people having 'faith' in them ('Faith' is a word that means 'having to pretend', O best beloved). Not one of those stupid, weak, powerless gods that simpering people invent to try to keep them warm in the endless freezing void of the true reality, in the aching futility of our fleeting, impotent lives. We know a song about that, don't we?

(Text illegible due to scorching)

No, Great Cthulhu does not need us to worship him – he is real whether we do or not. But we better had, because one day he will wake in his cosy little sunken city of R'lyeh (which is at 47° 9′ S, 126° 43′ W in the South Pacific Ocean, make a note), have a lovely big yawn and a stretch I should think – 'Yaaaawwwwwwn!' – and then kill everyone. But if you've been good little boys and girls and worshipped him properly, he might not kill you first. Isn't that splendid?

Chapter 3

IN WHICH CABAL LEADS AN EXPEDITION BEYOND THE WALL OF SLEEP

The mountain stood taller than any mountain had any right to stand without liquefying its own base with the sheer weight of rock upon it. Even close by that base, the four men looked out and stood speechless at the astonishing vista spread before them, like the world before gods. Well, three of them stood speechless with awe, the fourth was entirely preoccupied with beating dust from his trousers where he had stumbled on escaping the rapidly closing Gateway of the Silver Key.

'My God,' breathed Corde, finally rediscovering speech. 'It's . . . magnificent. I never dreamed . . .'

'No, you doubtless have,' said Johannes Cabal, as he smacked dust from his calves. 'You have forgotten it, though. That is the nature of dreams.' Finally, about as satisfied as he was going to be without a valet with a clothes-brush to hand, he straightened and took in the vast world that stretched out before them. He sniffed, stuck out his jaw and picked up his Gladstone. 'If it were a view in the waking world, I would be impressed. As it is, it is the shared fantasy of a hundred billion sleepers. Impressive in its own way, but I shan't be buying any postcards.'

'A hundred billion, Mr Cabal?' said Shadrach. 'You are mistaken. There are not even two billions in the world today, and fewer than half are sleeping at any one time.'

Cabal turned to him and gave him the sort of look a teacher might give a disappointing pupil before correcting him, and then thrashing him. 'You are correct in as far as there are no more than two billions in the world. You are in error if you believe that I am only considering the Earth.' He paused and looked Shadrach up and down. 'What in the name of Azathoth's little drummer boy are you wearing?'

'What am I wearing? That's an . . . Good Lord!'

Shadrach no longer looked nearly so much like an undertaker. Instead, his clothing fell more into the category of 'gorgeous', not a description that had ever before been attached to him in all his years. He wore a burgundy simarre in the Tudor style, trimmed with fur of a curious pattern, over a doublet of cream samite, slit upper hose of the same burgundy but with a brave crimson silk within, black lower hose double gartered in yellow, and square-toed shoes. He reached up and removed the slouching brown velvet cap from his head and looked at it in wonder. The overall effect was of a successful merchant of the sixteenth century, an Antonio before all that unpleasantness with Shylock.

'I – I don't understand,' stammered Shadrach, his usual bloodless composure shattered. For his answer, he received an equally astonished cry from Corde as he, too, discovered a change in his wardrobe.

Corde's profoundly unenterprising twill three-piece, trilby and woollen tie had been replaced with something altogether more dashing. Again the tone was a strange mix of very late medieval and Tudor, but the cut seemed to owe more to the cinema: a brown leather jerkin with slashed sleeves over a white doublet, black breeches and knee boots, a sword at the hip, a soft black hat with a black feather tipped in red, held in place by a small brooch of a dagger bearing a single tiny ruby.

After all the crying out and holding out of hands in astonishment, Bose's thunder had been too thoroughly stolen for him to do much more than look down at his own clothes and mumble a slightly surprised, 'Oh.' For he, too, had experienced a transformation. Gone were his previous clothes which, while conservatively stylish and expensively cut, had not made much of an impression on anyone. Now he wore a simarre much like Shadrach's, but where that had complacently proclaimed wealth, this was of profound blackness, such that the moleskin collar seemed verging on the gaudy. The whole ensemble, from shoes to the four-sided flat hat perched upon Bose's surprised head, was black, the only touches of colour being his pale face, the wide red-gold chain he wore running across his shoulders and down to a medal in the middle of his chest, and the blue carbuncle in the ring he wore upon the middle finger of his gloved left hand.

They spent some moments gawping at themselves and one another before turning their attention to Cabal who, they were confounded to discover, was still dressed much as he had been back in Arkham, although a scuff on his right shoe's toecap that he had suffered on the street was now gone and a button on his left jacket cuff, formerly depending upon a loosening thread where it had caught in a doorway, was now perfectly secure.

Bose spoke for them all when he said, 'I don't understand, Mr Cabal.'

For his part, Cabal seemed to find something secretly amusing about the whole scene, although the smirk was in a sense psychic, for his expression did not change at all. 'Herr Shadrach, you remind me of a portrait by Holbein the Younger. A successful merchant. Tell me, did you ever harbour ambitions towards a mercantile life?'

'No,' said Shadrach, immediately. Then he frowned. 'Well, briefly . . . once, long ago. When I was a boy, I visited my uncle's warehouse. He was a trader in teas and bric-à-brac from the Orient. He travelled a lot. I wanted . . . My father told me not to be foolish. There was a family business to inherit, his business.' Shadrach paused, looking at his hands. 'Shadrach and Son, *undertakers*.' He looked up at Cabal, frowning. 'Is this . . . *this* what I could have been?'

'You could have been anything, but you wanted to be a merchant, evidently. Herr Corde, I surmise, read far too many twopenny papers when he was young.' Mr Corde was not listening. He had freed the sword from its scabbard and, while not fully drawing it, was admiring the blade. It shone white and blue as it caught the light, steel of such beautifully patterned perfection that the swordsmiths of Damascus would have torn their beards in frustration at the very sight of it.

'You, however,' said Cabal, turning to Bose, 'you, sir, intrigue me. What is your heartfelt boon? Your great sublimated desire?'

'Well,' said Bose, before becoming distracted by the gold

chain. He lifted the medal and tried to read it, without success. 'Well, I was thinking that, perhaps, one day, I might like to be a magistrate.' Everybody looked at him. He blushed and smiled awkwardly. 'It's good to have an ambition.'

Cabal nodded. 'A chain of office, of course. Another historical trapping. The Dreamlands seem incapable of letting any lily go ungilded.'

'Yes, yes,' said Shadrach, profoundly uninterested in Bose's long-term ambitions to hand out small fines and morally improving lectures in court. 'But what about you, Mr Cabal? Why haven't your clothes changed?'

Corde slammed his sword back into its scabbard with jaunty gusto. 'Because you're already what you want to be, eh, Cabal?'

'Just so,' said Cabal, and this time the spectre of a smirk flittered around his mouth. He turned to look down the slope of the valley, and the smirk diminished to nothing. 'Now, to business.'

He reached down for his bag, and paused. It seemed that he had not managed the transition into the Dreamlands quite as unaltered as he had thought. The bag was open, as it should have been. He had left it open on the floor of the garret, the Silver Key lying within. When he had abandoned his post at the top of the stairs, he had dropped his pistol in before snatching up the bag and throwing himself into the vortex. The Key, he was relieved to see, was still where he had left it. His cane still remained secured to the bag by the leather straps that ran up the sides. Of his gun, however, there was no sign. Instead, lying along the open maw of the bag, like a stick in a toothless dog's mouth, there was a sword, scabbarded and attached to a belt.

Cabal bit back a snarl. Of course the Dreamlands would not tolerate something so prosaically mechanical as his Webley. Here, progress was held back by a vast romantic inertia as great as that of the mountain on which they stood. One day, it might finally allow flintlocks, perhaps at some future date when the waking world was using death rays and germ bombs.

Cabal took up the sword by the belt and strapped it on. It hung neatly at his left hip, and added a pleasing weight to his stride that he knew a real sword would never match. Demonstrating none of Corde's bashfulness, he drew the blade in a swift motion and tested its balance. Predictably, it was perfect, although it was no sort of weapon that he had ever held or even seen before. It was a rapier of sorts, but of a combative nature rather than for fencing: flat-bladed with a shallow curve that swept up to a right angle a finger's length from the sharp tip. Cabal slashed and thrust at the air for a few seconds. An interesting weapon, he concluded. At heart a rapier, but with just enough sabre in its family tree to allow the easy hacking of unfortunates when the mood took one.

He returned it to its scabbard with precision, and looked up to see Corde watching him with interest. 'You've fenced before, Cabal?'

Cabal noticed that familiarity was breeding sufficient contempt for them no longer to address him as 'Mr Cabal'. 'I have. Have you?'

'Oh, yes.' Corde drew his sword, and it was as different from Cabal's as a Viking one-and-a-half-hander bastard sword is, unsurprisingly, from a rapier with a bit of sabre on the side. 'Nothing like this, I grant you.' He whirled the sword in the air and it seemed for a moment that its path was made of a gleaming arc of solid steel. He swept it back again and then around his head, his eyes filling with undisguised joy. 'It's wonderful . . . wonderful!'

Suddenly his sword stopped in mid-air with a sharp cry of steel on steel. Cabal stood with his own once again drawn, halting Corde's in an exact parry. 'It is a dream, Corde.' He lowered and scabbarded it. 'Time is pressing, and we shall have plenty of time for you to demonstrate your dazzling swordsmanship. I would remind you that we have an entire world to search and we are by no means immortal.' He took up his bag while Corde reluctantly slid his blade into its scabbard.

Cabal took out his folder of notes on the Dreamlands and found a flattish section of ground on which to unroll a map.

'You have a map, Cabal?' said Shadrach. 'By all that's wonderful . . . !'

'Please do not become overly excited by it, gentlemen,' Cabal warned. 'It was drawn from the fancies of poets and the ravings of maniacs – which is to say much the same thing – and is therefore only slightly more useful than a blank sheet of paper. Why it is always poets, who are at the laudanum trough or gulping down absinthe, instead of somebody useful like cartographers, I have no idea. In any event, we have an unreliable map. And upon it, we are . . .' Cabal stabbed his finger down '. . . here.'

The others crowded around and looked at the map. After a few moments of angling his head this way and that, Shadrach asked, 'How can you be so sure?'

Cabal took up the map, rolled it and put it into his bag. 'In all the Dreamlands, there is one particularly famous mountain, Mount Hatheg-Kla. We are about one mile up it.' He turned and pointed towards the cloud-wreathed summit. There was something unpleasant about the mountain's perspective, as if there were simply too much of it and it had somehow furled itself just enough for it to be acceptable to the human psyche. Once inside the mind, however, it popped open like an umbrella with an unreliable catch, jabbing the sensitive fleshy parts with the spiky tips of its ribs and poking about with its contradimensional ferrule. Cabal, from long mental exercise, firmly closed the umbrella again and dropped it into the elephant's foot of his super-ego. The others, less prepared, were struck dumb by the immensity of the prospect.

Insensitive to his fellows' state, Cabal continued: 'Seven miles further up is the highest any human has ever climbed. Barzai the Wise was his name, which just goes to show that names don't tell you everything, for two miles further up is where the gods themselves sometimes sport. I have no idea what comprises sport for a god – don't ask. In any event, they took exception to Barzai getting close enough to irk them.'

'What happened to him?' asked Corde, the first to discover that the best cure for an umbrella in the psyche was simply not to look.

'Oh, something ghastly. It usually is with gods. They have no sense of proportion. If you are particularly interested, there is a rock at the eight-mile point that has the full story carved into it as a warning to the curious. Why, Corde? Curious?'

Corde was, but not enough to risk either the climb, or the possibility of getting his very own memorial, courtesy of the gods.

Cabal smiled, technically. He turned his back on the peak and pointed out over the land. 'That river is the Oukranos.

If we follow it down to the sea, we shall find ourselves in the city of Hlanith. Hlanith is a useful sort of place for dreamers, as it is close to the Enchanted Wood.' He pointed at a great forest visible south of the river a good way off. 'A twee name, but furiously dangerous. It is where most mortals who enter the Dreamlands through the usual route of sleep first emerge. On the other side of the river is the Dark Wood. A less twee name, but no less dangerous, just in case you were hoping for some sort of inverse relationship between names and peril here. Almost everywhere is dangerous, so you should get used to that idea as soon as possible, if you wish to survive this world.'

Shadrach and Bose had finally managed to tear their eyes away from the peak of Hatheg-Kla with the help of Corde, who had taken firm hold of their chins and steered their gaze in a safe direction by force. 'How will this . . . Hlanith,' Shadrach chewed on the unfamiliar word, making it sound like a small mining village in Wales '. . . how will it help us, Mr Cabal? We are not dreamers.'

'Not in any sense,' said Cabal. 'But as a result of every Tom, Dick and Harry with a talent for the particular mode of dreaming required to travel here, Hlanith is a gathering place for people whose minds are not altogether mired in the sticky romanticism of this place. In short, gentlemen, there we will find people who will give us straight answers to straight questions.'

Bose shielded his eyes against the sun, an orb whose light seemed a little more golden than that which shone over the Earth they had so recently left. 'I can't even see the coast from here. How long will this journey take? How far must we go?'

'Time and space are not measured in the way we are used

to,' warned Cabal. 'To give you a time in hours or a distance in leagues would be useless.'

Corde gestured over his shoulder with a jerk of his thumb. 'Just a minute ago you were telling us that this boulder commemorating Banzai the Wishful –'

'Barzai the Wise.'

'– is eight miles up the mountain. Now you're telling us that units of measurement are meaningless. Well, which is it?'

'Ah,' said Cabal, sagely. Before anyone could complain that 'Ah' did not really answer anything, he said, 'We have over a mile of treacherous mountainside to traverse before we reach gentler slopes, gentlemen. Perhaps we should begin.'

'A mile!' exclaimed Corde, in an attempt to make his point again, but Cabal was already stepping from the promontory that the Silver Key had dumped them upon, and on to the great steep field of scree and bare rock beneath them.

The most peculiar thing about the descent was how it seemed to take hours, yet when they reached the bottom of the long, ragged escarpment, the sun had barely moved a degree in the sky. Cabal muttered something about subjective objectivity, and there the matter lay. The second most peculiar thing was that, while Shadrach and Bose were neither of the utmost physicality nor especially well dressed for shinning down a mountainside, both arrived at their destination winded but not exhausted, their clothes as pristine as when they had set off.

They walked down towards the bank of the Oukranos in near silence, taking in the wonders around them. At this point they consisted largely of a ruined mansion off to the south, through whose abandoned orchards – in themselves covering the area of a small town – the party made their way. At first glance, the only truly unearthly thing about the environment was the sheer scale of everything: Mount Hatheg-Kla was huge, the ruined mansion was huge, the orchard was huge and contained trees of ancient growth; even the river before them was Amazonian in proportion. To Cabal's searching eye, however, there were more details that proclaimed the alien nature of the place, and the more he looked, the more subtle they became.

He saw a creature that was neither caterpillar nor butterfly, but rather a caterpillar with broad wings projecting from a chrysalis-like band about its upper third, as if a butterfly's life cycle had been cut and stitched into a single stage. He saw a rat scurry into a hole, but when it peered out again he thought he must have been mistaken for it had a little flat face like a capuchin monkey's. He finally realised it had the body of a rat but forelimbs ending in apelike phalanges, and the face of a tiny man with sideburns and a widow's peak. It glared at him with a mixture of angry hatred and curiosity until it understood they had no interest in it. At which point it grinned like a happy little man, and vanished deeper into its burrow.

The most subtle of the anomalous details, however, was all around them, its very ubiquity making it difficult to notice. The Dreamlands did not, quite, make sense to the eye. The most overt expression of this had been Mount Hatheg-Kla's ill-mannered refusal to be comfortably comprehensible to the viewer. It was not only big, it was the very epitome of bigness, and it wedged itself into the viewer's perception like a fat man into a small armchair. All around them now, however, the same perceptual unwillingness was always apparent. It was never quite clear just how far away the ground beneath one's feet really was. As they passed a tree, the degree by which the trunk's hidden side was exposed never quite matched up with the degree by which the trunk's side previously visible was turned away from them. Nothing worked quite as expected. Very nearly – 99 and a good number of percentage places – but never quite perfectly enough to escape a keen eye and an analytical mind. Cabal had these attributes, in addition to something verging on an allergy to whimsy, so he noted these anomalies early, and he noted them often.

This, then, was the stuff of dreams, and it nauseated him. Sloppy, half-baked fancies oozing from a countless multitude of sloppy, half-baked minds. He could hardly wait to conclude his business with the Fear Institute, the quicker to quit that land of the dazed. Those of an artistic bent would doubtless find much to admire in the Dreamlands' hanging gardens, their crystal fortresses, their gargantuan waterfalls and their towers of brass and steel. To Cabal, however, they were fripperies; momentarily impressive, but ultimately risible. His interest in the place was predictably prosaic.

Many necromancers had travelled to the Dreamlands before him for a variety of reasons – to speak with gods, to seek dark knowledge, or even to grow powerful and gather wealth, respect and a harem of houris who found names like 'Wesley' or 'Cecil' inexpressibly exotic. Not a few of these predecessors had come with the express intention of never returning, and so they had come as sleepers, engineering the death of their sleeping physical forms by strange rites that guaranted their spirit lived on in the land of dreams. It was an immortality of sorts, as they would never age or die naturally, but Cabal sneered at them as failures. While real knowledge, even experimental knowledge, could be gathered in dream, it was of no consequence if it could not be communicated somehow to the waking world. With the Silver Key in his possession, Cabal planned to make several unannounced visits on such reprobates, and gather their knowledge, by hook or by crook or by the patient application of thumb screws. Cabal didn't mind: once in the Dreamlands, he had all the time in the world.

There was the small question of the Institute members' notable naïveté. It was customary for payment to come after the service, yet here he was with the Silver Key in his bag, which he wanted, and the company of three idiots dressed like mechanicals for a production of *Henry VIII*, which he didn't. It would be simplicity itself to zig when they zagged, or duck into the shadows while they were otherwise occupied, or, if all else failed, shove them off a convenient cliff. The Dreamlands certainly didn't seem to be short of dramatic landscapes, so Cabal imagined there must be any number of convenient cliffs to choose from. That he did none of these things, no matter how personally amusing he might have found them, was pragmatic. The Fear Institute Expedition could and probably would run around until it was blue in the face and never discover the Phobic Animus, if it had the decency to exist. He truly did not care. What was important to him was that they would cover ground in doing so, establish protocols of behaviour, perhaps even make reliable contacts. All of these things would be useful to Cabal when he undertook his own projects. So, while the others were under the impression that all were united in the fool's errand, Cabal knew the true function of the journey was that of a reconnaissance. Plus, as he had realised earlier, there was safety in numbers, particularly when the rest of the party was made up of sacrificial victims to the higher purpose of Cabal's continued existence. 'All for one and one for all' would be their motto, even if only Cabal knew that the former 'one' would always be him, and the latter would not.

'You're smiling, Mr Cabal,' said Bose, smiling broadly himself. Cabal's own slight tightening of a few muscles was not in the same league as Bose's open and cheerful expression, but it was at least recognisable as a cousin. A fifth cousin of a disgraced forebear. Bose continued, 'You have faith in our mission, then? You see a happy conclusion ahead?'

Cabal thought of the Silver Key in his bag and pushed his face another few millimetres. The muscles creaked a little, but it had been some time since he had felt something akin to joy. 'Yes, Bose. I think with a little caution and circumspect prudence, combined with the will to take immediate action when the need arises, this could all go very well.' He looked on towards the river. 'Do those look like clifftops over there?'

Bose squinted. 'I'm not sure. Perhaps. Why do you ask?'

But Johannes Cabal said nothing.

As it turned out they *were* clifftops, but the drop below them was ridiculous rather than vertiginous and entirely unsuited for *ad hoc* murder. It was little more than a bluff overlooking, by a height of a few yards, a sandy bend of the riverbank where perhaps once the Oukranos had considered meandering before deciding it was too much effort.

They stood atop the bluff in silence and admired the view because the view was impossible not to admire. The Oukranos river: as mighty as the Amazon, as broad as the Mississippi, yet as clear as a mountain stream. Light penetrated a long way down, allowing them to see the stony riverbed from the water's edge out until the water grew too deep and blue and shadowed. Fish, extraordinary fish that had never swum in the seas of Earth, passed by or lazily beat their tails to hold position close by the rock- and pebble-strewn bottom.

Beside him, Cabal heard Shadrach breathe, 'It's beautiful . . . magnificent.'

'I wonder what it's like to swim in,' said Corde.

Cabal had his notebook out again and was flicking through it. 'Apparently it is safe, at least by Dreamlands standards. There may be a few things in it that will eat you, but they're not common.' He became aware of Corde's expression. 'Really, Corde, people swim in waters populated with crocodiles, alligators and sharks every day. Whatever happened to your defeating of fear, hmm?'

'It is not fear. It is a rational caution,' said Corde, falling back upon what Cabal now recognised as the standard Institute member's response when scared. It was not a refutation nearly so much as a mantra intended to settle the speaker's nerves.

'As you wish. We should keep moving. The Animus awaits us elsewhere. Unless that's it behind us.' Any shame at the childishness of the trick was handsomely outweighed by the pleasure of seeing three grown men leap into the air, spinning about-face as they did so.

After the recriminations and finger-wagging – all of which Cabal ignored – were over, Bose said, 'Look over there, about a mile or so downriver. Is that a quay?'

Cabal's binoculars had also undergone a transformation, but only as far as becoming an unforgivably ostentatious telescope, all chased brass and inlaid with semi-precious stones. Cabal held it for a moment, glaring at it with downturned lips as if it were a mortal insult. Then, without comment, he snapped it out to full length and looked through it in the direction Bose was pointing. 'Yes,' he said, having finally got the telescope focused to his satisfaction. 'There's a small jetty with a boat moored there. Some sort of fishing boat, I think. The mast's unstepped. I can see three people.' He snapped the telescope shut and dropped it into his bag, ignoring Shadrach's outstretched hand. 'Hlanith is days away on foot, but perhaps only a day or so by boat.' He started walking.

'But what if they want payment?' protested Shadrach.

Cabal didn't pause, but called over his shoulder, 'You are a rich merchant here. You can pay.'

'I? But, sir, what shall I ...' At which point he noticed the bulging purse hanging from his belt. He opened it and, before the astonished eyes of his colleagues, discovered a multitude of thin golden coins of the Roman style. Each coin, however, was not stamped with the countenance of a Caesar but of a beautiful youth in profile, wearing a laurel that was not laurel. His expression was of tolerant indolence, almost sleepy, but the eyes beneath the half-closed lids were somehow ancient, knowing, and perhaps even wicked. Shadrach shuddered, and dropped the coin back into his purse. He hastened with Bose and Corde to catch up Cabal.

The fishermen, for fishermen they were, were taciturn, though not hostile. They listened in silence as Shadrach explained how urgently he and his colleagues needed to reach Hlanith, and did not bargain greatly when the subject of payment came up. They accepted a little of Shadrach's gold, although later none of the party was sure how much had actually changed hands, only that it was 'a little'.

Still in near silence, but for the occasional softly growled command from the boat's skipper, they made ready to cast off while their passengers settled in for the journey. Cabal did not like the fishermen, although he was unsure why. They were quiet and competent, qualities he usually found admirable in people, but there was something more about them that gently raised his hackles by the mildest degree. He could not define this sense, however, so he disregarded it as much as he might. Which is to say, he gritted his teeth and attempted to ignore the nagging sense of wrongness that badgered him at an intensity roughly equivalent to the product of a mild headache and a child with a kazoo. He sat in the bow upon a small barrel, oblivious to the conversational gambits from his fellows, and wishing bitterly that he still had his gun.

It was probably nothing, he told himself. The entirety of the Dreamlands was 'wrong'. This was just another manifestation of that. As the fishermen cast off and guided their boat into the centre of the great river, Cabal tried to distract himself by watching Shadrach, Corde and Bose. Their earnest pointing and muttering soon bored him so much, however, that he returned his attention to the fishermen. They were swarthy men, but no more than most who worked outdoors for a living, and wore breeches, shirts of rough cambric and scruffy turbans in pale shades of yellow and blue. Their gait was not that of sailors, and Cabal concluded that they rarely if ever left the river. Venturing out of the estuary and hugging the coast to Hlanith was probably a major expedition for them. Yet they seemed unexcited, even blasé, to be going to Hlanith, and uninterested in their passengers. Cabal shrugged inwardly. Perhaps this was normal here. Giving up on them, he turned his attention back to his colleagues for the best part of fifteen seconds before giving up on them, too. Perhaps, he hoped, the changing landscape might give him some distraction from the tedium of the company.

Here, at least, he was not disappointed. The river and the wide valley through which it ran had a curious quality about them that, while just as mysterious as the curious quality about the fishermen, was far more pleasurable. After some careful analysis of his feelings, Cabal abruptly realised that this quality was 'beauty', about which he had heard so much and seen so little. On either bank, trees crowded nearly to the waterline, willows by the thousand. He had never heard of the like, never mind having ever seen such a mass of weeping boughs all together. Further into the forests – calling them 'woods' was not merely understatement, it was a barking lie – he could see taller trees, oaks, elms, scatterings of evergreens and even a few isolated palms and banyans. These were no forests that ever were, but had merely been dreamed of once, and the fruits of that strange vision had settled and grown. Cabal wondered what sort of man could have dreamed a dream of such a dream and dreamed it so strongly. He watched the trees slide by for another few minutes before concluding that this ancient dreamer, this weaver of the very fabric of the Dreamlands, was an idiot. He'd got it all wrong. Banyans, indeed. Such a dolt.

And as in contemplation of matters arboreal Cabal sat and mused, the Dreamlands sudde

Chapter 4

IN WHICH THE FAUNA OF THE DREAMLANDS PROVE UNPLEASANT

nly changed. It was not a slow transformation but, rather, the abrupt sense of dislocation one might suffer when feeling tired on a train journey, closing one's eyes momentarily, and reopening them to discover that one is two stations past one's destination and can't go back until you reach Crewe. Suddenness and shock are conjoined in that moment, and that was what the four hopeful adventurers experienced when, abruptly, they found themselves no longer on the river but standing in a small clearing in a wood. They reacted differently, as befitted their humours. Shadrach cried out and whirled around as if beset by invisible imps. Corde's hand fell upon the hilt of his sword, and he looked about, alert and ready. Bose simply stood stock still while his face warred between two expressions of astonishment, one wide-eyed and open-mouthed, the other furrow-browed and jutted-jawed. The resultant facial indecision caused his ears to flap slightly.

Cabal, for his part, stood very, very still. Only his eyes moved as he gathered data in an attempt to deduce what had happened. To one side of the clearing, the tree cover seemed thinner, and the sunlight penetrated, as if they were by a larger clearing or even at the edge of the wood in which they had unexpectedly found themselves. Ignoring the others, he moved quickly that way, pushed by a barrier of bushes between the trees and found the latter case was true. Before him was the bank of the Oukranos, the river stretching away to the other heavily forested bank. There was the flow, running from right to left (*Typical*, he thought. *We are in the Dark Wood*), and there was the fishing boat, beating into the wind and the flow as it headed back upstream, presumably returning to the jetty at which they had first seen it. Shadrach appeared at his elbow.

'Hey! Hey! Halloo! Come back!' he shouted, but the fishermen just waved and grinned. Shadrach's shoulders slumped. 'They're grinning at us. Is that a friendly grin, or a wicked one?'

Cabal was otherwise preoccupied. '"Halloo"? "*Halloo*"? Has anyone ever actually responded to that cry with anything but derision?'

'The hounds like it,' said Shadrach, somewhat ruffled. Cabal did not reply, but simply looked at him as a lady mayoress might look at a good-hearted but simple-minded orphan on a civic visit to the county and district simple-minded orphan facility. 'I'm a member.' This did not seem like news to Cabal. 'A member of the Ochentree Hunt.'

'Tally-ho,' said Cabal, in sepulchral tones. 'But, to answer your question, those are wicked grins. Definitely.'

Corde and Bose joined them as the boat turned a bend in the river and slid out of sight, the crew still waving, still grinning, still wicked.

'What happened just then, Cabal?' demanded Corde. 'How did we end up here?'

'I don't know,' said Cabal, opening his bag. It was interesting that he still had it, he thought, that both he and Corde still had their swords and, by the look of it, that Shadrach still had his purse full of coins.

'You don't know?' said Corde, putting his fists on his hips, unconsciously striking an heroic pose. 'We hired you because you were *supposed* to know your way around this place . . .' He paused at Cabal's index finger, raised in admonition.

'No,' said Cabal. 'You secured my services – and do not refer to me as a hireling ever again – on the basis that I have dealt with unusual circumstances of a supernatural type before, and have survived with life and mind intact. As I emphasised at the time, I have no direct experience of the Dreamlands, and my knowledge is strictly second-hand. This was accepted by all of you, and it is rather too late in the proceedings to start whining about it now.'

Corde lifted his chin, the better to glare down his nose. 'I was not whining about it,' he said, nettled.

'You were whining like a teething baby,' said Cabal, watching Corde's hand drift to the hilt of his sword. 'Herr Corde. If you show steel, I shall kill you.'

Corde's hand paused. 'You're very confident about that, Cabal.'

'Why should I not be? I have had practical experience of fighting with swords, as distinct from fencing for sport. I am still here. You may draw your own conclusions.'

'Gentlemen! Please.' It was Bose, moving between them. 'We are marooned and lost in a hostile land! Now, surely, is not the time for divisions within our party? United we must stand, gentlemen, for the alternative is oblivion.'

Corde's hand twitched, then fell back to his side. Cabal, who had been on the point of verbally agreeing with Bose, instead kept his silence and allowed a carefully pitched mild smirk to cross his face. Thus, he was in the happy position of allowing Corde's own pride to infer that Cabal considered him a coward, without actually having to go to all the trouble of implying it. It was the most effortless insult he had ever delivered, and its elegance charmed him.

Apparently unaware of the current of animosity that still ran between Corde and Cabal, and the potential differences it augured for the future, Bose seemed pleased by his peacekeeping efforts. 'Mr Cabal, time seemed to jump. Is this something that you have ever read of in this or any similar context?'

'It is not, which is suspicious in itself. One would expect such an effect to have been mentioned at least once in the great heap of portentous drivel that has been written about this place. Furthermore, it is not simply a skip forward in time, or – strictly speaking – the subjective perception of time that they use here instead of the real thing.'

Shadrach was nodding. 'The fishermen. They seemed completely unmoved by what had happened. Indeed, they seemed party to it.'

'Exactly so,' said Cabal, quickly regaining the expositional high ground. 'It is hard to imagine a chain of events by which all four of us would meekly agree to be marooned in the woods, so one is drawn to the conclusion that this has been engineered in some way by an external agency.'

'To what end?' asked Shadrach.

'With that sort of ability, why didn't this hypothetical agency of yours just kill us?' said Corde, dismissively. 'I don't believe it.'

'Believe what you will. You are in error if you attempt to ascribe Earthly motives to every mind in the Dreamlands. This could all be in the nature of a prank. Our death was not sought, only our inconvenience.'

'A *prank*?' This concept clearly did not sit well with Shadrach. If the Dreamlands were home to entities that could make time hiccup for a bit of a jape, then what they were capable of doing when they applied themselves hardly bore thinking about.

'Or a distraction, or a pleasantry, or a comment, or something that cannot be interpreted by the human mind.' Cabal shrugged. 'Or it may just have been a fluke. A random fragment of awareness that momentarily settled upon us, Azathoth belching, the stars being not entirely wrong. Who knows? I doubt any mortal does. Whatever the intent, we must deal with the results. The very inconvenient results.' He took the map from his bag and unrolled it once more. 'Yes, there we are. The Dark Wood. We shall have to walk to Hlanith.'

The others gathered around, crowding into Cabal's personal space and galling him immeasurably. 'Whereabouts are we in the woods?' asked Bose.

'Somewhere.'

'How far away is Hlanith?' asked Corde.

Cabal measured out the distance from roughly the middle of the long length of riverbank where the Dark Wood met the Oukranos to the dot labelled 'Hlanith' between finger and thumb, then held up his hand. 'About three and a half centimetres, I'd say.' He rolled up the map, put it back in its tube and restored it to his bag. 'You really must grasp the overriding principles at work in this place. Distances are measured in the difficulty of travel, time is measured by a sense of being either quick or slow. This is a world of subjectivism, loathsome though that may be.'

'So the journey to Hlanith is what? Quick or slow?'

Cabal gestured carelessly at the trees standing densely behind them. 'Is that not already painfully apparent?'

They tried to stay on the riverbank as they headed eastward, but quickly ran into an inlet that forced them inland. It was little more than a stream, but the cut it had created was steep and sharp and looked to be a great deal more trouble to climb out of than fall into, so nobody argued with taking the diversion. Soon, however, the wisdom of not risking the inlet became questionable.

The trees grew closer, the areas between them populated with bushes and tangles of high weed and briars. There seemed to be few paths, whether made by animals or people, and the ones they did find wound randomly about until they petered out into undergrowth and shadows. Cabal had anticipated the journey to Hlanith taking some time, but in the face of the extraordinarily hard going, he was forced to re-evaluate his estimate from 'some time' to 'some considerable time'.

It was dark in the Dark Wood, indicating that in the Dreamlands, at least, things functioned as advertised. It was not simply the dappled verdant darkness of a normal wood, however, but a heavy, hungry darkness that seemed to sap the brilliance of every ray of sunlight that somehow penetrated the canopy of leaves until the light fell upon the ground attenuated and ghostly. No insects buzzed, no animals cried.

'Anybody frightened yet?' asked Cabal, suddenly, from a position of scientific curiosity.

'We do not succumb to fright, Mr Cabal,' said Shadrach, not at all convincingly. 'Only rational concern.' The grunts of agreement from his fellows lacked conviction also. These grunts are worth mentioning if only because, if there had been a little less disconsolate grunting, they might have heard the crying a moment earlier, and subsequent events might have gone a little better for them.

It was Bose who heard it first, pausing and looking off to one side, while waving a hand for silence. 'Can you hear that?' he asked.

The others listened intently. The woods were unnaturally quiet, but even so the sound was distant. 'Good heavens!' said Shadrach, finally. 'It's a baby! Do you hear it?'

'I hear it,' said Cabal. 'And it causes me *rational concern*. We should be going.' He took a moment to gauge the direction the crying was coming from, then pointed diametrically opposite. 'That way. With speed.'

'It could be a child, lost and frightened,' said Corde, unwilling to take any advice from Cabal. 'We should investigate.'

'Excellent idea,' agreed Cabal. 'You investigate just what sort of child can move through this difficult terrain with such remarkable rapidity while the rest of us run away.'

It was true: where a moment before it had been necessary to demand silence and yet still barely hear the crying, now it was easily audible and becoming louder by the second. There was also the unpleasant realisation that more than one voice was crying.

Corde blanched and made to run, but paused as the sound spread around them as quickly as a forest fire. They were being flanked. 'Oh, my God.'

Cabal, too, had given up hope of escaping on foot. His sword was already in his hand as he scanned the trees. 'You know,' he said, with a tone of mild distraction, 'people keep saying that, but he never turns up.'

Corde did not reply, but his sword was drawn in a moment, and he fell into a fighting stance that, to Cabal's mixed surprise and relief, looked competent. Bose and Shadrach inspired less confidence, having drawn the curved daggers that had come with their costumes (Cabal could not bring himself to think of their clothing as anything other than fancy dress). They stood there, eyes wide, the largely ornamental daggers held as awkwardly as if they had just been drafted in from the street to murder the Duke of Clarence. Cabal expected little of them apart from acting as distractions to whatever was coming. With luck, they would be identified as the easiest targets and attacked first, giving Corde and himself a moment's advantage.

But the attack didn't come immediately. 'Back to back, gentlemen,' said Cabal, tersely. 'Cover all approaches. No, Shadrach on my left, Bose the right.' This left Corde directly behind Cabal; it seemed better to have two weak 90-degree arcs in their defence than the uninterrupted 180-degree arc that would result from Shadrach and Bose standing together.

'Come on,' he heard Corde growl. 'Show yourselves.'

Cabal didn't bother commenting upon how one should be careful what one wishes for, partly because it was rather trite, but mainly because they had come on and shown themselves.

He heard Shadrach gasp, and Bose sob with rational concern.

The things were not children – or, at least, not human children. They had cherubic faces and golden curls upon their alabaster pale brows, and lips as red as rose petals. Their compound eyes, however, went a lot of the way towards ruining the effect, as did the large chitinous bodies split into two tagmata in the same way as a spider, but with only six legs, much like an insect. The angelic little faces were mounted at the front of the cephalothorax, just as a true spider carries its seeing and biting apparatus. Unlike a true spider, however, the creatures made as ungodly a din as a kindergarten at feeding time. An unhappy simile, Cabal inwardly admitted.

They crept out from between the trunks of the trees, and peered down from the boughs, each at least a yard long. A swift count gave Cabal a result of eleven, approximately ten more than he felt they could comfortably deal with. Perhaps, he thought, they would be lucky and the creatures would not be as formidable as they looked. Perhaps, and there was a degree of irrational optimism here, they would not even attack, but were just gathered around out of natural curiosity. Then one of the creatures let out a scream like burning cat, and leaped in a single effortless strike at Bose.

Bose, to his credit, saw it coming. Bose, to his debit, reacted by moaning and fainting. The creature sailed through the space where he had been a moment before and crashed into Shadrach's back, sending him sprawling with a shout. Two more darted out from the trees at the defenceless undertaker, but were met by Corde's steel. He roared and whirled, hitting the first hard across the side closest to him, severing two legs in a spray of brown ichor and sending it rolling and shrieking miserably into its partner. This one scuttled quickly over the wounded monster only to be met by Corde's second blow, delivered down and across. The creature slumped, its legs spasming madly as its baby head sailed across the clearing to strike a tree trunk with a wet thud.

The creature on Shadrach's back was far too excited by having a helpless victim to hand to pay any attention to the fates of its siblings. It gripped him fiercely by the shoulders, the barbed claws along the inner edges of its forelegs stabbing him painfully through his layers of clothing and making him cry out. Its mouth opened wide and a wet proboscis, tipped with a flexing rasp, slid smoothly out and towards the base of Shadrach's skull. In a small part of a moment, the proboscis was joined by a second, but whereas the first was tubular and pulsingly organic, the second was flat, and steel. The creature was clearly baffled to find the tip of Cabal's rapier driving out from between its eyes, but after a moment it seemed to conclude that it had been stabbed through the top of its skull where the face joined the carapace and the sword tip was merely exiting. In this, it was correct and died in a state of intellectual satisfaction, a nice enough way to go.

Corde stamped down on the intersection between the body segments of the creature whose legs he had cut off and was rewarded with a satisfying squeal of pain that ended abruptly with a crunch of splintering chitin. He stepped back to his mark and fell once more into a ready position. 'Eight to go,' he called to Cabal.

Cabal grunted in reply, secretly quite relieved that he had not got as far as fighting Corde earlier; it might not have gone as well as anticipated. Not that he felt that it had extended his life by very much; Bose and Shadrach's limited usefulness in the fight had already been expended, which left Corde and himself to deal with the remaining spider-ant-baby things. The creatures seemed surprised with the speed by which three of their number had been dispatched and the remainder hung back, communicating with one another in a high cacophony of whines, screams, sobs and howls in a language that was both complex and uniquely irritating. The next attack, Cabal had no doubt, would be well co-ordinated and tactically sophisticated. He hefted his sword and wished once again that it was still a pistol.

The assault would certainly come in the next few seconds, and when it did, Cabal and the others would die. Therefore, waiting was a poor decision. Any chance of survival depended on taking the initiative. It fell into two categories: attacking first, or escaping. Escape was clearly hopeless: even if they were somehow to break the cordon around them, they would still be stumbling around in this warren of a forest, an environment that the creatures knew well and were admirably adapted to. Therefore, the best chance was to combat them somehow. Sheer force of arms would probably fail, but perhaps a bluff might work. The creatures had a level of intelligence, it seemed and a language. If a species has speech, it can be lied to.

These were the Dreamlands, after all. The place was littered with ancient sorceries and all that airy-fairy nonsense, Cabal reasoned. He *was* a magician of sorts, and even if his magic depended more on extensive laboratory time and a lot of glasswork than on waving staffs around and calling down damnation upon his enemies, the creatures were not to know that. He racked his mind for a suitable abjuration, quickly reaching down to pull his cane from the straps on his Gladstone. He levelled it at the nearest creature.

'*Aie! Fhtagn!*' he began, *Aie! Fhtagn!* generally being a good place to start when dealing with abominations such as these. It even impresses shoggoths – and it takes a lot to impress a shoggoth. He spoke the words again in the most impressive tone he could manage. Encouragingly, the creatures stopped their infernal noise and gawped at him, their cherubic faces agog, like a bunch of choirboys discovered raiding the sherry in the vicarage. Choirboys with compound eyes, shiny black carapaces and far too many legs for polite society, it was true, but otherwise the expression fitted.

He glared steely-eyed at them, while internally his mental cogs whizzed fast enough to burn oil. *'Ph'nglui mglw'nafh Cthulhu R'lyeh wgah'nagl fhtagn,'* he tried next. It wasn't much – everybody in the Dreamlands surely knew that dead Cthulhu was happily dreaming in his house in R'lyeh: it was probably sewn into innumerable samplers on innumerable parlour walls – but at least it demonstrated that Cabal was willing to call on some big names. 'Aie! Nyarlothotep! Chaos that crawls . . . messenger, mind and will of the gods . . . the haunted dark . . . devourer of grey lilies . . .' The creatures twitched in a way that seemed to Cabal to indicate growing unease. They shied back a little. This was going well, he realised. Cthulhu was all very well, but Nyarlothotep was known and active. A few more threatening phrases and their morale might break altogether. 'Aie! Nyarlothotep! See and smite my enemies! Crumble them to dust, and their kin, and their homes, and their . . .' He dried for a moment, fumbled for a continuation, and made do with '. . . and their pets. Strike them down, your humble servant implores thee! I . . .' And that was all he had to say.

It would be pleasant to report that Cabal's ruse worked exactly as he had intended, that the creatures would decide that even if he wasn't a great sorcerer, he was convincing enough not to trifle with, and scamper off into the woods, never to threaten Cabal and his party ever again. Unhappily, only the very last part of this came true.

The creature that Cabal had levelled his cane at was the first to die. It looked startled, then truly afraid. Its lips drew back in an expression of terror, the eyes grew wide, exposing even more of the vile tiny lenses of which its eyes were made, the skin grew ashen and then the whole beast became ashes – thin grey ashes, as if sieved from an intense fire. A rapidly advancing tide of colourless death swept from its head to the tip of its legs and abdomen, and where it passed, the creature just fell away in silent drifts and plumes.

Corde and Shadrach cried out in wonder and horrified joy – and Bose snored in innocent deep sleep – as the grey death came to every one of the creatures, striking them down where they stood or as they tried to run from that circle of destruction. After no more than a minute, the men stood alone, and they were triumphant.

'By all that's wonderful, Cabal!' said Shadrach, his thin, joyless face temporarily invaded by a smile. 'I thought the jig was up then but, by heavens, you showed them what for, eh? I knew he was the man for this job! Didn't I say so, Mr Corde? Did I not say so?'

Corde regarded Cabal with new respect. 'That was a nice piece of work, Mr Cabal,' he said, wiping his sword clean on the swathe of dust-covered grass at his feet.

Cabal, however, was not exhibiting any signs of exuberant happiness. To the contrary, he was pale, and beneath his dark glasses, his eyes were as wide as the creatures' at the moment they had met their doom. '*Ach, Gott*,' he said, in a hoarse whisper. 'What have I done?'

'Done, old man?' said Corde. 'You've saved our bacon, that's what you've done, and we're all very grateful, believe me.' He went to rouse Bose.

'No. No, you don't understand,' said Cabal. He was breathing heavily.

Shadrach was appalled to recognise the symptoms of fear. 'What is it, Cabal? Did something happen to you when you performed that magic?'

'Magic?' Cabal looked at him as if just realising that Shadrach was speaking to him. 'Magic? I performed no act of magic. It was a ruse . . . a ploy. I intended only to fool those creatures, to scare them into thinking I am the sort of magician who goes around casting spells.'

Shadrach frowned, perturbed and surprised. 'But they . . . You destroyed them.'

'No, I did not.' Cabal was recovering control of himself, but he was only hiding his fear, not dispelling it. 'I called on other powers. I have done so before in similar circumstances on the basis that at least it buys me some time. The calls are hopeless, you see. They have no effect.'

Shadrach started to say something, but thought better of it. He looked around the trees and the scatterings of fine grey ash that lay about the place. Then he turned back to Cabal, but he did not voice the obvious question. Neither did he need to.

'I called upon Nyarlothotep, the most vicious, arbitrary and sadistic of them all. Loki, Anansi, Tezcatlipoca, Set . . . All faces that it has worn over the millennia. A trickster god. Do you understand?

'I called upon Nyarlothotep, *and he heard*.'

Shadrach tried to think of something comforting to say. As an undertaker, it was his stock in trade to be able to comfort people at difficult times, to mouth platitudes and make them sound worth something, to help people see the light of the next dawn. Now he could not think of a thing. Never, in all the burials and cremations that he had planned and attended, had he ever had to commiserate with somebody who had just gained the attention – the probably baleful attention – of a real and malevolent god. A god that, when prayed to, did not depend on or even expect faith, but simply smote one's enemies. A price would surely be imposed later, at some future, unspecified Damoclean date. What can one say to somebody in such straits?

Instead he gave Cabal his most professional pat on the shoulder. It was his best pat, the one that said, *You have my most sincere albeit non-specific sympathies*. It was all he could do.

Cabal's stoicism was enough to make a Spartan seem prone to the vapours. A casual observer would have seen no obvious signs of the great metaphysical disruption within his mind and spirit, but it was there none the less. For the first time, he truly understood what Nietzsche had meant when he had yammered about looking into abysses. Not only had the abyss looked into him, it had noted his name, address and shoe size. He was disturbed and distracted, and these made him voluble.

'How bad can it be?' he asked rhetorically, as the subdued party made their way in what they had judged was probably more or less the direction of Hlanith. 'I've encountered worse. I'm sure I've encountered worse. I went to Hell. I met Satan.' He didn't notice the shocked expressions on the faces of the others. Whether they were shocked at the admission or perhaps at the possibility that Cabal was losing his mind hardly mattered. Whatever the reason, their faith in him and his abilities was as shaken as he was. 'Satan was nothing,' Cabal muttered to himself. 'I spat in his eye.' There was a short pause. 'Figuratively. I figuratively spat in his eye. I couldn't really spit in his eye.' Another pause. 'He was too tall.'

Mercifully for his unwilling audience, any further memoirs of supernatural entities into whose eyes he had expectorated, figuratively or otherwise, were curtailed by the discovery of a path through the wood. It was not much of a path, but it was the first time they had seen anything approaching a cleared route and it heartened them, as surely such a thing would only exist close to the wood's edge.

After a moment's quiet discussion as to whether they should follow the path this way or that, then a quiet argument, then a quiet flip of one of Shadrach's golden coins, they went *this* way, and hoped that Fortune would favour them. Fortune seemed a much better travelling companion than, say, Nyarlothotep.

But even Fortune may behave wilfully on a slow day when she is looking for amusement. They followed the path in as much silence as they could manage, listening for the distant cry of babies. None came. There was only the oppressive quiet, punctuated frequently by their own poor efforts not to punctuate it.

The path turned sharply to one side and suddenly they found themselves in a clearing, a *true* clearing in the forest, not just one of the patches of slightly lower tree density that had been all of their previous experience. It was not, however, unoccupied.

With the expenditure of great effort, sections of fallen

trees, anything from three to six yards long, had been dragged from elsewhere and placed on their sides. Then the cores of the logs had been patiently removed, apparently by many hours of gnawing. The result was crude but effective dwellings, a whole village of perhaps fifty or so. Each log was swathed with sheets of some organic substance that at first glance appeared to be webbing but that, seen close to, must have been extruded as great flat sheets, addled and crazed with imperfections.

The explorers were just wondering what sort of creature could have made such a place when they noted evidence at their feet which answered that question. The stunted grass and weeds were dusted with thin grey powder of a shade and consistency they had seen all too recently.

'It's their village,' said Corde, his sword never having left his hand since they had discovered the clearing. 'Those creatures, this is theirs.'

'They are all dead,' said Shadrach, strictly unnecessarily, yet it still needed underlining. He peered inside a slightly more complex structure of two tree sections that had been bound together to create a small hall. Inside, football-sized egg sacs hung from the walls. Within every one, there was no movement. They dangled dry and flaccid, half filled with grey dust. 'Even the unborn,' he whispered.

As he stepped back, his shoulder brushed the rough lintel. With a loud crack, a great section fell away, dropping to the hard-packed soil and smashing to dust. As if the sound had been all that was required to start the collapse, the roof fell in, breaking into greyness as it tumbled down. The men instinctively clustered together as the destruction spread. Hut after hut came crashing down, the sound of destruction starting harsh, but ending soft. Inexpressibly disturbed, they withdrew to watch the creatures' village vanish as suddenly as any baker abducted by a snark.

'They are all dead,' said Shadrach again, looking at Cabal with fascinated repulsion as if he were a cobra. 'They, their kin and their homes are destroyed.'

Bose was watching the last of the tree huts become nothing very much with childish amazement. 'I wonder if you got their pets, too, Mr Cabal? If they had pets.' He considered for a moment, then shook his head. 'No, they looked the sort to eat anything vaguely petlike. I don't suppose they were nearly so keen on companionship as they were on dinner.'

Nobody was listening to Bose's ruminations. They were all too busy staring at Cabal, except Cabal, who was glaring back.

'I say again, I am no sorcerer. The rules here, however, are apparently very different from our world in ways that we had not previously considered.'

'That *you* had not previously—' began Corde, but he was cut off by the increasingly testy Cabal.

'Yes, that *I* had not previously considered. This world is disturbingly arbitrary, random . . .' he looked for some term that would effectively communicate how repugnant he found it '. . . *whimsical*. I ask you, who spent so much effort planning for contingencies, did you ever consider anything even approaching our current situation?' The question was only partially rhetorical, but Cabal was glad of the silence it provoked.

Into that silence crept the ever-perturbable Bose. 'So . . . what do we do next? Shall we abandon the endeavour?'

Cabal shook his head, angry with himself for the weak leash on which his temper tugged eagerly. 'That is not a decision for now. We cannot spontaneously leave the Dreamlands whenever we want to. We must either exit via another gate opened by the Silver Key—'

'Will it be necessary to destroy some other hapless soul, Mr Cabal?' asked Shadrach, coldly.

'Usually not,' said Cabal, blithely unaware of any implied criticism. 'Gateways of the Silver Key rarely manifest in living creatures. Luckily, on this occasion it chose to do so in a poet and writer, not somebody important or useful. As I was saying, that is one way of re-entering the waking world. The other is to find a rising path, which brings one up and out physically from the Dreamlands. Those are few, and extraordinarily dangerous.'

'As opposed to the nest of security and comfort in which we find ourselves now, eh, Cabal?' said Corde.

Cabal looked at him coldly. 'By comparison, yes, Herr Corde. This *is* a nest of security and comfort.' He looked down the path leading away from the clearing that had once held the creatures, their kin, their homes and, presumably, their pets. 'This must lead somewhere,' he said, and without waiting for agreement, he set off down it. The others quietly followed.

Chapter 5

IN WHICH CABAL WANDERS FROM THE BUCOLIC TO THE NECROPOLITIC

The path did indeed lead them somewhere – and somewhere practical rather than to a cottage made of gingerbread or full of bears or dwarfs or all three. They emerged from the Dark Wood on a long, rolling meadow that sloped down towards a tree-lined road bounded by small fields of corn. The heavy silence that had travelled with them was lifted by clear air and sunlight, and their mood – but for the impenetrable sullenness of Johannes Cabal – lifted too.

'That will be the road for Hlanith down there, eh, Cabal?' said Corde, unaware of or unconcerned at Cabal's metaphysical torment. 'Finally, a bit of good luck on this expedition.'

'Perhaps so.' Cabal signalled a halt by the simple expedient of stopping and expecting everybody else to follow suit. He took out his telescope and surveyed the terrain. 'There are a couple of people down there by the road. We shall ask.'

'Isn't that risky?' asked Bose.

'In this place, even blinking is fraught with peril. Yes, it is risky. They look like a pair of yokels doing whatever it is that yokels do during the day, but they may turn out to be hideous monsters intent on chewing out our spleens.' He shrugged. 'It happens, but what is one to do?' He started walking again.

Bose pattered along in his wake, like an anxious pug. 'Do you think that is likely?'

'No. Yes. Perhaps. How should I know? I am a stranger here myself.' And so, having put Bose's doubts to rest, or not, he fell back into a ratiocinatory silence from which he would not easily be dislodged.

As they approached the road, Shadrach commented disapprovingly, 'Look at those sheep. They're in among the corn. They'll bloat and die from eating it.'

'You seem very knowledgeable on the matter, Mr Shadrach,' said Corde.

'I come from a farming family,' said the tall, thin, ascetic and thoroughly unbucolic Shadrach. 'We kept sheep on the top moor, and Heaven help anyone who let them get into the cornfields down by the river.'

They were now only a few dozen yards from the couple by the road, and conjectures could be made without recourse to a telescope. If they were hideous monsters with a penchant for spleen, they carried it well; Cabal's guess of 'yokels' seemed far closer to the truth. They were young people: he a shepherd in a blue smock and red vest, brown-booted and gaitered, a wooden flagon hanging from his belt, his hair a coarse, wiry brown, his sideburns hedgelike; she equally rustic, though apparently wearing her best red dress and white embroidered blouse. A young lamb lay in her lap, crunching sour apples.

Judging from Shadrach's angry intake of breath, this was also something sheep should avoid. They were sitting by the edge of the road between the trees, chatting and giggling, and altogether unaware of anything else outside their sphere.

'Excuse me,' said Cabal, 'how do we get to Hlanith from here?' He did not ask if this was the right road for, on closer acquaintance, it clearly wasn't much of a road at all, just a narrow avenue between two rows of unkempt trees. Perhaps once it had led to a great house or estate, but now it was overgrown and even pitted deeply enough in places to create small shadowed pools, one of which the girl was cooling her bare feet in.

The shepherd boy looked up at them with dull surprise, the natural stupidity in his rubicund face plainly enhanced by drink. Behind him, the girl leaned over to look at the newcomers. Her action was coy, but her expression was knowing, and Cabal disliked her for that just as much as he disliked her beau for his bovine inanity.

The boy scrambled to his feet, belatedly alive to his dereliction of duty. 'Jus' a moment, yer 'onours, jus' a moment.' He ran off to drive the more adventurous sheep from the corn, leaving Cabal's party in an awkward silence with the girl. She, for her part, did not rise, but remained seated on the green swathe, idly playing with a strand of her russet hair and smiling slightly at them. Corde smiled back, to Shadrach's disgust, Cabal's incomprehension and Bose's blithe ignorance.

'I wonder, my dear,' ventured Corde, eliciting a quiet snort from Shadrach, 'if you could direct us to Hlanith. It can't be far from here.'

She did not speak, but replied by pointing at the end of the avenue to the south and gesturing vaguely eastwards. Then she went back to toying with her hair and smiling at him.

'Thank you,' said Corde, low and slowly, and there was a definite air of twiddling a thin moustache, if he had been wearing one.

'Thank you, miss,' said Shadrach, in a tone of subdued outrage. 'Come *along*, gentlemen.' And he led off to the south, followed by Cabal, Bose and, in a desultory fashion, Corde.

As they walked away, the shepherd came back, his hands cupped around some interesting insect he had found. He watched them go with a dull lack of understanding or even remembrance. Then their presence slipped from his mind altogether and he sat down by the girl again to show her this new treasure. Corde watched all this over his shoulder and laughed. 'As pretty as a picture,' he said to the others.

Shadrach would have none of it. 'A particularly vulgar picture. The product of a coarse and depraved artist.' But that made Corde laugh all the more.

The girl, for all her dubious taste in suitors, was at least a reliable guide. The avenue ended beside a road between high embankments and topped with trees and bushes. It was clear and frequently travelled; they met a tinker coming from the east who confirmed that they were on the Hlanith road, and shortly thereafter they got a lift on a wagon taking fodder into the city. The four men perched on the swaying pile of hay with differing degrees of assuredness and dignity, and even gave voice to their belief that the expedition was past its stumbling stage and was now properly under way.

'Yes, indeed,' said Cabal. 'Apart from the trifling facts that we have no idea where the Animus is, whether its whereabouts are known to anyone in Hlanith, or – and this is my personal favourite – if it even exists. Apart from those caveats, yes, everything is going swimmingly.'

Hlanith, however, was no disappointment on first sight. The land around it was low and marshy, but approached from many directions by causeways both natural and artificial. These converged on a great sloping plateau no more than a few dozen yards higher than the surrounding marshland, a plateau that sloped gently down towards its seaward side. The granite walls that ran around the town proper were almost unnecessary to the defences – the approaches could be made very difficult to any enemy – but it seemed that the town architects had felt that walls were necessary, so there they were.

Their wagon clattered up an artificial causeway whose length was broken here and there by bridges to let the highest tides wash in and out of the marshes unimpeded. The illusion of reality was remarkable, Cabal admitted to himself. The sea breeze blew in and brought the smell of brine with it. Gulls, identical to the birds of Earth, as far as he could see, wheeled and cried over the hummocks of harsh sea grass growing across what seemed to be the estuary of a great river that had disappeared. He watched as a gull flipped a fish out of a shallow pool where it had been stranded, immediately starting a fierce squabble among the rest of the opportunistic flock.

The wagon paused briefly at a guard post close to the end of the causeway. The guards' questions and search were so cursory and disinterested that it seemed Hlanith had little need of any defences at the moment, natural or artificial. The wagon was directed onwards across the drawbridge and under the portcullis of a small keep that was built across the full width of the causeway – an artefact from a less settled time and a precaution against a dangerous future – and ten minutes or so later, they were clambering down and thanking the wagon driver outside a gate in the town wall. He, for his part, surprised them by refusing to take payment, and wished them a pleasant stay in the city before parting from them.

The guards on the gate were only fractionally more interested in Cabal's party than the ones on the causeway had been, but only as far as discovering that they were new to the Dreamlands. They asked if they had come via the Enchanted Wood, and Cabal lied, and said that they had. He suspected that if the guards heard that their route had taken them through the far more dangerous Dark Wood, then there would be more questions, starting with 'So, why aren't you all dead?'

Once the guards' initial prejudices that they were dealing with a bunch of tourists was confirmed, the expedition was allowed into the city proper. None of them were quite sure what they had expected Hlanith to look like, and this was as well for every expectation would have been beggared. The town was medieval in flavour, yet peculiar in execution. There was something very Scandinavian about the tall, peaked roofs, yet the crossbeams and plaster seemed more Tudor, and the mixture of thatching on some buildings, while their immediate and otherwise identical neighbours were tiled in the Mediterranean style, just seemed wilfully contrary. Bose looked around with hands on his hips, every inch the gormless tourist. 'Well I never,' he kept saying, which was both true and redundant.

'Well, Herr Cabal,' said Shadrach. 'How do we proceed from here?'

'We search, and we research. Herr Corde, you strike me as a man who would be at home gathering intelligence in a tavern. I would suggest you find somewhere busy and not too disreputable and start there. Herr Bose, there must be some form of library or university here. In your persona as a magistrate, you may be able to gain access to an archive that we cannot. Learn what you can, or at least gather lines of investigation that may prove fruitful. Herr Shadrach, Hlanith is primarily a trading centre and the mercantile guilds will surely be strong. Merchant ships criss-cross the world from here and may have brought back some useful data for us. I would suggest you make the acquaintance of the local merchant princes and discover what you can. We should all make our own arrangements for somewhere to sleep, then meet on the morrow.'

This seemed like a sensible use of their time, and none had any problems with it, beyond an understandable lack of confidence as to how well they might get on with the locals. This was quashed by a heavy implication from Cabal that they were subject to the influence of the Phobic Animus and so were behaving like – and this is not the exact phrase he used, but certainly gives a sense of it – a 'big bunch of jessies'.

'And what will you be doing all this while, Cabal?' asked Shadrach, as he doled out coins to the others, mostly to Corde, who reckoned he might have to get in a few rounds of drinks, a duty he seemed very happy to be taking on.

Cabal did not answer immediately, but looked down the long avenue at whose head they stood to the defensive wall that would seal off the docks in case of seaward invasion, and beyond to the oaken wharves and ships, and still further to the great blue-grey Cerenarian Sea. 'There are other questions to be asked, and other sources to be questioned,' he said distractedly. Then, drawing himself back to the present, he added, 'We will meet here at midday tomorrow to exchange what we have discovered and to decide what to do next. Are we agreed?'

And so they parted.

Cabal did not make enquiries: experience had given him instinct. He simply followed his whims until they brought him, as they always did, to the graveyard. In this particular case 'graveyard' was a poor sort of term for a true necropolis, a labyrinth of lanes and alleyways bordered by tombs like stone huts, opening out into fields of grave markers, and squares where the municipal buildings were great mausolea and temples to the departed souls. It might seem strange that there was death within sleep, but the truth of it was that the Dreamlands were as real as anywhere else, at least while you were within them. Judging from this town of the dead that nestled within a city of the living, many would never leave.

Cabal had entered the necropolis at its western gate, and walked until he found himself at its heart, a great circus – in the 'metropolitan' rather than 'three-ring' sense – of white gravel encompassed by great curving kerbs of stone tall enough to sit upon, which Cabal did. The kerbs were periodically broken by the beginnings of avenues that radiated outwards to every corner of the enormous area. Cabal watched a funeral enter the circus and depart down one of the avenues, a long column of figures in all encompassing black veils fore and aft, with a much smaller group of soberly dressed men and women following an open hearse drawn by six black horses. These latter people were dignified rather than mournful, unlike the veiled figures that sobbed and wailed and struck postures of extravagant spiritual distress. Cabal waited until the funeral had largely processed on to the avenue before getting to his feet and walking after it.

He caught up with the rearguard professional mourner and coughed until he gained its attention. 'Excuse me, madam,' he said. 'I was wondering if you could perhaps help me?'

'You can start by calling me "sir",' said a bass voice from within the veil.

'Yes, quite. My mistake,' said Cabal, after the shortest of pauses. 'I was thinking that in your profession you must have a good knowledge of the layout of this necropolis and—'

'Look, squire, I'm working,' interrupted the mourner, continuing to strike attitudes of mortal grief. 'The punters have forked out for forty mourners, not thirty-nine. If you want to talk, keep up and look mournful, savvy?'

'I don't have to be extravagant about it, do I?' Cabal was watching the others, who looked like nothing so much as a dance troupe extemporising on the theme of electrocution.

'You couldn't if you wanted to. Takes years of practice and three guild examinations to get to this standard. No, just look as if you gave a bugger about the departed and follow along.'

Cabal doubted he was a good enough actor to manage that, but he had spent his whole life polishing sombreness to a dignified mahogany glow that looked much the same to the unpractised eye. Thus, he followed at a steady funereal pace, and that did very nicely.

'So, what did you want to know, mate?' said the mourner, when he was satisfied that Cabal's presence was an asset to the procession.

'I was wondering if you could direct me to the oldest part of the necropolis.'

The mourner almost stumbled in mid-mimed declamation. 'You want to go where? What for?' he said, in open astonishment. 'That's the bad place.'

'It is also the interesting place and, for me, the necessary place.'

'No, seriously, chum, you don't want to go there. There's ghouls up there. The gardeners only go once a month and even then under armed guard. You're looking to get chewed if you go up there.'

'I'm not afraid of ghouls,' said Cabal. 'In fact, I might even learn something of interest from them. They are not my current concern, however. Does anyone live there? Any soothsayers? Oracles? Anybody like that?' He had the impression that the mourner was looking oddly at him.

'How'd you know?'

'It is a principle of the Dreamlands that themes of folklore are followed, even if they are altered or corrupted. Oracles and soothsayers are associated with shunned places. Therefore it seemed rational to seek out such a place. Given the predilection of ghouls to populate old graveyards and cemeteries in both worlds, I guessed their quarter would represent such a shunned place.' The impression of being oddly looked at had not diminished, although its timbre had changed. 'Well, you did ask,' said Cabal, perhaps a little tetchily.

The mourner looked at him a moment longer, then started striking attitudes once more, albeit at an accelerated pace to catch up with the procession. When they were back in place, he said, 'There's supposed to be a witch.'

'A witch,' Cabal repeated. He shrugged. 'Good enough.

When you say *witch*, do you mean the sort with a cauldron and potions, or just a mad old lady who feeds stray cats?'

'How should I know? Never been up there. But there *is* supposed to be a witch.'

A witch, then, would have to do. Cabal took leave of his short career as an amateur mourner with directions to the purportedly doom-haunted old cemetery in the north-eastern quadrant of the necropolis, and set off at a swift stride. Finding the right place had taken longer than he had anticipated and the sun was already low in the sky. While he truly did not fear the ghouls, he equally truly had a rational concern about being near one of their warrens after sunset. Between threats and a large Webley, he could keep a horde of them back for hours, but threats and a less immediate engine of extermination such as his sword offered no such certainty.

A decision to forgo the directions in an attempt to cut corners turned out to be unwise, and he wasted still more time while he backtracked first to where he had made the rash decision, and then to the circus. The shadows were long indeed by the time Cabal finally arrived at the old cemetery, where ghouls reputedly cavorted and a witch made her home.

The city of Hlanith had stood in the Dreamlands for as long as men have dreamed, and they have been dreaming for a very, very long time. It was a different place then, of course; crude and barbaric as those who dreamed it were crude and barbaric, but even from the first, it had known death. The necropolis was just a plot of land, then, in which the dead were interred with a few grave goods, their resting places marked with sticks and rocks and bones. Over time, the sticks and bones were discarded as too ephemeral in the former case, and too attractive to the local scavenging dogs in the latter. This left the stones, which grew larger, eventually sporting inscriptions of differing measures of accuracy, sincerity and spelling. These levels of increasing sophistication had travelled out, like ripples, from this original site until the differences became aesthetic and modish rather than fundamental. Seen from on high, however, the original burial ground still stood out like a black wart on a grey face. It had been shunned when it was first marked out, and it was shunned ground now, ancient, primal, dangerous.

There had been sundry ill-omened attempts to rehabilitate the area down the centuries. Every few generations, somebody would take it into their head that the ideal place for their inhumation or that of a respected family member, friend or client would be the oldest part of the necropolis. The builders would enter cautiously at dawn, and stampede out at dusk, spending the meantime erecting whatever tomb or crypt or mausoleum had seemed like such a good idea in the architect's office. After the things were built, and occupied, they were rarely visited again when it had become plain that, rather than civilising the atavistic nature of the place, the new structures might as well have been built in a war zone. So, abandoned if still remembered, these tombs, crypts and mausolea stood around like gentry who had inadvertently wandered into a rough pub, and there they grew grubbier as the years passed.

Johannes Cabal stood at the edge of the old cemetery and paused to take in the ambience of the place. The last shunned burial ground he had been in had been more than two years before, an unusually long period between shunned burial grounds in his working life. That one had been beautiful in its way, misty and artful in its slow, entropic descent into ruin. It had also borne an air of waiting for death, of hungering for new inmates, of taking the role of a great pointing skeletal hand in a misty, artful *memento mori*. It had not been a pleasant place to dawdle for reasons beyond its aesthetics, but it had never felt especially malign.

This old cemetery, on the other hand, reeked of malevolence. There were no true paths through it; nor had there ever been. Just jumble and tumble, weeds and briars, markers and ancient bones, some belonging to local scavenger dogs who had allowed their hunger to override their sense that the nature of this land was changing. The newer structures stood sloped and grimy, overwhelmed and embarrassed by their incongruity in this place of primordial death. Some had already collapsed, and from where he stood Cabal could see a smashed marble sarcophagus on its side amid the ruin of the tomb once built to hold it. The sarcophagus was empty, which did not surprise him. In this place, it had probably been emptied within a day of the funeral ceremony. To the ghouls, these structures were not hallowed resting places: they were larders.

Cabal loosened his sword in its scabbard and walked slowly forward. He wished he had a canteen of water with him: he was probably going to be speaking ghoulish soon and it always played havoc with his larynx. Some water to moisten his vocal cords would have been very helpful. He took up station upon a mound, under which lay the mouldering bones of a tribal shaman, and waited as the shadows flowed like ghost blood and the darkness grew deep.

He was not sure when he first became aware of the eyes that watched him. They did not blink, nor did they move, but they watched him with unwavering intent as their faint phosphorescent glow, an unhealthy greenish yellow, slowly made them stand out from the growing gloom. While there was still light in the sky, he knew they would be too cautious to attack, so he decided that now would be a good time to start his entreaty to them.

He cleared his throat, and began with a creditable attempt at meeping: 'I bear you no ill-will. I only seek counsel with one who lives in this place. My name is—'

'I have told you once before,' said a ghoulish voice from the shadows, and it spoke in English. 'I know who you are, Johannes Cabal.'

'Ah,' said Cabal, his concern at the reappearance of the ghoul who had spoken to him in Arkham at least slightly offset by his relief that he could speak a more civilised tongue. '*Guten Abend*. We meet again, it seems. You still have me at a disadvantage, though.'

'Only one, Herr Cabal? You are surrounded by sixty of my brethren. Your disadvantages multiply.'

'I have made provision for that,' lied Cabal. 'No, I am more interested in who you are.'

'Who I am is what I am, and I am a ghoul. That is all there is to me, and I am content in that.'

'Obviously I am delighted that you have found satisfaction in your current employment, but you hide in semantics. As you wish, then. Who *were* you?'

A pause. Then, 'Does it matter?'

'It might.'

Another pause. 'I forget. It all seems a long time ago when I walked in the light, and ate burned meat . . .' There was a liquid throaty growl from the other ghouls, a sound Cabal knew to denote disgust. From a race that routinely ate gamey human cadavers, it wasn't a sound that received much use. '. . . and vegetables.' The liquid throaty growl sounded again, louder this time. Cabal noted that the Ghoulish language certainly maintained a higher level of incipient threat than human languages. It was hard to imagine sixty people managing to be so menacing while chorusing, 'Eew . . .'

Cabal did not believe for an instant that the ghoul had truly forgotten its human identity, but they were inclined towards a wanton abstruseness. When one is a burrow-dwelling anthropophagist, one must seek entertainment wherever one can, so the ghouls had raised the sport of being mysterious to a level worthy of admittance to the Olympic Games. Not that they would ever actually turn up: they would just send some cryptic clues to the opening ceremony hinting that they might. Thus, this ghoul was almost certainly hiding its identity for some reason. That was comforting, as it implied that since the ghoul had a long-term plan for Cabal, it would not spoil it by eating him. At least, not by eating him prematurely. It was a toxic sort of guarantee but, for a man in Cabal's profession, it was much better than he was used to.

As the ghoul did not wish to discuss its personal history at this juncture, Cabal decided that it was permissible to skip the pleasantries and get on to the real reason for his visit. 'There is one who lives here . . . who I believe lives here.'

'You speak of the witch,' said the ghoul, barely before Cabal had finished. 'Yes, she is here.'

Cabal was too shrewd to be elated by this statement: the ghoul had specifically not said that she lived there, only that she was there. It might mean nothing, or it might mean everything. 'She lives here?' he said, with some emphasis.

'She lives,' said the ghoul, and Cabal thought he had heard

a note of amusement. *Ah*, he thought. *So teasing people as to whether somebody's alive or dead is what passes for humour in ghoul circles*. Then the ghoul said, 'You must speak with her. It is your destiny.'

Cabal's hackles rose slightly. In his experience, people who talked in terms of destiny were those without sufficient reason to be doing what they were doing. Not so very long ago he had suffered the misfortune of being in conversation with a military man intent on starting a war with his country's neighbours. He had spoken in terms of destiny, too, because, if that had been forbidden him, he would have had to admit that his motives were little better than rape, pillage and seizing the land of others. Calling it 'destiny' made it seem so much more noble. So it has always been, and so it will always be.

As if understanding his reserve, the ghoul said, 'If you prefer, it would be *wise* to speak with her.'

'Just to be clear,' said Cabal, 'do you mean *wise* purely as in pertaining to wisdom, or was it just an implied threat, with a flavour of *or else* about it?'

There was another pause. Cabal thought he heard the ghoul sigh. 'Which will induce you to speak to the witch, Johannes Cabal?'

Cabal thought about it for a moment. 'Under the circumstances, either.'

'Then it hardly matters, does it?' The ghoul was beginning to sound angry now. 'You are just as contrary as your reputation suggests.'

'What reputation?' asked Cabal, slightly taken aback. It counts for something when ghouls consider one *infra dig*.

'Go beyond the jade pagoda and look for the firelight. You will go unmolested by my people, but go quickly.'

The glowing eyes vanished quickly in scatterings of pairs. In moments the sense of being observed lifted from Cabal and he knew the ghouls were gone.

Breathing a sigh that might have been of exasperation or might have been of relief, Cabal looked around until he found a pagoda a few yards into the clutter of tombs. It stood some six yards tall, and was decorated with great slabs of jade. One lay by the pagoda's base, along with the tools that a foolish thief had used to remove it. It seemed that they had found to their cost that this particular part of the necropolis had no need for night-watchmen. Cabal walked slowly around it – pausing *en route* for a moment when something that he suspected was part of the thief crunched under his foot – and finally reached the rear of the structure.

The firelight was easily visible from there, flickering by a Grecian temple that had been built by students of Socrates, according to logical paradoxes rendered in architectural form. Given this provenance, it was no surprise that it had long since fallen over. Amid the tumbled columns, a figure sat upon a large bust of Socrates at his most disgruntled. She wore a black cloak that made her outline difficult to discern against the encroaching shadows, made deeper around her by the inconstant light from the fire. As Cabal approached, he saw she was wearing her cloak's hood over her brow and eyes. He could see the pale skin and red lips of a young woman but little else.

'Pardon me, madam,' he said, in the uncertain tones of a store detective running in a dowager duchess, 'are you, and I hesitate to use the term, a witch?'

She smiled, and while it was a pleasing smile in purely aesthetic terms, there was something knowing about it that he did not like. It reminded him of the peasant girl with the lamb's smile, not in appearance so much as in import. 'What were you expecting, Johannes Cabal?' she said. 'Somebody uglier? Wartier?' That smile again. 'Sluttier?'

'Who are you?' he asked. 'Do I know you?'

She shook her head slowly. 'No. We have never met, although . . . although you may know me by reputation.'

Cabal grimaced. 'It's all reputations around here.'

'Not around here. Back there,' and he knew she was speaking of the waking world. 'You need a clue. Very well. Do you recall the last little book of Darius?'

'The *Opusculus V*? What of it?' Realisation was sudden. 'You? I . . .' He somehow rallied his dignity in the face of astonishment. 'Madam, I was very much under the impression that you were dead.'

'Death is a very relative term here, sweetie.'

Cabal was briefly unsure whether to be more rocked by the discovery that he was talking to a woman whom he knew beyond all reasonable doubt was dead, or being called 'sweetie.' He decided 'sweetie' could wait.

'Miss Smith? That *is* you, then?'

'Smith . . . That is a name I haven't heard in a very long time. Here, I am simply the witch of the old cemetery, and it suffices.'

'I heard that you killed yourself when they came for you.'

'Then you heard the ramblings of ignorant minds. I was not dead, only sleeping. The *Opusculus V* contained a formula for a certain narcotic that allowed dream travel here, into the Dreamlands, even for somebody unskilled in focused dreaming. I was in a coma, as they would have discovered if they had had a doctor with them.'

'Yes,' said Cabal, gravely. 'Torch-bearing mobs tend to be very weak on bringing along medical personnel.'

'The first I knew that something was wrong was when the ritual of return failed, and I realised that it was because I had no body to return to. Tell me, Johannes, what did they do to me?'

'Outside, they had hanged you in effigy. So . . .'

'There was a rope handy. How cowardly. And what became of my body?'

'They realised belatedly that they were in a lot of trouble, buried you in a shallow grave, and disappeared back to their homes to carry on the charade of being decent people.'

She cocked her head slightly, and Cabal had the unnerving feeling that she could see him perfectly well, despite the lowered cowl. 'And how is it that you know all this detail, hmm, Johannes?'

'You know full well that I wanted the *Opusculus V* for myself. I have the first four volumes, but they are of limited use without the fifth.'

'Let me guess. You ransacked my rooms after the coast was clear? But . . . you did not find it.'

'Because it was not there,' said Cabal, finally feeling better about his searching skills.

'And when you could not find it, you cut your losses by taking my body for experimental material.' Cabal blanched. The witch laughed with delight and pointed at him. 'Ha! Just an educated guess, Johannes. It's what I'd have done in your position.' She paused. 'Oh, God. You've seen me naked.'

'You made a very beautiful corpse,' said Cabal, making an ill-judged attempt at gallantry.

She smiled at his discomfort, but it was not a cruel smile.

'So here we are.' Then the smile slipped away and she said, in the steady, forceful voice of an oracle, 'Johannes Cabal, you are in terrible danger. You should never have accepted the commission of the Fear Institute. You should never have come to the Dreamlands. Now it is too late to avoid. You must face the coming dangers. You are a scientist, and the very idea of destiny is anathema to you, but there is more than one sort of destiny. Yours is not predetermined, but it is a narrow path. You must cleave to this path, for if you step from it you will fall.'

Cabal listened, impressed despite himself. 'And how will I know this path?'

'Your own will shall guide you. You must search for the Phobic Animus, and you must find it. You must do so with urgency and determination, never permitting distractions, never losing your way.'

'But there will be false leads, wasted time. How can I be sure that I am staying on the path?'

'To err is human, Johannes. Mistakes do not matter as long as they are honest, as long as you never, ever hesitate or give up. Do you understand me?'

Cabal was thinking hard. 'Why are you doing this? Why are you helping me?'

'Because this is the Dreamlands, and we all have a role to play here. You are the hero on the quest, and I am the wise woman who gives you counsel.' She laughed, breaking character. 'Neither of us is ideal for our job, but you just have to do what you can.'

'Then why don't you just tell me where the Phobic Animus is, Miss Smith?'

'Oh, lots of reasons. First, that would make this a *really* short quest. "Oh, here's the Holy Grail. It was down the back of the sofa the whole time." Second, I honestly don't know where it is. "Wise" isn't the same as "omniscient", you know. Third, one of your little pals is going to turn up at your meeting tomorrow with a strong lead. You should follow it.'

Cabal frowned suspiciously. 'I thought you said that you're not omniscient.'

'I'm not. I'm just very well informed.'

'And this is the extent of your power? *Scientia potentia est?* You have a spy network, and ghouls for bodyguards.' He sighed. 'You have no power to divine the future. So all that dramatic soothsaying was just that? Drama?'

'I am doing a great deal for you, Cabal, even if you don't realise it yet. As for power, the Dreamlands are different.' Her voice had become dangerously calm. 'A few weeks ago, a thief came here to steal jade from the pagoda. I like the pagoda, and told him to leave or face the consequences. He didn't leave.'

'So you set the ghouls on him. Yes, yes, I stood on his skull.'

'How big a fool do you think that thief was? He came in broad daylight.' Cabal furrowed his brow in surprise. The sun would drain the life from a ghoul. 'No. It wasn't the ghouls that made his eyes boil in his head or his roasting flesh peel from his bones.' She lifted her face a little and, as she did so, the cowl fell back far enough for him to glimpse her eyes. Then he knew that she was telling him no more than the truth. 'Not that the ghouls thanked me for doing their job,' she concluded. 'They hate cooked meat.

'You should go now, Johannes. There's nothing more that I can tell you.'

Cabal coughed awkwardly. 'Thank you.'

She shook her head slowly. 'No. Don't thank me. I'm sending you into the worst trial of your life, and the only consolation is that the alternative is infinitely worse. I'm sorry. I wish it wasn't like this. You've attracted attention of the wrong sort now, and there's no going back.'

Cabal nodded grimly. 'Nyarlothotep.'

'*Don't* say that name here,' she snapped. 'I may have power, but I'm a long way short of bullet-proof and I don't need that sort of trouble.' Then she laughed, surprising Cabal. 'You know, I never have got into the hang of *thee* and *thou* and *prithee* and all that sort of stuff. "Bullet-proof." I guess I'm just too modern for this place.' She sobered a little and regarded Cabal through shadowed eyes. 'But you're right. You've caught on about *him* already, eh? You always were a clever one. The best rival a girl could hope for. I was so pleased with myself for nicking the *Opusculus V* before you. I knew you had the other four. You must have been *so* pissed off with me.'

'Mildly,' said Cabal, with extravagant understatement.

'I'm sure. Look, you remember that town? On the high street, there's a branch of Winwicks Bank with a safety deposit facility. You want box number 313. I can't give you the key, but I doubt that will slow you down. A gift from me, Johannes. I hope you live to enjoy it.'

On the way out, Cabal happened upon two men doing a poor job of hiding bags of tools behind their backs. They looked at him, then back along the way he had come with some consternation. ' 'Scuse us,' said one, 'but have you just come from the old cemetery?'

'Yes,' said Cabal, casually resting his hand on his sword hilt in a not especially casual way.

The two men looked at where his hand lay, and the option of an impromptu mugging was almost palpably crossed off their inner 'To do' lists. 'An' you didn't see no ghouls about?'

Cabal was interested if not surprised to see that, even here, the vast majority of criminals were stunningly stupid. 'No,' he said, with a pleasant sense of duplicitous honesty. 'There were certainly no ghouls around just now. I was just admiring a magnificent jade pagoda there, and I felt entirely safe.'

The two men grinned at one another, thanked Cabal hastily and trotted off in the direction of the old cemetery. He watched them go with no ambivalent feelings. 'A gift from me, Miss Smith.' Then he continued on his way.

Surviving fragments of Cyril W. Clome's manuscript for *The Young Person's Guide to Cthulhu and His Friends: No. 2 Nyarlothotep, the Crawling Chaos*

Oh, **Nyarlothotep** is such a naughty god! Full of wheezes and wizard pranks – which often involve wizards – he is more fun than the human mind can comprehend. So all we poor mortals can understand of his jolly clever jokes is the agony and the suffering and the blood and the madness. Yes, humans just don't have much of a sense of humour, I'm afraid.

Now Nyarlothotep is one of the Outer Gods, who are terrifically powerful and see we humans as less than germs, which is only right. Nyarlothotep is super-special, though, because he has lots of different faces and lots of different personalities. It must be so much fun to wake up in the morning and decide not only who you will be today, but even what species you will be. If *you* were Nyarlothotep, what form would you like to have today? I think I'd like to be a dense, oily mist that could creep into people's homes as they slept and give them acute radiation burns. That would be a splendid jape, wouldn't it?

He has lots of names, too, to go with every mask he wears, but really he is always good old Nyarlothotep. He isn't just a very funny clown, though. He is also the soul of the Outer Gods and their messenger, so he is terribly, terribly busy. But don't worry. Nyarlothotep always finds time to play his tricks. What fun!

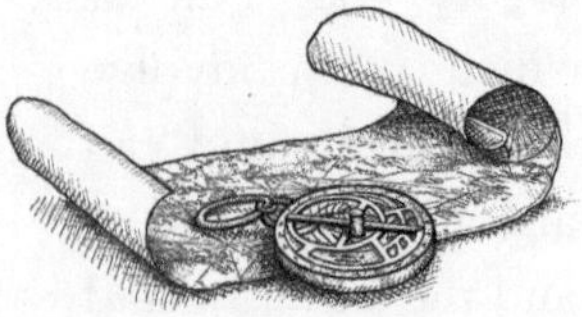

Chapter 6

IN WHICH THE EXPEDITION CROSSES THE SEA AND CABAL TAKES AN INTEREST IN THE LEG OF A SAILOR

They met as arranged the next day, and immediately retired to an alehouse where they could drink wine or beer or a local tea, as they so desired, and eat seed cakes as they told of what they had discovered. All but Cabal, who said that he had researched the strange glitch in time they had experienced, but had discovered nothing of use. This was true, in a largely false way: he had asked a stablehand, who had said he'd never heard of the like. Then again, the stablehand had likely never heard of Damascus, apoplexy or soap, but as no one queried Cabal on the size or demographics of his sample, he did not feel the need to burden them with such details.

Cabal's disappointing luck aside, everyone had something exciting to report.

Bose was the first. 'I spoke with the archive keeper and

asked him if he had ever heard tell of something called the Phobic Animus –'

'Hardly likely,' said Corde, 'since we coined the term.'

'– or anything similar,' continued Bose, a little testily. 'He *had* heard of something known as the "Frozen Heart", which is described as being the epitome of all fears.'

'The "Frozen Heart",' said Cabal. He was looking out of the window, drinking his tea slowly. His seed cake sat untouched. 'How poetic.'

'Yes, that was what I thought,' said Bose, happily, entirely missing Cabal's tone. 'This whole world is built on poetic principles. That is what led me to believe in the veracity of this line of research. I asked if these reports had a specific locale or locales associated with them. And they do!'

He produced a rolled-up piece of parchment from his sleeve and unfurled it on the tabletop. At its head, he had written in careful block capitals, 'LIKELY LIST OF PLACES (SHUNNED)'. Beneath it was a list of perhaps twenty locations.

'Well, it's a start,' said Shadrach, uncertainly. 'But those places must be hundreds of miles apart. Checking every one of them will take months, if not years, subjectively speaking at least.'

'This one's handy,' said Corde. 'It's the old cemetery right here in Hlanith. We can go there now.'

'You can cross that one off,' said Cabal, with a bored languor he did not feel. 'I went there myself last night.' They all looked at him in astonishment. He shrugged. 'I'm a necromancer. Cemeteries and the like are my meat and drink.'

'Not literally, though,' said Shadrach, smiling.

Cabal gave him a dusty look. 'One has to drop in. It's a

professional courtesy. There's nothing there but a bunch of ghouls and a mad woman who fancies herself a witch. The ghouls seem to believe it, as they leave her alone.'

Corde looked sceptical. 'You just strolled in and had a chinwag with some ghouls?'

'Hardly a chinwag. I walked in, they threatened to eat me, I threatened to destroy them, there was some sabre-rattling, literally in my case, and that was that.'

'And then what?'

'And then I had my dinner. White wine and chicken *al fresco* upon the tomb of a pair of tragic star-crossed lovers.'

Corde was not sure if Cabal was toying with him. 'And that was all?'

'Alas, yes. I had wanted some cheese, but couldn't find any at short notice. It was a shame. Cheese goes so well with tragedy.'

Corde stared hard at Cabal, and it took Shadrach's proclamation of his own results to regain his attention. 'I was invited to a dinner at the merchant adventurers' hall last night,' he said, with due deference to his own importance. 'This truly is a fascinating world, mixed from the epic poems of Greece and the sagas of the Vikings, the thousand and one nights of Scheherazade, the mystical tales of the Orient, and the Dreamtime of the antipodean Aboriginals. I heard so many strange stories . . . but none of the Animus. One place came up in conversation, however. By all accounts a terrible place, and it may be the one.' He drew Bose's list to him and cast an eye down it. 'There, the sixth one down, Oriab Island. There are supposed to be some ruins where something terrible happened once upon a time, although nobody seems to know what.'

Cabal already had his bag open and his notes folder out. 'Oriab Island is not small, and the ruins might be anywhere. We need more exact information before investing effort in going there.'

'The ruins are on the banks of Lake Yath,' said Corde, a little smugly. He leaned back in his chair, and took a decent draught from his flagon of beer before elaborating. 'I got talking to some sailors . . .'

'What you do in your own time . . .' muttered Cabal.

'. . . and they said Oriab Island was the place to go. *Not* because there's much likelihood of the Animus being there, but because in the ruins by Lake Yath lives a hermit. He will speak to one person a year, and will answer one question that they ask. It doesn't matter what it is, he will always know the answer.'

The others considered this. 'How do we know that nobody has already asked him this year?' said Shadrach.

'Because,' said Corde, with a wily grin, 'nobody has asked him a question for at least two years, and the person who asked on that occasion died shortly afterwards from his wounds.'

Bose's eyes had gone very large. 'Wounds?' he asked tremulously.

'There is something in those ruins that doesn't like strangers,' explained Corde. 'That's the scuttlebutt, anyway.' He took up his flagon and raised it to Shadrach, whose expression of moral outrage indicated that he thought 'scuttlebutt' was some act of frightful sordidness.

'We shall have to book passage, then,' said Bose. 'Ah. How do we do that? I assume that we cannot simply walk into a shipping agent's and buy tickets in the same way that we travelled to America.'

Shadrach took the opportunity to demonstrate his utility and, in so doing, distract himself from theorising as to exactly what scuttlebuttery consisted of. 'I know the very man. I made his acquaintance last night. Captain Lochery, owner, master and commander of the *Edge of Dusk*. A galleon.' He settled back to bask in the plaudits.

'Galleon' was putting it a little strongly. The party had proceeded down to the stout, oaken wharves, where stout, oaken ships waited at anchor, quite possibly crewed by stout, oaken sailors because, after all, this was the Dreamlands. Almost the only thing at the docks that was not stout and oaken was the *Edge of Dusk*, a ship that had probably looked like it had seen better days right from the hour it was launched. It was not a galleon, that was clear to all of them, but it was Corde who correctly identified it as a cog, an earlier and smaller form of ship. As a galleon is to a cog, a cog is to a small toy with a sail that one splashes around in the bath to amuse oneself when one is either very young or an admiral. It was something of a disappointment, but Cabal pointed out that a true galleon, one looking like a refugee from a Spanish plate fleet, would have been greatly surplus to their requirements and to their budget. The *Edge of Dusk* was not pretty, but she was small, and on closer inspection bore an air of competence and functionality about her that Cabal, for one, preferred to her romantic neighbours, their sails blowing like the ruffled shirt of a hero in a novel for spinsters.

Captain Lochery himself was on deck as they approached the ship. He positively grinned with delight when he saw Shadrach and bounded down the gangplank to meet them.

'Master Shadrach!' he cried, grasping Shadrach's hand in

both of his and pumping it firmly. For Shadrach, who was used to handshakes with all the vigour of a cucumber sandwich left out in the rain, this was a surprise, and all he could manage were a couple of 'Oh!'s and 'Ah!'s in response.

Lochery, who outmatched his vaguely Scottish name with an accent that would have made Robert Burns sound English by comparison, was introduced to Shadrach's companions and was polite and friendly with them all. When he reached Cabal, however, his mood faltered. He took in Cabal's clothing, and said, 'You'll be a strong-minded one, that's plain enough. This place will be a trial to you, no doubt.'

Cabal remembered the witch's reference to a trial, but decided that he was not so foolish as to see meaning where there was only coincidence. 'It has been noted before now, yes. Thank you.'

Lochery shook his head. 'No, son, you don't understand. The Dreamlands were built by dreamers, and dreamers are what they expect. Like a body fights an infection, this world will fight you.'

Cabal's lips thinned. 'Then I shall fight back.'

Lochery laughed, a fatalistic laugh of the sort reserved for gladiators, soldiers on suicide missions, and explorers leaving tents who 'may be some time'. 'I like your pluck, Master Cabal, but this is a world you're talking about. You can fight it, but you *will* lose.'

Cabal looked around him. 'I have no sense of the Dreamlands going to war with me, Captain. Do you? No black clouds, water spouts or monsters come to destroy me. I feel no more threatened than I might on Brighton beach.' He spat into the water for punctuation. 'Heaven forfend.'

'Oh, it won't be anything like that,' said Lochery. 'But I've seen men like yourself come here, and one of two things always happens.' He leaned closer and spoke in a hushed tone. 'The Dreamlands either destroy 'em, or absorb 'em. I'd buck up your ideas and try to fit in if you don't want the 'Lands to do it for you. For an example, I went to sleep in the wrong opium den. Well, wrong in one sense. I don't know what they'd mixed their stuff with but it brought me here. I guess it killed me too. My old body, that is. No goin' back for old Cap'n Lochery. But, as you see, I fitted in. You should try to do the same, sir, or things won't go so well for you.' Seeing Cabal's expression he raised his hands in conciliation. 'Not a threat, son. Just a friendly warning.'

'Do you always hand out metaphysical advice to your passengers?' asked Cabal, growing a little heated.

'Only those that looks as if they need it,' said Lochery, with infuriating good humour. 'And, for the truth, you're not passengers yet. No negotiations have been made, no bargain has been struck.'

Shadrach held up a handful of gold from his purse and said, 'Passage for we four to Oriab Island, Captain Lochery.'

Lochery's grin widened. 'And now they have, and now it has.' He stepped to one side and bowed them to the gangplank. 'Step lively, gentlemen. The tide turns soon, and then we'll be away to Baharna, capital city and – 'tis no secret – the only city on Oriab Island. The only one standing, at least.'

It was their second experience of nautical travel on the expedition so far, but taking passage upon a form of ship that had been obsolete for the best part of six centuries was a very different matter from eight days aboard a modern steam liner. In the first instance, the *Edge of Dusk* was small, barely fifty tons, and lacked the comforts that Messrs Shadrach and Bose, in particular, had enjoyed so much while crossing the Atlantic. To be precise, the *Edge of Dusk* lacked any and all comforts, including privacy. The vessel's single toilet was a cubbyhole in the rear quarterdeck with a piece of cloth held across the entrance by two nails. Inside was a bench with a hole and the ocean ten feet below. This, Captain Lochery proudly believed, was the very cutting edge of hygiene technology. Indeed, in high seas, it doubled as a bidet. This intelligence Shadrach and Bose received in a pallid silence, while Corde laughed, and Cabal looked at the horizon in the direction of Oriab Island.

They would be expected to sleep in hammocks along with the crew – as captain, Lochery had a small closet aft that he called his 'cabin' – and during the day were expected to stay at the rail and therefore out of the way as much as possible. Shadrach had suggested that, since they were paying passengers, seats upon the quarterdeck might not be unreasonable, but had quickly learned that, to a sailor, this was *deeply* unreasonable. Instead they had grudgingly been given permission to sit on barrels on the foredeck with the proviso that they get out of the way immediately if ordered by any member of the crew. Going from ordering stewards around to being ordered around by any passing sailor was a great humiliation for Shadrach in particular, and he spent much of the first two days of the trip standing by the bowsprit, stony-faced and uncommunicative, to the extent that the crew started calling him 'the spare figurehead' behind his back.

The time between standing at the bowsprit he passed much as the others did; swinging unhappily in a hammock, putting off visits to the frightful cubbyhole as long as possible, and being gloriously and violently sick on a regular basis. During the Atlantic passage, they had all suffered some sea-sickness for the first day or so, but had quickly overcome it and had mistakenly come to the conclusion that this was all the time necessary to find one's sea-legs. Compared to the steam liner, however, the *Edge of Dusk* was like spending every hour of every day being blindfolded and lobbed at short, random intervals on to a trampoline. The horizon wantonly flung itself around at peculiar angles and the contents of their stomachs followed it faithfully, even while their inner ears told them that everything else was lying, and 'downwards' was actually *this* way. The crew found the sight of their passengers leaning over the rails hugely amusing in the absence of any other form of entertainment, although they quickly got a sense that it was unwise to laugh at Cabal. He never seemed particularly stricken, barking up his breakfast in a perfunctory way as if he had planned to do so all along, then strolling over to the water-butt and taking a mouthful from the scoop to rinse his mouth before spitting it out over the rail to follow his bacon and biscuit. None of the crew had ever seen a man vomit in a dignified manner, and it worried them in an disquietingly undefined fashion.

There was some commotion on the third day when the lookout sighted a sea serpent about a league off the port bow. Cabal barely felt it necessary to use his telescope to examine it; the creature was vast, a mile long and thicker than the *Edge of Dusk* was tall. They watched it swim by in a series of undulating humps that barely disturbed the waters, the sun glistening off the slick grey scales, unaware or uncaring of the tiny ship that sailed so near.

Corde noticed the captain watching it, his arms crossed and a ruminative expression on his face. His calmness did much to still Corde's own nerves at being so close to such a giant, and he said, 'I gather such creatures do not attack ships, Captain?'

Lochery looked sideways at Corde, and raised an eyebrow. 'Oh, aye? And what makes you say that, Master Corde?'

Corde laughed. 'Why, your unconcerned attitude, of course. You do not look like a man who suspects imminent death.'

'Ah,' said Lochery, returning his attention to the diminishing serpent, now beginning a descent back into its native depths. 'Well, you see, if we had been in its path, it would have devoured the ship whole. They can do that, you know, and we would not have been able to do a thing to stop it.'

'What?' Corde's sang-froid fractured abruptly. 'We were in danger the whole time? How could you be so calm, man?'

'I repeat, we would not have been able to do a thing to stop it. If we are to die, Master Corde, we can at least die well.'

Ten days, the trip took altogether, and the majority were much like one another. Once, when the ocean grew shallow over a submarine plateau, Corde excitedly pointed out that he could see a sunken city clearly beneath the waves. Lochery was unhappy to hear it and put a greater press upon the sails, the sooner to be clear. Nor was Cabal delighted by this remarkable sight, refusing even to look at it, instead pacing up and down the deck, muttering about how greatly he resented the loss of his pistol.

Everyone was relieved when, on the early evening of the tenth day, the lookout called, 'Land, ho!' and shortly thereafter Oriab Island crept over the easterly horizon. There was sufficient light to study the architecture as the *Edge of Dusk* glided between two lighthouses to rival the Pharos on either side of Baharna harbour, and approached the quayside before lowering her sails and sculling in the last few yards. Sailors leaped easily to the quay and, within a minute, were tying her off to the bollards. After such a long and occasionally harrowing journey, the sense of anticlimax was intense.

'Well,' said Bose, as they gathered their few items of luggage bought in Hlanith, 'that was an adventure in itself. Sea serpents and sunken cities! Tell me, Captain, is this journey always so exciting?'

Lochery considered for a moment. 'No pirates this time,' he said, shrugged, and then bade his passengers a good evening before turning his attention to unloading cargo.

Baharna was a very different city from Hlanith, even larger (in their experience to date, the Dreamlands didn't seem to do small – except for ships) and seemed to owe less to Earth in its architecture. Or at least, as Cabal commented, to any surviving architecture known on Earth. The city was terraced, but in such a way as to make the ranks of Hlanith seem very modest indeed. The streets of Baharna rose and fell steeply and, as a result, were frequently stepped. The visitors guessed that loads were carried on the sharply zigzagging roads that ran across the terraced levels, but people still managed to ride up and down the interstitial stepped highways by an unexpected method.

'Oh, I say,' said Bose. 'That chap's riding a zebra.'

It seemed that the zebras of the Dreamlands, or at least the zebras of Oriab, were far more biddable creatures than their terrestrial counterparts. A smiling trader in an orange silken robe, saluted them with something similar but not exactly a salaam gesture, and rode by on his patient and sanguine zebra, laden with panniers.

They watched him pass and then watched him ride off down the stepped road towards the quays. The observation grew to a slightly irritating length until it was halted by Cabal's curt, 'Oh, hallelujah. We have seen a man on a zebra and may now die content.' He stalked off up the hill, looking for an inn the captain had told them of, and did not deign to make sure the others were keeping up.

As he walked, and they pursued him in a desultory we-were-going-this-way-in-any-event sort of way, he looked up at the huge archways that bent upon the highways of the city, archways upon which stood more buildings of the same dark purplish porphyry from which much of the city seemed to be built. It gave an impression of great solidity and great age. Cabal knew that an igneous stone like porphyry was difficult to cut; the ancient Egyptians had certainly made heavy weather of it, loathing the stuff for its hardness but loving it for its colour, finish and resistance to the elements. Or so the mummy of a master architect had once told him during a not entirely legal experiment at a respected science academy held long after normal hours. In fact, the virtues of building materials were all that ancient worthy had been prepared to talk about, probably because the rest of his brain was in a canopic jar somewhere.

The vast quantities of the stuff in evidence here, however, raised the question of just how large a quarry would have to be opened in the side of a nearby volcano to supply such gargantuan – indeed, Cyclopean – loads of the distinctive rock. Cabal considered the hypothesis that if all the porphyry were to be dumped neatly back into the quarries it would produce a good-sized hill after filling the holes. In short, that most had never been mined but dreamed into existence, long, long ago by men or things like men. The hard stone had been chosen because it reasonably matched the environment, but mainly because it emanated permanence, and permanence in the land of sleep is better than gold in the world of wakefulness. Cabal's chosen profession meant that he must perforce dabble frequently in history and folklore and the misty hinterland between them. Over time, he had developed a sense of what was likely and what was not, which historical theories were probably true, and which were bunkum. To this sense, the Dreamlands stank of bunkum, a rank, musty smell like old sacking. Real history was unromantic, steeped in greed and blood and abject eye-rolling stupidity. An endless parade of putative Ozymandiases marching off to glory before snapping off at the ankles in the depths of the desert: *that* was human history. Every now and then there would be the pretence of civilisation, but soon enough the restless, hateful, atavistic hearts of humanity would tear down the towers and slide back into barbarism, squealing with glee. Decadence loves the taste of blood, even though it is poison.

The Dreamlands had none of that. The town squares had statues to poets and artists, philosophers and writers, not generals and statesmen. Cabal had heard of no wars or even border squabbles in living memory. Oh, there were tales of great wars and toppled states, but these all dwelled in the distant past. When an Ozymandian empire fell here, it was explicitly for the convenience of any passing Shelley looking for a subject for a sonnet.

Yet, Cabal concurred, the Dreamlands should have had all the necessary ingredients for conflict and anarchy. There were fat merchants with vast wealth, so money was important here, and where there was money there were jealousy and violence. There were pirates, mercenaries, marines and soldiers. There were kingdoms that chafed under ancient enmities with other races and neighbours. All the elements were here, so why did no spark start a conflagration?

Perhaps, he concluded, wars could only start here for aesthetic reasons. Tawdry little land grabs simply didn't happen because they were revolting and wrong. Noble crusades and heroic ventures, on the other hand, were romantic and right. Perhaps, Cabal thought, when he had more leisure he might try his hand at starting a conflict here, just for purposes of scientific enquiry. The Trojan model looked simple and effective. He made a mental note to foment a war at some point, and returned his attention to finding the inn.

It took another twenty minutes to locate the place, ten of which were spent in a small square, the centre of which was a compact but beautiful garden, arranged around a statue of a middle-aged man of patrician features, dressed in a toga. The statue was of striking craftsmanship, but the reason for the pause there was because all of the party – Cabal included – were astounded to discover that they were able, at some curious subconscious level, to hear the statue think. Several people were gathered around, sitting on the pale wood benches that bordered the square, in poses of deep concentration, 'listening' to the thoughts and occasionally nodding in slow comprehension.

When one of them arose from his meditations to make a few notes upon a waxen tablet, Corde asked him, 'That statue, how is it that we can hear its mind?'

The man laughed, a small polite laugh of the type reserved

for ignorant foreigners, and said, 'That is not a statue. It is the great thinker Arturax, he who has travelled so deeply into the inner realms of thought and intellect that he has been transfigured by the very nature of his ideas. He has no need of food, drink or rest because such things are animal and unsuited to a man of thought. Thus, he has dispensed with them. He is a hero to all mankind, as he addresses question after question, slaying them with his wisdom.'

'These problems,' asked Johannes Cabal, 'I was wondering, do they include how to deal with urban pigeons?' But his colleagues shushed him and took him away before the student of Arturax could hear.

The inn was called the Haven of Majestic and Bountiful Rest and, worse yet, deserved that name. Cabal rarely visited inns, except to secure the temporary services of ratlike men with names like Tibbs, Feltch and Crivven to do the basic shovel work in moonlit cemeteries when he was in too much of a hurry to do it himself. The inns such men frequented in turn had names like the Friendly Gibbet, the Sucking Wound and the Sports Bar, vile places with vile clientele. The Haven, by contrast, was a lively, bustling place full of open-faced men and more than a few women, all wearing bright silks, drinking golden mead and ice wine, singing *risqué* but by no means obscene songs, and never getting more than pleasantly tipsy. Even the sawdust upon the saloon-bar floor was fresher than that in a busy woodwork shop. Bose and Shadrach were delighted to see it thus, Corde seemed slightly disappointed, and Cabal simply scowled, as was his wont.

The food was good, the drink was good, and the company was bearable, so Cabal bore it where once he might have gone to bed, leaving the others with an unspoken curse to be visited upon their next of kin. Two hours later, Bose waved over Captain Lochery, fresh from completing the offloading of the *Edge of Dusk*'s cargo and looking for a soft berth for the evening. As they were buying, he joined them with the practised alacrity of a seaman who scents free booze and, in return for a drink and a meal, regaled them with tales of the Dreamlands' seas. These frequently ended with the words '. . . and he was never seen again' so Cabal quickly lost interest. He was on the point of going to his room when he noticed that Lochery was – while cheerfully telling nautical tales of shipwrecked desperation, ingestion by sea monsters, the sodomite proclivities of pirates, and some unexpected combinations of these elements – feeding his right leg.

'Captain Lochery,' said Cabal, as he watched the man offer a piece of sour bread to his calf, which gratefully devoured it, 'I cannot help but notice that you are feeding your leg.'

'Aye,' said Lochery, unabashed. 'It gets hungry.' In explanation, he rolled up his right pantaloon leg to reveal what Cabal had assumed would be pale flesh but was actually a beautifully carved wooden prosthetic. In the outer right calf there was a small hole, and from this hole an inquisitive rodent's face was peering out at them.

There were cries of astonishment from the others, but Cabal went down on one knee to look more carefully. 'I don't recognise the species. It looks a little like a guinea pig, and a little like a dwarf rabbit, but is barely bigger than a hamster. What is it, Captain?'

'Guinea what was that? Rabby? I don't know anything of those, Master Cabal, exotic though they sound. But this is a dreff. They're only found on this island.' He slapped his thigh, but gently, so as not to disturb the creature. 'I lost this leg when I was a lad. One day out from here. The weather was strange, and the creatures of air and water were disturbed. My ship – she was the *Fool's Wager* out of Ulthar, under Captain Mart, dead these twenty years – was attacked by seagaunts.' Some interested bystanders made a sympathetic groan. 'Twenty or thirty, driven mad by the green sun.'

'I've heard of nightgaunts,' said Cabal. 'Slick, rubbery, faceless black creatures with horns and wings. What are these seagaunts?'

'Much the same,' said Lochery, 'except at sea. They fell on us. I saw poor old Jecks Pilt borne off by them. They tried to do the same to me, filthy flapping things, but I got a deadman's grip on the rigging of the foremast – she was lateen rigged, by the bye – and I was not going to let go, not with Jecks's screams still echoing in my ears. But the 'gaunts, they wanted something for their trouble. So . . .' He waved at the wooden leg.

'Well, Captain Mart, he was a good man, he said to me, "You're a sailor through and through and no leg-thieving seagaunts are going to take that away from you." At least, that's what he said later, 'cause I'd flaked out at the time from loss of blood. Anyway, he had a favour owed to him by a sorcerer in the city, and he took me to him – big tower at the northern end of the Spice Quarter, some dodgy evoker's got it now, last I heard – and he comes up with this little beauty. See, dreff live in trees from the Sinew Wood, south-east of the Lake of Yath. The trees can move, but they got no brains. The dreff have brains – pretty good ones, considerin' how little they are – but they can't look after themselves. So, the dreff and the sinew trees are sort of . . .' He looked for the word.

'Symbiotes,' supplied Cabal, intrigued by the insight into an alien ecology.

'Pals,' continued Lochery. 'Now, this sorcerer says dreff are clever and they know a good thing when they see it, which is a roundabout way of saying that they train up easy. Keep 'em fed and happy, and they'll be your pals for life. This little fella in here, Checky, he knows that when I throw my hip forward, it's walking time, and he makes the leg – finest sinew wood, this is – shift at knee and ankle. Fact is, that he just seems to know now, we been together so long.'

He fed the dreff the last of the sour bread before gently nudging its head back in and bunging the whole with a stopper perforated with air holes. 'They live about ten years. Takes about six months for you to understand each other, and they go a bit mad a few weeks before they die, sleeping a lot, making the leg bend all ways, so you know it's time to get to the Sinew Wood with a box trap and some sour bread. They love the stuff.'

He looked off into the middle distance, lost in the past. 'But you know the worst part of all of this? Not my leg, no, there's people suffer worse. No, I still think of Jecks, the poor sod. You know what?'

The rhetorical question was interrupted by Cabal rising. 'He was never seen again. Goodnight, gentlemen. An early start tomorrow.'

Chapter 7

IN WHICH THE EXPEDITION EXPLORES A NAMELESS CITY OF EVIL REPUTE

'Wamps,' said the sergeant, as he checked the ties on his scabbard.

'Wamps!' replied Bose, hand held up.

'Wamps,' said Cabal, 'are a species. Not a greeting.'

'Oh,' said Bose, unabashed. 'They sound rather harmless, though, don't they?' He tested the name several times with different intonations, each implying wamps were cuddly, warm, docile and fun to have around the house.

Sergeant Holk, a man with his experience measured in scars and a hard, weather-beaten face, looked at Bose as a father might look at a child who wants a wolverine for Christmas, ideally one with rabies. 'They're bigger than a man. They have nine legs and heads like great bats with no eyes at all. They're disease-ridden killers . . . Just a scratch from one can kill you, even if it takes a year of miserable, agonising sickness to do it.'

'Do be quiet,' said Corde. The sergeant's predilection for gruesome hyperbole was proving counterproductive. It was Corde who had found him at one of the ill-regarded dives he was becoming quite adept at locating. The sergeant had agreed to tell them what was known of the empty and partially ruined city to the east in exact, non-folklorish terms for he had been there.

So far his advice had been very much of the 'Don't go there' variety, of which the presence of wamps was the newest variant. Warming to his theme, the sergeant said, 'Six years ago, I went in there with a platoon to raid the old library. Special commission, you see. We got the scrolls we went in for, but it was dusk by the time we were ready to move out. The wamps ambushed us. They've got a few brains, and they don't fight like animals. They're cunning, see? They can creep up walls and drop on you from above. That's what happened to us. Thirty of us went in, only four of us got out.'

'Without a scratch, I presume?' said Cabal, drily.

The sergeant just laughed and pulled up the left side of his jerkin. Beneath, the flesh was not simply scarred but missing down to the ribs, which showed as slats beneath a thin covering of skin. His audience watched, fascinated, as the slats rose and fell with his breathing. 'No, sir. Not without a scratch. Within half a day, that scratch was a mass of worms. The chirurgeon had no choice but to cut out all the tainted flesh before it spread. I cursed him. Gods, in my delirium, I cursed the eyeballs from his head. But he saved my life.'

Shadrach was caught in the flux between repulsion and fascination. 'Worms? You mean maggots, surely?'

'I mean worms. Filthy, fat things that swallowed strings of my flesh at one end and shat out pus at the other.'

'But where did they come from?'

'From the same place a worm that causes a toothache comes, Shadrach,' said Cabal.

Shadrach looked sourly at Cabal. 'Don't talk nonsense, man. Worms don't cause toothache. That's an old wives' tale.'

Cabal made a noise often heard from the parents of ungifted children just before explaining for the tenth time *why* it's bad for Timmy to put Timmy's arm in the big fire. 'Herr Shadrach ... this is a world in which old wives are authorities. How many times must I reiterate this, gentlemen? This is the Dreamlands, where theories of micro-organic infection carry far less weight than the realities of myth. In the waking world, one may profitably avoid plaque and gingivitis. Here, dental hygiene consists of avoiding the attention of tooth worms.'

The sergeant listened to this, nodding with approval. 'Flossing helps,' he added. 'They hate that.'

'It all sounds a bit dangerous,' said Bose, quietly.

'It all sounds remarkably dangerous,' corrected Cabal. 'We don't even know if this marvellous hermit is still alive, or can help us if he is. Perhaps we should look elsewhere for data.'

Shadrach took a firm grip on the edges of his simarre and jutted out his jaw. 'Mr Cabal. We have crossed a sea to find this man. If you had any caveats with this plan, the time to say so has long since passed. We are committed, sir! We are committed!'

'Are we? Are we indeed?' Cabal could feel an old and pleasant feeling stirring in his breast. He had shown great patience with these fools to date. He had not failed them or abandoned them. Neither had he murdered even a single one of them. Yet for all these kindnesses he had received no thanks, only whining and, now, undiluted stupidity. The delightful sensation he could feel was his temper slipping the leash.

'Your argument is as specious as it is fallacious. I do not give a damn that we have crossed a sea to be here. By your logic, if one was to circumnavigate the globe before being given the option of jumping off a cliff or *not* jumping off a cliff, you would fling yourself off immediately because – oh, my goodness – you've gone all that way and it would be a shame not to do something memorably stupid at the end. Not memorable to you, of course: you'd be dead. But everyone for miles around will always remember the day the idiot from afar threw himself to his death because, well, it would have been a shame not to.'

'Mr Cabal!' Shadrach was scandalised.

Bose, meanwhile, had become very wide-eyed and was muttering, 'Gentlemen! Gentlemen!' under his breath, while Corde and the sergeant were smiling.

Shadrach was appalled that Cabal – a hireling, for heaven's sake – should be so . . . 'The impertinence, sir!'

'Are you going to challenge me to a duel, Shadrach?' Cabal drew back the edge of his jacket to show the hilt of his rapier. 'I very much hope you are.'

Corde stirred himself enough to step between them. 'That's enough, gentlemen. I think Mr Cabal is simply giving vent to some inner issues.'

Cabal's face tightened. 'I am angry, Herr Corde,' he said, in a severely calm tone. 'Not flatulent.'

Corde ignored him. 'But he makes a valid point. Rational

caution, eh? Remember that? These ruins out by the lake are not safe, not even close to safe. I think we must still go there – *pace*, Herr Cabal – but we must take every precaution and learn all that we may. For example, Sergeant, you said the wamps only attacked you on the way out. Was that because darkness had fallen?'

The sergeant nodded. 'Like I said, they don't have eyes. They don't see like we do. They can see in the dark, and they know we can't. I can't say if they hate the light, but I'm sure they love the dark.'

'There, then.' Corde held his hands wide in a supplicatory gesture. 'We have the beginnings of a plan. Nobody has to go jumping off any cliffs.' He considered momentarily asking Shadrach and Cabal to shake hands and make nice, but one look at their faces, Cabal's particularly, dissuaded him immediately.

Cabal released the edge of his jacket to cover his sword's hilt once more, and as it was apparent that this – a tacit agreement not to run Shadrach through *right this minute* – was the closest he would be offering in the way of an olive branch, it was duly accepted by all present, again tacitly.

'So,' he said, his narrowed eyes never leaving Shadrach, 'of what does the rest of this plan consist?'

As it transpired, it was not nearly so much a plan as a list of things to be careful about. They would be careful about the wamps. They would be careful to get in and out during daylight. They would be careful never to split the party. They would be careful not to tickle any dragons, antagonise any ogres, irritate any trolls. They would also – and this was Cabal's contribution to the plan – be careful to let somebody else go first.

Sergeant Holk was apparently used to the role of professional Judas goat and was easily able to lay hands upon a likely trio of bullyboys to traipse into danger in return for a decent reward. Shadrach was irked that he had to use more of his gold than he felt comfortable about to change what had first been envisaged as a relaxing stroll into a scenic set of ivy-entwined ruins to seek the counsel of a wise old man, and had now taken the character of an armed assault upon a Hellmouth.

Certainly the logistics of the matter had stretched out over three interminable days while equipment and mounts were secured. That the mounts were zebras did nobody's humour much good.

'They look ridiculous,' said Cabal, on the morning the expedition left Baharna from the Lava Gate in the eastern wall. He was standing by his zebra looking at it at least as caustically as it was looking at him. The irony that he himself was dressed entirely in black and white passed him by, his self-awareness not being of a high enough pitch to detect this resonance. The zebra, on the other hand, felt a nebulous sense of indignation that it would be ridden by another zebra, albeit an odd bipedal one with not much of a mane. This indignation would have manifested as kicking and biting among the zebra's Earthly brethren, but the zebras of the Dreamlands are a breed apart, intellectual and dignified by their own lights, so it communicated its disdain with a basilisk stare accompanied by a monstrous and lengthy micturition, during which it did not even blink.

Holk's three handpicked men – Cabal had watched him pick them out of the gutter outside an alehouse, and Holk had definitely used his hand to do it – were looking more presentable now that they'd had a chance to sober up and were wearing a uniform of sorts. Holk had found a reliable manufacturer of good cuir-bouilli armour and bought four suits in a striking shade of crimson. Corde, who had gone along on the shopping expedition, had bought himself one in grim sable, set with acid-blacked studs. He developed an inordinate attachment to it, and wore it with great frequency even while they were within the safety of the city. 'I'm just wearing it in,' he would say, but no one believed him. For his part, Cabal purchased a leather strap that he used to make a baldric for his Gladstone, allowing him to carry it slung across his body, and so leaving his hands free.

And so, on the morning of the fourth day, the expedition embarked upon its journey to the ruins by the Lake of Yath, with Holk and one of the mercenaries riding in the vanguard, the other two in the rearguard, and the four explorers in file in the middle, Corde to the front. Oriab Island was no small rock in the sea, and they knew it would take four or five days to reach the lake, even assuming easy going and no unwelcome adventures *en route*.

For his part Cabal bore it all with the same grim detachment that he had brought to the ocean journey. He was intrigued by so much in this world that he had little time for the small-talk of the others. He was interested in the way that distant places were not merely distorted by the haze of the air but – to his eye – seemed actually unfinished. There was nothing he could definitely give a name to, but there was a distinct sense that details clustered on these far vistas as they were approached, like coral accruing around a simple rock. He was surprised to find Bose, of all people, thinking along the same lines.

'Well, they *are* the Dreamlands, I suppose,' said Bose, swaying gently from side to side in time with his zebra's gait.

'And what we can't see close to has no need of . . . I have no idea what to call it . . . this stuff of dreams, until it's right there in front of you.'

'I'm not sure that is how it works,' said Cabal. He did not need to refer to his notes: he had reread them so many times by now that they were thoroughly ingrained in his always rapacious memory. 'We are not dreaming the Dreamlands. Others dreamed them before us, and the superimposition of their dreams has given it permanency. One may dream of the Dreamlands, but the Dreamlands are not a dream.'

'Yes,' Bose conceded, 'yes, that is very true. We, for example, are awake.'

We hope, thought Cabal, giving inner voice to the most recurrent of his concerns.

'Well, whatever the metaphysics of it,' said Bose, rising in his stirrups to look ahead, 'it is beautiful here. Great men must have dreamed some very wonderful dreams to have wrought such a world.'

'Perhaps,' said Cabal, for this had raised another concern: a suspicion verging on a certainty that the majority of the creation here was not of human origin. He had not spoken again of what had happened in the Dark Wood, but it rarely left him. Nothing else of the same sort had happened since the dislocation in time and space, and the destruction of the spider-ant-baby things, and the others seemed to have forgotten about it. Cabal had not, any more than a man kneeling in prayer would forget if the clouds parted, God Almighty poked his head out, and demanded, 'Yes? What is it?'

He had gained the attention of a god, and could not be sure that he had lost it, or would ever lose it. On a purely pragmatic level, if he had not called for the intervention of Nyarlothotep, they would doubtless all have died in the wood. He still wondered, however, if being prey to a spider-ant-baby thing was potentially preferable to whatever the infamously capricious god might visit upon him in return for the favour.

The small column rode on, and on, and on.

One of Holk's men turned out once to have been a restaurateur who – while under the influence of an experimental mixture of spices – had been murdered by a jealous *sous-chef*. The spices had included some unusual powders from the Orient, and as a result the restaurateur was sitting up blinking in the Enchanted Wood while, back in the waking world, the dirty deed was done. Divorced from his body and therefore a now permanent immigrant to the Dreamlands, he had briefly considered setting up a restaurant in Hlanith before realising that all he had ever really wanted to do in life was strap on a sword and do some serious swashbuckling. The swashbuckling had quickly deteriorated into roister-doistering, and thence to lying in gutters outside alehouses. Cirrhosis of the liver being unknown in the Dreamlands, this was a career path he had heartily enjoyed, right up to the moment when he had run out of money and had had to go back to full-time swashbuckling until he had made enough to be a drunk again.

This was all of very little interest to those around him, except for the detail about restaurants because he was a very decent chef. As a result, the evening meals were of surprising complexity, sensually challenging, and the uncontested highlight of every day. His *pièce de résistance* was *the-thing-I-shot-with-my-crossbow-au-vin*, which was universally praised on the second evening.

On the third evening, just as it was growing too dark to

travel further, they crested a hill and saw, glittering beneath the light of the Dreamlands' large and disquieting moon, the Lake of Yath stretching out before them. Perhaps four miles away, visible as a hulking mass of shattered rooftops and fallen columns showing pale, like bones in a giants' graveyard, stood the unnamed city of legend and dread. Certainly Sergeant Holk regarded it with stony-faced stoicism, but his gaze moved constantly, looking for the shadows of nine-legged things scuttling around the archways and byways.

'We should go back half a league,' he said finally. 'We don't want them knowing we're here. Getting most of this hill between us and them should hide us from them until dawn.'

Nobody argued. Even Cabal forwent the opportunity to make a snide comment about Holk's bravery because, having seen what the slightest wound from a wamp could do, he knew that almost any precaution could be regarded as reasonable. So they turned their zebras and cantered back down the hillside to make camp near a stream, their fire masked from the hilltop by a copse of trees. They ate quietly that night, and the guard rota was arranged more carefully than previously.

When morning came, none were dead, or alive and mortally diseased, or alive and rotting, so they regarded their precautions as effective. They rose, performed their morning rituals, ate, organised their equipment with great thoroughness, and then struck camp. Foreboding hung upon them like a cloud as they rode back up the hill and down the far side.

Cabal had gone to great pains to discover everything that could be discovered about the mysterious nameless ruined city while the expedition was being prepared in Baharna, and had raided every library and archive he could find, including several that were not open to the public. The collected intelligence thus uncovered agreed on three main points:

- The city was in ruins.
- The city's name was unknown.
- The city was a tad mysterious.

As far as could be ascertained, the city had once been a great conurbation, renowned far and wide for the strength of its commerce, the creativity of its artists, the skill of its artisans and the depths of its depravities. In its hubris, however, its collective wisdom had been insufficient to stop it angering something or somebody.

Probably a god.

Probably Nyarlothotep.

Cabal had paused when he saw this, closed his eyes for a long moment, breathed heavily, then returned to his reading.

The somebody or something had sent a monster or, if it really had been Nyarlothotep, assumed the form of one of his larger and more antagonistic avatars. Beneath a red and gibbous moon, doom had crawled from the lake and crept through the city, entering every home and every hostel, every bed and every cradle. By dawn, the city was dead and empty, with not a person or animal left in the place. A merchant caravan that had left the day before and had returned after a night of vile portents was the first to discover the horror.

It was not the first time such a fate had befallen a city in the Dreamlands – Cabal noted that the tale was very similar to the infamous fate of Sarnath – but this event seemed to predate even that. The lesson seemed to be twofold: do not anger the gods, but if you must, at least make sure your city isn't next to a lake, as that's just asking for trouble.

The lake looked, if anything, more forbidding than it had the previous evening. The sun was barely above the horizon, so was too low to cast its light directly upon the waves that jagged across the surface to lap at the banks. It left the waters themselves dark and unknowable, doing little for the approaching men's mood. The Lake of Yath was huge, only the distant hills and mountains giving any indication that it was not a sea, and its depths could only be guessed at.

'The hermit moved here only about three years ago,' said Corde, repeating a briefing he had already given before they had left Baharna and again the previous night as they ate. 'He is believed to reside in a temple on a hilltop in the most regal canton. Presumably some aspect of the temple, its construction or perhaps its significance, keeps creatures like the wamps at bay. That would be useful to discover straight away, as it would give us a secure camp overnight. Failing that, we must be out and clear of the city by dusk.' He looked at Holk, the image of exposed ribs covered only with scarred pink skin evidently large in his mind. 'That is imperative, for all our sakes.'

The city walls were still standing in long stretches, but breaches were common and large. They found a tumbled gatehouse with the remains of a tariff-taker's house outside and hitched their zebras' reins to a dead tamarind tree that grew by the ruin. Then, heavy with misgivings, they picked their way over the rubble and entered the nameless city.

Cabal had wandered around a few ruined villages and towns in his time, but this was the first city he had entered that still looked anything like a city. Nature reclaims quickly, especially when there is sufficient water to support significant plant growth. Oriab was a temperate island, with no shortage of fresh water, yet the city seemed in remarkably good condition. Scrubby grass grew in patches by the roadsides, ivy tangled the statues, bushes grew at cornices, and some buildings even had trees thrusting up through shattered walls, but it all seemed very mannered and controlled to Cabal's eye, as if it were the work of an artist portraying an abandoned city rather than the natural actions of time.

'Sergeant,' Cabal addressed Holk. He spoke quietly: the city pressed tightly upon the nerves and there was a sense that speaking loudly or even normally might somehow awaken the place. 'How long ago was this city abandoned?'

Holk did not answer for a moment as he adjusted the buckler strapped to his left forearm. 'Centuries ago, Master Cabal. Perhaps millennia.' He drew his sword – his men already had theirs in hand – and scanned the rooftops for movement.

'Impossible,' Cabal said. He turned to Shadrach, Bose and Corde. 'This place would be a forest in less than two hundred years.'

'On *Earth*, Cabal,' said Corde.

'Yes,' admitted Cabal. The way this place failed to behave scientifically never ceased to irritate him. 'On Earth.'

The city clustered up the hillside above the lake. On their approach, they had seen the remains of the docks and the simple housing that huddled near them. It seemed likely that the 'most regal canton', in Shadrach's phrase, would be at the top of the hill, and this area they therefore headed towards as quickly as they dared. They discovered a great city square and followed a broad road that led straight up the hill from there. Holk made a point of keeping the party in the middle of the road: if there had been any risk of coming under arrow or quarrel fire, he would have used cover, but as the primary concern was wamps, some dead ground between them and any potential ambush places could give them vital seconds. At least they had light: there was barely a cloud in the sky, and the sun made the pale volcanic stone of the buildings gleam.

They had been on the road for only a minute or two when Cabal saw the skull. He signalled the sergeant to form a perimeter while he examined it.

'It's a city of the dead,' muttered Corde. 'A skull is hardly a surprise.'

'You forget the story, Herr Corde,' said Cabal, not paying him much attention as he crouched by the skull and examined it cautiously. 'Whatever happened to the citizens of this place ultimately, the point is that they all vanished from the city beforehand. Besides, this skull is evidently not human.' He pushed it over with the tip of a stick and examined the jaw. 'It is similar to a bat skull, but obviously much larger. The orbits are atrophied. This creature had no eyes.'

'A wamp!' gasped Bose.

'Well, of course it's a wamp. Why do you think I'm not touching it directly? What intrigues me is how it died. The skull is broken.'

'It's how they breed,' said Holk. 'They can burst out of the skull of anything that's dead in an abandoned place like this. If the skull's big enough to house a new wamp – and a human skull works fine – they just grow in there and smash their way out when they're ripe. They can grow in adult wamp skulls, too. They're not fussy.'

'They lay eggs in skulls? I'm confused,' said Shadrach. 'How exactly do they reproduce?'

'They don't,' said Cabal. 'Spontaneous generation. It doesn't happen on Earth but, as has been made apparent to me on many occasions so far, this is not Earth. An abandoned place of foul repute and a large corpse. That's all you need for a wamp infestation. However,' he tapped the broken side of the skull with the stick, 'this skull has not been burst from the inside. It has been smashed from the outside. Nor is the damage directly over the brainpan. The fact that there is no skeleton or bones around is also significant. This wamp was killed with great violence, and the skull damaged in such a way as to prevent a new wamp forming in it.' He straightened up and looked around, throwing the potentially contaminated stick into an overgrown garden as he did so. 'We must consider the possibility that wamps are not the main threat here. There may be something or things here that efficiently hunt wamps and that are, in all likelihood, not going to want to be our friends.'

Three hundred yards further up the hill they found a more complete skeleton, albeit one that somebody had played 'She loves me, she loves me not' with. Cabal stood by one of the skeletonised legs while the others located others, around the roadsides. None was closer than three yards to its nearest neighbour. 'These limbs were torn off and thrown away when they still had flesh upon them,' said Cabal. 'See? The bones lie close to one another as they did in life.' He walked over to the torso and skull in the middle of the avenue. The skull had been crushed in the same way as the previous example. 'This creature was torn limb from limb while it was alive. So, we can conclude that whatever killed it was very powerful physically, and entirely undaunted by the diseases wamps carry.'

He looked up the hill and then back in the direction they had come. 'Interesting.'

'Interesting?' said Bose. 'Mr Cabal, I must admit that I have been in a state of trepidation verging on fear ever since the matter of these wamp creatures was first raised. Now you tell us that this city contains something that preys upon them – that preys on *monsters* – and you characterise it as "interesting"?'

'You seem pale, Herr Bose. Something you ate, perhaps?'

'There was nothing wrong with that *Hasenpfeffer*,' said their resident cook, from his position on the perimeter.

'*Hasenpfeffer*?' said Cabal. 'I'm very familiar with that dish, but it's a rabbit stew. I haven't seen any rabbits, just those furred creatures like wingless turkeys . . . Oh.' He considered for a moment. 'They were delicious.' He turned his attention back to Bose. 'My apologies, I interrupted your panicking.'

'I am not panicking!' shouted Bose.

Somewhere off to the east, there was the sound of collapsing masonry.

'No rubble's fallen since we arrived,' said Holk, tersely.

'The stuff must fall over occasionally,' said Shadrach, the paragon of reason. 'It *is* a ruined city, after all.'

'It may be a coincidence that it happened at the same moment Herr Bose gave away our position,' said Cabal, picking up his bag and starting to walk up the hill at a quick pace, 'but it may not be. It would be nothing more than a practical application of the rational caution that you are so quick to espouse if we were to start running. *Now*.' He did so, the mercenaries – professionally attuned to danger as they were – joining him in a dogtrot.

Messrs Shadrach and Bose looked at one another in astonishment before looking to Corde, only to find him already well up the road, running also.

Then more rubble fell, to the east, but now it was closer. Shadrach and Bose decided that keeping their dignity came a poor second to keeping their limbs attached to their torsos, and set off after the others as quickly as their robes would allow.

The change from a stealthy progress through the totterdown city into a headlong charge did not reduce the tension that ran through them in the slightest. Headlong charges do not offer many opportunities to look back and, on the snatched glances they did take, they saw nothing but the empty houses and tenements, eyeless yet noble in their slow death. Of the wamps, they saw no living examples, but every alleyway and courtyard seemed to contain their skeletons, all torn, all smashed. The expedition saw them and their sense of growing threat intensified with every snapped bone. There were no longer any unexplained sounds to haunt them – or, at least, none that could be heard over the sound of eight men running – but this did not settle their nerves: if there is one thing more disquieting than an unexplained sound, it is a silence after an unexplained sound.

Around them, the city became steadily grander and more impressive as they passed fallen gateways that marked off the different areas. Each gate had been more massively built and heavily ornamented than the one before as they progressed from being simply markers to show where the scum lived, to actually restricting access to keep the scum out. Cabal ran by a basalt basilisk lying on its side at the end of a line of rubble where a gatepost had fallen, the basilisk's beak open in challenge, but gagged with a growth of dandelions. On its head was a diadem of gold; one of the mercenaries paused by it, and made to lever it off with the tip of his sword, but Holk swore sharply at him, and the man ran onwards with only one regretful backward glance.

They arrived at the corner of a plaza close to the top of the hill, and as they turned it, the ones at the front came to an abrupt halt, the others piling into them with cries of mixed anger and dismay.

'The greatest temple of the most regal canton, wasn't it, Shadrach?' said Cabal. 'Does this qualify?'

The great cathedrals of Europe are massive affairs, and would frequently have been larger yet, but for the soil beneath their foundations being unable to bear their prodigious weight. Aachen, Paris, York, all have mighty houses of worship that are known throughout the world. Yet if the Kaiserdom of Aachen, the Cathedral of St Peter in York, and Notre Dame in Paris were placed side by side, there would still have been room for a horse track and a shopping precinct within the temple to an unknown god before them.

'That's . . .' started Corde, but words failed him.

'Cyclopean?' suggested Shadrach, who read a lot.

The temple was a vast circular building, as far as could be made out, with a large flight of steps, as wide as a football field is long, leading up to a colonnaded terrace upon whose rear wall was the temple's main entrance: massive twin doors of wood and brass. The colossal edifice was topped with a shallow dome that glowed with the reflected light of the Dreamlands' sun upon copper that had never and would never suffer the touch of verdigris.

Behind them, some five or six hundred yards away, and

perhaps a hundred yards from the road, whose head they had reached, stood a thin, delicate tower that must once have been the domain of an ancient sorcerer or mystic. It rose above its neighbours unbowed and unmarked by the passage of the ages, a fine stalk broadening to a complex series of petal-like walls in different stones, a great stone flower topped by a peacock palace. Sergeant Holk was covering their backs, so he was the only one facing in the right direction to see it when the tower abruptly lurched bodily to one side, stood as if in injured dignity for a long second, then fell headlong and out of sight behind the closer buildings. A second later, a muffled *whump* reached them.

'What was that?' squeaked Bose.

Cabal watched a plume of brick dust blossom out into the wide avenue behind them. 'Good news, Herr Bose. It definitely wasn't wamps.'

Without another word, they ran across the plaza for the temple, passing wamp bones all around.

Chapter 8

IN WHICH CABAL HAS A SURPRISINGLY CIVILISED CHAT WITH A MONSTER

The great size of the temple on the hill confused the eye as they closed on it; they had preconceptions as to the limits of heavy stone construction and therefore the greatest size the temple could realistically be. The Dreamlands, however, was always pleased to squash the preconceptions of the waking world, blithely ignoring building restrictions, health and safety considerations, and – most rudely – physics. The overall effect was to reproduce one of the most common and least enjoyable of dream experiences: running very hard yet barely seeming to get anywhere. The square before the temple simply could not have been that huge, the temple could not have been so vast, yet the square was, and the temple was, and the flagstones beneath their feet seemed never to end as they ran and they ran and they ran.

And then, as is also the way of dreams, they were suddenly

there, so abruptly that there was not even the sense of having covered the last hundred yards. They ran up the steps, all ninety-nine – Cabal counted – and arrived in front of the great entrance into the building.

'Oh, for crying out loud,' gasped Corde, as he tried to recover his breath. 'Have you ever seen such enormous doors?' Behind him, Shadrach and then Bose staggeringly reached the top of the steps and promptly fell down, wheezing pathetically.

'Yes,' said Cabal, as indeed he had. 'But they had the decency to have a porter's door set into them. How is anyone supposed to open these things for worship? Did they have mammoths for ushers?' He turned and looked out across the square, which, typically, now didn't seem anywhere near as enormous. The glare from the morning sun on the pale stone made his eyes water, and he instinctively felt for his glasses in his jacket pocket.

As he did so, something twisted uncomfortably in his mind. Something like *déjà vu*, except instead of having the sense that he had done all this before, he had an unaccountable sense that he had never, not even once, in all the time that they had been in the Dreamlands, checked his pockets for their contents. It didn't make sense, and almost immediately small fragments of memory, like ants, clustered around and he thought, perhaps, that he had after all. Yet the scent of an unreliable recollection, a false memory hung around it, and it was with considerable effort that he pulled himself back to the present. He found he had his blue-glass spectacles out, and was staring at them as if he had just noticed that he had eight fingers on that hand. How many fingers *did* that hand have? Eight. No, five. That was right. Five. Five phalanges; four fingers and an opposable thumb. That was what he had. He counted twice to be sure.

Shadrach had managed to regain his feet by leaning on one of the massive columns that supported the portico over the temple gates. He was looking at Cabal oddly. 'Mr Cabal? Mr Cabal, are you well, sir?'

Cabal put on the glasses quickly, but his hand shook as he did so. 'I am perfectly well, Mr Shadrach,' he said, taking care that there was no tremor in his voice. 'Simply exhausted after the run. I'm sure you can sympathise with that.' Without waiting for a reply, he turned his attention to the square. It was empty of all but wamp bones and scrub grass forcing its way between the slabs. Of their pursuer, if there *was* a pursuer, there was no sign. 'It isn't showing its face – assuming it has a face – yet,' he said to Corde. Corde ignored him: he and the mercenaries were at the crack between the great wooden doors, trying to get enough purchase to open them. Normally Cabal would have been happy to watch them scrabble away for a good long while, but as his own survival was also at stake, he decided he should make a few constructive comments.

'Don't be such *verdammt* fools,' he snapped. They turned to him with differing degrees of curiosity and resentment. 'If this is the correct temple, and I hope for all our sakes that it is, then a lone hermit lives here. I hardly think he manhandles those doors open and shut every time he wishes to dash out for some milk. There must be some other way in. I had hoped it would be at the top of the stairs by the main gates and that we could not see it as we approached because of the curvature of the frontage or the occlusion of the colonnades. A forlorn hope, it appears. The fact remains that a frontal assault on these doors is doomed to failure, and that time may be limited before whatever destroyed the wamps locates and does the same to us.'

'The man's right,' said Holk, brushing grime off his hands. 'We would need a platoon and ropes stapled to the door edge to stand any chance of getting this thing open. If there's another way in, we have to find it, and soon.' Without waiting for orders from either moneyman Shadrach or 'Captain' Corde, he turned to his men. 'Right, you two go around widdershins and take Masters Bose and Shadrach with you. The rest of us will go the other way. If anybody finds a door, send a runner immediately to tell the other party. Understood? Then jump to it!'

Going down ninety-nine steep stone steps in a hurry was less tiring than going up ninety-nine steep stone steps in a hurry, but comfortably made up for it in terms of perceived danger. Hand rails and other such nods to safety had apparently been regarded as somehow heretical, and it was better that some of the faithful should finish as broken lumps of flesh at the bottom with bones sticking out at odd angles than there be any backsliding into being blasphemously careful. After the first few steps taken at a rapid pace, it became obvious that stopping was no longer an option so all eight men found themselves having to apply their full concentration to a descent that was quickly developing an aspect of 'headlong'. All it took was for one little mincing step inadvertently to be a long, manly one, and the owner of the recalcitrant leg would shortly find himself at sixes and sevens, and possibly eights and nines, depending on how many sharp-edged corners he encountered on the way down.

They reached the square at a gallop, the more adventurous jumping the last few steps, the less adventurous losing any remaining dignity as they had to keep running while bending their legs to absorb the downward momentum, overall giving the effect of a drunken uncle at a party doing the hilarious going-down-to-the-cellar visual gag, and doing it badly.

They split off into the teams Holk had suggested and began their circumnavigations of the great round bulk of the temple. 'You realise that we shall be travelling far faster than the other party, Sergeant?' said Corde. 'Shadrach and Bose are exhausted. They'll have to keep stopping.'

'He knows,' interrupted Cabal. 'That's exactly why he did it. If he'd split Shadrach and Bose between parties, both would be impeded. This way at least one is making decent time.'

They were indeed making decent time. Cabal had realised some time ago that much in the Dreamlands depended on one's state of mind. If one expected to be exhausted, one would likely be so that much sooner than somebody with more faith in their own endurance. Similar aspects were equally affected by expectation and, it seemed, aesthetics. Cabal and the Fear Institute expedition had been in the Dreamlands weeks already, yet none of them had had any need to change their clothes. Well, there was Corde and his studded black leather, but that had been by choice, not necessity. If their situation changed to one in which the popular imagination decreed bad smells – if they were taken as galley slaves, for example – then bad smells there would be. But for doughty adventurers, there would be nothing more than the smell of fresh sweat and, when the need arose, blood. Such was Cabal's observation, his conviction and his expectation.

All of them now and then looked back at the top of the avenue by which they had reached the square. Cabal found himself half expecting the appearance of some monster rendered in painted latex upon a wire armature, lent life by stop-frame animation and scale by back projection, like a film he had seen when he was young and had time for such nonsense. The harsh light and hard shadows gave the whole vista an artificial air that chimed with the thought, and Cabal made a conscious effort to suppress it: this world seemed to take far too much notice of one's inner musings. *Or day-dreaming*, he reminded himself, which seemed to explain a great deal. As they continued to dogtrot clockwise, the top of the avenue slowly became hidden from view, and not one of them was sure that they preferred it that way.

When they finally found an entrance, it was not quite of the nature they had been expecting. Something discreet and bijou like a castle's postern gate, perhaps, or a theatre's stage door, by which, in days of yore, theological groupies might have clustered in the hope of a glimpse of some superstar preacher. Instead they discovered a great yawning cavern of destruction, a ragged hole in the temple's rear wall sufficient to provide disabled access for a wheelchair-bound diplodocus. Blocks of stone, Brobdingnagian in scale, lay tumbled about like a child's toys amid drifts of rubble. The four men had slowed to walking pace when the first pieces of debris had become visible, and now were all but walking on tiptoe. There was no chance that this was a natural collapse: the top of the hole remained firm and the blocks had not simply fallen but had been thrown some distance.

Cabal moved up first, to peer cautiously around the edge of the breach. Beyond, he could see a trail of demolished internal walls going deep into the building, until all was lost in gloom.

'It got in,' said Corde, defeat heavy in his voice. 'It got in and killed him. The whole journey out here has been pointless.'

'Not necessarily,' Cabal admonished him. 'Observe – the rubble from the walls, right from the inside to out. This damage was not caused by something monstrous going in: it was caused by something monstrous coming out.'

'Well . . .' Corde thought for a moment. 'Mightn't whatever did this have gained entrance elsewhere and just created destruction on the way out? For all we know, Shadrach's party are standing by an equally massive hole, but one in which much of the debris lies inside the line of the wall.'

'I don't think so,' said Cabal, impatiently. 'Look, man! If there is another breach, would we not be able to see light somewhere within?'

Corde opened his mouth, failed to think of anything more intelligent to refute this argument than an arch, but in this case unsupported, 'Not necessarily,' and therefore shut his mouth without saying anything at all.

'There is, of course, a chance that this mysterious colossus has returned here and is lurking deep inside, presumably with one hand over its mouth to stifle its giggles, as it waits for us to stroll in and consequently suffer blunt trauma and detached limbs.' The others looked at him uncertainly. Cabal shrugged. 'But it's unlikely. Well, this represents an entrance, I suppose. Sergeant Holk, we should alert the other group to our discovery.'

Apparently Holk was still having trouble getting past the image of a snickering colossus waiting to do him harm. 'Eh? Oh, yes. At once, Master Cabal.' He turned to the other mercenary and sent him off to continue clockwise around the building at a run until he met the rest coming the other way.

He was to make a mental note of any other entrances he passed *en route*, but the important thing was to reunite everyone as quickly as possible. With a hasty salute, the soldier ran off, his hand on his sword hilt to keep his sword angled up and away from his heels as he went.

'Right,' said Corde. 'Very well. Good plan, Sergeant.' He plainly felt keenly the way he was not being consulted, but was endeavouring not to show it. 'When the others get here, we shall decide how to proceed.'

'Yes, you do that.' There was a faint hollow quality to Cabal's voice that made Corde turn, and then gasp audibly, for Cabal had already climbed over the sill formed by the shattered stone and was advancing into the temple. 'I shall just have a little wander around while you wait.'

'But!' Corde realised he'd shouted, and lowered his tone to *sotto voce*. 'But, Cabal! What if the – the *thing* really is still in there?'

Cabal had just vanished behind the first broken internal wall but he leaned out and put his finger to his lips. 'Hush, Herr Corde,' he said. 'I need to be able to hear a snickering giant if I am to survive this.' With which he vanished into the shadowed interior, leaving only a faint tang of sarcasm upon the air.

Once he was out of sight and – longed-for and glorious – by himself, Cabal's artfully angled flippancy fell away to be replaced by a cool wariness, honed by a hundred unauthorised sorties into other people's laboratories, other people's libraries and other people's graves. He could see that the damage caused by the mysterious Goliath was in no way wanton: it had simply decided that it wished to leave, had had its own reasons for not going by the main door – it was very hard to believe that a creature capable of such destruction would have had any problems with the great gates – and had made a dash for the outside, swatting away several hundred tons' worth of pesky intervening walls in the process. Cabal could not know why the gates hadn't appealed to it, but he was inclined to think that it was simply because it had not understood the concept of doors. He was also inclined to think, and here he was very sorry that he did not know, that since it had been so very keen to leave the confines of the great temple, then it would not be in any great hurry to return. This was supposition, however, and supposition could often cause one to die at an inconvenient time and with one's work left unfinished. Therefore, he backed it with a generous portion of caution.

He paid little attention to the chambers he climbed through, beyond checking for possible threats: he found none. The light was becoming dim as he clambered through ruined offices, storerooms, subsidiary chapels and libraries, all raised in the honour of a god who seemed to care little enough now, perhaps even the god who had visited the city's doom upon it. Gods had so much power here, and so little wisdom: like a child with a howitzer, they rained death on those who displeased them, and as for those who did please them, the gods did nothing. It was a poor sort of deal, to be left alone in return for tribute, a bullying sort of worship, but one common in the Dreamlands, and implied often enough on Earth.

He was just negotiating a route through some sort of chapel of rest, which must have been used on an industrial scale in its heyday, judging by the number of empty funereal biers, when he met with mishap. He stood upon a tumbled pew, and its end seesawed down alarmingly. Too far down: the floor was broken deeply through not just the sombre black tiling but into the very fabric of the Romanesque cement that lay beneath. The floor beneath the pew tipped steeply, pivoted on a structural beam beneath, and Cabal – unable to keep his feet – fell heavily and slid into the dark depths. Without his weight upon it, the floor swung back to equilibrium. Of the gap in the floor where Cabal had vanished, there was no sign but a crack.

It was not the first time Johannes Cabal had been dumped into darkness, and the experience had lost its dubious allure on his very first outing. He was thus already in a vile mood as he crumpled on to an unseen floor, his right knee driving up hard enough on impact to strike him in the face and to draw blood from where his canine ripped the inner lip. He spat out blood, saliva and invective as he sought to reorientate himself in this new and troublesome environment.

First, he took in what he could through his available senses. Wherever he was, the floor was even and worked so at least he hadn't fallen into a cave system or a cavity formed by natural subsidence. This was good: there must therefore be a way out. He could taste dust that had been thrown up by his undignified entrance and, from his extensive experience of long-abandoned places, could tell that it was largely inorganic in nature, indicating that at least he was unlikely to be sharing the space with anything else at that exact moment, a small comfort. The air was cool and musty and, even after standing, he could wave his hand over his head without touching the ceiling, which accorded with the second and a half it had taken him to reach the floor. The light in the room from which he had fallen had been attenuated at best and none of it could make it past the obliquely spalled crack. He listened for a full two minutes before sharply stamping, and listening for the echoes.

They confirmed what he had gathered in the moment of poor light as he fell, that he was in a room with hard walls, more likely stone than brick, and that it was no more than forty feet across in any dimension.

Now it was time to cast a little light on his situation. He had two option: to use a match from the silver matchbox in his pocket – a technological innovation that the Dreamlands were apparently prepared to countenance – or to try out a device he had spotted in an artificer's shop in Baharna while trying to explain the concepts of percussion caps, powder corning and the special joy of putting a lead ball into any person who presents a nuisance.

The device consisted of a beautifully filigreed brass cylinder topped with a sphere of solid glass. Into the space beneath the sphere one placed a small capsule in which there was a beetle of a particular species, kept alive but sluggish through the agency of a small quantity of drugged food. The beetles were the Dreamlands' equivalent of glow-worms or fireflies but, unlike their mundane cousins, they did not generate their light as it was required through a chemical reaction but, rather, stored sunlight during their pupal stage and released it at will through adulthood. Cabal had, at this stage of the artificer's explanation, pointed out several scientific implausibilities in this explanation, stated a distinct lack of faith in the artificer's truthfulness, and offered to nail the artificer's fingers to the counter in full knowledge of the detrimental effect this would have on the artificer's subsequent livelihood. At this point, the artificer decided that this would be an ideal point to offer a small lagniappe of sorts, in return for good will, future business and not having his fingers nailed to the counter.

Cabal had studied the device only briefly at the time, and

had not loaded one of the capsules into the cylinder beforehand. Now he sat cross-legged and, in total darkness, carefully unscrewing the glass from the end of the cylinder. Once it was off, he dropped it into his right pocket for easy recovery later, and opened the parchment tube containing four capsules of fine wound wire. The parchment bent in his hand, and he was rewarded with the sound of the four capsules falling to the floor and rolling off in all directions. He bit back another testy comment, and started patting the floor around him carefully, with his open palm, in an attempt to find one.

'Try by the tip of your left shoe,' said a voice in the dark. It said it in Ghoulish.

Cabal started, his head held up, his ears keening. 'Who are you?' he meeped slowly.

'Oh, do not attempt my language,' said the voice. 'Your accent is terrible. Speak in German, or English, or Latin, or whatever tongue you prefer, without that awful parody of a pharyngeal stop. I will understand you perfectly, and not be offended by your butchery of my elegant and poetic tongue.'

'Ghoul speech sounds like somebody vomiting up halibut heads in syrup,' said Cabal, stung by the attack on his pronunciation. He had worked hard on that pharyngeal stop. As he spoke, he reached out cautiously with his hand and discovered that, indeed, there *was* one of the lost capsules by the tip of his left shoe.

'For somebody whose native language is German, you should be very careful about casting aspersions on the artistry of any other tongue.'

'It is the language of Goethe,' said Cabal, dropping the capsule into the open end of the cylinder. He recovered the glass sphere from his pocket and began screwing it home.

'An accident of birth, not an informed choice. Forgive me if I am underwhelmed.' There was a pause, then the voice said, 'You are forgetting that it's a left-hand thread. You will never put the thing together like that.'

Cabal had indeed forgotten that it was a left-hand thread, such had been his concentration on the voice and wherever it was coming from. 'You don't mind me using this, then?' he said, as he finally finished screwing the sphere back into place.

'Not at all. I know you cannot enjoy being in the dark, unable to see me, when my eyes can see you so very easily. Go ahead, Johannes. Cast a little light on proceedings.'

'As you wish,' said Cabal, and gave the lower end of the cylinder a vicious twist. Inside, a piston drove upwards, crushing the tiny cage and its soporific occupant. As the beetle was smashed flat and partially sieved through the mesh of the capsule, captured sunlight was released, refracted through the glass ball, and emitted all around in a yellow glow with an unhealthy green tinge. Cabal held the cold torch aloft and took stock of his surroundings.

The room was perhaps forty feet along its long axis, and thirty feet broad, built from rough brick. Around the walls were marble slabs, and Cabal realised that the room had once served as a mortuary for those of insufficient standing to take a place in the chapels above. At one end of the room there was a ramp broad enough for a coffin to be borne along, upon the shoulders of bearers. By the ramp on either side were deep alcoves at waist height, and in one of these sat a ghoul. Cabal risked a glance over his shoulder and saw that the brickwork had been broken through in the far corner. Beyond it doubtless lay a ghoul warren. Something caught his eye, and he walked over slowly to the pile of bricks as the ghoul watched him with mild interest.

Unlike house bricks in the waking world, they were square prisms so had no specific upper or lower sides. 'Some of these bricks have mortar on four sides,' said Cabal. 'They've been reused. Why is that? Why has this wall been broken down once, rebuilt – less expertly by the look of the mortar – and then been broken down again? By you, I would guess.'

'Well, let's see,' said the ghoul. It unwound its long betaloned fingers and began counting off points as if it were a professor in a lecture theatre. 'First, this room used to have food in it.'

'You mean corpses.'

'Of course I mean corpses. I'm a ghoul. What did you think I meant? Sausage rolls and fairy cakes? Yes, human corpses. Not only delicious, but good for you too. You should try one some time.'

Cabal watched the ghoul with carefully concealed worry. Ghouls were not necessarily ruthless killers all the time, just most of it. They were strong, resilient and unpleasantly flexible, armed with vicious teeth in their canine jaws and sharp claws upon their powerful fingers. Once they had been human, though, and vestiges of that humanity still showed in many of them. Most had been nothing more than vile cannibals in life, and joined the tomb legions of the ghouls as their appetites overwhelmed their physiologies, altering them in these loathsome ways. They were beasts long before they ever became ghouls, and their chaotic, insane minds had long since fragmented completely. Others, however, had come to this transfiguration voluntarily via decadence and intellectual preference, and held on to much more of their previous life. He had never heard of a ghoul being quite so jocular before, though.

'They don't taste like chicken,' mused the ghoul. 'I don't know why people think that. They should try some before spouting such rubbish. Much more like pork.' The ghoul sighed. 'But I digress. I was explaining the state of that wall. First, this room had food, corpses if you prefer, in it. So we broke open the wall, took a few bodies and replaced the bricks after we went.'

'And nobody noticed?'

'Administration is poor in the Dreamlands,' said the ghoul. 'They come down here, think, *Wasn't there a body on that slab?* then think perhaps they imagined it, and wander off to write a *haiku*. We got away with it for years, sneaking in and out as necessary.'

'Hold hard,' said Cabal. 'This city has not been populated in millennia. How could you have been here when it was occupied?'

'That? Two reasons. Ghouls are effectively immortal, barring accidents and foul play. Thing is, being a ghoul invites accidents and foul play. It all evens out. Second, the ghoul warrens, the great underworld beyond that wall, obey the confines neither of time nor space. I can enter here, and exit in Massachusetts sixty years ago, or on the Moon sixty years hence. Time and place mean a lot less to me than they do to you.'

Cabal was silent for a long moment. 'You can travel through time.' His tone was distracted, thoughtful.

The ghoul chuckled, an unpleasant sound. 'Then one day all the bodies went – living ones up above, and dead ones down here. All gone. The city was abandoned. No, that's not a good word. *Abandoned* makes it sound like they had a choice. *Depopulated*. That's better. Like *deforested*. Chopped down where they stood and taken away. Much better. That has a sense of it. Then we knew they would come. The many-legged ones, with the bat faces and no eyes, full of fever and corruption. And people think *we*'re disgusting.' The ghoul laughed once, a bark. 'Then the big thing came and killed the many-legs. Crack! Crack! Crack! Off come their legs! Then, crunch! Crush the skulls so no new little baby many-legs pop out of the dead brains. Have to admire the big thing. Thorough. Methodical. Never stopped until the many legs of the many-legs were dangling from gutters and thrown over rooftops and anywhere at all except on the bodies of the many-legs. Every skull . . . *crunch*! Good job, big thing! Of course,' it added, rubbing its chin in a very human gesture, 'if we go up top it will pull off our legs and crunch our skulls too. So we don't go up there. That hole was blocked when the many-legs came, unblocked when the many-legs died. Now we peek out – careful and crafty – but the big thing is never about. Haven't seen it,' it giggled, as if at a private joke, 'only hearsay.'

'What is this "big thing" of yours?' asked Cabal. He had never had such a lengthy conversation with a ghoul before. Normally they consisted of little more than 'Get back into your holes, you damned cannibals, before I shoot you,' and rarely developed into a discourse.

'Not of mine,' said the ghoul. 'Not of mine, oh, no. Of somebody's, but not mine. They've gone away now, but the big thing will be here for ever. Oh,' it added conversationally, 'it will kill all of you. Pull off your legs and break your skulls. Will probably pull off your arms, too. A limb's a limb to the big thing.'

'We got in easily enough,' said Cabal, not sounding quite as confident as he would have preferred.

'It didn't know you were there. It was bored, lying down in Artisans' Square, eating weeds. Very bored. Then you made lots of noise and it came looking for you.'

'We did *not* make lots of noise,' snapped Cabal. Then he thought of Bose's indignant squeal. 'Well, not very much.'

'Made enough. The big thing has little ears, but they are very keen.'

Cabal frowned suspiciously. 'I thought you said you'd never seen it?'

'Oh, I haven't.' The ghoul smiled innocently, which went about as well as could be expected. 'Not in person.'

'Why are telling me all this? Why are you talking to me at all? You could have killed me in the dark. What do you want?'

The ghoul's smile vanished in unexpected ways, as if its face was made of melting wax. When it spoke, the light, bantering tone was gone. 'I want you to succeed, Johannes Cabal. It is your destiny. If you fail, more than your puerile Fear Institute will be disappointed.'

'I don't believe in destiny,' said Cabal. 'We make our own futures.'

'So we do. But I have seen your future, Johannes Cabal, and if you do not find the Phobic Animus, you will lose more than your life or your soul.'

Cabal's eyebrows raised. 'I'm not sure I have anything more than those to lose.'

'Oh, yes, you do. Believe me, necromancer. You do.' The ghoul paused and looked up at the ceiling, as if listening. When it looked back at Cabal, it said, 'Your colleagues – I am sure you don't think of them as friends – are above us now.

The two parties are together and they have entered the temple. They are following your tracks through the dust. Soon they will find the disturbance at the place where you fell through into this room and they will attempt to rescue you.'

'Attempt?' said Cabal, slowly.

'Attempt,' confirmed the ghoul, 'because you will already have freed yourself.' It nodded up the short ramp that ran beside it. 'The door is not locked. I know you would not wish to be indebted to them for rescuing you.'

'I'm their guide,' said Cabal. 'They would be lost without me. Don't delude yourself into thinking they would rescue me out of any finer feelings.'

'Guide?' The ghoul laughed again, a sound like a choking dog. 'You think they could not hire a hundred reliable men who know these lands better than you, Johannes Cabal? Your usefulness ran out the day you got them to Hlanith.'

'That is not so,' said Cabal, although he was racking his brains for a good reason why it was not so, and having little luck in the process.

The ghoul leaped from its resting-place and bounded past him on all fours in a long, fluid lope, like a great whippet with rubber bones. It reached the hole in the brickwork and vanished through it in a blink. A moment later, it leaned its head and shoulders back out and leered at Cabal.

'Johannes Cabal. Just remember him in your greatest extreme in the next few hours. Remember him.'

'Remember who?' said Cabal, raising the light sphere high.

'Remember Captain Lochery,' said the ghoul, and vanished back into the shadowed breach.

Chapter 9

IN WHICH A HERMITAGE IS DISCOVERED AND A GREAT TERROR REVEALED

The others were on the point of standing in the wrong place and falling through into the underground chamber, when Johannes Cabal said, 'Step back from that pew, please. It is the beginning of a short if entertaining ride into the mysteries of the temple's cellars.'

They turned to see him, standing in a doorway behind them, beating dust from his clothes. 'We thought—' Corde stopped himself.

Bose, however, had no such form of manly internal censor. 'We thought you'd been got! By it! Or something! Oh, Mr Cabal, we were so worried, I can't tell you!'

'I think you just did,' said Cabal, unsure whether to be amused at their childishness or offended that they thought he couldn't look after himself. Later, he would realise that he had actually been neither of these things but, instead, pleased. 'Did you see anything else outside?'

'No,' said Holk, straight to the point as always. 'No wamps, and no sight or sound of whatever killed them. Maybe it lost interest.'

Cabal shook his head. 'No. Whatever else it is, it is very single-minded. It knows we're here now,' he looked pointedly at Bose, who blushed, 'and it won't stop looking until it finds us and kills us.'

'It is curious that it is so precise in the way it kills,' said Shadrach. 'Not only dismembering its victims, but always making a point of crushing or piercing the skull to prevent a new wamp infestation occurring. For something possessed of such Herculean power,' and here he gestured at the pathway of shattered walls through the temple, 'it shows remarkable precision in some of its acts.'

'It does,' agreed Cabal. Seen in that light, however, the dismemberment was a strange embellishment. It seemed vengeful and petty, where the skull-breaking was pragmatic and sensible. Still, conjecture was of little use when based upon such a paucity of data. 'We should move on. The sooner we can find this mysterious hermit and get clear of the city, the happier I think we shall all be.' There were a few nods to his words, largely from the mercenaries. Cabal picked up his bag from where it lay beside the treacherous pew, and led the way.

They continued further into the interior. Four more smashed walls later, they found themselves in a great open space. The light from Cabal's dead-beetle-powered device did not penetrate nearly far enough for them to see the whole place, but the mercenaries lit torches and spread out until the limits of the room, at least, were discovered, although the upper reaches of the vast dome within which they found themselves were lost in gloom. Ranked around were scores, hundreds of pews facing a great lectern that rose from the base of one wall, like the prow of a rakish ship, to stop some fifty feet above the ground.

Cabal considered it for a moment. 'Either this place has excellent acoustics,' he said, 'or the priests of old were very loud.'

'What?' called one of the mercenaries from a far wall.

'Well, that answers that question, anyway,' said Cabal to Corde. 'Practical archaeology.'

Elsewhere, there were signs that the dome had been undergoing renovations when the city had been attacked. Great wooden beams and scaffolding lay among heaps of wood chips and shavings. Shadrach was wandering among them, illuminated by a beetle light of his own that he must have bought independently of Cabal, to Cabal's petty and irrational irritation. Suddenly he paused, and looked around the floor by him, patently confused. 'Over here!'

They hurried to him rather than ran; he was plainly in no danger. When they reached him, it quickly became apparent what had bemused him so. Scattered among the wooden wreckage were several man-sized wooden dummies, like great marionettes. They were crude and bore no features but for a single eye drilled through the forehead, opening into a brain-sized cavity. Cabal peered inside, and then, using a foot long splinter that lay by his feet, probed inside the cavity. It came out with more wood shavings on it. Cabal sniffed them before letting them fall to the floor. 'Ammonia,' was all he would say. His brow furrowed, and he shushed Shadrach in an offhand fashion when he tried to speak. Finally, Cabal nodded, and muttered to himself, 'So that is what it meant.'

'What was that?' demanded Shadrach. 'What do you mean, sir?'

'I mean nothing just yet, *mein Herr*,' said Cabal. 'But I have suspicions. Here, see.' By the wood debris there were several clay pots, thick hairy string handles tied at their necks. Cabal took one up and held it out to Shadrach.

Shadrach shied back a little, uncertainly. 'And what, sir, is that?'

'It does exactly what it says on the label.'

Shadrach peered at it. Indeed, under the dark patches that ran down from the stoppered neck he could make out a label. He squinted closely. ' "Wood preservative",' he read slowly. He straightened up and looked at Cabal with undiluted bafflement. 'Is that important?'

'Important? To somebody, yes. To us, it is suggestive. Look how many pots there are. There must have been gallons, but now it's all gone.'

'I'm afraid I don't follow you,' said Shadrach, slowly.

'I'd recommend that you do. There is little time to waste.' He put the pot back on the marble floor with a hollow *klop*, and walked to the temple's main door. 'Barred from the inside. Of course it is.' He shook his head and came back, a rare smile on his face. For all that, it was a predatory sort of expression. 'There's ingenuity here. Also a terrible oversight on his part, but an understandable one. Regrettable, but understandable.'

'Cabal,' said Corde, 'none of us know what you're talking about. Speak sense, man.'

'Speak sense? I *always* speak sense. Apart from that time

with the mild concussion, yes, but apart from that, I *always* speak sense. Don't you see it? You've seen everything I have. Don't you know what that monster out there is? There's just one missing factor.' As he spoke, he was walking quickly down the aisle between two columns of pews, his light held high, looking this way and that. Suddenly he halted and bent down. When he stood up it was with a skeletal limb in his hand.

'Right arm. Belonged to a Caucasian male in his fifties.'

'How can you possibly . . .' Corde paused. 'Oh, my God.'

'Gentlemen,' said Cabal, holding the arm aloft. 'Allow me to introduce you to the object of our expedition to this place. I give you, the Hermit of the Nameless City.' He dropped the arm, the bones rattling on the marble floor in an awful silence. And then a terrible thing happened.

Johannes Cabal giggled.

He felt giddy, ebullient, strange. Something was wrong. Something was terribly wrong at the edge of his understanding, and he feared it. It waited for him, and he knew he could not avoid it. *Soon*, he thought, *I shall be dead*.

His sojourn in this strange fugue was short, but even so, he was treated to the sight of his seven comrades in adversity all wearing similar expressions of horrified bafflement, the sort of expressions they might have worn if he had vomited millipedes while toy trains shot out of either ear. 'Look at you all,' he said, scorn in every syllable. 'Gawping like simpletons.'

'You . . .' Shadrach was momentarily unable to communicate the full enormity of what they had just witnessed. 'Cabal . . . you . . . *giggled*.'

'Which is cause for standing around like moonstruck zebras?' They had all commented upon the zebras' vacuous expressions on seeing a full moon during the journey. Cabal permitted himself the indulgence of a luxuriant sneer. 'You do not know me. Do not presume to imagine that you do.'

It was a magnificent act, for behind the façade he was as astonished as any of them and, more, he was unnerved. He doubted he had giggled since his teenage years; its sudden reappearance, and at such a fraught time, smacked of hysteria. He had never been hysterical – angry, yes, incandescently so, on several occasions – but he had never so utterly lost control as to make that horrible tittering sound.

He faced them down until they looked away rather than meet his eye, his stoic aspect dispelling any fears as to his state of mind. He was very clearly a man in control of himself, and therefore they might permit him control of their destinies, at least in the short term.

Now all business, Cabal looked around, sidling up and down the aisle and occasionally pausing to look under pews.

'Mr Cabal?' said Bose hesitantly. 'What are you looking for?'

'His skull,' replied Cabal, without pausing. 'It may prove useful.'

'For what?' asked Corde, but Cabal was not in the mood to enlighten him, and from the looks the others were giving him, Corde decided that it was not the time to press the matter. They scattered and started searching in the same slightly mannered way that one might adopt while helping a stranger hunt for lost keys. After five minutes of quiet diligence, Thirsh – one of the mercenaries – held up his hand and called, 'Here, Master Cabal!'

Cabal was with him in a few moments, and between them they dragged out the semi-mummified torso and head of a long-dead man. 'Over here,' Cabal ordered Thirsh, 'in the open area.' They pulled the partial cadaver up the aisle to the clearing beneath the lectern, Cabal by putting his hand inside the empty right arm socket, Thirsh rather more fastidiously by gripping the left clavicle. Still, he was glad to let go when Cabal told him to, and stood off to one side, dusting off his hand on the side of his Romanesque centurion's skirt for quite a long time afterwards.

Cabal, meanwhile, was studying the body. 'Evidently he died in the same way as the wamps,' he said, carelessly gesturing at the empty places where most people liked there to be limbs. 'The skull is partially crushed, too. Enough to prevent a new wamp spontaneously generating within, but not quite as violently as we've seen previously. Sloppy. Very sloppy.'

'Does it matter, Mr Cabal?' said Shadrach, snippy with disappointment and frustration. 'We should be getting out of here with all possible dispatch! Come along! If we are quick, we can gain the outskirts by nightfall.'

'Yes, we can do that,' admitted Cabal, as he opened his bag and looked through the contents, 'but wouldn't you rather learn the whereabouts of the Phobic Animus?'

Shadrach gave a short, unamused laugh. 'From whom, Mr Cabal? From whom? From the dreadful monster that apparently seeks to kill everything in this city? Shall we ask it, hmm? Clarify the etiquette in that conversation for me, Mr Cabal. Do we ask it before, after, or while it is tearing our arms and legs from us?'

Cabal sighed. 'Everybody is *such* a critic. No, I do not suggest that we interrogate the monster, not least because it is not a monster in the sense that you imagine, nor because it will have little of import to tell us even if we found a way of communicating, and finally – most tellingly – because we have a far more immediate and useful source right before us.' And here he made a distracted gesture at the corpse while he continued to search through his bag.

There was a silence, during which the mercenaries frowned even as the penny dropped for the Fear Institute members. 'Ooooh,' said Bose, the slowest to cotton on. 'Of course. I keep forgetting. You're a necromancer.'

This was news to the mercenaries, who all took cautious steps back from Cabal.

Cabal hid his exasperation that, even here in this land of wonders, his profession was held in much the same opprobrium as it was in the waking world. He did not hide it well, however. 'Yes,' he said, allowing the *s* to draw out into a sibilant expression of dangerous resentment. 'A necromancer. Shaking facts out of dead heads is more traditionalist than most of my experiences, but it's always nice to do something that harks back to the old school.' He removed a small padded case from his Gladstone bag and opened it to reveal several small test-tubes, each stoppered with wax. 'One of these might do the trick,' he said conversationally, laying the case to one side. Then he took the head of the hermit firmly between his hands and, with a sharp twist and the sound of tearing dry skin, muscles and tendons, and the clacking of vertebrae scraping over one another, wrenched it off. He turned away from the hapless torso, placing the head on its stump to glare eyelessly at him. 'There,' he said, pleased. 'Much more convenient.'

'How much . . . Cabal, how much will this . . . thing be able to tell us?' Shadrach was as fascinated as he was appalled.

That Cabal was a necromancer they had known all along, of course, but they had not been anticipating him actually having a need or an opportunity to practise his skills while in their company. One may travel with a slaughterman from a knacker's yard for the knowledge he has on a related subject, but one does not necessarily expect him to fish a poleaxe out of his jacket and use it on a passing horse. This was the scale of the dismay Cabal's companions felt as he sorted through test-tubes, and prodded the dead man's head as if it were a potted plant.

'Back in the real world, next to nothing. I would expect the procedure to fail. If, against all expectation, I actually got a reaction, he would probably just discuss his last breakfast, or his favourite colour, or what a splitting headache he had. Here, however, things are generally more puissant on the thaumaturgical side. I have hopes, but we shall see. We shall see.' And, so saying, he flipped the wax seal off one of the test-tubes, using his thumbnail, and scattered the contents over the head. The fine powder, blue-grey with tiny flickers of reflected light from the minute crystals within the mixture, fell upon the desiccated scalp with all the magical effect one might ascribe to a test-tube full of powder paint, and it sat there, besmirching the dead man's brow, to no obvious purpose.

Cabal rocked back on to his haunches and regarded the head with evident disappointment. 'Oh. Perhaps I overstated my case.' He frowned, and then said, '*Ashmarakaseer*,' in a spirit of experimental optimism. It was, in vulgar parlance, a 'magic word', and had its uses in a few of the less impressive feats of necromancy. It was, however, of roughly the efficacy of 'abracadabra' when applied to anything greater, such as the matter currently at hand.

The powder burst abruptly into a brilliant shuddering blue-green light amid a thick cloud of rising fumes within which shapes writhed and contorted. Everybody else was so busy jumping backwards and swearing volubly in surprise that nobody noticed Cabal fall from his hunched crouch on to his arse and swear too, albeit in a much pithier fashion. Things had gone from very disappointing to almost unbelievably successful in the time it takes eight men to be violently surprised, and Cabal did not know whether to be delighted or horrified. Cautious exploitation fell somewhere between these extremes and he settled upon it quickly, gathering himself into a crouch over the head once more, and saying in the no-nonsense tones of one who has dealt with the dead before and isn't about to take any backchat, 'Speak to me! You, who once knew this face and this skull, as his own, you will speak to me! I command you! I draw you back from the shadows into the sight of men once more, and compel you to speak!'

'All right,' said the head.

There was more swearing and jumping back from the spectators. Cabal ignored them and demanded, 'What is your name?'

'My name . . .' The head did not move its jaw. It did not move at all, but they all heard the voice as clearly as if a living man stood before them rather than a decapitated head, the scalp aflame with an unnatural eldritch fire. 'I am Ercusides. Who are you people?' The voice altered in tone and volume slightly, as if an invisible speaker was looking around as he spoke. 'I came out here for a bit of peace and quiet! Why cannot you all just leave me be?'

'I assume you used to live in Hlanith,' said Cabal.

'And what if I did?'

'In a tower, in the north of the city? I believe you sold it to an evoker of dubious reliability.'

'A bloody fraud, you mean. Still, his money was good.' The head faltered, and when it spoke again, its tone was suspicious. 'Who are you? You know too much of my business!'

Bose said, in a quiet and somewhat tremulous voice, 'Aren't you going to tell him he's dead?' Shadrach and Corde shushed him immediately.

'I have a question or two that only a man of your great wisdom and knowledge can help me with. Then, sir, I shall be delighted to leave you to enjoy your hermitage.'

The head of Ercusides was not about to be distracted so lightly. 'How did you get past the wamps, eh?'

'We travelled into this city by day. We are aware of the risk.'

'Risk? Heh! Not for much longer. I've had enough of those nine-legged bastards, a-creeping and a-crawling around the place. You can hear them at night, you know, trying to get in. Lucky they're as thick as they're filthy. Still, when I'm done with them, they'll be sorry they ever bothered me. Do you want to know what I'm going to do, eh?'

'At a guess,' said Cabal, growing bored with the dead man's egotism, 'you have parlayed your knowledge of the curious foibles of sinew wood, the same knowledge you used to make that remarkable prosthetic leg for Captain Lochery, to create homunculi as your helpers. These were then used to bring substantially larger quantities of material in from the nearby Sinew Wood,' he turned to the others and added, in an undertone, 'which you recall grows "by the Lake of Yath", according to the redoubtable Lochery. Then,' he returned his attention to Ercusides, such as he was, 'from these long beams you created a weapon to prosecute a war of extermination against the wamps. You trained the dreff rodents to hunt and kill, to tear away the limbs of their targets – which may have started as a necessary way of immobilising the creatures but was allowed to descend into petty sadism – and then to damage the skull to prevent any more wamps coming into being.' He sniffed, drew a handkerchief from his breast pocket and blew his nose. 'That's just a guess, of course,' he concluded, as he put the handkerchief away.

The head was silent for a long moment, the only sound being the gentle growl of the supernatural flame. 'Bit of a smartarse, aren't you?' it said.

'You have no idea,' said Shadrach.

'Yes, I've done all that, I've got the dreff trained, and tonight they're going wamp hunting. I can hardly wait. By tomorrow morning the streets will be full of wamp legs, all over the place. That'll teach them, the ugly bastards.'

Bose went to say something, but Cabal quelled him with a hard stare and a raised index finger. 'All very ingenious,' said Cabal to Ercusides. 'I am sure it will go swimmingly. In the meantime, however, perhaps you could assist me with my little problem. I promise you, we have no desire to linger here, disturbing your peace.'

The head sighed heavily. 'Oh, if you must. Go on, then. What is it?'

'We seek something that goes formally by the name of the "Phobic Animus", but you may know of it by some other name. It is the spirit of fear, the epitome of terrors. It dwells somewhere in the Dreamlands. Do you know where we might find it?'

'You seek the spirit of fear?' The voice Ercusides spoke slowly, disbelief evident in its tone. '*Phobic Animus*: that is a good name.'

'Thank you,' said Bose, before being punched in the arm by Corde.

'You are fools to seek it. You will all surely die.'

'Yes, well, be that as it may,' said Cabal, trying hard not to retaliate with a comment upon Ercusides' own current state. 'The fact is that we still need to know where it is. Can you help us?' He paused, but the head said nothing. 'O great and wise philosopher,' he added flatly, an unconvincing attempt at flattery and shameless buttering-up.

Being dead, fortunately, had done nothing for Ercusides' perceptiveness, and when he spoke next, it was with unwarranted smugness. 'Oh, I can tell you where to seek it, all right. But whether you will want to, now that is another matter.'

Cabal bit his tongue, and consoled himself with a mental image of punting the recalcitrant head clean across the temple with a well-placed kick. 'Quite so, O celestial sage, but let's assume that we're going to ignore all warnings and go anyway. Where might we find it?'

'The Frozen Heart you seek,' continued Ercusides, plainly enjoying saying sooths so much that it was affecting his sentence constructions. 'Look you to the distant Island of Mormo, deep in the Cerenarian Sea. Far it is from the sail-roads of mortal men. Unseen it is by living eye. Unmarked it is in book or chart.'

'Hold on,' interrupted Cabal. 'Do you mean to say that nobody knows where it is?'

The head paused, a trifle testily. 'Far it is,' it repeated, 'from the sail-roads of mortal man. Unseen it is—'

'Annoying it is to hear you talking in such a ridiculous fashion,' retorted Cabal. 'To get straight to the point, you don't know where it is? *Nobody* knows where it is?'

'The Frozen Heart you seek,' Ercusides said, starting from the top. 'Look you to the—'

'Distant Island of Mormo. Yes, yes, I got that gem of information. But knowing the name of the place is not of much help if I cannot then look it up in an almanac. Where *is* the *verdammt* Island of Mormo? And if you say it's deep in the Cerenarian Sea, I shall not be responsible for my actions.'

'The location of the Island of Mormo is unknown and unknowable, a secret of the gods themselves, and one that they guard jealously, for how much of the adoration of their worshippers comes from fear? But . . .' Ercusides added quickly, for he had heard Cabal's grunt of hot exasperation and had suddenly experienced a psychic glimpse of a possible future that involved travelling at great speed and height across the temple to smash into the wall '. . . *But* . . . that does not mean the island is unachievable. Once, the great sorcerer Hep-Seth of Golthoth was minded to seek the island. Not for the Frozen Heart, but for the great weapons that were said to be stored there by the gods against a future in which even gods may war. With even a single such treasure, none would stand against him, and even the gods would fear him, for he could strike them down with their own weapon. It was a fine plan, but a vain one, for he did not consider everything that might befall him before he gained such a weapon.

'He bragged that he knew how to reach Mormo and spoke of a seven-sided gate that would guide the way.'

'And then?'

'And then ... nothing more is known.' Ercusides managed

to give the impression that he was shaking his head without moving an iota. 'That is *all* that is known.'

'Golthoth.' Cabal drew his notes from his bag and flicked through them. 'Oh, by all that is holy and many things that aren't . . . I feared as much. We must go back the way we came and . . .' He was silent for a few moments while he read some more, and then he shoved them back into his bag with an expression of violent exasperation. 'The Brothers Grimm can have this abominable place,' he said finally, when his temper was under some tenuous form of control, 'and I hope it chokes them.'

He replaced the test-tubes in their case, and then in the Gladstone. 'We should make our plans to escape this place,' he said quietly. 'Something colossal, wooden and remarkably dangerous this way comes.'

'My colossus?' said Ercusides. 'You are mistaken. It has not yet been animated, and even when it is, it will obviously not attack men. That would be ridiculous. I have trained the dreffs to attack only wamps.'

Cabal picked up the head and looked into the gaping eye sockets. 'Sir,' he said, 'your training techniques leave something to be desired.'

'I . . .' Ercusides faltered. 'What happened just then? The floor . . . Where *is* the floor? Why can I not move?' He sounded curious and inconvenienced rather than scared, as if a rather *outré* practical joke had been played upon him. 'Why can I not see?'

'Ah,' said Shadrach, entering his professional mode in which he was adept at dealing with the recently bereaved, and those deep in denial.

'You're dead,' said Cabal, whose professional mode

employed a very different set of skills, even if they also applied to the dead. 'Your creation pulled off your arms and legs, threw them around the place willy-nilly, then cracked your skull. Look on the bright side: it didn't damage your head anywhere near as badly as it has those of the wamps we've seen around the city. I think the dreffs may have been gentler with you because you had looked after them and trained them.'

'You speak nonsense, man!' cried the head. 'I taught them carefully! I even wore a wamp costume I'd made so . . . Oh. Ooooh . . .' Ercusides thought about it for a moment, during which the others looked looked uncomfortable and somewhat embarrassed. Finding out that one is a decapitated head is a private sort of experience. 'No. No! They wouldn't misunderstand what I meant. They couldn't . . .'

'They would, they could and they did. They were probably a little bemused that you wanted them to kill you – if they even understood that that was what they were doing – but training is training. They saw a wamp, but they also saw a man, and gained the impression that you wanted both species dismantled on sight. You're talking to me at the moment only because I am a necromancer. You can work out the ramifications of that for yourself.'

'Oh, well, this is just wonderful.' Ercusides' tone indicated that, no, it wasn't. 'I left Baharna in the first place to get some peace and quiet. Sold my tower, and came here. I knew there would be wamps, but I thought, The place was stripped of its population. Without bodies to spawn from, just how many wamps can there be, anyway? Hundreds! That's how many! Hundreds! All that fiddling about with dreffs and sinew wood and creosote and for what? So the little bastards could pop my limbs off and cave in my skull!'

Cabal had had enough. 'You want peace and quiet?' he asked, then opened his bag, dropped the head inside, and closed it again. Ercusides' complaining stopped. Cabal stood, hefting the bag to analyse its new weight, and found it acceptable. He turned to find the others looking at him with a variety of expressions, none of them admiring. 'What?' he asked.

'You've . . . put his head in your bag,' offered Shadrach, after some hesitation.

'So I have,' agreed Cabal. 'How astute of you. Now,' he turned his attention to Holk, 'Sergeant, we really should be getting away from this temple now that our business here is concluded. This idiot's wamp-killing machine . . .' here he illustrated who 'this idiot' was by holding up his bag '. . . will certainly return. Even if it doesn't know we're here yet, this is familiar ground to it. We must leave before it gets bored tearing up the city looking for us and comes home.'

Given the likelihood of Cabal's hypothesis, and the generous amounts of evidence for what they could expect if they were discovered, the general consensus was to stop being appalled at what Cabal had in his Gladstone, and to get out of the city as quickly as was safely possible.

'Gesso,' Holk called to one of his men, 'you're the quietest. Go out and scout the area around the breached wall. If it's clear, we'll head for the buildings over yonder. They're close together and should give us enough cover to hide from it as we move.'

Gesso did not seem pleased to be delegated to the rank of forward guard, but he was a disciplined soldier and, besides, Holk was right: he was light on his feet and could move like a cat when necessary. They moved as a group through the fallen internal walls until they were close by the outer breach. It was indeed getting dark out there; all the stumbling around inside the temple had eaten away at the time more quickly than anyone had realised. They hid in the deepening shadows around the hole in the wall, and Holk gestured to Gesso to scout the area outside.

Gesso made to draw his sword, hesitated, as if realising how useless it would be against the man-made monster they knew was out there, then drew it anyway. If he was going to die, he could at least die with a sword in his hand. He crept close to the lintel formed by the shattered blocks and paused there, looking left and right. He scanned the visible part of the square and the buildings at its edge – the painfully distant buildings that might be their only refuge – and then moved forward, silent and graceful. He slid across the broad stone surface of the broken block like a shadow, and all those observing were in the process of being impressed when a great claw came down from above and snatched him out of sight.

'Oh, dear God!' cried Shadrach. Outside they heard Gesso shout in surprise, then roar with rage, and then he screamed, a high-pitched cry of mortal terror and disbelieving horror. A moment later, his arm fell on to the stone. The hand still held the sword.

'Oh, dear God!' cried Shadrach again, but this time it was more like a sob. 'What shall we do? Whatever shall we do?'

Cabal slapped him hard. Perhaps harder than necessary, but he felt he deserved a little recreation. 'You can stop blubbering like a child for a beginning, Shadrach,' he snapped. 'Sergeant, my analysis is that if we stay here, we shall all suffer the same fate ...' a leg fell wetly on to the square a hundred metres away, a long trail of blood splashing down after it '... as Gesso. Agreed?'

'Aye, Master Cabal,' said Holk. 'It's a desperate business, and we won't all make it.'

'What?' said Bose. 'What? What is he talking about? What are you talking about, Sergeant?'

'He means,' said Cabal, slinging his bag on to his back with the aid of a black sash he had bought in Baharna for exactly this purpose, 'that some of us are going to die when we run for it. We must move now, while that thing is absorbed in dismembering Gesso. Get out there and scatter. Head for the buildings as quickly as you can. Well? Come on!'

He drew his sword, and rushed at the breach.

Chapter 10

IN WHICH THERE IS A BATTLE AND CABAL MAKES IT QUICK

As with many aspects of Cabal's life, charging at a great monster that has been specifically designed to kill other monsters looked, to the untrained eye, like arrant suicide. Johannes Cabal, though, was a man who lived a life of calculated risk. He knew, more or less, what he was up against, and he appreciated that, while the wamps were dangerous foes, they were not great tactical thinkers. Holk had been impressed by their ability to organise an ambush, but ambush predators are hardly unknown even in the waking world.

Ercusides, for all his many and varied failings, had created a device for efficiently wiping out the city's wamp infestation, and he had based his plan on the wamps' observed behaviours. They were cunning, but no more cunning than a fox, and foxes were regularly exterminated by fleets of horse and hound marshalled by folk with the collective wit of an umbrella stand. Wamps had three modes: hide; attack; flee. They only used the first as part of an ambush since, being towards the top of the food chain, they had no natural predators; its use as a defensive tactic escaped them. The second was the default, but so simple had they previously found killing that it lacked flexibility. Cabal had no doubt that the wamps' nemesis carried scratches and bites about its feet, shins and claws, but this was the equivalent of trying to defeat a sequoia with one's teeth, when one is not a beaver and when the sequoia is intent on tearing your legs off. Orphaned limbs scattered about the dead city gave mute witness to the futility of that. Finally, there was fleeing, but the nine legs of a wamp were there to allow easy climbing and not sustained running beyond that required to bring down escaping prey. Soon those nine legs would grow tired, unlike the long-striding doom bearing down upon them.

Therefore, Cabal had decided that fleeing was pointless, and hiding would only delay the inevitable. Instead he would apply himself to the attack, the exact nature of which he would evolve on sighting the colossus.

His forward foot coming to rest on the leading edge of the broken wall, he jumped down, landed on the ground running and jinked left, the direction he guessed the colossus to be standing, based on the angle of the claw's descent when it had taken Gesso, and the subsequent observed trajectories of his limbs. In this he was proved correct, almost running into a leg the thickness of a tree trunk, largely because it *was* a tree trunk. He ducked and dodged, whirled and looked, even as he backed away in an undignified reverse skip.

Colossus, he admitted to himself, was probably something of an overstatement. To his mind, something would have to stand at least a hundred feet tall before it could really be termed 'colossal'. He recalled that the Colossus of Rhodes was reputed to stand somewhere around the 110-feet-tall mark, commensurate with the Statue of Liberty, which their ship had sailed past in what already felt like a lifetime ago. Ercusides' effort lacked that scale, measuring certainly no more than perhaps sixty feet from the base of its great flat pallet-like feet to the top of its conical watchtower head. The design was innovative, perhaps, but inelegant in the extreme. So, no, *colossus* was not an ideal description. *Giant*, though, was certainly acceptable.

It was structured identically to a great wooden mannequin, a larger cousin of the homunculi they had discovered within the temple. The finish was crude: the bark had been sheared from the logs and treated with whatever variant of creosote Ercusides had bubbled up in his pots and cauldrons. Here and there, holes were cut into the wood, and Cabal was confident that each was the entrance to a snug little chamber containing bedding of wood shavings and a trained dreff. The head had three such holes equally spaced around its sloping sides, which must contain the cleverest specimens, for they commanded the whole by some strange binding of intellects into a single intent and impetus: a hive-mind of hamsters; a *Gestalt* of guinea pigs.

Irritatingly, it also gave the giant a full 360 degrees of vision, and when Cabal saw a beady-eyed little face peering down at him from the aft hole, he knew he could expect trouble in the immediate future. He still had a few seconds' grace, however. The giant was just tearing loose Gesso's remaining leg, the right, and seemed a slave to procedure. It would finish removing the leg, toss it away, deliver the *coup de grâce* to Gesso's head, drop him and then, finally, it would apply itself to providing the same service to Cabal.

He was just formulating a response to this state of affairs when Holk and his two remaining men burst out of the temple, swords drawn, and immediately split up, running for the edges of the square and shouting like maniacs. Cabal was impressed by their professionalism; they had been hired as, essentially, bodyguards and here they were, doing their best to distract the giant from their clients even though it would probably result in their deaths.

Tellingly, they were visible to two of the three head holes, and therefore two thirds of the fuzzy little committee that directed the giant. The other was the only one that had seen Cabal, but it was promptly outvoted in the 'Who shall we kill next?' stakes. Gesso was reduced to a torso and his skull punctured with a sharp jab of a great wooden index finger, whittled to a stake at its tip, in a hurried perfunctory way, and tossed aside, a broken toy.

The giant seemed to consider Holk and Thirsh as equally likely or, at least, one third of its mind wanted to go after Holk and another wanted to go after Thirsh. Since both options were known directly to those thirds, these were the only options they would willingly consider, and the remaining third was left lamenting a lost opportunity to kill the four-legged wamp that lurked just behind it. The outvoted dreff withdrew its head and disappeared back into its snug little chamber, presumably to play music loudly and write bad poetry about how nobody appreciated it.

Cabal saw the situation changing and immediately rubbed the current list of plans off his mental blackboard in preparation for some revisions. As he did so, he slipped the baldric over his head and left his bag at the base of the wall, his jacket joining it a second later. The best defence was looking to be an offence, and he did not wish to be encumbered when the moment came. That moment was delayed for a few more seconds as the two thirds of the giant's brain psychically bickered, the shoulders of the great homunculus shuddering from facing Holk, then Thirsh and back again, as the dreff repeatedly failed to arrive at a consensus. Cabal had already arrived at his own decision, proving that two heads are not always better than one. With no apparent trepidation, he stepped on to the heel of the giant's flat right foot, wrapped his arms around the shin, and waited for the inevitable. At last, one of the command dreff capitulated, and the foot lifted, swung forward in a great arc at unexpected speed, and slammed down again, several yards closer to the fleeing figure of Sergeant Holk than it had been a few seconds before.

Cabal saw the giant's intent and committed himself to preventing it if at all possible. A year or two before, he would not have cared, but then he had been a soulless creature. Now he found himself very occasionally making decisions that were not entirely logical. It was easy enough to rationalise attempting to save Holk: he was a useful soldier who might prove useful again subsequently. Beneath that, however, there was the hint of a shadow of a faint possibility that Holk had impressed him with his professionalism and competence, and that Cabal did not care to see such a man die while there was any chance of saving him.

Then the leg was rising again, and all of Cabal's concentration was required just to hang on to the dizzying rise, swing and fall. He had the presence of mind to use the fall as an opportunity to shin his way a little further up the leg as it descended faster than he would drop. In that moment of freefall, he was able to shift himself almost a yard up the shin. Then the foot slammed down and, once again, he had to hang on hard to avoid losing this gain. He looked back, and saw Shadrach, Bose and – with a notable lack of swashbuckling bravado – Corde sneaking out of the temple and quickly around its edge while the giant was fully engaged in heading away from them. Cabal permitted himself a curled lip before looking up. He was glad he was climbing up a giant and not a colossus. Better yet, a giant with insensate legs, or he would have been scraped off by now and would probably be adjusting to life as a sticky patch under one of the giant's feet. The knee was a tad over four yards from the base of the foot, by his reckoning; easily attainable in most situations, but not when he was swinging up and down as if he were on a demented carnival ride. Cabal, who had briefly run a demented carnival, knew this to be a reasonable simile. By his reckoning, he could reach the knee in two more strides providing he exerted himself and did not fall off. Unhappily, Holk was no more than two strides away.

Another sweep of the leg, and Cabal was so close to the knee that he bared his teeth with frustration. There was his goal. Bored into the leading face of the laboriously smoothed barrel hinge there was another dreff hutch hole. He could almost reach it. Just one more . . .

The leg lifted again, but instead of performing a full walk swing, only came as far as its neighbour. The giant was going into a stand, and even as it did so, the torso was rotating on the hips, the right arm was swinging out, and Cabal realised he was too late. 'Holk!' he shouted. 'Dodge, man! Dodge it!'

Holk was a calm, focused, exemplary warrior right to the

end. Of their charges, he had long since identified Cabal as the only one to trust in crisis, and on hearing Cabal's cry he did not look back or falter, but immediately dodged. If he had dived to the left, he might have got away with it, but he dived to the right and straight into the palm of the wooden hand that was swooping down to capture him. He realised his mistake at once, and tried to roll out again, but the fingers curled quickly and he was held firmly.

The giant took no pause for gloating, for what it did it did through training, not inclination. It derived no pleasure, except that of fulfilling a function, as the left hand swung up in a practised arc and grasped the first limb it reached, Holk's right leg. With a sharp tug, like a farmer's wife plucking a dead chicken, it tore the leg off, and threw it sharply over its shoulder to whirl away into the darkening sky. Holk screamed, a hoarse roar that faded into sobs when he wanted to scream more but could not draw breath. The great left hand, dripping with his blood and Gesso's before his, swept forward again.

For all their practice at hunting and killing, the dreff were still essentially shy woodland creatures, albeit of an unusual wood in a strange land. Thirsh's furious battle cry startled the whole ambulatory warren – nothing they had yet encountered had prepared them for such a thing – and the giant jumped as if another giant had stealthily approached before exploding a paper bag the size of a pup-tent behind it. Cabal hung on for life itself as the giant leaped some ten feet into the air, but loosened his grip as it fell, sliding up its shin and grabbing the splayed upper front of the lower leg attached to the barrel hinge. The impact slapped his face and body hard against the wood, and he felt something give in his shoulder that ideally should not, but he was alive, and he was in position. He snorted blood out of his nose, and felt hatred blossom deliciously in his heart for small furry woodland creatures. Retribution was at hand.

Thirsh rushed at the giant, his sword held high. Cabal could see that he must have almost reached safety when the sound of Holk's agony had reached him. He had exchanged survival for peril purely out of loyalty, and in doing so had bought Cabal an extra few seconds. Thirsh would probably be dead at the end of those seconds, but that – Cabal concluded – was none of his concern.

Thirsh made the most of those seconds. He arrived at the giant to find it still in a state of nervous paralysis analogous to a skittish terrier being rushed by an unexpectedly aggressive rat, and capitalised on this by hacking fiercely at the giant's left leg while swearing furiously, like a lumberjack with coprolalia. A real giant of flesh and blood would have been mightily discomforted by such attentions, but this giant, being more like a collection of diligently murderous telegraph poles than anything else, only regarded them with mute incomprehension until the initial surprise dissipated and it noticed that Thirsh had more limbs than was permitted locally. Ercusides had considered the possibility of too many targets to deal with concurrently, and had provided the dreffs with a simple but useful tactic to give themselves a little leg-plucking time when challenged. With a fast sideswipe, the giant's left arm swept down out of a darkening sky and Thirsh was suddenly travelling backwards much faster than he had charged, and doing it a yard off the ground to boot. Its immediate situation thus simplified, the giant was returning its attention to the fitfully struggling Holk when part of its group consciousness reported that something was peering into its chamber and asked what the standard operating procedure was for such an occurrence. The three head dreffs were considering how to respond to this, when the reporting dreff added a slightly panicky addendum to the effect that the face had gone and now a snake or possibly a limb, yes, definitely a limb, one of the ones without the foot on the end, was in through the entrance hole and was tipped by something shiny and *PAIN! PAIN! PAIN!* At which point the report stopped, and the dreff Brains Trust was left fairly sure that this was a good thing as obviously the problem had gone away, until they noticed that the group consciousness was definitely a member short – and why were they tilting dramatically to one side?

Cabal withdrew his hand from the dreff hole on the front of the right knee and examined the dead animal impaled on his switchblade. Not a zoologist by training or disposition, his examination was perfunctory and finished with him tossing the corpse away with the same dismissive flick that the giant had so often used to dispose of wamp legs and man limbs. He snapped the blade back into the knife's handle and dropped it into his trouser pocket, before hastily shinning down the leg, dropping the last metre and running clear, keeping an eye on the giant as he waited for the inevitable. Nor did he have to wait long: there are only so many contingencies rodents can be trained for, and the loss of control over one leg was not on that short list. The sinew wood hung as a dead weight, stylishly carved with three points of articulation, from the giant's right hip, and all the dreff panic in the Dreamlands would not keep the construct upright any longer. With some unhelpful waving of arms, the giant fell sideways very heavily, the right side smashing to splinters on impact, the head falling off and bouncing across the square to a muffled cacophony of dismayed squeaking.

Cabal had intended to make a circuit of every dreff hole in the fallen giant to introduce them all to his switchblade, but the destruction had been greater than anticipated and, apart from some spastic flexing in the wrecked timbers, it seemed unlikely that it would ever again represent a threat. Thus, when one of the surviving dreff emerged stunned and disorientated from the head, he made no move towards it, but simply watched it wander in a circle, sniffing the air and trying to understand what had just happened to it.

Shadrach's foot stamping down hard probably came as something of a surprise to it. Cabal watched, unconcerned at the animal's death, but unimpressed with the motivation for it. Shadrach stamped on the animal again, his expression one of pure petulance. 'Horrible creatures!' he spat. 'Disgusting little rats!'

'They bear no resemblance to rats whatsoever,' said Cabal, tetchy rather than angry. Shadrach's pomposity and pettiness seemed to define him as a person, and neither endeared him to Cabal. If he had hidden qualities, they had been very well hidden indeed. Cabal turned his back on him, and went to Holk.

He reached the still clenched hand around the sergeant just as Osic, the mercenary with culinary leanings, reached them at a run. 'I thought the others would find cover before me,' he panted. 'What happened?' He saw Holk's terrible injury and his shoulders sagged with dismay. 'Oh . . . Oh, by Nodens – not the sergeant.'

'Thirsh is over there somewhere,' Cabal gestured off into the darkness. 'He may still be alive.' Osic nodded, and ran to investigate.

Cabal knelt by Holk. The sergeant was terribly pale and deeply unconscious. Cabal opened the giant's hand with little difficulty: robbed of its motivating force the sinew wood was just wood, and the fingers swung back easily on their knuckles and joints. He took a deep breath, and weighed up the options. Movement made him look sharply to his side. Shadrach, Bose and Corde were hesitantly shuffling forward, none of them offering any help, appearing to Cabal's eye to be little more than the oafish onlookers drawn to any disaster. Cabal suddenly realised how much he hated this 'Fear Institute' and its selfless members. 'You,' he snapped, pointing at Shadrach. 'Get my bag. It's by the wall.' Shadrach hesitated, unused to being spoken to in such a way, but Bose made a move to comply. 'Not you!' Cabal barked. Bose stopped, looking quite similar to another stunned dreff that limped by at that moment. Cabal pointed very deliberately at Shadrach. '*You.* Get me my bag.'

As he waited, he checked Holk's pulse. It was weak and thready, and Cabal expected the worst. The blood loss was heavy, and although he made impromptu knots in the severed major blood vessels, the segeant's chance of surviving the shock seemed infinitesimal. Shadrach arrived with the Gladstone bag and dropped it by Cabal with ill grace. Cabal ignored him, taking out his surgical instruments and the very few chemicals he carried that might conceivably be of use. It was a loathsome thought, and he banished it as soon as it started to coalesce, but just this once, he wished he were a doctor. That he was not could not be helped: he could only try to apply his skills in raising the dead to preserving the living. He had no great expectations. 'I will do what I can,' he said, in an undertone to Holk, and began.

*

Holk did not die that night, much to Cabal's apparent satisfaction and inner consternation. Thirsh, too, was alive, although he had to discard his cuir-bouilli breastplate, which had crumpled under the fierce impact of the gigantic backhanded blow. Better that than his chest, which, while bruised and painful, was at least still where it was supposed to be, as distinct from snugly fitting against his spine, his lungs crushed and heart burst by the new arrangement.

Even though the city was now safe, at least until some new horror moved in, the zebras refused to pass through the line of the outer walls. Osic and Thirsh constructed a litter from bedrolls and lengths of wood culled from the fallen giant, a curiously pathetic object in the clear light of day, and placed Holk upon it to drag him from the city to where the zebras waited. What was left of Gesso that they could find, they gathered up and hauled out of the city, too, to be buried in the gently rolling hills below the sinew trees. Thirsh had at first suggested burying him in a small overgrown garden he had noticed on their approach, where beautiful flowers grew, but Cabal had remembered the ghoul in the temple cellar and intimated to the others that anyone who was buried within the city would not rest there long.

He also took with him a block of sinew wood and a captured dreff, but would not explain why. He strapped the block to his saddle, and kept the dreff in an extemporised cage fashioned from Gesso's helmet and a length of quarter-inch chain that had once formed part of the dead man's sword belt, criss-crossed across the helmet through holes he had punctured for the purpose. The dreff sat behind the chain bars and regarded Cabal with curiosity, as did the others, but still he would not discuss his intent.

The journey to the city had not been especially rambunctious or as thigh-slapping as an adventure of a different hue might have been – the city's reputation had done a lot to undermine that sort of ebullience. The journey back, however, had been envisaged as a far more joyful event; they would not, after all, be dead, and that's always nice. So pre-eminent had the possibility of a total massacre with no survivors been in their minds, however, that none had ever considered a result midway between annihilation and complete success. One man dead and another dying had never been seen as possibilities.

On the first evening of the return trek, it became apparent that the hand that had torn Holk's leg away had carried some contamination from the blood of the wamps it had slaughtered previously. Holk's skin became drawn and wrinkled like wet paper, and beneath the yellowing surface, small bumps moved freely like protozoa upon a microscope's slide. It seemed that Holk had survived one wamp-induced parasitic infestation in his life only to succumb to another. Thirsh and Osic spoke together in hushed tones, then came to Cabal as he watched Holk's symptoms progress. 'Is there anything you can do for the sergeant?' asked Thirsh.

'No,' said Cabal.

Thirsh and Osic exchanged glances, and Thirsh said, 'No, Master Cabal. We know he cannot be saved. We mean to ask, is there anything you can *do* . . .'

'His suffering,' said Osic. 'The sergeant does not deserve to suffer.'

'What we mean to say is, is there anything *you* can *do*?'

For a moment Cabal thought they were asking him to

resurrect Holk after his inevitable death, and his raised eyebrow communicated this.

'No!' said Thirsh. 'No, that would be wrong. Please, Master, that is not what we are trying to say.'

But Cabal had already moved past that misapprehension, and now understood their intent. 'You don't want him to suffer. Yes, I understand.' He knew they were soldiers, and had likely killed in cold blood as well as in battle before. This, however, was different. 'Start gathering wood. We shall have to cremate him immediately afterwards to prevent the contamination spreading or a new wamp forming.'

They left quickly, taking the members of the Fear Institute with them, the latter's confused objections being quickly silenced with barely cloaked threats. Cabal watched them go, then went to sit by Holk. He was deteriorating rapidly, his skin starting to become baggy and threatening to slough in places, his breathing thick and ragged as his lungs slowly flooded. The worst of it was that he could not slip into sleep, but remained conscious and lucid as his body turned into a swamp around him. His eyes, filmed and yellowish, looked up at Cabal as he sat and took in the extent and variety of symptoms. With difficulty, Holk gathered enough breath to speak.

'I did not want to die this way,' he said, in a hoarse whisper that bubbled up from his chest.

Cabal shook his head. 'No.'

There was silence for some minutes but for the crackling of the campfire. Then Holk said, 'Make it quick, Master Cabal.'

When the others arrived back, carrying wood, Cabal was already sewing Holk into his bedroll. 'Better it were done quickly,' he said, as they stood over him. His eyes were not cold, but they were empty, and when he looked up, at least one of them wondered if they had left all the monsters behind them.

'But,' said Thirsh, both horrified and relieved, 'you said . . . a wamp . . . you said . . .'

'I took a leaf from Ercusides' book,' said Cabal, calmly. Covered by the sheet, none could see the thin stake Cabal had fashioned from a fallen branch, then driven through Holk's eye and into his brain once he had breathed his last breath. There would be no wamp cracking its way out of Holk's skull.

They made a pyre and placed Holk upon it. As he burned and the wamp filth in his veins boiled and died, Cabal threw the block of sinew wood he had been carrying on his saddle pack into the flames, and they watched it twist and flex as the fire took it too. It would have been about large enough to carve a wooden leg from, but that happenstance was now gone for ever. When the fire finally burned low, Cabal gathered up Gesso's helmet, unfastened the chain lattice running across its mouth, and let the dreff free. They watched it run up the hillside towards the treeline. Two thirds of the way there, a white eagle with lines of black and gold upon its wings stooped down from the cloudy sky and took the dreff cleanly, flying away with the unmoving animal in its claws. If it was an omen, it was an uncertain one.

Their arrival in Baharna was unheralded. They rode in during the morning of a market day, overtaken by farmers, traders and lava gatherers, and the little troupe of dusty travellers sitting silently on their zebra mounts drew little attention, or even that two unridden zebras followed the column, led by their tied-off reins.

Their passage through the eastern gate was untroubled: the guard who dealt with them had been on duty the day they left and already knew where they had been. He eyed the trailing zebras, but said nothing.

Once within the city, Shadrach concluded their dealings with Osic and Thirsh. Holk had no family, but Gesso had a wife and a young daughter. Shadrach refused to be taken to see them, but gave the zebras to Thirsh, with a fistful of gold, and told him to see Gesso's family all right. As the mercenaries walked away, Corde moved alongside Shadrach and said, 'How do we know they were telling the truth? Gesso never spoke of a family – we only heard of them after he was dead. How do we know they haven't just taken you for a fool?'

Shadrach just looked at Corde with something like loathing in his face. 'We *don't* know,' he said in disgust, and turned away, abandoning a dialogue before it had even started.

Cabal had noticed that Shadrach had seemed to be ageing rapidly ever since the battle in the nameless city on the banks of the Lake of Yath. His hair was greying at the temples, the lines of his face deepening, and now he walked with a stoop. It seemed that the Dreamlands were not the only thing that could be physically influenced by the psyches of dreamers.

In contrast, Corde was developing a distinctly lean and hungry look. Whereas earlier he had only been play-acting the role of a latter-day Caesar, now his profile was becoming more patrician, his eyes hooded and predatory, and his armour seemed far less of an affectation than it once had. There was something thoroughly rapacious about the way he watched Osic and Thirsh carry on down the Great Market thoroughfare, the string of zebras behind them. It was the expression of a man denied his spoils and already scheming to regain them. Cabal did not care for it at all, and put part of his intellect to the task of devising ways to dispose elegantly of Corde should he prove troublesome.

Having placed an abeyant death sentence on Corde's head, he turned his attention to Bose, who, for his part, looked vapid and without a shred of malice or machinatory instinct about him, a soft toy in the great department store of life. In short, just the same as he always did. He seemed to bimble around the Dreamlands like somebody at a museum exhibit of how frightful foreigners are. He would look, and gasp, and be appalled, then go home, have a boiled egg for tea and be utterly untouched by what he had seen in any lasting sense.

Inevitably, Cabal wondered if he, too, was changing in appearance. If the mechanism was one of altered perceptions, then it was unlikely; he was as sure as he could reasonably be that he was of the same mind and worldview as he had been the day that the Fear Institute had first come to call. It's difficult to be objective about the subjective, but Cabal maintained assorted mental checks and balances to confirm that he was reasonably sure his mentality remained recognisable, and that he had not gone inconveniently mad. As Descartes would have been quick to tell him, his perceptions could not necessarily be trusted, but – then again – if he was so mad that he didn't realise he was utterly mad, it was academic anyway. He would have failed in his life, and that was that. He could just get on with learning to enjoy institutional food and the sure knowledge that electricity makes your eyes go black.

Still, things were progressing, at least. They had a faint idea where to go next, to speak with someone else who was probably dead, who might not be able to help them whether he breathed or not, and who might be able to direct them to somewhere that might or might not hold the Phobic Animus, but which was ludicrously dangerous in either case. Cabal had a sense that the whole expedition had long since taken on the character of certain doom, but was dooming them all so very, *very* slowly that it was difficult to get upset about it. It was like travelling by glacier to be hanged.

True, they had also lost two men, but neither had been him, so that was of limited concern.

Surviving fragments of Cyril W. Clome's manuscript for *The Young Person's Guide to Cthulhu and His Friends: No. 3 Azathoth, the Demon Sultan*

Azathoth is as huge as anything (except Yog-Sothoth, who is as huge as everything), but do you know, O best beloved, he's as mindless as . . . Well, there's the thing. *Nothing* is as mindless as Azathoth (who is sometimes called the 'Demon Sultan', although never to his face, but then he doesn't have a face). Think of the most stupid thing you can. A flatworm? No, that's cleverer than Azathoth. A rock? No, that's still brighter than he. A Member of Parliament? Shocking as it may seem, O best beloved, far more obtuse even than that. Azathoth is so cosmically stupid that he saps the intelligence from those who see him, big old chaos beyond angled space that he is. Why, if you were to take the biggest fool in the world to see him, the fool's wits would still steam out of his ears. And if you took the thousand cleverest people in the world, their minds would spill into the void, like water from overturned goblets, but all their cleverness would not even dampen the burning void of Azathoth's mindlessness. Still, it's fun to try.

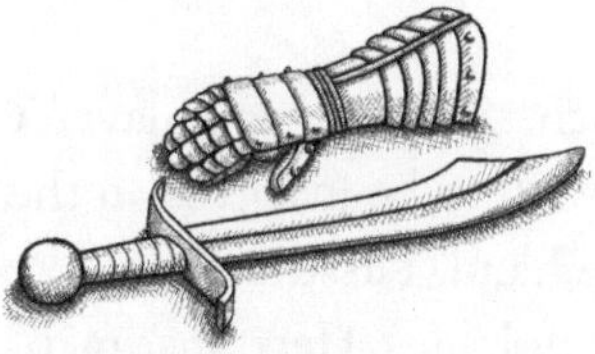

Chapter 11

IN WHICH IT TRANSPIRES THAT DYLATH-LEEN IS NOT VERY NICE

Captain Lochery was at sea, it transpired, and they therefore had to make alternative arrangements to go westwards from Baharna. This was how they came to be sharing a table with two merchants swathed in heavy black robes that left only their faces exposed, an unfortunate oversight in Cabal's opinion. The merchants smiled and chuckled and smirked and giggled and rubbed their heavily bejewelled gloved hands and tittered and were so transparently evil that he spent much of the time watching his colleagues for the moment when the penny must surely drop. After almost an hour of oleaginous dickering, Shadrach and the others were all set to buy passage aboard the merchants' black galley. Wearily Cabal realised that he would have to save the day again. Luckily, he could do it by being monumentally rude.

'So, gentlemen,' he said to the merchants, 'you undertake

to transport we four to Dylath-Leen in safety and comfort. That is the deal, yes?'

'Yes, O most perspicacious one,' said one of the merchants – it barely mattered which – smiling and nodding and smiling some more.

'Really, Mr Cabal,' said Shadrach sharply, 'you haven't said a word in an age, and now you wish to be involved in the negotiation. I have the matter well in hand, I assure you.'

'Oh,' said Cabal, chastened. 'My apologies, Herr Shadrach. Forgive my interruption. Please, carry on . . .' he leaned back in his chair and then added, quietly but clearly '. . . selling us into slavery.'

'What?' said Corde. He looked at Cabal in surprise, then swung his gaze to the merchants, his expression hardening. He did not much care for Cabal's company, but he knew his instincts to be good.

'These creatures before you, and I say "creatures" advisedly, mean to capture us all and use us as slaves. At the conclusion of your discussion they will call for wine to celebrate the agreement. The wine will, of course, contain enough soporifics to stun a shoggoth. The intention is that, when we wake, we shall find ourselves aboard the fetid black galley, which – incidentally – is safe and comfortable only for these . . . people. Finally, we shall be dumped upon the Moon. Yes!' (He said it quickly to overrule Shadrach's dismissive 'Oh!') 'The Moon is a viable environment in the Dreamlands, and it is inhabited by these . . . people's employers, who are white and toad-like and hideous. They get through slaves quite rapidly, by a dual process of attrition and peckishness, hence a steady demand for replacements. It says little for the acuity of the Dreamlands' citizens that the merchants of the black galleys have been plying this trade for millennia, using precisely the feeble technique we see this evening, and people still fall for it.'

'Is all lies,' said one merchant, cheerfully.

'We has deck quoits,' said the other, happily.

'No doubt you do,' said Cabal, climbing to his feet, 'and that is another excellent reason not to travel with you. Good night, gentlemen,' he said to Shadrach, Bose and Corde. 'I shall see you in the morning, when we shall look for a real captain who has a real chance of getting us to Dylath-Leen. If I do not see you, I shall assume you have decided to ignore my advice, have accepted the offer of these . . .' he couldn't bring himself to flatter them with *people*, given he knew full well that, beneath their robes, they were not even faintly human '. . . these *things*, and that you are bound for an interesting, if short and miserable, lunar experience.' With that, he left.

On one side of the table Shadrach, Bose and Corde turned to regard the two merchants with manifest suspicion.

'We has deck quoits,' repeated the second merchant, blissfully, a sweetener that had always sealed the deal in the past.

'We'll try the docks tomorrow,' said Corde to Shadrach, and left the table. Bose followed quickly, and a moment later, with some reluctance, Shadrach.

The two merchants sat smiling but nonplussed, looking around the room as if for an explanation as to why their infallible ruse had failed. After a few moments, two adventurers walked up to them, fine, swashbuckling types with chiselled jaws and declamatory voices.

'Ho there, sirrah!' cried one, putting a knee-booted foot upon one of the recently vacated stools and resting his forearm on the raised knee. 'Rumour has it that if a couple of bullyboys like meself and me companion here –'

'Ho-ho!' boomed his barrel-chested companion, fists on hips.

'– should seek passage to Dylath-Leen at the turn of the next tide, then you're the swarthy coves we should be talking to!' He grinned, and his teeth gleamed as brightly as the golden ring in his ear.

The merchants were only swarthy by dint of a layer of preservative upon the stolen faces they wore, faces that had once graced the skulls of two previous passengers. The chemical layer contracted over time, giving the faces a manic rictus that people simply interpreted as the open smile of an honest visage.

'We has deck quoits,' said the second merchant, gleefully, the only phrase in human speech it knew.

'Done then!' roared the first adventurer, confident that good voice projection and a waxed chest would see him through every predicament. He shook the hand of each merchant in turn, failing to notice that their arms each had two elbow joints. 'Done, and double done! We sail with the morrow's tide!'

'Ho-ho!' boomed his barrel-chested companion, all unaware that in a week he would be giant Moon toad food.

Next morning discovered Cabal and the others – they in a variety of moods from indifferent to disgruntled, he supremely unconcerned – negotiating passage aboard a weathered but serviceable caravel to Dylath-Leen. There was a clear advantage in travelling aboard the lean and rakish ship in that she would make significantly better time than a fat cog hybrid like

Lochery's *Edge of Dusk*, a coastal vessel pressed into sea-crossing journeys with a few alterations to hull and sheets that ranged from canny to optimistic. The captain of the *Audaine*, Wush Oleander, was short and fiery, and came with an unusual prosthetic, apparently an entry requirement for the job. In his case, it was a scrimshaw left hand, beautifully carved to show a tiny vignette of a screaming Captain Oleander dangling by the stump of his wrist from the jaws of a great sea serpent. Bose was particularly taken with it, and plied him with questions about the event, and whether Oleander was filled with an obsessive desire to pursue the sea serpent to the four corners of the Dreamlands, seeking vengeance, but Oleander just looked at him askance, and said, no, these things happened and you just had to accept them. Bose nodded sagely, digesting this shimmering truth, then asked about meals.

After passage to Dylath-Leen had been agreed, and their few belongings secured, Cabal and Corde stood by the rail as the ship made ready to depart on the running tide. They had little to say to one another, and instead watched the docks and the other ships departing the Oriab Island. One was a large black galley that slid by, its ranks of oars working strongly, silently, and with inhuman synchronisation. On deck, two merchants, swathed in black, played quoits. As a breeze blew toward the *Audaine*, it seemed to carry a scrap of sound with it, a voice raised in righteous indignation, apparently somewhere below.

Corde frowned as he listened intently, then said to Cabal, 'Did somebody just shout, "Release us at once, you varlets!"?'

Cabal watched the black galley glide by and out past the harbour mole, a great breakwater of natural and worked stone. 'No,' he said, and went below.

*

The journey back across the sea was largely uneventful. They happened upon the sunken city again and, as before, the crew became anxious and hastened to clear it as quickly as they could. This time, however, they crossed it at dusk, and during the night the ship was paced by something that never came closer than a hundred yards off the starboard beam, churning the sea into a phosphorescent glow as it went. Captain Oleander stood by the wheelsman for five long hours, quietly warning him to hold his heading and to change course neither closer nor further away from their submarine shadow. Eventually, whatever it was dived deep, leaving the surface to the waves and the white horses, and the *Audaine* as she sped away from those unhallowed waters. Oleander stayed watching until the sky started to lighten in the east, and only then did he go to his bunk.

Cabal had little interest in such things: he was entirely of Captain Lochery's liver here. If a sea monster attacked the ship, there would be some screaming, men falling off rigging and the other usual accoutrements of such an attack, and then they would all die and that would be that. As he would have no say in the outcome, he failed to see any reason why he should spend time fussing about it. Besides, he had a much more immediate and more intriguing happenstance upon which to apply his intellect.

He had been waiting for Ercusides to die again, but Ercusides hadn't, and Cabal found this perplexing in the extreme. The agent he had used to bring some sort of life back to the slightly crumpled skull had been a long shot, and he had been pleasantly surprised when it had not only worked but worked magnificently. From past experience, the best he had been hoping for was a few sepulchral sentences from Beyond the Veil, yet instead Ercusides had been loquacious to the point of actually being rather exasperating. His personality seemed to be much as it had been in life, which was unfortunate but there it was. Cabal had not even had to mutter the mandatory incantation to complete the ritual, indicating that perhaps in the Dreamlands 'mandatory' was not so terrifically mandatory.

Every day or so, he would open his Gladstone bag and be unsurprised, if increasingly perturbed, that cold ghost fire was still rolling off the skull and that the spirit of Ercusides was still there, still aggravatingly chatty.

'Is that you, Cabal?' the skull demanded, as Cabal took it out of his bag and placed it on the small table in the cramped cabin the four men shared. The others were up on deck at the moment, taking the air, and – by the bye – watching out for more sea monsters, although they would never admit that.

'How did you know I had opened the bag?' asked Cabal. 'I was very quiet.'

'I could feel the light on me,' said Ercusides. 'Do you think I might be getting my sight back?'

Cabal looked at the mummified eyelids over the empty sockets. 'No,' he said. He leaned back in his chair and regarded the flaming skull thoughtfully. 'Whatever shall I do with you, Ercusides? Once upon a time I would have dropped you over the side and been done with you. That would have been the convenient thing to do, for me at least. These days I am minded that you are only talking now because of me, and that I am, in some tiresomely moral way, responsible for you. So,' he leaned forward and rested his chin on his hands on the tabletop, regarding the skull, nose to gap-where-the-nose-used-to-be, 'what am I to do with you?'

Ercusides was silent for a time, and then said, soberly and without resentment, as one learned man speaking to another, 'Shall I ever know rest again?'

'I do not know. You should have returned already, but the Dreamlands seemingly amplify my powers, and do so unsystematically. I could destroy your skull, but I strongly doubt it would do any good. The bone is only an anchor for the fire, and the fire is you. You would still be here, but in nowhere near as convenient a form. But tell me, you were an aesthete and a hermit in life. Is this new existence really so execrable to you?'

'No, and *that* I find execrable. But . . . I have time to think now. Nor am I totally isolated while I still have one sense left to me.' A pause, and then, 'Ask me in a year, Cabal. Do that for me.'

'If I am still alive myself in a year,' said Cabal, 'you have my word.'

Where Hlanith was virile and lively, and Baharna was exotic and vivacious, Dylath-Leen was built from basalt and made no further claims. The *Audaine* glided slowly into port soon after dawn, having sighted land too far to the south and hugged the coast back to the north until it found the city. Captain Oleander made no apologies for the navigational misstep, pointing out that changing course at the correct time would have made them cross paths with the thing in the sea, in which case they would probably all be dead by now. Given that as an alternative, a few extra hours afloat seemed far preferable.

Even having arrived at the city, the event was not one of

great joy for crew or passengers. Their first sight of the docks lined with black galleys drew a pall over any such positive feelings. Oleander cut a wad of Ogrothi baccy and chewed it slowly as he eyed the ships with undisguised jaundice. 'Never seen so many,' he muttered. under his breath. 'I'm guessin' we won't be callin' at Dylath-Leen agin fore too long.' On the decks, they could see figures swathed in black robes, their gloved hands glinting with rare yet vulgar gems, strolling around, or conversing with one another in little gaggles, or playing deck quoits with an obvious ignorance of the rules, such was the depth of their depravity.

He found his dock at the far end of the wharf, as far away from the ominous vessels as he could. Even as they were tying up to the broad bollards along the dockside, Oleander was already engaged in conversations with other captains who had congregated nearby. Cabal, who was leaning on the rail, was able to make out the gist of the news, and it did not make comforting hearing. The scuttlebutt – a marine term for 'gossip' that might amuse or bemuse the casual listener depending on personal interpretation – was that Dylath-Leen was in serious trouble. The council, which had always maintained at least a cosmetic distrust of the black galleys, had suffered a reversal when all its leading members disappeared in a single night. The lesser members, all men of luxuriant tastes and representative of the city's trading guilds, had slid into the senior executive roles aboard a carpet of greased palms and their first act had been to revoke the limitations upon the black galleys, imposed some years earlier after a previous slavery scandal. There had been little surprise among the citizenry that the councillors' luxurious tastes had subsequently been gratified to a disgusting level by nameless benefactors. Many people were finding excuses to leave the city, but since the captains of the guard had all been replaced with foreign mercenaries, it was becoming more and more difficult to get through the gates.

Oleander walked back up the gangplank, scowling. He saw Cabal and said, 'You mayn't want to be leaving the ship at this place after all, Master Cabal.'

'It doesn't seem very friendly here, Captain,' agreed Cabal. He was thinking of what inevitably lay ahead: there would be a slow erosion of liberties within Dylath-Leen, and then, when the inhabitants were prepared to accept anything because they were permitted to do nothing, the patrons of the black galleys would regard this little patch of ground as safe enough for them to visit from their lunar cities. They would bring with them their unholy appetites and exercise them upon an unwilling populace. After that, it could only be a matter of months at most before Dylath-Leen joined the Dreamlands' slowly growing list of abandoned and shunned places.

By this point, the Fear Institute contingent had appeared on deck, carrying their small bags of belongings and eager to disembark. The captain and Cabal's sour expressions gave them some small inkling that they were going to be missing out on hugs and *lei*. 'Is there something awry, Cabal?' asked Corde.

'Oh, I say! Look at all those black boats!' cried Bose, inadvertently answering the question. 'And look! There are more coming!'

Swearing an oath salty enough to make Dagon purse his lips, Oleander ran aft and looked to the harbour mouth. Bose had spoken nothing more than the truth. Perhaps two miles off, three black galleys in line astern were heading implacably towards Dylath-Leen. 'What are they doing?' he demanded of nobody in particular. 'That's madness! They'll never get by the gates beam to beam like that.' Then he understood, and his face grew pale beneath the tan. He ran to the rail and shouted down to the gossiping captains there gathered, 'To your ships! To your ships! The devils mean to blockade the harbour!'

Abruptly all the serious standing around and muttering ominously at one another turned into a mad and undignified dash back to their vessels. Even as they did so, Cabal saw that the city guard, in full mail and faceless behind their helmets, was approaching the docks at a lumbering charge. They ran oddly, as if their knees weren't in quite the right places for their greaves. Not for the first time, he wished he had access to something with rather more range than a rapier. 'Captain—' he began.

'I see 'em, Master Cabal,' snapped Oleander. 'Cast off, fore and aft! Cut the lines, damn you!'

Axes thudded and the mooring ropes parted. The gangplank, forgotten in the frenzy of intent, fell into the water between the ship's side and the dock as she started to move away, pushed back fiercely by crewmen wielding poles.

'Herr Corde,' said Cabal. He was watching several of the guards still heading straight for them, despite the widening gap between the ship and the quay. 'Draw your sword.' He drew his own, his eyes never leaving the charging guards.

Corde frowned at him, followed his gaze and scoffed. 'You're joking, Cabal. The gap's twenty feet if it's an inch. They couldn't make it even if they weren't weighed down in armour. Relax. They'll end up drowning themselves.'

'If they were men, I would agree,' said Cabal, as the first

guard reached the quayside and, without hesitation, threw himself towards the *Audaine*.

In a cool, rational world, the guardsman would have described a graceless parabola into the harbour waters and – wrapped in steel knitting as he was – made swift progress to the sea bed. The Dreamlands, however, do not present a cool, rational world, instead favouring a sequence of events such as the guard leaping the gap as if catapulted, crashing heavily into the rail without even a grunt, and then hurdling it easily, drawing its – we can no longer dignify such a creature with *his* – longsword, and looking for somebody to carve up with it.

Cabal backed away as the guard swung its helmeted head this way and that. 'Herr Corde? How much provocation do you need?' Corde said nothing, but let his cloak fall from his shoulders to reveal the leather armour beneath. The sound of his sword sliding from its scabbard was enough to engage the guard's attention.

There was another dull, gruntless thump against the rail, and then another, but this one was followed by a splash: the *Audaine* was finally out of jumping distance for even these inhuman creatures.

The first guard spoke, but it was an unconvincing attempt, full of gurglings and *basso profundo* boomings from deep within. It tried again, and this time managed to produce something like human speech, although it was as convincing a rendition as a dog saying, 'Sausages.'

'Ship . . . impounded . . . by authority of . . . impounded . . .' It swung its head from side to side, a poor impersonation of a man looking around. Cabal's misgivings deepened: however the guard was sensing them, it was not through eyes.

'Ye'll step off my ship, sir!' demanded Oleander. He

carried a polished falchion that Cabal had assumed uncharitably was for show. Now drawn and glinting in the weak sunlight, it looked far more like a device for creative hacking.

'Ship impounded . . . order of . . . council . . . Dylath-Leen . . .' Without allowing even the shortest moment for a reply, it launched into the attack.

Oleander met the slashing blow with a fast parry of his falchion that struck sparks. He thrust the guard's sword arm to one side and shoved it back with his free hand to gain a little space. Cabal, meanwhile, was weighing up the wider situation. All along the dock, the other manned ships were trying to cut loose while their crews engaged the wave of bestial guards. A swift glance over his shoulder showed that the three galleys were close by the mole and all had their tillers hard over, swinging across to block the harbour mouth. Then, to add to his rapidly populating list of concerns, he saw that some of the black galleys already in dock were moving out to engage the ships that had managed to cast off. They were in a rat trap and, his mind whirling through alternative plans, Cabal could see no way out of it. Then he noticed the second guard who had jumped, painfully hauling itself on to the rail, and noted with satisfaction that there was at least one small victory he could achieve.

'Corde! Help the captain, you idiot!' he shouted, as he ran for the second guard. 'You don't need to be invited!'

Corde, who at some deep and very English level was indeed waiting for an invitation to fight – a slap with a gauntlet or a strongly worded note, perhaps – shuddered into action. He ran forward and stood shoulder to shoulder with Oleander, jumping around a bit as if preparing to receive a serve in a friendly game of tennis. 'Get behind it!' said Oleander, angrily, as Corde ate into his room for manoeuvre. 'Stab it in the back!'

While Corde wrestled with his sense of fair play, Cabal had reached the rail at a charge. The second guard had just got its head above it when it found a rapier waiting for it. Cabal struck hard and precisely, the tip of the blade going neatly through the left eye of the guard's helmet. Cabal doubted he could blind it, but hoped it had something precious to it stored inside its head; a brain would be lovely, but an important nerve ganglion would suffice.

The guard made a sloppy wet noise as the blade went in, but Cabal could not tell if it was the sound of important flesh being parted or a vocalisation in whatever slithy collection of dripping, slobbering and burbling sounds it pleased the guard to regard as its native language. Then the guard shook its head angrily, as if getting a length of steel through the eye was a mild irritation on par with a snapped shoelace. Cabal realised that more robust measures than merely stabbing it through the head would be necessary.

The guard managed to get both hands on the rail and said something that sounded like a blocked sink clearing, yet still maintained the tonal *je ne sais quoi* that allows one with decent linguistic skills – and Cabal's were more than decent – to know that a frightful insult has just been uttered. Cabal did not tolerate insult, especially from burbling things that refused to die easily. Lying near at hand was a discarded axe that had been used mere minutes ago to part the hawsers. Cabal left his rapier in the guard's eye, took up the axe and severed the guard's wrists with two well-placed blows 'twixt gauntlet and bracer. The guard made a new bubbling sound, this time denoting surprise, and fell backwards. Cabal snatched his rapier from where he'd left it parked in the guard's head, and favoured the falling creature with a humourless smile as it vanished from sight, hitting the water a moment later.

On the deck, the two orphaned hands started to crawl away, presumably looking for a hiding place where they could plot their revenge. Cabal picked them up by the lames across the gauntlet backs as if handling particularly feisty crabs, and tossed them into the harbour. They could do their plotting in the mud, as far as he was concerned.

'It won't die!' Corde's shout, generously scented with more panic than rational concern, drew Cabal's attention. Oleander was barely holding his own in a vicious exchange of blows with the first guard, while Corde stabbed it repeatedly in the back with the enthusiasm of a masochist poking a wasps' nest. Cabal returned his rapier to its scabbard, recovered the axe from where he had left it embedded in the rail with a pool of whey-like blood around it, and went to assist.

'You fail to employ the scientific method, Herr Corde,' he said, as he approached. 'After sufficient experiments to confirm your initial observation – in this case, that stabbing is an ineffective strategy – one should move on to new hypotheses. This creature is concentrating entirely upon the captain, perhaps because his falchion is a slashing weapon. Does the creature regard being slashed as more deleterious to its general operation than being stabbed? Let us experiment.' So saying, he used the end of the axe to tip the guard's helmet forward a little, exposing flesh with the colour, consistency and wet texture of fresh blancmange. Then he drew back the axe and decapitated the guard.

The guard was definitely surprised. Not killed, or

apparently wounded to any significant degree, but certainly surprised. It turned to Cabal, the space over its neck giving every intimation of being very surprised.

'There,' said Cabal, pleased. It was always gratifying to see a hypothesis verified. It was less gratifying to have a headless and angry monstrosity bear down on one when its sword has twice the reach of one's axe. 'Some assistance here?' asked Cabal, as he backed quickly away.

Oleander needed no second prompting. Aiming at the top of the shoulder as the guard turned away from him, he swung the falchion with great force. The links in the mail separated easily – apparently such work went to the lowest bidders even in the Dreamlands – and the blade almost reached the armpit before running out of energy. The guard's right arm flopped down, boneless and skinless, less grown than extruded. Oleander pursed his lips, like an artist considering where to make the next brush stroke, and hacked at the thin sliver holding the arm on. It fell, the sword clattering free. After a moment, the hand started to drag the arm off behind it as it sought shelter.

Oleander and Cabal laid into the defenceless hulk of the guard, smashing it down with heavy blows until it toppled, then pounding its form until pale liquescent filth flowed from the ragged sleeve and the neck of the mail bernie, and the armour sank until it was empty.

'What . . . what was that?' said Corde, his eyes wide and wild. 'What sort of creature?'

'Something cheap and expendable,' said Cabal, but his attention was elsewhere. The trap was still closing. The fight on the *Audaine*'s deck had taken only seconds, and the crew who had moved to help were already back at their stations, trying to escape the wave of galleys that was nearing them. It was plainly a hopeless endeavour, however: the oars of the galleys swept mechanically and relentlessly, while the *Audaine* could make little steerage with her sails furled, despite the crew's hard sculling.

It was for the captain to call, and he stood watching the oncoming galleys as he considered the options. 'Captain,' said Cabal, quietly, at his side, 'if you give up the ship, you and your men will be slaves within the hour, and dead within a month. I intend to fight.' He drew his rapier, and awaited Oleander's decision.

Oleander took a moment to reach it, not least because every reasonable outcome ended in death. All that mattered now was choosing which particular path was most acceptable. 'Men!' he shouted. 'Stand by to repel boarders!'

It is a strange moment when one realises that one's life is now measured in minutes, and that whatever great plans might have been laid are now all moot and pointless and – in the great burning clarity of the instant – trivial. Cabal did not know what the others were thinking of, neither did he care. All he knew was that the course of his life had long been nothing more than a list of calculated risks, and that, finally, his luck had run out. All the work, all the hardships, all the sacrifices – both personal and of livestock – had been for naught; his work would never see fruition. He would never see her again. But that was not his fault, and he regretted nothing.

He gave the situation one last appraisal before committing to what would likely be the last decision of his life. Behind him, Shadrach tried to look dignified, but was leaning on the mainmast to support him as his knees turned to water. Bose had given up any pretence of bravery and was huddled in the angle between the quarterdeck steps and the rail, trying to will himself into invisibility. Corde held his sword in his hand, and was looking at it with new eyes, as if realising that the skill with which he might wield it would mark the difference between a fast and dishonourable death, or one drawn out a few seconds longer. It would mean at least that he hadn't died meekly and mildly, a sacrifice to alien gods.

Oleander and his men were armed and ready, facing the enemy with determination on their faces and not a whit of hope in their hearts.

Cabal felt something fluttering in his chest, and applied himself to crushing down the rising panic. Panic would only result in a confused, meaningless death. He would remain calm and rational to the end. The Phobic Animus would not have him for its prey in his last moments. He would continue being his own man to the final second. He could expect nothing less of himself. And so he stood, resolute and perhaps even a little heroic, as one of the approaching black galleys suddenly threw its tiller hard over, turned to port, and smashed into the forward side of the next galley.

Cabal blinked in astonishment, and as he blinked, so did the Dreamlands. There was a sense of waking from a nightmare, only to find oneself still in it. The harbour, the ships, Dylath-Leen, even the sky and the sea, seemed to flutter indecisively between possible meanings and the collateral paradigms. Cabal's sword became a pistol, then a sword, then some sort of extraordinary long gun, and then it was a sword again. The Dreamlands were changing, but in awkward, inelegant, stuttering steps. He suddenly realised that they weren't changing nearly so much as *being changed*. Somewhere, a great consciousness had placed them under the lens of its awareness, and the very act of being observed was making their reality waver, like a thumb flicking through a mail-order catalogue. He looked up, as if expecting an eye of cosmic proportion to be staring at him through the blueness and the high clouds.

Then he heard the screams, and around him the world gelled back into something similar to what it had been. Now, however, one of the attacking galleys was up to the bowsprit in the hull of its neighbour, and the wounded ship was *screaming*.

But, then, the whole world was screaming. Everyone, even the galley slavers in their shapeless black robes were looking to the sky and screaming, or howling, or sobbing. For the blue morning sky had burned back in a ragged hole, through which could be seen the Dreamlands' Moon, and the Moon, too, was burning.

Chapter 12

IN WHICH THERE ARE MONSTERS AND CATS, WHICH IS TO SAY, VERY MUCH THE SAME THING

'What is happening?' bellowed Oleander, over the fearful cries and the rising note of a strengthening wind. 'What have those devils done?'

By *devils*, he meant the masters of the black galleys, but even a glance was sufficient to assure anyone that not only were they not responsible for these new phenomena, but they were even more horrified by them than the humans of Dylath-Leen. The slavers tore away their stolen faces and threw them aside, pulling back their tagelmusts, thin white tendrils, the colour of cave fish, unfurling to undulate at the Moon like weed on the seabed. Then they screamed at the sight of the burning Moon, '*Ph'nglui k'ytholo mfagnul oseer'akff!*' – a phrase that translates to something far shorter in English.

The men who looked upon these horrors felt their sanity shift, and minds broke in that moment. Corde gave a shriek like a terrified child, and backed away, shaking his head to deny the existence from which his eyes could not be drawn, Bose still lay bundled up in the corner of the deck, his shoulders heaving with his sobs, and Shadrach made no noise at all. Cabal looked around to find the cadaverous Shadrach, and found him clutching futilely at his throat. There, the first guard's severed arm had him, the great gauntleted hand almost encircling his neck. Shadrach made no sound, but his face was dark and his eyes were starting from his head. Cabal started to run towards the stricken man, but he knew that it was already too late. The hand was not merely strangling Shadrach: it was crushing his neck. Cabal was only a matter of two yards from Shadrach when there was a percussive sound of collapsing cartilage, and the crunch of failing bone. Shadrach's face became slack, and he fell back against the rail, then over it. Cabal reached it just in time to see the splash and Shadrach's discreetly expensive shoes with the curled toes disappear beneath the water.

Cursing at an avoidable loss – he should have dealt with the arm after those limbs' tendency for awkward autonomy had already been demonstrated – he turned back, but the tableau had barely changed, beyond becoming fractionally worse. The fires on the Moon had changed from wide clouds into distinct red points of light, indicating a series of simultaneous explosions across the surface. They showed against the pale lunar rock like buboes on a dead man's face, and Cabal guessed that these were the cities of the Moon things, the creatures whose agents were even now standing awestruck, venting glutinous polysyllables of arcane vulgarity.

He went to Oleander and shook him roughly by the arm until he gained his attention. 'The sky,' said Oleander, a vacant look of shock in his eyes. 'The sky is broken.'

'So it is,' said Cabal, pointedly ignoring it, for the wise man avoids falling through the ice by never setting foot upon it. 'Oleander, you have to pull yourself together. The slavers are directionless at present, but we don't know how long that will last. We must press the advantage while they are disrupted.'

But Oleander would only murmur, 'The sky . . . the sky . . .' with a terrible expression of haunted loss upon his face, so Cabal hit him, which worked very well. He suddenly focused on Cabal like a startled drunk, and was drawing back his blade when Cabal grabbed his sword hand in one of his own, Oleander's jaw in the other, and shouted in his face, 'Time, Captain! We are running out of time. Burning skies and exploding moons are all very well, but aliens with a mass of *bavette* for faces are our more immediate concern.'

Oleander shook himself free of Cabal's grip and tried to rally the forces of his routed sanity, searching for a standard by which to gather them. He settled on pasta. 'What is this "*bavette*" of which you speak?'

'It's a form of spaghetti.' Cabal could see the answers to Oleander's next questions were in all likelihood going to be 'Pasta', 'Italy', and 'A country', so he cut sharply past such quizzical distractions with, 'Of no importance at the moment. Action, however, is. The creatures are defenceless and vulnerable – you will never get such a good chance to kill the slavers again.'

Finally, the captain's wits had their standard by which to regroup. The black galleys had long been distrusted among many of the races of men in the Dreamlands, but never before had their true nature been so publicly exposed, and never before had the opportunity for vengeance upon them been so advantageous. This would be a time of righteous glory, with a decent prospect of looting thrown in. It was too magnificent for any man with blood in his veins to resist. Oleander's blood was red and hot, and he had a strong, no, irresistible urge to see what ran in the slavers' veins. With a shout that overrode his crews' terrors, he rushed forward at their head, throwing grappling lines to draw in the nearest galley, a vessel that so recently they would have done anything to avoid.

Cabal didn't know what their chances were. If they died, at least they would be distracting the slavers as they did so, allowing him and his two remaining charges some precious time to make good their escape. The few inhuman guards scattered about the wharf were as fascinated and discommoded by the destruction of their home cities as the slavers, but how long that would last, he could not say. Neither did he care to bet his future safety against it being more than a few minutes. An alternative presented itself; if they got on to the northern harbour wall, they could follow it around until they were on the mole, then cut across and circumnavigate the edge of the city wall. Yes, there was a tower to protect the city against invaders performing exactly the reciprocal manoeuvre, but with luck they would be staring skywards with gormless expressions upon their pasta-like faces long enough. It was a gamble, but a lesser one than hoping to make it all the way through the city unchallenged.

Corde was staring fixedly at the hull of the black galley that had been torn open by its neighbour. Exposed within lay folds of brain-like tissue into which the shafts of the oars sank, secured with collar plates riveted directly into the living mass. It was screaming, a thin, ululating whine like an unappreciated shaman, but in such volume that it set the teeth on edge. Between the flesh and the shattered wood of the hull flapped thin leaves of a metal that seemed like lead one moment yet glistened with a rainbow of colours the next, colours not to be found anywhere upon the electromagnetic spectrum. The thin layer of metal had been placed there to keep the galley thing's compartment hermetically sealed; now that it was exposed to the air, its flesh boiled and melted, and the creature screamed endlessly without pause or attenuation.

Cabal quickly surmised that shaking Corde to gain his attention was too time-consuming, too likely to fail, and would involve spending far too much time within his personal space, so he just went directly to his tried and tested supplemental plan. It was more of a punch than a slap, but it proved as efficacious as it had with Oleander, dragging Corde back from the slippery slope of cosmic horror while simultaneously allowing Cabal to alleviate some of his growing frustration with the situation.

'Come along!' Cabal barked at Corde, as if he were a recalcitrant schoolboy on a day trip. 'No time for dawdling.' Without waiting for a response beyond an expression of outraged astonishment, he ran to Bose's side and pulled the sobbing man to his feet.

'Where's Shadrach?' demanded Corde, as he followed.

'Mr Shadrach's dead,' said Bose, in a pitiful, small voice. 'It got him. It killed him. He fell into the water.'

Corde tried to say something, but it failed in his throat.

'It was an arm,' added Bose, pathetically and parenthetically.

Cabal looked at Bose, his expression entirely neutral. Then he said, 'Herr Bose is correct. Shadrach is dead. The loss of the money he carried may present a problem later. Currently, however, we do not have time to discuss that, or what a splendid chap he was, or whatever other reason is making you stand there impersonating a guppy, Herr Corde. We must be gone immediately.'

The wind was rising, and both the *Audaine* and the galley to which she was grappled were being driven to the lee shore, close by the end of the wharf and the start of the sea wall. All they had to do was wait a couple of minutes, and they would be in position to jump ashore and make off. Corde started for the quarterdeck, but Cabal stopped him, and instead they went into Oleander's cabin, a much shorter jump from its bow windows down to the shallows. It also meant they didn't have to watch Oleander and his men engaged in a loathsome, nightmarish fight with the inhuman slavers, a fight rich with blood and ichors, desperation and despair. Finally, Cabal's plan furnished him with an opportunity to repair their financial misfortunes by breaking into the captain's strongbox and stealing a quantity of gold coin.

Corde watched him with evident disapproval, but did not stop him. He only said, 'The captain's been good to us. He's out there right now, fighting for his life.'

Cabal finished stowing a heavy purse in his Gladstone, and said, 'He will shortly be dead, and won't care. Or he will have defeated the slavers and will be in a position to loot their ship, in which case the loss of this footling quantity of gold will be galling but hardly devastating. In either event, our need is greater than his.' He paused as the ship shuddered, and grated against the pebbles of the harbour beach. 'Ah-ha. Our cue to run away like cowards and thieves.'

*

The great escape was miserable, wet and tiring. They trudged to freedom. Bose and Corde walked with their heads bowed, the better to ignore the torn sky and the wounded Moon. It seemed that lunar cities had decent fire-fighting arrangements, as the red dots grew fewer by the minute. Presumably even as the three men waded through the shallows by the sea wall, and marched with squelching steps up the mole, bloated white Moon toads in brass helmets were hosing down their predictably Cyclopean buildings. They would have to do it themselves, as it was hard to believe their slaves would be in any hurry to help. They would be standing by with space marshmallows on sticks, having the one and only good time they could expect as thralls of the toad things.

Cabal kept his head up and disregarded the heavenly apocalypse as easily as more mundane folk might disregard an unremarkable cloud. He had seen inferno and tempest, and had not only looked into the abyss but the abyss had looked into him, and then made disparaging comments. Some charred troposphere and a smoke-damaged Moon were hardly worth a footnote.

The guards in the watchtower were not of the same liver – should they have livers at all, which seemed unlikely – and were howling skywards with their facial tentacles in sinusoidal agitation. As a race, it seemed they were not used to suffering reverses, and would probably be sobbing into their beer analogue for many months to come.

Cabal's party followed the path around the outside of the wall, then stayed close to it until they came to a tumble of rocks that gave them cover to break away and head into the countryside. Even when they got a safe distance from the wall, however, they did not speak, Bose and Corde because they were subdued by what they had so recently experienced, and Cabal because he was Cabal and felt little need to jabber incontinently for the sake of conversation.

It was only when they had walked for some hours that Corde broke the silence. 'The expedition is a disaster,' he said. 'We have lost one of our number, and who knows what else we may have lost?' He looked to the sky, but the rent in the atmosphere had healed with only a dispersed, jagged pink line to show it had ever been there, and even this was slowly dissipating.

Cabal stopped walking and leaned against a dry-stone wall bordering a farmer's field. 'You mean Shadrach's money?'

'No! No, I do not!' Corde was speechless with rage for a moment, then blurted, 'I mean our minds, our very souls. Why did we ever come here?'

'The Phobic Animus,' said Bose, quietly, settling himself on a boulder by the road.

'Yes, I . . . I know that, Bose. I don't mean . . .' Corde shook his head, tired and defeated. 'We must go back.'

'I agree,' said Cabal.

'You would,' said Bose. Both Cabal and Corde looked at him with some surprise. Finding himself suddenly under observation, Bose couldn't meet their eyes, so he addressed the turf at his feet instead. 'You have made it very plain from the earliest stages of this venture that you thought us foolish and our quest pointless. I have no doubt that you've only stuck with us so far because of your own curiosity about the Dreamlands. We were foolish to leave the Silver Key in your hands, but I think . . . we all thought . . . that by your own lights you were honourable. Well, I release you from any remaining responsibilities. Take Mr Corde, and get back to the waking world. There is no use you both dying for a cause you do not believe in.' He straightened his legs and slid off the boulder to land on his feet. He took a deep breath, and started walking again.

'Wait, Bose. Wait!' called Corde, to the little man's back. 'Where are you going?'

Bose did not turn, but kept walking. 'To the Island of Mormo, in the Cerenarian Sea. I shall find it, and the Phobic Animus, and then I shall try . . .' He stopped walking. 'I shall try very, very hard . . . to destroy it.' He began walking again.

They watched Bose walk on without them in silence for a long minute. 'Hmm,' said Cabal.

'Oh, for Heaven's sake,' said Corde. Then he started running after Bose. 'Bose! Mr Bose! Gardner! Wait!'

'Hmm,' said Cabal again, and walked after the pair of them.

A hundred yards later he caught up with Corde and Bose, who were having a heated discussion. Bose was saying, 'Shadrach died for this. I cannot just give up immediately afterwards, as if that counts for nothing. I do not weigh my life as worth more than his. I *must* go on, don't you see?'

'Damn you, Bose!' It was hard to be sure if Corde was angrier with Bose or himself. 'Damn you! We'll all die in this misbegotten world if we don't leave, can't you see that?'

'No. No, I don't. Although I would be happier if Mr Cabal were to stay with us, or me, if you insist on returning.'

'Me?' said Cabal, intrigued. 'Why me?'

'You saved us all against the spider-ant-baby things, and against the black galleys. And without you we would never have known that our goal lies on Mormo.'

'Hold hard,' said Cabal, raising an admonishing finger. 'I had nothing to do with what happened back there.'

'Didn't you? I'm not so sure, Mr Cabal. I saw the hand of Divine Providence in what happened. Perhaps not the divinity that we usually look to, but any port in a storm, eh?'

Cabal's face hardened; he had been trying hard to forget about his inadvertent calling down of Nyarlothotep in the Dark Wood in the irrational but fervent hope that if he forgot about it so would the god. Unfortunately, it seemed likely that Bose was correct. It was stretching coincidence a little far to believe that the sky had just decided to split open and the Moon to explode at that exact moment on a whim. It seemed that Cabal was still being monitored by a supernatural force that, for reasons that remained alien and indistinct, had taken an apparently benevolent interest in his activities. There seemed to be no reason for it – Nyarlothotep was a deity more than usually well disposed to incandescent levels of mindless terror. Why it would see fit to aid an expedition to destroy the well of all irrational fear was a mystery, and perhaps one that transcended the human mind's ability to comprehend, even if it was explained very, very slowly with diagrams, models and glove puppets. Probably quite frightening glove puppets.

'The . . . entity to which you are referring, Herr Bose, is notoriously fickle. It did not intervene in the nameless city.'

'But that wooden monstrosity just fell over, didn't it? What caused that?' said Corde.

Cabal looked at him in offended consternation. They had not spoken of that night again, except in the broadest terms, Holk's death still throwing a pall upon events, but he had not realised that they thought the sinew-wood giant's fall was due to natural, supernatural or otherwise non-Cabalian causes. 'It just *fell over*,' he said icily, 'because I was on its shin, waggling a knife around inside its knee joint. I don't suppose either of you noticed that, due to all the intense skulking you were doing at the time.' This was slightly hypocritical of Cabal, who had done a great deal of skulking in his life, and was probably regarded as something of a master of the form among the skulking fraternity.

Bose nodded thoughtfully, but Corde was stung. 'Are you suggesting that we are cowards, Cabal?'

'Not at all,' said Cabal. 'I am stating it. Bose at least has the grace to admit it, by act if not by word. He has never pretended to be anything he is not. Apart from a magistrate,' he conceded, gesturing at Bose's judicial robes, 'but that was rather thrust upon him by the Dreamlands. Reach for that sword, and I shall kill you where you stand.'

For Corde's hand had strayed to the hilt. It wavered there for a moment, then fell by his side.

Once he was satisfied that Corde would not sully his discourse with any further murderous intentions, Cabal continued, 'That, Herr Corde, was reasonable caution. Your behaviour in the presence of Ercusides' great scarecrow was not. Any lucid, rational eye would quickly have discerned the thing's nature and evolved a strategy for dealing with it, as I did. I required no external agencies to do so.'

Yet as soon as he had said it he doubted it. He had not thought through every detail of that night, but now it occurred to him that there was a speck around which his deductions had been built, a few words of forewarning that had given him a head start on the truth. He thought of a whispering inhuman voice beneath a temple to a forgotten god in a city with no name: 'Remember Captain Lochery.'

He had focused purely on wondering how the ghoul had

even known of the captain and that Cabal was acquainted with him. He had concluded that the ghouls' unnerving ability to go almost anywhere and anywhen that amused them had been the cause of it, and that the ghoul was merely using the captain as an example of their wide-spanning intelligence, and as a warning to be careful. Now that he paused to consider his memories of the ensuing ratiocinations, however, he realised that the unusual nature of the captain's leg had flickered through his mind. This, truly, had been the seed from which his deductions pertaining to the true nature of the mysterious wamp-killer had sprung, the moment he had clapped eyes upon the evidence of Ercusides' exercises in arcane woodwork.

This was a disturbing revelation in itself, and Cabal hushed Corde's simmering outrage with an impatient flutter of his fingers and a pneumatic *pffft* of the type used for shooing off cats. Cabal needed to think, and he didn't need a histrionic solicitor distracting him while he did it.

The truly disturbing element, however, was the nature of the hint. It had been cryptic to the point of abstruseness, and not a reasonable bet for a hint to most people. For Cabal, and Cabal's thought processes, however, it had been precise and exact. How could some cadaver-chewer have known that? Unless, and he did not enjoy the thought, the ghoul had not been a ghoul at all. Nyarlothotep famously had a thousand avatars, a thousand faces to present, a thousand masks to wear. This was only a figurative figure, however: Nyarlothotep in reality had far, far more. It did not stretch credibility in the slightest to suggest that the ghoul was one of them. If anyone could gauge a clue with such terrifying meticulousness, surely it had to be a god.

Once one accepted in principle that their expedition was

being protected by the Crawling Chaos (one of Nyarlothotep's many names, along with others such as the Black Pharaoh, Ahtu, the Grey Man, Loki, the Child of Eyes, the Bloated Woman, Anansi, the Dweller in Darkness, the Smiling Killer, Tezcatlipoca, and Dave in Accounts), abandoning it became problematical. Nyarlothotep might just shrug and leave them to it, or he might take offence and then revenge. Given that Nyarlothotep's revenge would likely be biblical in scale, Dadaist in commission, and cruel enough to make de Sade wince, not offending the god seemed very sensible.

Cabal had many faults, several of which were also capital crimes, but he was in no wise indecisive. He shouldered the baldrick to which his Gladstone was attached, and started walking again. 'Come along,' he said. 'I am not abandoning our quest, and therefore will not be finding a reciprocal gateway for the Silver Key. Without it, you are trapped here, Herr Corde, so I suggest you have little option but to accompany us.'

Corde was furious, but still he did not reach for his sword. 'Don't I have any say in the matter?'

Cabal stopped to look at him. 'You have no say, but perhaps you do have a choice. Come or stay.' He considered. 'Yes, that covers all the possibilities.' Cabal made to start walking again.

'One day, Cabal, you will have your comeuppance.'

'Is *comeuppance* some mealy-mouthed way of saying *die*? One day I shall die, yes, and given my profession, it will likely be sooner than later. But it will also likely be random and stupid and pointless. It is to war against the very irreversibility of such deaths that I do what I do. In all your days as a solicitor, Herr Corde, I doubt you even once pressed the war against death with a minute of your time or an iota of your energy. In real humanitarian terms, your campaign against the Phobic Animus is the most selfless and noble thing you have ever done or will ever do. Do not miss your chance to be useful.'

If the logic convinced him, he did not nod. If the sentiments mollified him, he did not smile but, none the less, Corde followed, and the remaining 75 per cent of the Great Phobic Animus Hunt walked on.

Just over two weeks later, Corde died. It was random and stupid and pointless.

The icy atmosphere within the party had thawed a little, at least on Corde's part. Cabal was capable of only glacial coldness and incandescent fury; convivial warmness was well beyond him except as an exercise in play-acting. They had made good progress to the Karthian Hills, and the ease of their passage via the kindness of passing caravans, both commercial and military, had given them the easiest leg of their adventures to date. They had bought supplies at cost from the rearguard baggage wagons of a column of *húskarlar* accompanying a king on royal progress around his lands before saying their goodbyes and climbing into the hills.

The Karthian Hills were painfully bucolic and picturesque, as if planned by John Constable. Every view was striking, every weather condition heart-stopping, the light never anything less than blooming. It was like walking through an art gallery that contained only one piece, but one that surrounded the viewer and altered from one moment to the next, from one masterpiece to the next. As is usually the way in art galleries, they soon settled into a routine of largely ignoring it, but the transcendent beauty of their surroundings could not help but have a mellowing effect on them. Even Cabal found less to be sarcastic about, and so sank into a somewhat resentful quiescence, like a dormant volcano fondly remembering its last pyroclastic flow in which it had buried several hundred people, and now rather looking forward to its next.

There were farms and orchards in the hills, and the people were friendly, refusing as often as not to take payment for the food they gave the travellers. Bose was able to shake off the recent horrors they had witnessed as easily as a young child might, and took to chattering to Corde, or to himself, or to Cabal, which was much the same as chattering to himself. Corde bore the empty conversation well, ignoring much of it, and responding briefly and thoughtfully when the subject touched upon something that interested him. They did not speak of Shadrach. He was gone, and they did not care to consider how that had happened, or the consequences in the waking world when they returned. It would indeed have been easier if only his spirit had entered the Dreamlands, for then his body would have simply died in its sleep and there would have been a coroner's report of natural causes. Explaining a disappearance would probably turn out to be trickier.

Instead, they liked to consider what the world would be like when the Phobic Animus was finally destroyed. Strangely, despite all their preparations beforehand, they had never truly been examined the actual results of a successful expedition in anything but the vaguest terms of a 'golden future'. Now that they applied themselves to it, they were pleased and somewhat relieved that they could perceive no deleterious ramifications. Well, almost none.

'Nobody will care to read ghost stories again,' said Bose,

as they walked. 'Perhaps just for reasons of literary enjoyment, but certainly not to get the shivers because no one will believe in ghosts any more.'

'That,' said Cabal, in one of his rare utterances, 'would be foolish. One should be cautious of ghosts, for they certainly exist.' He flexed his shoulder and winced slightly as he said it.

Typically, he would not expand upon the subject having dropped such a boulder into the pool of their conversation, so Corde and Bose had to content themselves with telling one another ghost stories, both 'true' and fictional. Cabal sniffed disdainfully during some of these tales, and not during others, by which standard they came to understand which were most likely, given their taciturn companion's experiences. By this method, they amused themselves to the tops of the Karthian Hills.

The view from up there of the land ahead was less salubrious than that of the land behind. Off in the distance the rolling landscape grew less marked, and the colour drained from it by degrees until the verdant hills gave way to the pale brown sand dunes of the Cuppar-Nombo Desert. Nor was this shade of brown the usual golden brown of Earth's more scenic deserts, but rather the bland light brown of cold *café au lait*, a tired, sad colour, too depressing even for hospital walls. All three men looked at it, and all three drew long breaths that they allowed to sigh out of them as if they were deflating. Why the founders of Golthoth had decided to build their city in such a vile environment when the beautiful Karthian Hills were so close was a mystery for the ages. Perhaps the land had been different then; perhaps the Karthian Hills had belonged to some enemy; perhaps the Golthothians really, *really* liked nondescript brown sand.

Whatever the case, there was a strong sense that their pleasant interlude was drawing to a close, so they settled down to have possibly their last meal without sand in it for a while. They opened their jars and unwrapped their linen parcels, made a picnic of sorts upon the grassy swathe, and chatted about this and that as they ignored the brown expanse and ate their bread, cheese and salted meat.

They had just been discussing the careers that would abruptly wither away once fear was removed (fortune-telling, several branches of insurance sales, and a large part of the Stock Exchange, the latter principally comprised of fiscal pirates on a monetary sea kept profitably choppy by groundless panic and thick-pated optimism; Cabal asked if there was an equivalent form of the Phobic Animus that encouraged such wide-eyed hopefulness, and if so, would they be hunting this cosmic Pollyanna next?), when Corde noticed that the slice of meat he had just that moment arranged upon a cob of bread was no longer there.

After some undignified glaring in all directions, his eye settled upon a young cat, barely more than a kitten, that was padding away as swiftly as it might with a large slice of stolen meat in its mouth. It withdrew to what it believed was a safe distance some twenty feet away, and started tearing morsels from its booty, all the while keeping a watchful eye upon the three men in case they couldn't resist the desire to recover their food, grass-stained and cat-drool-coated as it was.

'Well I never!' said Corde, in righteous anger, but Cabal just made a soft bark of amusement in his throat, and Bose laughed out loud. Corde was suddenly aware that the only beings in that world or any of its immediate neighbours that gave a fig for the fate of his sandwich filling were himself and the cat that had stolen it. He smiled and laughed, a little forcedly, for inside he seethed with resentment at the animal.

'What sort of cat is that?' asked Bose, gesturing at it with a meat sandwich that Corde couldn't help but notice was unsullied by cats. 'What do they call those? It's a brindle, isn't it?'

'Brindle,' said Cabal, slowly, as if Bose had said something thoughtlessly hurtful, 'is a patterning. A brindled cat is a tortoiseshell.' He sat, watching the cat through narrowed eyes, a faint sense of disquiet growing within him. *How far from Ulthar are we?* he wondered.

'Well, whatever type of cat it is,' said Corde, with *faux*-joviality, 'it's a little rascal.' So saying, he took up a small stone and shied it in the general direction of the cat. When Cabal saw what he was about, he started to call a warning but it was already too late.

The stone was little more than a largish piece of gravel, and it was thrown without any great force. It should have described a leisurely parabola and bounced upon the grass near the cat, probably startling it. The stone did few of these things. With the horrible inevitability of nightmare it left Corde's hand like a bullet from a slingshot, spinning rapidly as it went, arced sideways, and hit the cat hard in the head. Even from where they sat, the harsh crack of bone was sickeningly distinct. The cat fell to one side, shaking violently in spasm. Corde leaped to his feet and ran to it, but it was already still and dead by the time he got there.

A man dressed as a great fighting general, he stood over the pathetic little form, put his hand to his mouth and gazed in horror at the blood, the exposed brain and the split eyeball.

The cat looked more as if it had been shot than hit by a casually tossed stone.

'Is it dead?' he heard Cabal say, in clear, neutral tones behind him.

'I didn't mean to . . . How is that possible?' Corde simply couldn't take in how bizarre the sequence of events was. 'I barely even . . . It makes no sense.'

Cabal was not interested. 'Gather up your things immediately,' he instructed. 'We must be on our way before they find out.'

'What?' Corde looked uncomprehendingly at Cabal. 'What are you talking about, man? Before who finds out?'

'The cats, naturally.' Cabal was already striding past him, heading westwards in the direction of the desert.

'Cats, Mr Cabal?' Bose was having difficulty in raising his voice to be heard through a mouthful of sandwich. 'The cat's owners, you mean?'

'I mean what I say, and I am in deadly earnest. There are plenty of things to be rationally afraid of in the Dreamlands, and not all of them are as overt in their threat as wamps.'

Based on Cabal's usual sang-froid, if he decided that killing a cat, even accidentally, was cause for a rapid decampment, that was sufficient motivation for Corde and Bose, who decided to hold their questions for later, quickly gathered up their belongings and headed westwards too.

When they caught up with Cabal his first words were, 'In the shade of the ivy on the wall to the left is a cat. We are discovered already. Our only hope is to reach the desert and hope that their notorious laziness and dislike of discomfort prevents them following.'

Corde risked a sideways glance and saw that there was

indeed the tumbledown remains of an old farm wall, upon which grew a generous dangling of ivy. Beneath it, he saw the glint of green eyes, and felt a strangely alien antipathy projected at him that did not make him think of tangled knitting and hairballs. He shuddered, and quickened his pace.

'What is this?' he asked Cabal. 'They're just cats. How is it that they're dangerous?'

'Because they are not just cats,' said Cabal, now starting to break sweat as he, too, lengthened his step. 'These are the Dreamlands, and what is here is the stuff of dream. Cats, as any rational person knows, are solitary, opportunistic, ambush predators, much like spiders, but with fewer legs and a better fan club. They are, by and large, stupid animals, the cleverest of the species being about on par with an average dog. I am no great admirer of dogs, either, I should add. My observations, while admittedly casual, are at least, therefore, objective. Cats, however, appeal to the anthropomorphising aspects of the human psyche like no other. They are credited with intelligence, cunning and an indefinable sophistication that, when regarded in light of their actual behavioural mores, will be observed to be pure phantasms. It is a deep belief, however, and that is where our danger lies, for the ridiculously inflated beliefs of generations of delusional cat devotees – and I use the term advisedly – are made concrete in the Dreamlands. Here they truly are intelligent, cunning, sophisticated and capable of the most exquisite malevolence, just as the dreamers who unwittingly weave them would want them to be. You have killed one of their number and, among far too many people, that is a capital offence. And so it is here.'

Soon the cats did not trouble to hide themselves, but sat erect like statuettes by the way, only their eyes moving as the three men hurried past. Then they rose and trotted along in a growing pack behind them, their tails low and twitching with anger.

There was no time to catch their breath and take stock. The horde of idealised kittery in their wake grew in numbers and in threat at every moment. It had long since ceased to be just a bunch of cats – now it was a furred stream that swept after them, an avalanche of claws awaiting the signal.

It was Corde who gave it to them. His evident panic increased with every step, every new recruit to the pursuing army, and his desperation grew with it. He was offered no comfort by his companions. Cabal was silent and focused purely on reaching the desert where the cats might desist. If he knew anything, it was that he loathed the thought of his last moments consisting of being swamped by an overindulged bunch of goldfish-botherers like their persecutors. Bose said nothing, but hurried along in a state of confusion, blinking furiously.

Then panic froze into hopelessness and a desire for some sort of resolution right at that very minute, and Corde stopped, spun on his heel, drew his sword, and bellowed, 'Come on, then, you damn'd fleabags!'

He was probably expecting a moment of indecision on the part of the cats, a beat before they were faced down, or flew at him, all claws and spitting, but they did neither. They did not stop when he turned, but continued to flow across the ground, and he had barely time to cry his challenge when they were flowing over him too. He was surprised, and did not call out or scream, as he became coated in cat. He struggled, but soon enough he could not see or hear anything. His hands flailed and his sword fell.

Bose said, 'Oh!' and went to help him, but Cabal caught his arm and said, 'If you hurt even a hair on one of their smug little heads, they will kill you too.'

'But Mr Corde isn't dead!' he cried. Cabal just held his arm tightly and watched as Corde fell, and the boiling, purring pool of fur where he had stood smoothed out, and became distinguishable individuals again, then poured off in all directions as if they had appointments elsewhere.

When they had gone, Cabal finally let go of Bose's arm. 'Now he is,' said Cabal.

There was little left, just an abandoned sword, a few scraps of torn cuir-bouilli and some tumbled pieces of equipment. Cabal watched a kitten a few yards away dragging off a finger bone, the joint gripped fiercely in its adorable little blood-smeared mouth.

'And then there were two, Herr Bose.'

Chapter 13

IN WHICH THE DOMESTIC WONTS OF SORCERERS ARE INVESTIGATED AND CABAL CANNOT BE CONCERNED

Much as a rubber ball deforms on impact only to spring back into its usual shape, so Bose's crumpled spirits soon rose above such small distractions as having two friends die in relatively rapid succession and in the most horrible ways. After all, life goes on, which in the case of Gardner Bose meant strolling along, whistling a jaunty tune and generally exhibiting a guileless, indeed witless, mien. On a village street, it would be acceptable. In the dun dunes of the alkali Cuppar-Nombo Desert, it was a little wearing.

At least it was not especially hot. The lack of water in the desert was more an accident of geography than extreme temperatures and, while it was a long way from cool, it was not unbearable. Of the environmental hardships, Bose's whistling was by far the worst. It came slightly muted –

although not nearly enough – by the handkerchief he had tied over his mouth and nose in imitation of Johannes Cabal, a measure to avoid breathing in more sand than was necessary. Cabal's second innovation of wearing his baffled blue-lensed sunglasses Bose could not emulate, so he was reduced to squinting fiercely against the fine dusty clouds that blew up into dust devils given the excuse of any faint breeze.

At least Cabal would not have to endure Bose's whistling for long, as this leg of their journey would be a short one: according to Cabal's maps and notes, the abandoned city lay a day's walk into the sands and was easily visible at range, so an error in navigation was unlikely. When the distant towers of ancient Golthoth appeared, only slightly off their set course, they were only as tired as a day's walking on sand would warrant and – since the sun didn't seem greatly interested in the Cuppar-Nombo – barely dehydrated at all.

Golthoth was a very different city from the one they had left by the Lake of Yath. Where that had been strangely vibrant, as if all the citizenry were just hiding out of sight and waiting to leap out in an impracticably large game of peek-a-boo, Golthoth seemed to have been built as a mysterious abandoned city right from the first stroke of an architect's stylus. As Bose commented when they first walked into its broad precincts, the place seemed very redolent of ancient Egypt, calling to mind the Memphis of the early dynastic period. Was it perhaps possible, he wondered, that the dreams of the first pharaohs had influenced this place? Cabal was quite certain it was the other way around.

The city contained a great deal of formal statuary, made from a dense stone of less scatological shades of brown than the desert. Gods and rulers they may once have been, but a thousand generations of sandstorms had eroded their faces into little more than arrays of suggestive bumps and contours that seemed to indicate that few had begun with human physiognomies. Cabal also noted that the doorways were uniformly a good twenty inches taller than normal Earthly doors, and that the more important buildings often seemed to sport additional doors of a curious squat hexagonal design, some larger examples lacking the upper edge to become pentagonal instead. Cabal kept his counsel, but suspected that these buildings had witnessed visitors for whom the strange doors were ideally suited.

The architectural style, however, was not homogenous. Here and there later additions stood awkwardly surrounded by the eldritch opulence of the original buildings. Some seemed to have been built in an attempt to claim the city for some interloping power, a strategy that had only ever been met by failure, judging from the current state of affairs. Other – rarer – forms were more enigmatic. These were uniquely towers, dotted randomly about the place as if they had been dropped from space, or had grown up through the pavements and squares. There were not many; Cabal counted five easily visible, with two or three more tumbled and broken, the brown sand grown yards deep in drifts against the shattered stone.

'Wizards,' he said disparagingly. 'The pretentious bastards just have to set up shop in towers situated in awkward places. It is a fault endemic among them.'

'And this wizard Ercusides mentioned . . .'

'Hep-Seth.'

'Yes, Hep-Seth. One of these will be his, then, Mr Cabal?' Bose allowed something like worry to travel across his beamish face. 'I say, though, it's all a bit . . . dead here, isn't it? Do you think he's still about?'

Cabal considered opening his bag to double check with Ercusides, but decided against it. The hermit-cum-paperweight had become recalcitrant since Dylath-Leen, and every time Cabal tried to speak to him, their conversations became shorter and more cryptic to the point at which he simply did not care to try any more. 'He should be,' he said, but did not sound very reassuring even to himself. The city felt dead to him, and he was better equipped than most to sense such a state. He just hoped that it would not be necessary to revivify any more skulls, although the thought of Ercusides and Hep-Seth being stuck in the same Gladstone and resenting it deeply cheered him up a little. 'It must be one of these towers. We shall work through them until we find the right one.'

Fortunately, the pretentious nature of wizards in general and the sort who raise obtrusive towers in other people's cities, without so much as a by-your-leave or planning permission in particular, worked in Cabal's favour. The first tower they approached was all basalt blades jutting into the air around the topmost reaches, with sinuous forms in black marble disporting themselves around the door. It was quite evident why this particular magus had got into the job in the first place. Over the door was carved a sphinx *couchant*, and when they approached, she turned her face to them and said, 'Whosoever wishes to meet with Calon of Serpes, the Sage of the Amber Star, must first answer me riddles three.'

'Calon of Serpes,' repeated Cabal. 'Wrong house. Good day, madam.'

'Wait a moment!' demanded the sphinx. 'I've been lying

here all *couchant* for three hundred years waiting to ask somebody my riddles.'

'Then your wait isn't over. Good day,' he repeated, a little firmly, and walked away, the sphinx's enraged shouting fading in the sigh of the desert wind behind them.

Bose looked at him, eyes wide with fright. 'The door spoke to us!' he managed eventually.

'Strictly, the door frame spoke to us, but yes. Now our next port of call.'

The next tower was oddly proportioned, in a way that would appeal to a student of Freud, and Cabal didn't have to make many guesses as to this magus's inner motivations either. Fortunately his name was on a sand-scoured brass plate upon an iron door, ancient but readable, and they were able to exclude it from their enquiries and move on.

The third tower belonged to Ukuseraton the Destroyer – at least, according to the animated stone dog that guarded the place, a glistening spire of woven glass and crystal. Then the dog attacked them, but it was only constructed from common sandstone and the desert storms had blasted it thin, so a well-placed kick decapitated it. It charged at Cabal, or where Cabal had been a moment before, and so completed its destruction by running into a wall and reducing itself to aggregate.

The fourth tower was as black as ebon night, and encouragingly bore the inscription 'HEP-SETH' over the doorway in Lorphic hieroglyphs that Cabal was able to enunciate with dismissive ease. Less encouragingly, the door stood open, swinging slightly in the low, endless desert wind.

'Perhaps he has an open-door policy?' said Bose, with optimism verging on delusion.

'Yes, of course. That will be it,' said Cabal, as he eased the door a little further open with his foot. 'He raised a tower in this distant damned place, wringing the very matter of it from the footnotes between quanta, and then he left the door ajar because he's so very sociable, really.' In the low afternoon sun, the ground-floor room of the tower could be seen to be several inches deep in fine sand. 'And he sacked his cleaner.'

He looked at Bose, but the little man was obviously trying to reconcile all these facts into a whole. Cabal sighed. 'Sarcasm, Bose. It was sarcasm. I'll hold a sign up next time,' he added, but as he wasn't holding a sign up at the time, Bose believed him, and nodded with a grateful smile.

They tracked cautiously through the entry hall, but if it had ever contained any defences, magical or mechanical, they had long since manifested or sprung. Round the curved wall stood a solid staircase of the same black stone that rose in a clockwise spiral, much like that of a lighthouse. Up this stair Johannes Cabal slowly climbed, followed at a judicious distance by the pallid Bose. The first floor consisted of an antechamber of sorts, the stair to the next floor being behind an elegant but sturdy door of suggestively molten forms, all rendered once more in the smooth glossy black stone. Fortunately it was not locked, and they were able to climb further upwards to what seemed to be an audience chamber or even a throne room. 'They never lack for egos, do they?' said Cabal, as they moved up to the third floor. This was the living quarters, informed with the decadent luxuriance so common among top-end wizards. There was a bathing chamber beside the bedroom that contained a great sunken bath, and beyond that a discreet privy, whose drainage plumbing appeared to be a transdimensional interface of some sort. 'Presumably waste is thereby conducted to some distant place where raining excrement is not regarded as unusual, like Tartarus,' he guessed. 'Or Ipswich.'

Cabal had already made some rough guesses as to the dimensions of the rooms, and he could not help but notice that they were growing steadily larger, unlike the external dimensions, which apparently tapered to a small lookout on the highest floor. Apparently, playing merry-hob with dimensions had been Hep-Seth's major stock-in-trade, and based on this conjecture he had already made a guess as to what the next floor would reveal.

Neither was he incorrect, as they climbed up into Hep-Seth's laboratory. It was a large room, some hundred feet in diameter, windowless yet illuminated by good, unwavering lights that seemed simply to emanate from the air close to the ceiling. In the centre of the chamber was an iron spiral staircase that seemed likely to re-enter the normal dimensions of the exterior at its peak and open into the small lookout deck. Cabal walked a few yards into the laboratory and looked around, uncertain what he should be searching for. Looking back, however, he spotted Bose's head from the nose up just peeping out of the stairwell.

'Is it safe?' asked Bose, a waver in his voice.

'That I cannot say. If you specifically mean, *Is there an ancient sorcerer up here who is outraged by our intrusion and means us harm?* the answer is no. Neither is there a body. The signs are that the tower is abandoned, just like the rest of the city. Hep-Seth either didn't need this place any more, or died elsewhere and never returned. I cannot say which.' He grunted irritably. 'Do come out from there, Bose. I feel like I'm talking to a mole.'

As Bose crept up the remaining steps, like a man entering a

maiden aunt's sick room, Cabal turned his professional eye upon Hep-Seth's arcane paraphernalia. He was inwardly disturbed by how little of it he could recognise. There were several things whose function he couldn't even guess at, and his ignorance chafed at him. Nor were they even comfortable to examine visually, their edges, angles and vertices behaving in ways so strange and ill-mannered that Euclid would have been brought to tears.

'This is the work of a man who was obsessed with reaching the Island of Mormo,' he said, half to himself, this being the half from which he expected a sensible conversation.

'Eh?' said Bose, the half from which Cabal expected nothing, so he ignored him.

'A genius, judging by his work here. A genius of dimensional engineering. If he wants to go somewhere, he doesn't call a taxi. He wants to go somewhere none can go, because nobody knows where it is. And he speaks of a . . .' He had been turning, slowly, as he talked, his eye sweeping around the room, and now he stopped and stared. 'A seven-sided gate.'

'Yes, he did,' agreed Bose, standing by a structure that, to the unjaundiced eye, looked a great deal like an asymmetric seven-sided gateway standing by itself some twenty feet from the nearest wall. It was made from thin, lath-like girders of a brass-like metal that was not brass but a strange alloy that Cabal had encountered once before in unenjoyable circumstances. 'That's what your head in the bag said, anyway. But what does it mean?'

Cabal walked over to him, grasped him firmly by the back of his collar, and twisted him to look at the structure. 'Count,' he commanded.

'One!' squeaked Bose. 'What's got into you, Mr Cabal?

There's one frame sort of thing! Should there be more?'

Cabal gave up and let him go while he himself stepped away to weigh up the next move. The gateway was as ambivalent to reality as anything else in the room, seeming to change form within flashes of perception, as if unable to decide whether to be two faces talking or a vase. In this case, however, the choice was between being one asymmetric seven-sided gateway and being any of a vast number of similar but different seven-sided gateways. Looking upon it for even a minute was very uncomfortable, as if the intellect was firmly and methodically unplugging and replugging the cables on the switchboard of the mind into new and ontologically challenging configurations. With difficulty Cabal managed to look away from it, and instead found himself gazing at the cheerfully gormless face of Bose, thereby going from the sublime to the ridiculous.

The work of creating the necessary gate of dubious physicality within the gateway built for it was not going to be a sudden great revelation any time in the next few minutes, so Bose repaired to the sorcerer's bedchamber to snore gently upon grey-silver samite sheets miraculously untouched by the passage of time, another boon of the tower's curious reality. Cabal, meanwhile, settled down in the laboratory with what writings of the great man he could find, and started sorting them into piles of graduated usefulness. Even for a man of Cabal's voracious intellect, this proved difficult. He was a long way from his specialities, and his problems were compounded by the growing realisation that Hep-Seth was not only a leading light in his field but that he was the only light. His notes used forms and nomenclature that were unique to him because he had originated this whole thaumaturgical subset of theory. So,

Cabal not only had to evaluate the notes, but he also had to learn a new and novel lexicon in which to do it. Muttering sourly to himself, he began to pore over the papers in the full knowledge that he might be days or weeks about it. Happily, they had discovered a large store of fresh food that was as fresh as the day the fruit had been plucked or the animal slaughtered. It was another of Hep-Seth's innovations, like the privy, applying the extraordinary to the mundane; neither had he overlooked a seemingly boundless supply of fresh, cool water. They would not starve here, at least.

The next morning – the rooms' mysterious lighting helpfully waxed and waned to give a sense of the time of day outside – found Cabal surrounded by notes in his own writing and possessed of a grudging admiration for Hep-Seth, albeit one overmatched by a solid dislike for the man based on his inability to write a glossary of terminology and leave it out where some passing necromancer might find it. That he himself wrote notes in a dead language and then enciphered them did not strike him as blinding hypocrisy: he could be executed for necromancy, whereas somebody who could create such magical conveniences as instantaneous travel, perfect food preservation and unblockable toilets had very little to fear, except being mobbed by a loving population.

Bose came in, the very epitome of ebullience and – in rapid succession – wished Cabal a good morning, asked him if he'd cracked the secret of turning the gateway on yet and, even as Cabal was looking for something heavy and spiky to throw at his head, patted it for purposes of illustration, thereby activating it.

Cabal froze, a heavy, spiky thing in his drawn-back throwing arm, and gawped at the shimmering portal that had appeared as easily and without fuss as blowing a soap bubble. The heavy spiky thing fell from his hand to heavily spike the floor.

'How . . .' He seemed momentarily incapable of forming the simplest sentence. 'Gateway . . . How? Created . . . did . . . How?' He leaped to his feet, the laboratory stool of Hep-Seth clattering over behind him. 'How in the Nine Circles of Hell did you manage to conjure the gateway, you dim-witted buffoon?' he roared, forgetting both diplomacy and some much more cutting insults in his passion.

On the other hand, it would have been wasted effort. Bose's ability to miss, misunderstand and generally remain unscratched by the most jagged verbal barbs transcended the usual simile of 'water off a duck's back'. In comparison to his happy indifference to insult, a duck was made of sponge with blotting-paper feathers.

'I just tapped it, old man,' said Bose. 'Hadn't you tried tapping it yet?'

'Look at this!' demanded Cabal, gesturing at the dozens of closely written sheets arranged into neat piles upon the table. 'Look at all this! This is just basic theory, the very least I would need to understand before going on to intermediate theory, then advanced theory and, finally, the extreme edges of theory where Hep-Seth was working before I could even think of touching that damnable thing! No, "just tapping it" was *weeks* away.' He swallowed, and took several deep breaths. 'Get your things together. We don't know how long the gateway will remain open.' Bose opened his mouth to say something, but Cabal interrupted him: 'If you were about to say that if it closes before we're ready you can just tap it again, don't. It would be more than your life is worth at present.'

They had few belongings by this point in any event, the few knick-knacks that Bose had collected being abandoned aboard the *Audaine*, while Cabal kept all he needed, and several things he might, in his Gladstone. It was the work of a moment to find something similar to a carpet bag in Hep-Seth's wardrobe (he was, it seemed, especially given to very high collars and wide sleeves judging by its other contents), and to load it with food, water and wineskins. Then they stood before the coruscating light contained within the shifting heptagonal gateway and paused a second. Cabal could not help but be reminded of a similar occasion, weeks before, when they had stood before a similar gateway in an Arkham garret – and just look at how that had turned out. Then, they had been hounded by a ghoulpack and time had been pressing. Now, the only pressure upon them was the possibility of the gateway closing, and that did not seem quite so urgent. Cabal had a sense that if he went through that wavering sheet of distorted reality, things would change, hugely, radically, in ways he could not predict. It was an irrational feeling, and normally he would have crushed it easily, but in that place it circled inside his mind, making his neck tense and uncomfortable, and he knew the Phobic Animus was at work again.

He considered briefly whether he should allow Bose to go first or give him a firm shove into the portal, should he demur. It would be pointless, however: there was no easy way to tell if a disparition was disintegration followed by a distant reintegration, or just disintegration followed by nothing at all. Besides which, the odd ill-formed conviction of change that flittered around his mental battlements, like a translucent sheeted ghost, assured him that the change would not simply be one of being alive to being dead. So, he took a deep breath in through his mouth, let it out through his nose, and stepped into the gateway.

It was a lot less pleasant than travel via a discorporated poet. Cabal had a momentary sense that he had turned to very fine sand, and that the sand was falling away from him. He especially resented it when his eyes flowed away from him like pollen in a breeze, but a moment later the rest of his skull followed and it subsequently became difficult to resent anything very much. He did wonder distantly if this was the nature of the change he had intuited, that he would spend the rest of eternity as a cloud of minutely powdered necromancer, wafting around the cosmos and unable to get very concerned about anything any more. He felt he should be concerned that he couldn't be concerned, but he couldn't be concerned enough to care, so he wasn't. A Jovian perspective, to be sure, but one hard to become enthusiastic about if the job didn't come with thunderbolts. But then he considered 'enthusiasm', and found his own memories of it drained of colour, dimensions and veracity, like a badly written strip cartoon in a cheap newspaper.

Falling apart had been so easy. Mildly disconcerting to begin with, but one got used to one's molecules going their separate ways, and then the atoms within those molecules trailing off by themselves, and then the electrons and neutrons, and the strangeness and charm, and down *ad infinitum* in far less time than it takes to say *ad infinitum*.

Coming back together, on the other hand, hurt like blazes.

There was sun, and there was sand, and there was a screaming, burning man being reforged from the stuff of creation, and he was not enjoying it in the slightest. It would have been a boon if his nervous system had re-formed a little later in the process than it did, but that's magic for you – even when it's helpful, it finds a way to be surly with it. Thus his nerves were in place to tell him just how shatteringly painful it is to be glued back together from cosmic clay and fairy dust. The only positives about the experience were that it was educational – being reconstructed is precisely *this* painful – and it was short.

Johannes Cabal flopped on to the beach, eyes wide with still vibrant memories of recent agony, and rolled on to his back, his hands clenched tightly enough for his fingernails to draw blood from his palms, his face in a humourless rictal grin. He had no idea how long he lay there, the sound of the waves breaking as ignored as the azure sky his eyes saw but did not comprehend. Then he blinked, and sense began to return to him.

'Gosh,' said a familiar voice. 'That stung a bit, didn't it?'

Cabal sat up. He was on a beach, a beautiful beach of golden sand, beneath a golden sun. It would have been idyllic but for the presence of Bose sitting on a nearby rock, a man with the ability to render the greatest wonders prosaic by his mere presence.

Reaction to the translocation set in a moment later: Cabal leaned over and vomited upon that golden sand, which was not improved by the addition. When he had finished bringing everything up, he felt febrile, weak and oddly ashamed, so he scooped sand over the vomit to hide it. He fumbled in his pocket to find his blue-lensed glasses and put them on to conceal his reddened, watering eyes and save them from the strong sunshine.

'It *stang* a bit?' he managed to say. 'How are you so composed, Bose? That was the single most unpleasant physical experience I have ever suffered, and I've had some bad ones, believe you me.'

Bose shrugged. 'Yes, it was rather horrid, wasn't it? But I was here for a full hour before your arrival, Mr Cabal. I've had a chance to get over it. Where were you?'

'Where was I?' Cabal rose shakily to his feet and dusted himself off. 'Neither here nor there, it seems.' He looked around. The beach stretched for about a mile in either direction before vanishing in the curve of the coastline. It gave way to palm trees, then thicker vegetation as it rose up sharply towards a great rocky crag that formed the centre of the island, assuming it was an island and not some promontory on a larger landmass. Directly between them and this feature, however, there was no forest at all, but only a hill of bare rock into which a crude zigzagging path had been carved. At its head, some five hundred yards up the rockface was an equally primitive great stone face cut from the living rock, a demoniacal countenance with a cave entrance for a mouth, befanged, behorned and terrible in its clichés. Cabal had seen a few scary cave entrances in his time, and this one scored low points for originality.

'This *is* Mormo, I presume?' he said, semi-rhetorically, as he expected little insight from Bose. 'I would hate to have to enter some hideous cave of secrets and face whatever terrors it contains, and then for it to turn out to be the wrong one.'

Bose shook his head. 'Can't say, old boy. But unless you plan to make a boat or just settle down here, I don't suppose we have much choice but to investigate it.'

'No,' admitted Cabal. 'I don't suppose we do.'

The day was still young, and Cabal felt enervated by the trip and empty by its effects, so they took a little time to eat slowly some of the food they had brought with them, and regarded the cave mouth frequently with guarded suspicion as they did so, just in case the Phobic Animus came galumphing out to share their meal and then, in recompense, kill or unhinge them with a torrent of pure fear. It did not, but the possibility that it might took away most of the small pleasure to be had from eating outside.

It was, however, an eminently suitable time to reflect on how far they had come, and the travails they had undergone to be on that beach. Or just to look at the sea and say how pretty it was, which sufficed for Bose.

Cabal ignored him, a skill it had taken little effort to bring to a high finish. For his own part, the forebodings he had experienced within the tower of Hep-Seth now doubled and redoubled. There was a terrible sense of imminent change, and not a change that he would care for. He was inevitably reminded that the thirteenth card of the tarot deck, Death, signified sudden change that was usually only a figurative death. Usually, but not always. That uncertainty between the metaphorical and the actual had never concerned him quite so much before. Death was waiting for him here; if he had drawn a card at random from a tarot deck right that moment, he would have been more surprised if it had been one of the seventy-seven others.

The sense was not rational, so he could not analyse it rationally. It was subjective to the final degree, so the only metric for it was previous experience. Was the sense imposed, or was its genesis within him? He could not tell. It might just as easily be the influence of the Phobic Animus demonstrating that it had subtleties beyond mortal terror. Cabal drew a long draught from his waterskin, and replaced the stopper with an awareness that this might be among his last acts.

'Come along, Herr Bose,' he said, as he stood and beat the sand from his seat. 'Our destinies, or something along those lines, await.'

The climb up the pathway did not take nearly long enough, and almost before they knew it, they were standing in the mouth of the great stone head. The daylight did not extend very deeply inside, and from what they could see, the interior was not a natural cave but had been cut from the stone of the hill.

Bose squinted into the darkness. 'I can't say I fancy going in there, Mr Cabal. It's awfully gloomy. We shan't be able to see our hands in front of our faces. I suppose we could try and make flambeaux.' He looked around and found a bit of dry wood, presumably carried up into the cave during a fierce storm in some bygone year. 'If we find another stick like this, and wrap something around it that we can set fire to . . . ?'

Cabal said nothing, but took the stick from Bose, and opened his bag. Instantly, cool green-blue flames licked up from inside. Cabal took out the eternally burning head of Ercusides, and stuck it on the end of the stick. 'There,' said Cabal. 'That will do nicely.'

'Eh?' said Ercusides. 'Is somebody there? What is going on?'

'You're earning your keep, sir,' said Cabal. 'Now, quiet, please. We are working.'

The cave extended back some twenty feet before narrowing into a stone gullet, ridged with shallow steps, that descended at an angle of some thirty degrees to the horizontal. Cabal walked down them without hesitation; if he was correct about the nature of the place, it would not require traps to protect its treasure, as its treasure was quite capable of defending itself. The gullet opened out into a jagged gallery, this time a natural formation that had been tweaked here and there, but was otherwise as natural processes had created it. Along one side a crevice in the floor wound as they walked alongside it, becoming first a crevasse, and then something like an abyss by the time they were close to the far end of the gallery, some two hundred feet long. The light from Ercusides' skull burned brightly and reflected from the semi-precious stones and quartzes that speckled the walls.

Cabal paused, looking first up a short ramp that led into another narrow carved corridor, much like the gullet from the entry, and then he looked into the abyss. Dank humours were carried up by a low wind that groaned on the very edge of hearing. Bose cautiously joined him.

'What do you suppose is down there?' he asked, curiosity and trepidation mingling in his voice.

'I am guessing at two things. One is a supposition, the other a good likelihood. First, I think whatever is left of the wizard Hep-Seth is down there, if he's lucky. The gods played a childish game with him, and they usually throw away what they tire of.'

'Really?' Bose's voice was a squeak. He sidled a little closer to the edge and looked into the shadowed deep. 'And the other?'

The powerful shove he received in his back from Johannes Cabal took him clear off the precipice, and then he screamed shrilly enough to remove any chance of him hearing Cabal say, 'You, any minute now.'

Cabal listened to the diminuendo screaming for a few

seconds, but had heard similar before and was unimpressed by this new rendition. He was making a calculated guess here, and if he was wrong, he was certainly in no more trouble than if he was right. Holding up the grumbling head of Ercusides on his stick, he went down the last corridor and into the chamber of the Phobic Animus.

Surviving fragments of Cyril W. Clome's manuscript for *The Young Person's Guide to Cthulhu and His Friends: No. 4 Yog-Sothoth, the Lurker at the Threshold*

Yog-Sothoth is never late for appointments, best beloved, and for the most wonderful of reasons. Yog-Sothoth is coterminous (coh-TER-min-US) with all time and all space, which means that clever old Outer God exists everywhere ALL the time! It is so terribly, terribly bright that even it doesn't understand what it's thinking about half the time, but luckily it's aware of the other half of the time all the time, so it can crib off itself. I don't think that counts as cheating.

Yog-Sothoth – who has lots of other names like the Lurker at the Threshold, the Key and the Gate, the Opener of the Way, the All-in-One and the One-in-All and log-Sotôt – looks like a big crowd of silvery bubbles but, unlike a big crowd of silvery bubbles, is stupendous in its malign suggestiveness. That's just another way of saying, 'I'm really not sure I trust those silvery bubbles.'

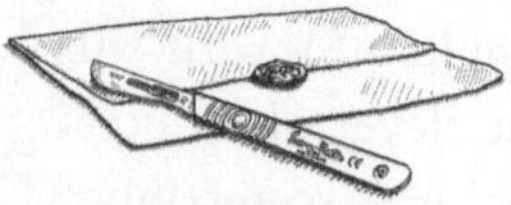

Chapter 14

IN WHICH WE CONTEMPLATE THE LIFE AND DEATH OF JOHANNES CABAL

As Johannes Cabal descended, he could see a flickering glow ahead, and realised he was approaching the final chamber. Once the glow was strong enough, he popped Ercusides off the end of the stick and put him away. Cabal had a strong presentiment that what was coming was going to be complicated and fraught enough without having to worry about a dead head on a stick. He drew his sword on the small chance that it was possible simply to jump on the epitome of Fear and do it to death with some fevered stabbing. It was a very small chance, he knew, but at least it provided a prop to his resolve. He considered turning around and going back out into the daylight. The Silver Key was useless without a gateway, so he could not escape via that route. Perhaps it would be possible to put together some sort of raft, given time, although the chances of negotiating the Cerenarian Sea without knowing where he was, and with all the terrors both meteorological and biological he might encounter *en route*, were vanishingly small. Or, he supposed, he could just sit around like Robinson Crusoe. No, he concluded, he would go mad with intellectual frustration before many years had gone by and end up more like Ben Gunn. No matter what its nature, its likely brevity, or its outcome, he must ultimately endure this encounter, so he might as well get it out of the way now.

The descending corridor reached its end, and Cabal stepped through into the chamber beyond. It was not hugely impressive but – given its occupant – it did not need to be. The chamber was circular, and some fifty feet in diameter. The walls rose some ten or twelve feet, then formed a hemispherical dome above. In sconces spaced some ten feet apart around the walls torches burned with a strange red fire that flickered black in its heart, yet cast a soft yellow light. Opposite the entrance upon a low dais stood a simple throne of grey and red stone, and upon the throne sat the Phobic Animus in all its preternatural glory.

'Hello, Herr Bose,' said Cabal.

'Hello, old man,' said Bose, as cheerfully as ever, but with a distinct underpinning of smugness. 'I gather you caught on to my little joke. Or did you just kill me because you finally got sick of the sight of me?' His expression shifted to Bose's habitual sheep-like foolishness. 'Oh, I say! Yaroo!' He relaxed again. 'If that's the case, you have far more patience than your reputation suggests.'

'The former is the case, which was the main reason the latter did not occur until this late juncture,' replied Cabal. 'It was a small thing, as is usually the way. It occurred to me far too recently that you knew I had cursed even the pets of the spider-ant-baby creatures of the Dark Wood, and yet you were in a dead faint when I had done so. At Dylath-Leen you knew Shadrach's fate, even though you were in a foetal ball facing the other way at the time. A neat trick for a man. Then, even as you were committing this *faux pas*, your eyes were dry and it occurred to me, just in passing although the idea grew on me, that you had not been sobbing in fear at all. You were laughing.'

'Yes, well,' Bose shrugged, 'it was funny.'

'The form that you have taken does you no favours. It is impatient and wilful. I feared I had gained the attention of Nyarlothotep by that ill-considered incantation in the Dark Wood, but my apprehension was a misapprehension. Nyarlothotep had taken notice of me well before then. When I realised that, it calmed me a little.'

'Did it?' Bose was frankly surprised. 'Did it indeed?'

'It did, because at least it meant I had not drawn down such misfortune upon my head. It was happenstance, the difference between being struck by lightning in a street and on a mountaintop during a storm while capering around with a silver wand.'

'That's a pretty allusion,' said Bose. 'I like that one.'

'The slip in time and space that put us into such peril in the first place was both calculated and impatient. At first I thought we were the objects of scrutiny for some wizard or another – the Dreamlands are rotten with wand-wavers – and I stuck by that thesis despite hints to the contrary.'

'Oh, I know where this is going . . .'

'Dylath-Leen, however, was blatant. No wizard holds that kind of power, to reduce the lunar cities of the Moon things, to make the Moon burn. That was . . .'

'Fun?'

'Heavy-handed.'

Bose wrinkled his nose. 'That didn't stop it being fun.'

'I must admit, I am disappointed. I thought there might be some grand design behind all this, but it seems I was mistaken. As gods go, you're just a brat.'

Bose's complacency did not slip, but he was silent for a long moment. Then he said, 'I am called the Crawling Chaos, the God with a Thousand Faces, but that is just a simple number for simple minds who like things simple. I do not employ Mr Gardner Bose often, and when I do, my sensibilities are filtered through his, just as with all my masks.'

'I'm reasonably sure that you're patronising me.'

'Oh, Mr Cabal, there has never been a human born, nor shall there ever be, to whom I do not have to talk down. You are all infants in a planetary nursery, and your lives are far too short for you ever to grow up. My point is that it doesn't matter what you think of me, because you don't matter so very much yourself. You have some small use, and you are already fulfilling it. I shan't explain it for reasons that must be terribly obvious even for a stunted intellect like yours.'

Cabal said nothing. He was not insulted, for the sting of an insult comes from the resentment the insultee feels towards the insulter's relatively weak position of superiority that nurtures a sense of 'How dare they?' When a god of unimaginable power and intelligence that quite surpasses even the theoretical limits of the human mind calls one a bit dim, however, one has to admit that, relatively speaking, they have a point.

Instead, he said, 'I have some small understanding of what

you have in mind. Satan himself regards me as an agent of evil and chaos in the world.'

'Satan?' said Bose. 'Oh, yes, Satan . . . Let me ask you something about that. How do you suppose that both Satan and I can exist in the same universe, hmm? I mean to say, I don't regard myself as anything so bland as an agent of evil and chaos. I have a job to do, however, and what you would call evil and chaos are the usual collateral results. Actually going out of one's way to create them, though . . . a tad immature, wouldn't you say? Unless . . .'

'What are you suggesting?' said Cabal, but he already knew, and so did Bose.

'Here's a little thought experiment. What if when you met Satan you actually met me in one of my many forms?'

'It would be irrelevant,' replied Cabal. 'No matter what your form, you're an unmitigated bastard. I don't care if you're Satan in your spare time.'

But Bose was not listening. 'And what if there was no God, except as a fictional counterweight to my Satan, hmm? Just think of all those people bowing and scraping to a deity that I made up in my lunchtime, hoping their grovelling will get them to some ill-defined Heaven, whereas everybody actually ends up in Hell.'

'You forget, I have been to Hell. Not all of the dead can be found there.'

'Well, maybe there is more than one Hell, or perhaps the ones who would have got to Heaven, if it wasn't fictional, I just allow to blink out at death. That would be quite merciful of me, wouldn't it? They die an atheist's death, but that's better than going to Hell, probably. I wouldn't know. Whenever I die, I get over it after a while. When I was

Tezcatlipoca one time, the locals murdered me. Not sure why – underdeveloped senses of humour would be my guess. Anyway, my corpse stank the place out and everybody else choked on the stench and died, which was pretty witty of me, wouldn't you say?'

'You require my validation? Then, no, it wasn't very witty. Ironic, I grant you, but witty, no.'

'Suit yourself,' said Bose, unabashed. 'The Aztecs thought it very droll. The ones who didn't die, obviously. Anyway . . . where was I?'

'You were congratulating yourself on your mordant wit.'

'So I was. Just think on it, though – every religion in the world, major or minor, worshipping things that don't exist. And the unbelievers being all smug about it, and saying that religions are products of human fear, ignorance and inadequacy, all unaware that they're actually products of some minor mystical jiggery-pokery by yours sincerely, so both the believers and the unbelievers are wrong. Now, come on, you must find *that* just a little bit funny, surely?'

'What of the ones who worship you?'

'Worship me? *As* me? Oh, they're just a handful, and they tend to end up dead or insane or whatever, and in any case, I don't care. I don't need followers. If they want to grovel to me, it might do them some good, it might not, but my needs transcend the awe and adoration of a bunch of filthy apes.'

'Yet here you are, burning up precious weeks and months of your immortality for some half-witted joke upon me. Perhaps you could explain that in terms a filthy ape might understand, O great and powerful Bose.'

Bose laughed, and swung around in his throne so that his legs hung over one arm. He smiled complacently. 'You're terrific, Johannes Cabal. You know that? Just about anybody else would be whimpering in the corner by this point with his sanity in his hands, not least because I would have got bored with them and gone out of my way to blow their wits out of their ears. You, though . . . I am talking to you because I am the Messenger of the Gods, and that makes me the great communicator. I am the only one who has any interest in humanity at all. The others occasionally turn up and blunder around a while, but if they can even perceive humans, they usually regard them as a bit creepy and exterminate them.'

Cabal tried to imagine dread Cthulhu rising from the corpse city of R'lyeh, seeing humans, and squealing like a *Hausfrau* who discovers mice in the pantry, before pounding them to death with a broom. Then again, perhaps Cthulhu *did* squeal, but in a form and context unimaginable to the human mind, or imperceptible to human senses. It hardly mattered if it were true; Cthulhu could still eradicate all life on Earth whether he was squealing like an enormous transdimensional schoolgirl or not.

'But know this, Johannes Cabal, you have a small part in a grand plan, and whatever you decide to do, it is destined. Fall on your sword or live until you are ninety, whatever you do, you do for us. And that is all you need to know. To be honest, it is all you are capable of understanding.'

There was a short, awkward silence. 'And the Phobic Animus?'

'That? Oh, there isn't one, not in the convenient package that the Fear Institute believed. No, irrational fear is always where everybody thought it was – sweating away in the human heart. Once I became aware of their brave little project, though, well, it was so convenient to my plans I just couldn't resist. I recovered the Silver Key from its last owner – that was Hep-Seth incidentally, and you were right, he *is* at the bottom of the crevasse – then inveigled it into the hands of the Fear Institute.'

'And sent them to me,' finished Cabal. 'I shan't bother asking why – you'll only get all mystical.'

'Reasons and reasons. But you might understand one.'

Bose looked steadily at him, and Cabal thought he caught the scent of brimstone. 'This "thought experiment" of yours,' he said slowly. 'Just how hypothet—'

'I told you we weren't done at the time, Johannes Cabal,' said Bose, but his voice was not his own.

Cabal swallowed very carefully. 'So,' he said tonelessly, 'what now?'

'What now?' Bose's voice was still of the pit, flaming and dangerous. Suddenly he smiled and sat up. 'How would you like your heart's desire?'

As Johannes Cabal gathered himself up from the grass, he wondered just how many times he was likely to be translocated around assorted plains of existence in his lifetime. He looked around as he dusted himself off, peeved but unsurprised that the Phobic Animus, or Nyarlothotep, or Gardner Bose Esq., or whatever else it might be styling itself this week, had not allowed him to keep his bag. The loss of Ercusides he could manfully bear, but the loss of his notebook, phials of reagent, his death's head cane and, worst of all, the Silver Key were nuisances great and small. He was wondering how likely recovering them might be when a large crow settled on a nearby boulder, eyed him with mercenary glee and croaked loudly, 'Kronk!'

Cabal almost groaned with rancour and disappointment. He recognised the crow. He recognised the rock on which it was perched. He knew exactly where he was, and he knew that his bag and its contents were lost beyond any reasonable chance of recovery. It was very annoying, but there was nothing to be done about it, so he put them aside in the vast mental jumble room he kept for memories of abject failure, and set his face towards a new day. He was nothing if not a pragmatist.

He allowed the crow to perch upon his shoulder as he walked along. The last time he had been coming this way, it had been to meet Messrs Shadrach, Corde and Nyarlothotep at the pub in the village. How long ago it seemed. Now they were all dead or alive in some metaphysical way that he doubted was expressible to poor creatures like himself. Whom the gods would destroy, the ancients tell us, they first make mad. Cabal often wondered why they would bother destroying anybody whose sanity they had already shattered. It seemed petty, but then, that was gods for you.

The house was just as it always was: bleak, solitary, and with a perilous front garden. He went up the path, ignoring the tiny eyes that watched him from within the shrubs and beneath the ivy, unlocked the door – hardly necessary, but old habits die hard – and let himself in.

And there, in his front hall with the black-and-white tiled floor, he stopped and stared in utter astonishment at what lay before him. For there, just by the mat, was an envelope.

It made not a ha'penny of sense. He collected his post, what little there was of it, *poste restante* from the post office in the village, both because he didn't care to have more people than necessary coming to his house, and because the post office did not enjoy having its postmen eaten by the recalcitrant fairies and other little folk of Cabal's front garden. For a while, he had trained the garden folk to acknowledge a list of people they should let by, which included the postman, but the training required constant refreshing as the gossamer-winged little proponents of chaos tended to forget it at the first hunger pang. Then there had been a moderately ingenious attempt to kill him by a disgruntled relative of somebody or another that he'd dug up for research material: they had dressed as a postman and actually made it into his house before becoming research material themselves. It was all too distracting, so he had made a *poste restante* arrangement, and everybody was about as happy about it as they were likely to be.

The envelope had not therefore been delivered by a postman, or anybody else who might reasonably be considered edible to tiny mouths full of very sharp tiny teeth. He looked suspiciously at the crisp white envelope for a second longer before reopening the door and calling into the front garden, 'Who has been to the house?'

'Nobody,' came a plaintive chorus of small voices. 'We are *ever* so hungry, Johannes Cabal.' Cabal grunted dismissively, and went back indoors. The garden folk were lousy liars, and on this occasion they seemed to be telling the truth. He crouched by the envelope and tried to see if there was anything obviously dubious about it, such as razors or the faint shimmer of a dried contact poison, but he could see nothing. Finally picking it up gingerly between finger and thumb, protecting his skin with a handkerchief, he took it up into his attic laboratory.

The letter remained inscrutable to close observation under

lens and ultraviolet light. Finally, wearing his heaviest rubber gauntlets and an army-surplus gas mask, Cabal opened the envelope with his favourite Swann & Morton No. 22 scalpel, being careful to cut the paper at the opposite end from the flap. Inside he saw nothing more malevolent than a folded sheet of foolscap parchment, which he removed with tweezers, and opened gently for fear of triggering some trap so subtle as to baffle conventional physics and, indeed, common sense. But then, as Cabal knew full well, nobody ever died from being *too* careful. Well, apart from that man who suffocated in cotton wool, but he was an idiot.

The sheet of parchment was, however, looking much like a sheet of parchment at present. That wasn't to say it was harmless: there are certain runic patterns that can draw the attention of unwelcome supernatural attention on whoever has the misfortune to look upon them, so Cabal continued to be delicately cautious long after the point when he had disproved the possibility of every form of magical trap known and several more open to conjecture. Finally, even after he had conceded that the letter was merely a letter – though it bore no name and address, and had somehow been posted without the knowledge of his front garden – he still felt misgivings as he opened it fully and studied its contents.

At first he thought he must be mistaken. Surely it was only a similarity in cursive styles. But as he read the short note of a little more than a hundred words that began with no greeting and ended with no signature, he recognised naunces in phrasing and came to the inescapable conclusion that it had been written by himself. He had no memory of ever doing so, however, and the content was of such startling originality that he knew he never had. He tore off the gas mask and gauntlets and read it again, and then again. It was ingenious, it was radical, and he knew in his heart that it was effective. What had Nyarlothotep said as he mooched around on his throne in the form of the inoffensive Herr Bose? *How would you like your heart's desire?* The note contained the basic principle for perfect resurrection, the secret of raising the dead just as they had been when they were alive – physically, mentally, spiritually.

Cabal took down his laboratory logbook from the shelf and opened it at a fresh page. All the experiments previously, all those years of work, were now as dross to him. Now he could see the beginning of the true path to his goal. He hung up his jacket and rolled up his sleeves. There was still much to be done, but now he knew what he knew, the fire burned in him again. This time he would succeed. One day, perhaps not so very far away, depending on where his researches led him, she would rise again, and she would see and speak and think, and Cabal would feel happiness for the first time in so long. He paused, angrily wiped at his eye with the heel of his hand. He was shaking. He had no time for this, he told himself. No time. There was so very much to be done.

It was true: there was a very great deal to be done. The note – which Cabal painstakingly transcribed into three different notebooks for fear that it might vanish as mysteriously as it had appeared – was only a beginning, an inspiration to explore some principles that might have been disregarded indefinitely without the note pointing out a subtlety to their applications that opened vast new vistas of fruitful research. But the note was short and of no help beyond putting him on the right path. More researches were necessary, more experiments, which meant more danger. Now, however, he knew the perils were worth it. No more stealing obscure books at great personal risk when he knew they would lead only to dead ends. No more canoodling with demons for scraps of dubious information.

Cabal did wonder, though: if Bose had been telling the truth in his little 'thought experiment', and he was also Satan, and Satan was therefore not a fallen angel but just another face of a trickster god, as Tezcatlipoca, Loki and Anansi must also be, what were the demons of Hell in reality? It was an intractable problem. There was only one sure way of knowing and that would involve communicating with Nyarlothotep, who would likely be in neither such a jovial frame of mind nor form should they ever meet again. Cabal's best guess was that the demons in that case would be constructs or creatures corrupted so thoroughly that they were no longer aware of ever having been anything but demons. It would be the final humiliation, that the eternal suffering of the damned in Hell was simply stage dressing. Ultimately, however, it was irrelevant to his current researches, and he considered those hapless multitudes only for a moment before moving on.

Early experiments were encouraging, and as Cabal's confidence in this new direction grew, so did his intolerance of distractions. He purchased a new Webley .577 and a replacement for his sword cane. Soon he was using both.

A seventeenth-century painting of the theologian Johannes Valentinus Andreae included a scrap of paper carelessly thrown on his desk that contained a complex diagram showing the relationship between certain esoteric humours. Cabal went to the private house where it hung and cut it from the canvas with the sword cane. When the owner attempted to stop him, Cabal shot him dead with the Webley.

Then there was the time a year later when Cabal was cornered by armed police in the chemical-engineering building of a university. He escaped by converting a fractional distillation column the size of a three-storey house into an impromptu explosive device and hiding behind a heavy concrete wall when it detonated. A dozen bystanders were injured, three fatally, and four university buildings burned down, but Cabal escaped with the materials he had sought, so all that was of no import.

Three years after that, it was necessary to relieve some inbreed – a member of the aristocracy, which is to say much the same thing – of a gem recovered from a meteorite four hundred years previously. It comprised the centrepiece of a tiara that left a vault only for very important occasions, and Cabal waited impatiently for such an occasion to arise. Finally, a benefit dinner for some worthy cause (Cabal thought it might involve orphans, but he was not overly interested) was announced at which some dowager somebody of somewhere would be wearing the tiara. The next morning, the newspapers were agape at the mass murder of everybody at the dinner through the agency of poisonous gas. Some days later, during the investigation, the tiara was recovered from under a side table where it had been carelessly thrown. The central gem was no longer in its setting.

And so it went on, an outrage here, an atrocity there, punctuating the onward and upward progress of Johannes Cabal the necromancer. His path was clear, and if anyone ventured upon it and became an obstruction, they were removed as quickly and economically as swatting a fly. Where

Cabal walked, he left gravestones and woe, yet he did not care and he did not pause. Where once he had killed with at least an iota of regret in aiding his ultimate foe, Death, now he murdered easily and without hesitation.

For the first time in his life, he was buying new fifty-round boxes of ammunition annually. He was on his third new sword cane, the first having been lost during an escape, and the second's blade having snapped in the ribs of a museum guard. Sometimes when he looked in the mirror to shave, Johannes Cabal saw his ultimate foe right there, looking back at him. He shrugged inwardly, and carried on shaving. None of that mattered, he knew. None of those people mattered. He had a plan, and it was more important than anything else in the world.

Nor were his crimes limited to the mundane world. He summoned the demon Lucifuge Rofocale for the second time in his life, and as the demon was halfway through saying, 'Oh, it's you again. Have you got your dread rod with you this time?' Cabal shot him through the head with a bullet made from the metal of Leng, sanctified on a lonely beach by Dagon himself, who had no love for demons. Lucifuge looked surprised, then dead, and Cabal hung him by his feet from a nearby tree for his blood to drain into a bucket. He left the demon dangling upside-down, the last droplets of his black blood tainting the soil. The carrion crows gathered around, but none cared to sample that particular dish.

Satan did not turn up that night, all in a bate because Cabal had killed one of his. Cabal hardly expected him to, because in his mind's eye he could see Satan sitting in his great basalt throne by a burning lake of lava, and – in some lights – he looked just like Mr Gardner Bose.

The wall of Cabal's laboratory contained a cork-lined noticeboard, and upon this were pinned yellowed newspaper cuttings of opening museum exhibitions and of forthcoming benefit dinners, carefully drawn alchemical charts and formulae of unusual chemical equations. There, in the centre of them all, was a sheet of parchment upon which was written a short paragraph in his own handwriting. It never yellowed or faded.

The path was clear, but it was also long. His experiments were not always successes, but the triumphs became more remarkable and more frequent as he closed in on his ultimate goal. He resurrected animals, first fish, frogs, insects and reptiles, and then mammals. He brought a cat back to life that seemed so delighted to be dead no longer that it positively tap-danced. A dog followed, but turned out to be an ill-tempered and poorly trained animal that had deserved its premature death, so Cabal was forced to repeat the experience for it, this time with no hope of reprieve.

Now there was a final test to make. It seemed advantageous to re-create a certain set of circumstances, so he travelled to the city and made the acquaintance of a woman in her late teens whose time was for sale, and when they were comfortably sequestered in a discreet hotel of a certain sort, he drowned her in the bath. He then conveyed her away in a large trunk he had waiting for precisely this purpose, by train and hired cart, and so to his house and laboratory.

Here, he applied his newly developed procedures and processes, which involved an extraterrestrial crystal, the blood of a demon and a great deal of new research hitherto unguessed at in the esoteric field of necromancy. Three hours and fifty minutes later, the young woman was sitting on the old sofa in

Cabal's front room, shivering with a blanket around her shoulders as she drank a cup of Assam tea Cabal had made her. He spun her some story about her collapsing and how, in a panic, he had brought her away. She couldn't remember any of the unpleasantness in the bathroom, and barely remembered meeting Cabal in the first place. He insisted that she stay the night, ostensibly because it was already the evening and the railway station was a long way away, but actually to observe her. She behaved much as any startled young woman might, and responded within norms when he lied to her about being a doctor and carried out some tests on mental and physical function. Among these, he sprinkled in a few to make sure that her spirit had not been corrupted or supplanted in the process, dripping holy water and garlic essence on her tongue under the pretence that it was a neural test to check that her senses of taste and smell were still working.

She reported that the water tasted like water, that the garlic essence tasted like garlic, and Cabal observed that at no point did her tongue burst into flames or her head explode, both of which would have constituted negative indicators. She behaved normally throughout, slept normally on the sofa, and at no point during the night was observed to fly around the house with her eyes glowing, or decide at breakfast that what she really wanted to eat was a nice plate of human brains.

He drove her to the second closest railway station by a circuitous route, and pressed a generous sum of money into her hand for her expenses, the inconvenience, and for being an excellent test subject, although he didn't actually mention this last point. He was breaking his original plan by letting a potential witness go – the rational thing to do would have been to kill her again, saw her up and get rid of the evidence in the house's furnace – but he was tired of death. He had never enjoyed killing, except in a few well-deserving cases. Now his time as a necromancer was drawing to a close, and he did not regret it.

He did regret, irrationally and momentarily, that he had failed to preserve Miss Smith in any sort of form useful for resurrection now that the secret was in his grasp. Then again, the good turn she had done him had been after her death and dissection, and he truly doubted that he could bring life back to the few bits of her that still existed, bobbing about in formaldehyde. Besides, she seemed happy in her *post mortem* career as the witch of Hlanith necropolis. Attempting to cram her spirit into a few bits of pickled offal would likely irritate her.

It took him a fortnight to gather the nerve to break the seals on the glass coffin. There it had lain all these years, concealed beneath the floor of his hidden second laboratory in the cellar, a secret within a secret. He spent the two weeks planning and preparing, again and again, assuring himself that this was not procrastination, not fear, but solid, sensible forethought. There reached a point where such rationalisations ceased to convince even himself, however, and so, early one clear Friday morning and after a good breakfast eaten slowly, he went down the cellar steps. He walked reluctantly, as if going to his own execution rather than to the sum of all his ambitions. He knew that there could be only one attempt, and that if he failed, he failed for ever.

His step wavered as he considered going to the city and carrying out his previous experiment again. After all, one can have confidence in one's results only if they can be consistently repeated. It was a lie to himself, though, and he had always been good at telling when he was lying. He continued the descent.

Once he was committed, he did not hesitate. The seals were broken quickly, for once the first was opened, the conditions within the glass coffin, filled to the brink with a fluid of occult formulation, altered, and its contents were no longer held outside time and from corruption. The coffin was a large structure, almost filling the four-by-eight-foot hole it occupied beneath the laboratory floor. Between the thick glass and the great weight of liquid it contained, there had never been any intention of removing it. Indeed, even shifting the lid required the use of the same winch he had employed to lift the false floor slabs that concealed the coffin in its pit.

It was a struggle to lift her from the coffin and he feared his plan might founder on this slightest of details. He had already lost almost a minute when he reached in and took her arm by the wrist. He had not touched her in so long, and for that minute he was overcome and could hardly breathe for the slow pulse of guilt and sorrow that he had managed to lock away for all those years. Time was wasting, though.

And so he carried out the procedures and the processes, the apex of necromantic science, the final catholicon, a cure for death.

Three hours and fifty minutes it took, just as with the woman from the city, and it succeeded perfectly, just as with the woman from the city.

She was shaking from the reaction, so he coddled her in a warm blanket, and made her tea, and she thanked him for his kindness, and asked where everybody else was, and how far downriver had she been swept before the kind gentleman saved her.

Cabal had been ready for anything, ready for any possibility, or so he thought. He knelt by her, took her hand in his and said her name, and then he said, 'It is me. Johannes. Your Johannes.'

Then her eyes widened with recognition, and she reached out to touch his hair, which had once been blond but was now grey. 'How long was I asleep?' she asked, her voice breaking.

She was stronger than him in so many ways. Everything she had known had faded away in the decades she had lain dead in her fairytale coffin. Only Johannes Cabal was left, but now he was old and, somewhere along the way, he had died too. The man she saw was not the man she loved; she consigned that man away into her lost years. This Johannes Cabal was kind, but just now and then something he said or something he did betrayed an inner desperation she pitied, and sometimes a heartlessness grown habitual that she despised. She was kind to Johannes Cabal, which pained him, and he could feel her pity towards him.

Thus it was no surprise to either of them, not really, when one day he walked her to the railway station, and put a bag containing all the wealth in paper and gold he could gather together in her hand, and sent her to the city. He left her there before she might try to kiss him. It would have been the kiss one gives an elderly relative whom one is moderately fond of, and it would have crushed his heart where he stood. He left her on the platform as the train approached, and he did not look back.

In his house, in the attic laboratory, he sat at his workbench and looked at the noticeboard upon which was still pinned that strange piece of parchment. He felt nothing, not any more. In the cellar the furnace burned fiercely as it consumed his notebooks, a lifetime flaming into light and smoke. He had made some adjustments to the boiler valves. Soon there would be a catastrophic explosion that would be heard from the village. He had little doubt there would be celebrations there that evening. Let them have their fun. He wouldn't even be alive to be taken by the explosion.

On the workbench before him lay his Webley Boxer .577, freshly cleaned and tested. It wouldn't do for it to fail now. He took it up, enjoying its weight for the last time, placed the muzzle in his mouth and fired.

Chapter 15

IN WHICH LITTLE IS SAID, BUT MUCH IS CONVEYED

Johannes Cabal was not expecting anything very much from death, but the dizziness surprised him. He opened his eyes to find himself in a hemispherical chamber carved into stone. Before him sat a happy man of puppyish demeanour, whom Cabal thought somewhat familiar.

'Well,' said Bose, 'how'd you like *those* apples, eh?'

Cabal could do little but stare at him for an incontinently long time. Then he looked at his hands. They were the hands of a man in his late twenties, steady and unmarked by liver spots. He looked back up at Bose.

'Nyarlothotep,' said Cabal, more calmly than he felt. 'You little bastard.'

Chapter 16

IN WHICH CABAL PLANS IN THE LONG TERM AND LAUGHTER PROVES TO BE THE WORST MEDICINE

'How'd you like those apples, eh?' is a ghastly, uncouth phrase to hear from anybody, and coming from a god did not improve it in the slightest.

'What a ridiculous waste of time,' said Cabal, trying to think of a verbal barb sufficiently sharp to sting even an immortal, cosmically puissant being. It was an endeavour doomed to failure.

'Not for me,' said Bose. 'Not a second has passed for me. Or for you, if we're being pedantic, and I *know* how much you enjoy your pedantry. Subjective time doesn't matter a jot, does it, old man? Well, I say *old man* but, of course, not as old a man as you thought.'

Bose's complacency was such that it took a gargantuan effort of Cabal's will not to stride over to him and slap him as the impertinent schoolboy he was affecting. That would, however, have provided only momentary satisfaction before Bose – it was so hard to think of him as Nyarlothotep – retaliated in some profoundly horrible though topographically challenging way.

'When I'm not running *billets doux* between my employers, Johannes, I deal in terror, and chaos, and madness primarily. Death also, but that's just a hobby, really. Sometimes you want something with a little piquancy, though, and despair does it for me. You say what I have shown you is a ridiculous waste of time, but I have not wasted a moment. What you should be realising is that your life up to now has been a ridiculous waste of time. Your goal is unachievable. You will die in misery just as you saw.'

'I will not die in a retirement home,' said Cabal, 'surrounded by strangers. Your vision was wrong on that count.'

'Details, details.' Bose curled his lower lip and wafted his fingers about. Cabal hoped this was an honest response and not a piece of play-acting to counter his own. He dared not test Bose's knowledge of what Cabal had experienced beyond this without drawing his attention unduly. It would have to do, and he would base his plans on the presumption that the details of the vision were his and his alone. He did this with a degree of trepidation. Nyarlothotep was the most psychologically human of the Old Ones, but the gap in intellects dwarfed that between, say, a border collie and Leonardo da Vinci. Galling though it might be to him, Cabal's best hope was that Nyarlothotep could not think down to his level.

Bose's next comment, however, scuppered at least part of that hope. 'I know what you're thinking, though, Mr Cabal,' he said, with an inscrutable smile. 'You're thinking that I've actually done you a big favour. I've saved you decades in research by letting you live through them in the blink of an eye, and that you can just go home and reproduce the latter stages of your experiments.'

Cabal's face was inexpressive, but inwardly he winced. That was exactly what he had been hoping. He was also hoping that this reality was the one he thought it was, and Nyarlothotep had not packed him away into a Chinese puzzle box of nested realities interconnected in unexpected ways from which he would never escape. It was a possibility, and the Dreamlands were the ideal environment in which to make it work.

'The secret you seek is as simple as ABC,' said Bose, demonstrating godly understatement. 'It was equally simple to concoct a likely but ultimately fallacious path of research and set you off on it, substituting the happy result that you experienced. It *was* a happy result, wasn't it? You must have wept tears of joy.'

'As practical jokes go . . .'

'My whoopee cushion is to die for,' said Bose. He smiled wistfully. 'Horribly. Oh, I meant to ask, your brother, was he there?'

Cabal felt anger flare and took a moment to damp it down again. 'My brother is dead.'

'Yes,' agreed Bose. 'Running around, drinking blood dead. I've heard of that. I may even have invented it.'

'No, not undeath. Not any more. I mean dead. Utterly irrevocably dead.'

'Really?' Bose rubbed his chin in contemplation. 'Well, I suppose the line between undeath and death *is* crossed rather easily, one way or the other. Very well, no brother. Any other family members to haunt your conscience?'

Cabal could feel his anger squirming its way loose of the leash, a development that probably would not go well for him in the present circumstance.

'I refuse to rise to your childish taunts,' he said stiffly. 'You've had your fun. I'm going now.'

'Hmm? Oh, yes. Of course. You must do as you see fit. I suppose I should crack on myself. Lots of little errands to run and chores to do that have been mounting up while I've been playing with you and those other two animals. Azathoth will want the newspaper reading to him, and Shub-Niggurath always wants help changing the nappies.'

'I'm sure the epithet *mother of a thousand young* is only metaphorical.' Cabal paused to consider. 'At least, I think it is only metaphorical.'

'Oh, don't I wish,' said Bose, and sighed. He stirred himself on his throne and sat up. 'Well, no time for dawdling. You had better see yourself out. I'm bored with being an inoffensive solicitor so I'm going to put on something a little less coherent that will probably shatter your sanity if you look upon it.'

'How exactly do I get off this island?' asked Cabal.

Bose's last few friendly affectations faded away and he looked stonily at Cabal. 'I wasn't joking about your sanity,' he said, in a gravelly voice that no longer sounded much like Bose or, indeed, much like any human. It sounded just like gravel might talk.

There seemed little more to be said. Cabal nodded curtly, turned on his heel and walked out with dignity, while all the time being unable to shake the thought that his exit looked no more decorous to Nyarlothotep than a cockroach attempting a dignified scuttle. As he climbed the corridor towards the crevasse-edge chamber, he could hear something particularly disturbing happening behind him, something that made wet noises, ripping noises and other sounds he could not categorise but which he suspected were generated by happenings neither common nor comprehensible to a mere mortal such as he. Curiosity is one thing, but there comes a point when a wise man sees all the dead cats lying around the place and thinks, *I'll just get along fine without that particular experience.* Cabal hastened his step.

The sunlight was harsh after the subdued illumination of the 'Phobic Animus' chamber, and Cabal flicked his blue-glass spectacles out of his pocket instinctively and put them on quickly. He walked down the zigzag path, and found a boulder to perch upon at the bottom. He would risk re-entering the cave again the next day, by which time even the most sluggardly of multidimensional creatures should have had ample opportunity to change form and leave. He doubted there was much of use in there, but all it would cost him was time and that, at least, he had plenty of.

He cast his mind back to his early musings on escaping the island and saw little to change his opinion as to the difficulty of the endeavour. He tried to recall if there was anything useful he might gather from a childhood reading of *Robinson Crusoe*. As far as he could remember, the trick was to avoid being eaten by cannibals, patronise anybody one might save from said cannibals ('Since today is Friday, I shall call you . . . Man Friday!'; 'I do have a name, you know. Just because you can't pronounce it . . .'; 'Be quiet! I haven't taught you English yet'), and then cunningly do nothing very useful for years until *ftrangely deliver'd by* PYRATES. No, that would never do. The local PYRATES were likely to be as bad as cannibals, and that was on the assumption that they weren't actually cannibals themselves. It was hard to believe, but Cabal had the distinct impression that Daniel Defoe had let him down.

He sat and watched the sun settle slowly towards the western horizon off to his left. Before him was a vast expanse of ocean without a hint of distant land. Once he thought he saw an island, but it grew closer and, before it finally submerged, he realised that it was actually a sea monster, approximately the size of Rutland. It was a memorable sight, but not one he felt improved him or his situation.

As the sun started to dip below the water, crabs began to populate the beach. In common with so much in the Dremlands, they couldn't simply be just like earthly crabs. These specimens had bodies roughly the size of dinner plates, their chitinous armour coloured a dismal brown-orange, puckered like warmed celluloid. They had four eyes, two mounted on stalks in a decent crably way, but the others were large and human-like, peering out of round openings in the front seam of the carapace between the upper and lower parts. These eyes, occasionally moistened with a meniscus that slid back and forth, looked permanently startled and cautious, but Cabal knew that was just an effect of their setting and nothing to do with their owners' actual dispositions. As he had no desire to be pincered to pieces by an army of startled-looking crabs in the early hours, he retired to the cave entrance, and blocked off the path with rocks. He hoped the crabs weren't substantially more intelligent than they looked, and settled down for a miserable night's sleep in the sandy cave mouth.

Next morning he discovered some useful information about the crabs (that they had probably intended to eat him if they could, but that their rapacious appetites fortunately far outstripped their intelligence), and breakfast (there was a small pile of crabs lying on their backs beneath the cave mouth that had fallen there while trying to negotiate Cabal's rock blockade. They were still alive and, if anything, looking more startled than usual). He cracked them open with a sharp stone, which startled them still further, and cooked them on a fire lit with one of his precious remaining matches.

He decided that he would keep the fire going as long as he could, and start supplementary fires elsewhere. He had no idea how long it might take to get off the island, or if he ever would, and permanent fires seemed like useful things to have. He might get lucky and find a supply of flint, but he probably wouldn't, and the whole idea of rubbing sticks together seemed very hit and miss. The smoke from the fire might also attract the attention of passing ships, should there be any, bearing in mind Mormo's reputation for obscurity. Admittedly, given the Dreamland's tendency towards the dramatic, should any ship come to the island it would probably be full of cannibalistic pirates, piratical cannibals, Jehovah's Witnesses or similar. That was acceptable, however. He was sure they could come to some arrangement that didn't involve any unpleasantness. Any unpleasantness to himself, at any rate.

Somewhere around midday, Cabal re-entered the caves and made his way with no great enthusiasm to the throne room. There was no self-proclaimed Phobic Animus in residence, and Cabal presumed that he was no longer of interest and Nyarlothotep was off elsewhere, doing incoherent alien things, incomprehensible to anybody who couldn't think in more than eleven or twelve dimensions. Somewhere between the realities floated a god's 'To do' list with the name

Johannes Cabal firmly ticked off. He did not know whether to feel insulted or relieved that he was no longer a person of interest, and settled on relieved, although he would have been still more relieved to have been put somewhere more convenient than Mormo at the end of Nyarlothotep's pitiless little game.

Cabal sat upon the throne to think, and presently sprawled upon it for comfort, incidentally and unselfconsciously mimicking Bose's attitudes of the previous day. In the first instance, he decided, it would be necessary thoroughly to explore Mormo to discover what it contained and then to make plans based on whatever resources were revealed. His options seemed to coalesce into a simple choice between making his home there and hoping for rescue, or building a vessel and taking his chances with the sea. The latter course was by far the more dangerous, but also the least maddening. The very thought of sitting around and feeling his life frittering away was abominable. No, unless his survey of the island turned up something unexpectedly useful, such as a marina on the north shore or even an isthmus to a mainland, then he would put together some sort of boat and bet his life on it neither falling apart nor being swallowed by Moby-Rutland. His mind made up, he went out to see what wonders the beaches and wooded slopes of Mormo might conceal.

The woods contained trees and the beaches contained sand and, occasionally, large crabs that seemed astonished by their own vicious aggression. It was a disappointing exploration, but Cabal did not begrudge the three days it took to circumnavigate the coast and to examine much of the forest and look up the open upper slopes of the rocky island heart. Food, at least, was not too uncommon. Aside from the vicious but splendidly stupid crabs, there were coconut palms, something like papayas and breadfruit groves, and even a couple of families of wild pigs that avoided him as carefully as he avoided them. It was good to know that they were there, though, should he ever decide the meat part of his diet was becoming tediously crab-orientated. His survey completed, he arrived back at the cave and considered the practicalities of his next move. He had searched the outer part of the island, true, but that still left the inner. The great crack in the throne room's antechamber might lead somewhere, and required exploration. A stone tossed experimentally into the void went a long while before a distant clatter of impact arrived back at Cabal's ears. Assuming the laws of physics were more or less the same as in the mundane world, and making an educated guess as to the effect of air resistance, he gauged a drop of somewhere between a hundred and twenty and a hundred and fifty feet. That was a long way to climb in near darkness and there were few handholds, from what he could see close by the upper reaches. He needed a rope and, he realised, he had the necessary elements to make one.

Coconut rope requires two things above all others: a lot of coconuts and a lot of time. He distantly remembered reading once how such rope was made, and knew that simply making the white coir fibre he needed would take the best part of a year, assuming that he was lucky with the current stage of the coconut's growth cycle. Cabal considered this, and decided that it would be a last resort if he could not find a more immediate alternative. The obvious one was to use jungle creepers, of which he had noted several varieties on his sortie.

An expedition specifically to investigate them returned with the results that one was covered with tiny thorns, another had the tensile strength of uncooked bread dough, a third was a fortuitously mild-tempered snake, and a fourth felt like weathered electrical cable. Of this last he harvested as much as he could find and dragged it back to the cave, leaving strange tendrilled tracks in the sand behind him.

It was slow, tedious work, and Cabal's mind wandered as he plaited the creepers into lengths of makeshift rope that he would tie or splice together when the time came. He thought of the future Nyarlothotep had shown him, of himself as an old man, and she still as young as when it had all begun. He remembered the pity in her face when he had said his last goodbye to her, the walk back to the house, his ageing knees, ankles and hips complaining. He remembered the taste of the gun in his mouth.

A strange flicker appeared at the corner of Cabal's mouth. An uninvolved and disinterested observer might have thought it was a twitch of amusement, a ghost of a smile. To anyone who knew Cabal, however, that was clearly nonsense. Unless Nyarlothotep, for all his vast intelligence, for all his wiles and experience, truly was not ever able fully to understand the shadows and light within the human heart. Unless Nyarlothotep had somehow missed a nuance in his dealings with Cabal that he simply could not comprehend. Unless Cabal had somehow pulled the wool over a god's eyes.

But no. That was not the case.

In truth, Cabal had pulled fully two layers of wool over a god's eyes.

The great problem with being a trickster god or, as in Nyarlothotep's case, *the* trickster god, was that anyone who deals with one from a position of knowing that one is a trickster is necessarily expecting to be tricked. The true trick that had been played upon Cabal was of such passing subtlety and arcane significance that, apart from the waste of time it constituted, he didn't mind greatly. His main intentions when agreeing to accompany the Fear Institute expedition had been to gain the Silver Key, and to reconnoitre the Dreamlands, and he had achieved both of these aims. He had never been convinced by the Institute's claim that such an entity as the Phobic Animus actually existed, and become increasingly cynical as clues and happenstance led them on a path that had been obscure to all others previously. Where others had paranoia, Cabal had a sense of self-preservation that bordered on the supernatural; it gathered every inconformity, every non-sequitur, every coincidence, and built deductions from them, as others might build models of the Eiffel Tower from discarded matches. Every such theoretical construct was measured against the metric of likelihood, and where it fell short, it was ignored for the time being.

On entering the Dreamlands Cabal had unconsciously lowered this metric, and it had served him well. Where the others had disregarded their unexpected appearance in the Dark Wood as some sort of Wonderland experience to be accepted without question, Cabal had filed it away under *Suspicious Occurrences*, and had been adding to the file ever since. Bose's great revelation had, therefore, been anticipated. This much has already been stated, but Cabal's guard against deceit was not lowered when Bose's true colours had been unfurled. So, when Bose – Nyarlothotep – had so obligingly given him the basic principle of perfect resurrection, he was already deeply suspicious. As has famously been noted, 'There ain't no such thing as a free lunch.' Thus, he had regarded Nyarlothotep's great banquet with particular caution.

When Cabal had first embarked upon the quest for the Phobic Animus – this most boojumish of Snarks – he had naturally considered where he might be most vulnerable to its tenebrous wiles. Physical injury and pain he regarded as unpleasant, but commonplace. Unless one lived one's life wrapped in kapok and under sedation, then injury and pain were certainties to be expected and dealt with rationally and promptly. He did not look forward to them, but neither did he fear them. He spent no time at all considering the more fanciful phobias: a man who is used to facing down the walking dead and battling ghosts as part of his job description is unlikely to be utterly unmanned by the sight of ducks or the sound of whistling. This left the quieter internal fears. The psychic cancers of doubt.

Among these Cabal's greatest was failure, but it was a clear and obvious one and he had long since armoured his heart against it. If ultimately he failed, then there was little he could do about it. Sometimes it still tormented him, but no great endeavour goes without the possibility of its coming to naught, a truism that no longer galled him as much as it might.

Nyarlothotep, however, was wilier than that. He had settled upon the fear of success. Total, absolute success in all respects save timeliness. This was something Cabal had no defence against except pointedly ignoring it and hoping it would not be so. The phantasmal personation of such a future that had been visited upon him was therefore perfectly pitched, and unimaginably cruel. It was also expected, given Nyarlothotep's reputation for unimaginable cruelty. Thus, Cabal settled down for several subjective decades of play-acting, carrying out experiments that he knew were useless in the real world. These were the experiments based on the core mechanism that had been provided to him on the parchment, in a forgery of his own hand. There were other experiments, however, apparently arranged as confirmatory or deductive exercises to support the central thesis. These were scattered over the years in an attempt, apparently successful, to hide their true nature as a single coherent line of research. Cabal knew that, for all their power, none of the Great Old Ones was truly omnipotent or omniscient, even if at least Yog-Sothoth managed the party trick of eternal omnipresence. The likelihood was that Nyarlothotep did not actually know what was happening in Cabal's false future beyond the planned sweep of it, but caution seemed wise all the same. Thus, it was not a complete waste of time at all. In his vanity, the Crawling Chaos had gifted Cabal several very useful years of research in the space of a single second.

This was the first layer of wool. The second was less involved, but far more important to Cabal. If its nature is enragingly opaque to the reader, who is likely to belong to the human race, then it may be understood how entirely incomprehensible it was to a mind as alien as a god's.

Cabal worked steadily and diligently on the vines to create his rope. He noted that they were drying as they were braided, and he hoped that this would increase rather than decrease their strength. Certainly, it would reduce their weight, which could only help. Even slightly dried out, the rope would have a formidable mass, and the possibility of it snapping under its own weight was a very real one. What might happen when his own weight was added to it was a concern. He would make a few experiments using rocks to simulate him, but he still had the baleful impression that his safety margin would be a narrow one. This wariness resulted in, over the next few weeks, the construction of a large balance scale on to which Cabal placed himself on one side and different quantities of rocks on the other until he had a pile that equalled his own mass, plus a little extra to allow for impulse strain caused by the act of climbing upon it, and a little extra more for safety.

Then his line of experimentation moved to dangling a woven sack of rocks on varying lengths of rope. Sometimes the rope snapped, or separated at the splices, and Cabal would swear volubly for a minute or two, and then get back to the project.

Every day, however, he made a point to give himself a moment or so in the domed room, just to say, 'You little bastard,' to the empty throne before getting on with his rope work.

Finally, some time after every possible variant of stupid crab, coconut, breadfruit and papaya had been tried, but shortly before culinary boredom sent him after the pigs, the rope was completed to his reasonable, if not absolute, satisfaction.

Cabal allowed himself a night's rest before embarking on the descent. He dropped a bundle of torches into the depths, crude items of wood with coconut matting heads moist with crab grease that he knew would burn for a disgustingly stench-filled half an hour when lit. Ercusides on a stick was certainly more reliable and less odoriferous, but also more voluble and inclined to testiness; Cabal would make do with his crab-fat torches instead. The bundle was wrapped around some food, although he doubted the little tetrahedral cage he had formed from the torches would survive impact. He knew the area he was descending to was reasonably flat, having cast several burning torches down in a survey the previous week, so that was one less thing to worry about. Muttering irritably under his breath, he fed the secured rope down into the darkness and then, muttering stilled, began the climb downwards.

Very aware of the old mountaineers' maxim that if one is going to fall off a rope, it is usually better to do so near the bottom, he made the best time he could without resorting to abseiling, which might put too much strain on the plaited creepers. Quickly he slid down into a thick, tangible darkness that closed in around him like oil. Above him, the glimmering light from the permanently alight – and very permanently fixed, as he had discovered – flambeaux grew attenuated and then seemed to flicker out altogether. Soon, the only way he had to gauge his progress was the number of times he had moved his hands down the rope, and that was a rough approximation at best. Then, with about forty feet to go, the rope parted.

He fell in silence, but inwardly he was thinking, *Typical*.

He awoke with no idea of how long he had been unconscious. This was low on his list of priorities at the time, it is true, lagging a long way behind a warranted sense of elation at not being dead and an equally justifiable sense of relief that his skeleton still seemed to be in the correct number of pieces. This miraculous escape was rendered less miraculous by the discovery that he was lying in a deep bed of some fibrous hair-like material that must have cushioned him on impact. While grateful for its serendipitous placement, he was less happy at what it might turn out to be. The image that leaped first to mind was a massive form of mucor, the threadlike mould often found on rotting vegetable matter, but this impression passed quickly when he realised that the threads were dry and not standing vertically but curled and balled. There was the smell, too: dry and musty, with a faint but distinct scent redolent of old crypts.

A suspicion began to form and he rolled slowly from the strange mound, ignoring the discomfort of the bruising he had suffered in his fall. He cast around on the rocky floor, finding only gravel and grit for several long minutes until his hand brushed against a piece of wood, and he realised it was one of his torches. The head of wiry coconut coir was greasy with crab fat and he realised that it must be one of the new torches from his provisions cache. That it was there by itself didn't raise hopes for the state of the cache, but he would worry about that in a moment.

He took out his silver matchbox and struck a light, allowing the flame to settle and grow in the still air before applying it to the torch. The grease melted and bubbled before the flame took and spread across the matting head, and finally he was able to look around.

The first thing he saw was the provisions bundle. It was not nearly as badly damaged as he had first anticipated. In fact, the only thing different about its state from the moment he had dropped it into the abyss was that one torch had become detached, and that was the torch with which he was now examining it. Serendipity again, it seemed.

The next thing he saw was what he had fallen on to. His second supposition as to its constitution was, he was very sorry to say, the correct one. It was hair – vast, vast quantities of hair, formed into an untidy pile. Moreover, it was human hair. Its length, colouration and, here and there, signs of dyeing and highlights gave no other possible origin. The fact that quite a few bits of desiccated scalp were still attached clinched the identification. Its presence posed two major questions. Where had such a huge multi-hued hairball come from, and why was it here now? Unless some sort of demon trichologist was haunting this dark passageway, Cabal was forced to admit to himself that he had no idea.

Then, when he raised his torch high to look around, the third thing he saw was the great ring of perhaps a hundred or so ghouls that encircled him, down on their haunches, silently watching. Once again Johannes Cabal thought, *Typical*.

He considered the wisdom of reaching for his sword and found it wanting. Besides, they could have killed him in any second since his undignified arrival into this darkness and had not done so. He had been, and remained, it seemed, an object of fascination among the ghouls. They just seemed to follow him around to see what amusing misadventure he might become embroiled within next. When one's career consists of haunting graveyards and eating human corpses of varied freshness, Cabal conceded, one has to find one's entertainment where one can.

'Well,' he said, clear and unwavering, 'how may I help you, ladies and gentlemen?' They all looked very similar with no obvious sexually dimorphic features, but he knew that every one of them had once been as human as he. Such niceties as showing basic politeness might make the difference between life and lunch.

The ghouls did not reply to him, but meeped and glibbered among themselves, as was their depraved wont. Neither, however, did they come any closer or retreat from the uncertain light of his torch. Cabal wondered just how long they would keep this up. It was like being threatened by wolves dressed as sheep, who had sunk so deep into their method acting that they were now unclear about the whole 'being dangerous' thing. Experimentally he took a step forward. The ghouls before him scuttled back a step, while those beside and behind him scuttled sideways and forwards accordingly to maintain the cordon. *Marvellous,* he thought. *I have my very own halo of ghouls. Oh, happy day.*

He was just considering, perhaps unwisely, the possible results of leaping forward, arms held high, and bellowing, 'Boo!' at them, when there was a disturbance in the circle off to his right. He turned as the line opened a gap and allowed through another ghoul. Physically, there was little to delineate it from its fellows, but there was a spark of recognition, psychic and certain, in Cabal's mind that this was the same specimen he had spoken to in Arkham and in the nameless city on the bank of the Lake of Yath.

'We meet again,' Cabal said, 'I'm fairly sure. What cryptic truths have you come to bore me with this time?'

The ghoul settled down on the grimy rock, crossing its legs with practised ease despite the way its knees bent back like a dog's. 'The last but one, Johannes Cabal.' It fell silent, watching Cabal with its head cocked to one side.

'Well?' said Cabal. 'If you could buck up and illuminate my ignorance I should be very grateful. Actually, if you want me to be very, *very* grateful, I would appreciate being led from here to the waking world. This darkness is clearly with your territories, so it shouldn't be very difficult for . . .'

But the ghoul was slowly shaking its head. It was hard to tell if it was grinning: the line of its muzzle and the flickering light made things uncertain. 'It is not for me to tell Johannes Cabal what the truth is. Johannes Cabal will see for himself very soon.'

'What? What do you mean? Am I intended to deduce it? Play Twenty Questions? This is ridiculous.'

And it *was* ridiculous. The more he thought about it, the more ridiculous it seemed. Here he was, in the depths of an abyss, within the bowels of an uncharted island, in an alien sea, on a different plane of existence, surrounded by monsters, playing guessing games. It was ridiculous, and soon he couldn't see anything else but how ridiculous it was, and that was when he started laughing. The laughing started with giggling, then full-mouthed guffawing, and it grew louder and more hysterical as the ghouls watched in silence and, perhaps, in sadness.

Within Cabal, he felt panic as the tightly held reins that had steered him from insanity on so many occasions suddenly flapped loose and useless. He felt his mental discipline turn to water as it bore him to the lip of another abyss. This abyss descended into far darker places than he had ever experienced before, and it was one from which even the most accomplished spelunkers would never return.

And then he heard his own laughter, shrill and humourless, gulping breaths beneath it. He heard those half-swallowed sounds and he recognised them, and the fear blossomed within him like flame. The Fear Institute had been right all along, it seemed. Here truly was the Phobic Animus, or his, at least. Where Nyarlothotep had failed, the ghouls had succeeded.

He dropped his torch and fell to his knees, and then to all fours. His hands were before him, and – would he had worn gloves to save him from that sight! – he saw the fingers were perhaps a little too long, the nails a little too pronounced, the skin a shade too grey. He stared at them, making despairing little barking sounds under his breath, and so was unaware when the leader of the ghouls crept close and sat by him.

'Do not fear, Johannes Cabal,' it said, though not in any human tongue. 'We shall look after you. Now you are family.'

Surviving fragments of Cyril W. Clome's Manuscript for *The Young Person's Guide to Cthulhu and His Friends:* No. 5 An ABC

A is for Azathoth, all mindless in space,
B is for Bugg-Shash, a god with no face.

C is for Cthulhu, the Father of Screams,
D is for Deep Ones, who watch while he dreams.

E is for Elder Things that lived long ago,
F is for Fire Vampire, they don't like the snow.

G is for Ghouls, who look much the same,
H is for Hastur, but don't say his name.

I is for Ithaqua, you'll freeze to the bone,
J is for Juk-Shabb, of whom little is known.

K is for Kadath, lost in cold wastes,
L is for Lloigor, of decadent tastes.

M is for Mi-Go, clever if fungal,
N is for Nyarlothotep, not prone to bungle.

O is for Oorn, a mollusc from Hell,
P is for Pluto, called Yuggoth as well.

Q is for Q'yth-az, a strange deity,
R is for Rhogog, who looks like a tree.

S is for Shub-Niggurath, her prey are dismayed,
T is for Tsathoggua, whose needs are depraved.

U is for Ulthar, cat killers be warned,
V is for Vhoorl, where Cthulhu was spawned.

W is for Witch House, down Old Arkham way,
X is for X'chll'at-aa, which is tricky to say.

Y is for Yog-Sothoth, who's everywhen and where,
Z is for Zoth-Ommog, Great Cthulhu's third heir.

Read this right through, and then you may see, That

(The MS halts abruptly at this point. The author remains largely missing, but for his finger- and toenails, and his eyes.)

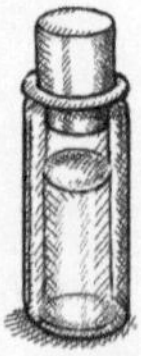

Chapter 17

IN WHICH CABAL EXPERIENCES OMOPHAGIA, ANNOYS THE VATICAN, AND ENDURES MUCH

The physical transformation was rapid, the mental one slow. More than once, Johannes Cabal wished that the reverse had been true. He sat in the darkness, chewing on the haunch of a newspaper proprietor who had just been buried a day or two before. The meat was rich with avarice and mendacity, rendered salty by the crocodile tears of his heirs. Cabal had balked at eating human flesh at first, despite the rising appetite for it within him. The leader of the ghouls had come to him then and pointed out the obvious truth that most people were little more than dumb animals and that, in any case, this could be regarded as a form of recycling and therefore was terribly sensible as well as delicious. Cabal had still been reluctant, but then they had brought him best joint of archbishop and, after that, he had no problems at all.

If the dietary changes were eventually acceptable, the

physical ones were less so, and the inevitable mental degradation concerned him most of all. The ghouls were not stupid – they were about as intelligent as an average human – but their intelligence rarely wavered much higher or lower than that, and the thought of being reduced to merely average human intelligence appalled Cabal. Indeed, if he were to be honest with himself, it terrified him.

Less dismaying than the cannibalism (though, as he rationalised it, he was no longer truly human and therefore no cannibal), but almost as troubling as the imminent collapse of his mental faculties was the nudity. Ghouls had little use for clothes, a mode that Cabal was sure he would not adopt. As time passed – and in the eternal darkness beneath the worlds, he had no idea how much time that meant – his garments grew constrictive and he felt intolerably swaddled and contained within them. He shed them in an isolated tunnel, and left them there, neatly folded, the last memorial to Johannes Cabal.

It should hardly have surprised him, this change. It was not even unknown in the history of his profession. The basic precepts of necromancy involved hanging around graveyards, tinkering with corpses and inevitably having dealings – friendly or otherwise – with ghouls. Given that the triggering events for a ghoulish transformation are psychic rather than material and include an interest in human cadavers, an empathy if not necessarily a sympathy with ghouls, and the ingestion of human remains, Cabal could only conclude that he should have washed his hands more thoroughly between dissections and lunch. Somewhere along the way, he must have inadvertently enjoyed a morsel of meat that had not come from the butcher. It served him right for eating in his laboratory. Still, it could have been worse. He'd only changed species instead of, say, picking up hepatitis.

So, he sat with the others in a lightless cavern, chewing a media tycoon's thigh and wondering what would become of him. He had failed. It had always been a possibility, but he had imagined the path would be abruptly halted by his death. It had never occurred to him that he might be turned aside from it, watching helplessly as potential success paled into certain failure. He looked at the others scattered around, industriously rationing out parcels of stolen meat among themselves. He didn't even need visible light to see them. Everything was limned in a strange and beautiful incandescence that showed details in the most mundane things that he had never dreamed might be there. This was a gift of his new physiology and, it was true, this he did not mind so much.

'But,' meeped a voice, 'you are not happy.'

Cabal turned to see the leader squatting nearby, watching him with calm interest. 'No,' he replied. 'I am not happy. I did not complete my work, and soon I will not even be able to remember why it was important to me.'

'You will,' laughed the leader, a sound like a choking terrier. 'You will remember.'

'But I won't want to.'

'You are so sorry for yourself. All your power and knowledge and books, and you are sorry for yourself. We have heard so much about Johannes Cabal. A clever man. A clever man. But sorry for yourself.'

Unused to being chastised, least of all by a creature that used crypts and tombs as All You Can Eat buffets, Cabal snapped, 'The process is irreversible. Everybody knows that.'

'Oh, yes,' said the leader, nodding understandingly. 'Everybody.'

'Yes. Everybody. Well, except for Culpins, but his theory of countermorphic residual transfiguration pertained only to lycanthropes, where the process is essentially reversible in any event, not this sort of transformation where, once the new morphic form is achieved, it is retained.'

'Achieved,' said the leader, nodding. It looked off into the cavern, apparently already bored with the conversation. 'Retained.'

'Exactly so,' said Cabal. It was nice to use his intellect. It was like looking over the old mansion he had grown up in before being permanently evicted and spending the rest of his life in a small studio flat. 'Once the full morphotypical state has been . . .' He paused. 'The destination is final, but the journey . . .' He leaped to his feet, and wobbled slightly. His knees were midway through the transformation of bending backwards to bending forwards, and currently bent both ways, which was good for yoga and bad for almost everything else.

'But the journey may be aborted! Quickly! Tell me! How much longer before I am entirely a ghoul? Days? Weeks? Months?'

The leader looked sideways at him. 'You do not like being a ghoul?'

'No. I don't. No insult intended, but I have plans, and eating people for eternity isn't among them.'

The leader looked at him fully. Then it grinned the mad-dog grin that ghouls do so well, exposing every fang it had. 'That is fine, and we are not insulted. You are Johannes Cabal.' It gestured at the others. 'We have enough numbers. There are lots of ghouls, but only one Johannes Cabal. You have at least six weeks, Johannes Cabal. At most, eight.'

Cabal's initial enthusiasm abated a little in the face of what he needed to do, and the time in which he had to do it. 'A stabiliser elixir won't be easy to synthesise. I'll need a laboratory, chemical reagents, books.'

The leader made a dismissive gesture with a paw. 'We steal bodies. My people, we have stolen three dead popes. The Vatican was very cross. Glass things, chemicals, books, they will be no trouble. Much easier than dead popes.'

'Why on Earth did you steal three dead popes?' asked Cabal.

'First, to make the Vatican very cross. That was funny. Second reason, delicious.'

Considering the ghouls' bad reputation, Cabal had found them astonishingly affable creatures: when the leader gathered them together to tell them that Cabal was going to attempt to stop his own transformation, they were not insulted, and when it called upon them to help in any way possible, they were happy to do so. If his life had been a little different, Cabal concluded, being a ghoul really wasn't so bad. While they were intellectually stunted, at least by his standards, their aesthetic senses went unblunted. He had discovered one ghoul painting a study of a London Tube station, in which ghouls watched the inattentive commuters on the platform from the shadows of the tunnel. The execution was exquisite, even if the subject matter was not. As a race they were mutually supportive and sanguine in their outlook. Previously Cabal had always reckoned them to be rivals in his graveyard harvests, nuisances at best, dangers at worst. Now, however, he saw them for what they were, stoic opportunists, and he respected them for it. Should his efforts over the next few weeks prove successful, he would be far more tolerant of their activities, and never shoot one again. Unless *really* irked.

First, it was necessary to possess a copy of the thesis, published to universal dismay by Erast Culpins, renowned lycanthropologist, son of a Russian *émigré* and a Kentish haberdasher, and now a permanent patient of Brichester Asylum. This the ghouls stole, in an excess of mischief, from the Vatican's very own *Index Librorum Prohibitorum*. Apparently, the theft made the Vatican 'cross'. Cabal didn't care if it made it livid, just so long as he had a copy.

Flicking as quickly as his increasingly long and distressingly rubbery fingers could manage it, Cabal disregarded the other artefacts of Culpins's peculiar genius – consisting of crude pictures of women bathing amid unnecessarily Byzantine plumbing – and concentrated on the fragmentary references to the metamorphic process. Culpins's terminology was imprecise and as mutable as his subject, but over the period of fifteen precious days, Cabal succeeded at shaking out the seed of the idea. On the sixteenth day, Cabal drew up a shopping list, and the ghouls were dispatched to gather the items therein requested. They went joyfully, apparently enjoying some petty larceny in their lives to make a change from the drudgery of workaday grave robbing.

There was a rash of thefts not only across the Earth, but across its history, and across the histories of other Earths and counter-Earths, and Earths that never should have been, and Earths that never shall be, as the ghouls happily voyaged through strange dimensions to play in Cabal's scavenger hunt. They came back, eventually, with many of the things he had requested, some things similar to those requested, and quite a lot of things they had just taken a shine to in passing.

'Another dead pope,' said Cabal, to one such returnee. He peered into the sack again and sighed. 'Though this one shows signs that he wasn't dead before he was folded up and put in here. I imagine the Vatican was quite cross about this, was it?' To which the ghoul nodded happily.

As Cabal worked at putting together a laboratory down in the ghoulish caverns, he would sometimes turn to find the ghoul leader there, hunkered down in the shadows, watching his progress in silence. Cabal had noted that the leader was also changing in strange ways, his speech becoming simpler and more like that of the others in the pack. This, he gathered, was because he had once been a man of great intellect himself, but that the steady erosion of his humanity had reached even this last bastion as inexorably as an incoming tide. The ghoul didn't seem to be so very concerned about it, so Cabal never broached the subject.

'It's coming along,' Cabal told him. 'I should be able to start experimentation soon.' He paused in unpacking a condenser tube from its box, stolen from the chemistry lab of a small boys' public school in Hampshire, and turned to the leader. 'I am appreciative of all your help in this enterprise, sir, but I must know: why exactly are you doing so?'

The ghoul lifted its long index finger, a finger graced with too many joints to be seemly, and counted, 'One thing. Johannes Cabal is necromancer. Necromancers get respect from gravefolk. From ghouls. Johannes Cabal needs help, Johannes Cabal gets help. Two things. If Johannes Cabal is unhappy as gravefolk, he should not be gravefolk. Three things. Stealing is fun.'

Cabal nodded, satisfied. He had certainly heard less worthwhile reasons given to commit the most appalling crimes in the past. A willingness to help and a *raison d'être* for a bit of racial kleptomania were better than most.

The apparatus was constructed rapidly, though some of the more unconventional reagents intended for its retorts took longer to procure. One in particular required special care, and Cabal led a party of ghouls to help him acquire it. He returned sombre and quiet, bearing the skeletal tip of a left-hand little finger. 'That grave remains sacrosanct,' he told the leader. 'Spread the word among the gravefolk: if any break into it – man or ghoul – they will regret it.' He held up the small bone and regarded it with melancholy. 'Apart from me, obviously.'

The leader did not need to enquire why, for it had already been informed that the gravestone above the coffin they had so respectfully robbed bore the words,

Gottfried Cabal. Survived by his wife Liese,
and son Johannes, gone to join his elder son
Horst in God's Grace.
REQUISCAT IN PACE.

Instead it watched Cabal painstakingly clean the bone and then carefully powder exactly as much as he needed before placing the remainder in a fresh test-tube, sealing it and stowing it in his Gladstone bag.

Cabal's motivation was high: every day he found it a little harder to remember things or to carry out mental calculations. He was heading towards average human intelligence, and he found the experience stifling and claustrophobic. On the one hand it appalled him that people were content to live with such small intellects, although on the other it went a long way to explaining so many things about society that otherwise defied belief. At least the ghouls seemed as highly motivated as he: he had only to suggest that an item might be useful for a gang to run off and return anywhere from hours to a couple of days later with it in paw. That at least was one less thing to worry about, but the narrow window of opportunity the elixir presented and the impossibility of securing further supplies of some of the reagents needed meant that he had little latitude for supporting experimentation. The few tests he was able to conduct were highly encouraging – it seemed that Culpins's obsessions with werewolves, plumbing and naked ladies had actually borne fruit – but there could only be a single acid test, and as much as he wanted to hold it off until he could be sure he was doing the right thing, its time was growing inexorably closer.

At last, Johannes Cabal ran out of excuses for himself. Time was short, the principles of his work were already beginning to escape him, and he knew he must act now or for ever be trapped in the Stygian places beneath the Earth and its close neighbours in dream and out of it. He carried out the last reactions, filtered away an unnecessary precipitate, added another reagent drop-wise until the contents of his test-tube went from sepia to colourless and clear. He added the powdered bone, marking the elixir with a trace of his own former humanity, and shook it vigorously for ten minutes until the bone had entirely dissolved. Then he neutralised the remaining solution, and distilled it. He was left with perhaps a fluid ounce of clear, slightly oily liquid, which he gathered in a small test-tube. He allowed it to cool, and then stoppered it.

It was so small, little more than an ampoule, yet everything rested upon it. He gathered his faculties, arose from his laboratory stool – obligingly stolen from a Brazilian university by the ghouls – and went out into the main cavern.

He stood before them, straining to stand upright as a man stood, instead of the slight crouch that the ghoul form encouraged, and held up the elixir. 'Friends,' he meeped, and it was true that he had rarely felt so friendly towards anybody or anything. 'Friends, I come before you today to thank you for your aid in my work.' The ghouls were already scampering over on all fours to be close and catch his every word. 'This transformation clearly suits many of you, and is, I think, a more honourable and honest career than, say, the judiciary. It is not, however, a career suited to everyone.' Cabal could see the ghoul leader standing nearby, nodding slightly in silent appreciation of these sentiments. 'I have found my stay with you highly educational, and a wide expansion of my horizons, and as I have come to know the gravefolk, I have also come to understand you, and to respect and appreciate you. When I return to the world above, I will never forget you. Indeed, I believe that we may combine our forces in many mutually advantageous ways.' Cabal had learned to see expression and emotion in the muzzled grey rubbery faces, and he could see sadness there now. They were sad to see him go, he knew, and probably sad that all the justified thieving had to stop. Despite himself, he felt quite fond of them.

'Now?' asked one to his right.

'Well, let me get home first, and then . . .' began Cabal, but the ghoul was not speaking to him.

'Now,' said the leader, quietly but firmly.

Suddenly Cabal was being held down, his arms and legs

pinioned. 'What?' he shouted. 'What are you doing?' He thrashed in their grip, but there were too many of them, and they were far too strong. Then he felt his paw being gently but inexorably forced open. He could only swear and damn them as the elixir was taken from him. 'No! Get off me, you *verdammt* animals! It's no use to you! It's too late for you!'

He fought until he was exhausted and weeping with anger and fear of his certain future. The ghouls continued to keep him still as their leader stood before him. He held up the small glass tube that held all Cabal's hopes and said, 'I am sorry, Johannes Cabal. I am sorry as you will be sorry, too. But not yet.'

'It's useless to you,' rasped Cabal, through a larynx grown unused to human speech. 'You cannot use it. You are fully transformed.'

'Yes. Full transformation. Sorry again. I lied.'

Cabal looked up suddenly at him. 'You did what?'

'Body change, yes, six . . . eight weeks. Mind change, much longer.' Still looking thoughtfully at the elixir in its right paw, it batted self-referentially at itself with its left. 'Mind finally going but not gone yet. Not too late for me.' He looked at Cabal. 'Long as you fight it, not too late for you either.'

'If you take that away from me,' said Cabal looking at the test-tube, 'then it *is* too late for me.'

'No,' said the leader. 'You do not understand yet. You will understand.' It started to turn away and paused, looking back guiltily at Cabal. 'I am sorry, Johannes Cabal. Wish there was other way.' And suddenly it was off at a bound, running into one of the tunnels and, from there, to anywhere and anytime.

'No!' Cabal called weakly after it. 'It won't work for you.

You don't understand. It wasn't formulated for you, it isn't keyed to you. Please. Come back.'

The leader did not, and the other ghouls held Cabal prisoner until pursuit became hopeless. Then they released him, and slunk away, ashamed.

Cabal sat alone, unable to take in the enormity of what had just happened to him. No, that isn't quite correct. Cabal was a man who had bandied words with gods and devils, and had yet to experience anything of sufficient enormity to prevent him functioning. It wasn't the scale of the disaster that distressed him so, vast though it was. It was the irrationality of it. The ghouls might be childlike sometimes, but they were no fools, their leader least of all. Cabal had made no secret of the elixir's specificity, so what did the ghoul leader hope to gain? To crush Cabal's spirit? Possibly, but everybody – every*thing* – had seemed almost as upset about it as he did. He tried to visualise the ghoul leader stopping in some lightless tunnel to open the phial and gulp down the contents, waiting for several minutes while nothing at all happened, then looking faintly put out. Cabal could not understand it. It made no sense at all.

Until the slowing mechanisms of his mind stumbled upon an idea, and he considered it and found it was not wanting in any respect, and realised that it was therefore likely enough to be the truth. He sat frozen by the idea as its ramifications rippled out and illuminated his ignorance like a flare down a pit. It was at first breathtaking, and his breath was duly taken. Then he started to laugh. It was an open, full-throated laugh, with an air of relief so strong in it that it occasionally tended a little to hysteria, but was reined back whenever it did so. It was an honest laugh, and it was the laughter of a man, not that of a ghoul.

When finally he was able to bring it under control and it quietened to sobbed chuckles, he said, loudly enough that anyone nearby would hear it, 'Oh, I won't forget. I won't forget what I am. I will never forget *who* I am.' Then he stood and bellowed into the empty darkness. 'I am Johannes Cabal! Necromancer! Mildly infamous in some quarters! Rise up, ghouls, and come to me! There is work to be done! There are preparations to be made!'

From every corner, every tunnel they crept and slunk and crawled and scampered to form a great mass of a corpse-eating audience before him. They were no longer filled with guilt and regret at what they had done, because they knew he now understood. They grinned their mad-dog grins, happy again.

The ghoul leader bounded through blackness, the curving rocky tunnel flaming in smudged colours to his eyes. It wasn't perfect sight – light was required for that – but it was substantially better than running into walls and off precipices. He had wondered how it worked for some time, but had known that that was beyond his ability to deduce. Still, that would be changing shortly, just as soon as he drank the stolen elixir. He felt no guilt at its theft. Why should he? He knew that Cabal would soon understand his reasons, then come to regard his new ghoulish existence not as a malign curse but as the great opportunity it truly was.

It turned a corner, scurried across a nexus in the great deep darkness frequented by the fearsome gugs, and darted into a new narrow tunnel that had been melted through the rock by a juvenile cthonian twenty millennia before. The ghoul knew the giant worm-like cthonian in question, at least by repute; it was now a young adult of truculent demeanour and a burden to all seven of its parents. But the ghoul had more important matters to concentrate on today than the soap opera lives of the selfish and invertebrate.

It paused, sensing the eddies in time that surged in those strange places as gentle as breezes. The hackles of its neck arose and it knew it was close, sniffing the air for a scent of a particular time and space. The creatures in those tenebrous extents wandered up and down the years, like cows in a field, unaware and uncaring, but the ghouls understood instinctively the opportunities and dangers since they were among the few who ever ventured into the worlds that abutted the Dreamlands, and among the even fewer who cared.

Soon the scent of fresh air would have been apparent even to a sense of smell less perceptive than a ghoul's. The ghoul leader stopped, and looked back as if half expecting pursuit, but the tunnel was empty except for himself and an explosion of roots that entered the space from above. The ghoul searched roughly within them, quickly locating a hollow from which it withdrew a brown-paper parcel, packaged as incompetently as only a ghoul or a schoolboy could manage. It reached further into the hollow and pulled out Cabal's Gladstone bag and cane, both stolen only hours before while Cabal's attention had been on the latter stages of the elixir synthesis. Stolen by subordinate ghouls, hidden here at their leader's command.

The ghoul fumbled with the parcel's string, quickly grew frustrated with trying to untie the knots and tore away the paper instead, with its long powerful fingers, snapping the string as easily as it could a neck. Within lay Cabal's sloughed skin: the carefully folded and stored bundle of clothes. The ghoul measured its arm against that of the suit jacket and grimaced at how much shorter the sleeve was than the distance from its shoulder to its wrist. Still, there was a solution to that. Holding all the stolen goods in its arms, it moved onwards in a stooped lope, up the sloping path until the rock turned to clay and compacted soil. The tunnel stopped abruptly in a convex wall of cut stone, each block about the size of a loaf. With no hesitation, the ghoul drew the stopper from the little tube of elixir and gulped it down. Now, working quickly, it removed the stones and stacked them carefully on the tunnel floor until there was a gap large enough for it to manoeuvre its scrawny frame through, and take the stolen things with it.

The village was asleep, its occupants deep in sleep, though few sank deep enough to visit the lands from which the ghoul had so recently departed. There was nobody around to see the long-fingered hand, tipped with gore-stained talons, rise from the shadows of the well on the village green, and grasp the edge, or to witness the grey, hideous form that rose up after it. The ghoul looked cautiously around before jumping soundlessly into the moon shadow of the quaint little roof that stood over the well shaft. Behind it, the water bucket swung slightly where its shoulder had touched it. Possessed of a surprisingly tidy mind for a grave-robbing cannibal, the ghoul reached out and stopped it. It had already given orders that the stones in the well wall some thirty feet down the shaft would be replaced before morning, and was in no doubt that it would be obeyed. It was important that no trace was left of this journey.

Across the green, the only light in any building burned in the windows of The Old House at Home. No doubt Parkin had interrupted his evening patrol for a quick half of bitter about two hours ago, and was now on one of its many successors. The ghoul's long ears flicked back and forth as it listened to the police sergeant, and anyone else in no hurry to go home, quietly talking. Nobody was saying their goodbyes. Excellent: nobody was likely to exit the pub and see a lean dark form dash from the cover of the well, across the green and down the road.

The ghoul could feel the elixir working. The flaring colours of its dark-penetrating sight were becoming attenuated; it no longer loped but was starting to walk more upright; its skin was becoming lighter and more human in texture. Unexpectedly, it was also growing weaker. Humans had not a fraction of the strength of a ghoul, but as its ghoulish strength left it, it seemed to drain deep into the human strength that lay beneath it too. Soon the ghoul's indefatigable trot became a walk, then a slouch, and finally a stagger. It paused at a rock by the path, having left the road a mile or so before, and sat heavily upon it. It looked at its limbs, at their increased girth, their shortened length, and found them disgusting. At least the clothes would fit now.

Dressed, although not a sartorial triumph in any sense, the ghoul lifted Cabal's bag and discovered it to be far heavier than it remembered. It ran its hand – it could no longer really be called a 'paw' – over its head and was gratified to discover hair growing there, so quickly that it could almost feel it doing so, driving out of his scalp like clay extruded from a nozzle. Belatedly, it realised that the sheer speed of the transformation was also the reason for the overwhelming weakness. It was too fast for his body to bear. If it didn't stop soon, it might kill him.

He dared not abandon his bag, and half carried it, half dragged it for the next mile until at last he saw the house. It looked cold and forbidding in the moonlight, but it was his salvation, and he must reach it if the long plan he had mapped out was to see fruition. It was another quarter of an hour before he finally reached the garden gate and slumped down by it, mortally tired. He tested his face: the muzzle had gone and his skin felt like human skin, just as it had before his transformation, just as it had before he had been forced to trick himself.

Cause and effect were never certain things in the Dreamlands, and what was objective there was subjective here. Time and place shifted in chaotic patterns between the two realms and it had always astonished him that the ghouls, free travellers that they were, had never taken advantage of it. Now he had come within a hair's breadth of assuming full ghoulhood, he understood very well. The ghouls simply didn't care, any more than a rat on a warship or a spider in a clock might care about the greater possibilities of its environment. He, however, had realised how this could save him. He wasn't sure at what point he *had* realised this or when he had acted upon it. Paradox had stolen the exact sequence of events from his mind and he doubted it would do his sanity much good to try to re-evaluate it, but what was sure was that he *had* acted upon it, and now the ghoul warrens housed among its many unpleasant material artefacts this one gloriously elegant temporal one. He knew Cabal would settle into the role of ghoul leader easily. After all, he always had.

Cabal sat by the wall of his house and remembered how he had realised the truth of it from the depths of despair when the ghoul leader had stolen the elixir from him for no apparent reason. He had known what he must do, and he had done it with precision: the 'attack' on the house in Arkham, making contact with the witch of Hlanith, and being there to hint to himself about the sinew-wood construct in the nameless city. He had known where he would descend into the crevasse in Mormo, and had marshalled his ghouls to harvest several thousand dead heads of hair to ensure he had a soft fall when the rope broke, as it always had and it always would.

He had not enjoyed deceiving himself into making the elixir, but it had been necessary and, after all, he had done the same to himself when he was at that point in the loop-the-loop of events. All these things had happened before and were already happening again, albeit in the subjective past. They were foretold and already lived, and it was to Cabal's advantage that they remained so. Once he had left the loop, however, Fate arose from her figurative armchair, stubbed out her figurative cigarette, put down her figurative newspaper, and started to take an interest in him again. Now he no longer knew the future, as was borne out by the evidence of him sitting by his garden gate, slowly dying.

In the silver light, tiny faces peered under the gate at him. Bound into the limits of the garden by magic Cabal had used to contain them where he could keep an eye on them, the garden folk watched and speculated.

'It's Johannes Cabal! Johannes Cabal!' they cried, in tinkling high voices like the sound of fairy bells.

'He smells like a dead dog,' said one.

'He looks very ill,' said another. Then, in a slightly calculating tone, 'And weak.'

There was some excited muttering. Then they chorused, 'Come into the garden, Johannes Cabal! We will help you to the door! We will help you in! We are your little friends!'

'And we won't eat you. Honest,' said a voice belonging to one of the less human-savvy Fey. There was angry shushing and the sound of a tiny Fey creature being punched.

Cabal had not needed the hint. The garden folk were capricious at the best of times, but at least they respected and feared his powers. Currently, though, he knew he couldn't intimidate a skittish kitten. He also knew that unless he got to his laboratory and made a simple counteragent to slow the elixir's effects to a bearable level, he might not live much longer. He had no choice, but to attempt to bluff the garden folk into believing he was not as ill as he was.

His master plan of deception and obscuration failed at the first step. He couldn't stand up. 'Damn,' he said out loud. 'Damn, damn, damn.' It had been such a good plan too. He had fooled himself, after all. How difficult could it be to fool a bunch of criminally insane pixies? 'Damn,' he said once more, and lapsed into unconsciousness.

He sat propped against the low garden wall, quietly dying. As he faded, he dreamed of how he had raised her from the dead, and how he had felt to see her live and breathe again. How he had not cared about the years, but only about the result and the truth that there were some people in this benighted world who were worthy of sacrificing oneself for. This was the second thing that he had denied Nyarlothotep, Crawling Chaos and bastard, and he might have laughed in his sleep as he dreamed of it.

Slowly he slumped over, and sank too deeply towards death to dream any more.

For five more minutes he faded.

A figure detached itself from the shadows beside the house and walked to him. Cabal was unaware as his eyelid was drawn back and the pulse at his throat checked. He didn't feel it when he was unceremoniously picked up and slung easily over the figure's shoulder, his bag gathered. The garden gate was opened and he was carried down the path to the front door of his house. The garden folk scattered in panic. They knew danger when they saw it, and the figure reeked of threat.

The front door was locked. Cabal doubtless had the key about his person or in his bag, but the figure had neither the time nor the inclination to search. Instead it put down Cabal's Gladstone, punched the door with its now free hand, smashing the bolt through the frame, picked up the bag again and carried it, with Cabal, into the hallway, past the door that still shuddered from the impact. The figure, a tall man in a long coat, didn't bother to secure the door. The house was warded against intrusions by the garden folk but, even if it hadn't been, none of them would have dared to enter while he was there.

Stirred from deep sleep, Cabal was muttering in delirium, and the man listened intently without even having to put his ear to Cabal's feverishly quivering lips. Cabal was running through the last things he had been thinking about before passing out. The scheme to get into the house was now moot, but the cause and cure for his quickly evaporating life was not. The man listened gravely to the burbled imperatives. Time was short, it was true, but he proved remarkably rapid. He opened Cabal's bag, was only momentarily surprised to find a flaming skull in there, removed the notebook that Cabal had fastidiously kept even during his descent into ghoulhood and flicked through it quickly. At least the relevant sections weren't encrypted – Cabal's failing intellect had preventing him doing that. The man read quickly, stopping once to look at Cabal with disgust. He went to the bookshelves and took down a slim volume entitled *A Treatise on the Induced Retrocessation of the Physiological Transformation in cases of Lycanthropy, Including Notes on the Metamorphic Processes Catalysed by Ghoulish Anthropophagy* by Erast Culpin. Then, in long strides, he was out of the room and up the stairs to the attic laboratory.

Cabal did not die that night, the next, or the next, but neither did he awaken fully. He was nursed through the illness by the man, fed slowly and patiently like a baby, washed and looked after. Sometimes, during the day, Cabal would almost manage to awaken, and would look around his room before lapsing back into sleep, but the man was never there.

The man looked after the house, too, repairing the front door, cleaning the rooms, and laying in provisions. One evening, he opened Cabal's Gladstone bag and removed the skull of Ercusides. 'Who's there?' Ercusides demanded. 'There is something going on, isn't there? Isn't there? Is there?'

The man did not answer, but instead carefully placed the skull with its cool blue-green flames in a varnished wooden box that had once contained a reflecting mirror galvanometer until Johannes Cabal had inadvertently destroyed it in an unhelpful if exciting experiment. The empty box had been left in a corner of the attic laboratory for years, which was where the man had discovered it. Ercusides' skull fitted neatly, and the heatless flames did not start a fire in the wood shavings the man had provided as packing. The lid was closed and clipped shut, and the box placed on the high shelf by the fireplace in the front room, beside another wooden box of similar dimensions.

Ercusides wasn't sure what was being done with him, but he was reasonably sure it was outrageous. 'What is this? Is that you, Cabal? Speak to me, you vile man!'

The stranger who had placed him there was already gone, but the other box, Ercusides' new neighbour, answered in a fashion. It whistled, a slow, haunting, melancholy air that spoke of optimism through adversity. Ercusides' shouts grew quieter, and died away altogether as he found himself listening. Finally he said, 'You . . . whoever you are. That tune, what is it?'

The other box replied, its voice rich and mature. ' "Blimey, I'm a Limey",' it said.

'What's a *limey*?' asked Ercusides. 'Who's "Blimey"?'

'That doesn't matter,' said the box, and began whistling again.

Soon, when he had heard the tune all the way through, Ercusides joined in.

Four days after he had collapsed at his own front gate, Johannes Cabal finally awoke fully. It was late evening, almost eleven, according to the clock on the mantel, and for a moment he felt content. Then he realised he had no idea how he had got there, and his contentment quickly turned to concern. He was wearing pyjamas, which he never wore because he had long since fallen out of the habit of wearing pyjamas to bed, the closest thing he had to a decadent characteristic. They had been sitting in a drawer in his dresser for years. Why was he wearing them all of a sudden? Why was there a carafe of fresh water by his bed? There had been next to no coal when he had left on the Fear Institute expedition, and he had not bothered to order any, so why was there a full scuttle by a healthy fire in the grate? With some difficulty he sat up, and – some ghoul instinct still in place – sniffed the air. There was an ineffable sense of intrusion in the air. Somebody else was in his house.

In *his* house. He looked at the desk and wondered if the interloper had searched it. If not, then the Italian revolver he had in the upper-right-hand drawer should still be there.

The door opened and he had no chance either to reach the desk or pretend he was still asleep.

The anger on his face at the intrusion into his home melted like wax beneath a blowtorch. Entirely forgetting himself, he gawped, and continued to gawp as the man sat on the edge of his bed, and looked at him without saying a word.

It was Johannes Cabal who spoke first, when his wits began to return having been temporarily expelled by mountainous astonishment.

'You,' he said at last, his voice thin and weak from illness and disuse. 'It's you.

'But . . . you're dead . . .'

Author's Note

It would be remiss of me if I were not to emphasise that the titular society does not exist, and one would be ill-advised to search for it, not least for reasons that must be apparent from the text. There *is*, however, a real Fear Institute. The organisation in this novel was briefly called the Phobos Society, until I gave in to the temptation that descended upon me every time I walked along the high street in Keynsham, Somerset, England, the town in which this book was written. There stands the J. N. Fear Institute, a building bequeathed to the people of Keynsham by John Nelson Fear in 1917. I feel obliged to underline that while the Institute is home to bridge and chess clubs, that one may learn to dance within its Fear Hall (I ask again – how could I resist?), and that it holds frequent country markets, it has never at any time instigated, funded or pursued the goal of eliminating irrational fear from the world by natural or supernatural means, least of all through the offices of a sarcastic necromancer. Or, if it has, it hasn't mentioned anything about it on its noticeboard.

With respect to the map, H. P. Lovecraft did not, as far as I know, create a map himself. From clues given in his stories, however, assorted examples have been drawn up over the years. I used a combination of elements from maps by Carolyn Schultz and Jack Gaughan as a starting place (although my lovely crinkly bits around the coastlines are somewhat different), but then naughtily shifted the entire Eastern Continent a bit further north to give me space to pop in the island of Oriab where I thought it looked nicer. I then – does my hubris know no bounds? – shoved the Lake of Yath into a different position and moved the ruins of the unnamed city to stand by its northern shore. Why did I do these wilful things?

Well, because that's the way I dreamt it.

Acknowledgements

It is usual to thank those who have helped out in the creation of a book, but in this particular case, it is a larger community than the norm. Ever since H.P. Lovecraft created the Dreamlands it has been a playground for generations of writers and artists, and to all of them – especially those whose additions I have made use of in this novel and likely altered horribly – I offer my appreciation and thanks.

As always, there is a great unsung army behind the business and production side of every book. Mentioned in dispatches are my agent Sam Copeland, my editor Claire Baldwin, and the thoroughly perspicacious Hazel Orme, who copy edited *The Fear Institute*.

Thanks once again to Linda 'Snugbat' Smith for her splendid chapter head art. There never seems enough time between the finalised chapter list and art deadline to get them done, yet she always manages it.

I'd also just like to say a few words about George H. Scithers, who died last year (2010). I never met him in person, but we corresponded after he bought the very first Johannes Cabal short story – 'Johannes Cabal and the Blustery Day' –

for publication. He was a clever man, experienced in the ways of the world of science fiction and fantasy (he had four Hugos to his name), and wise too. He offered me good advice and strong encouragement, and I was grateful to have him in my corner. He's missed.